DRAW THE LINE

WITHDRAWN

WRITTEN & ILLUSTRATED BY
LAURENT LINN

Margaret K. McElderry Books
NEW YORK • LONDON • TORONTO • SYDNEY • NEW DELHI

Margaret K. McElderry Books

An imprint of Simon & Schuster Children's Publishing Division

1230 Avenue of the Americas, New York, New York 10020

This book is a work of fiction. Any references to historical events, real people, or real places are used fictitiously. Other names, characters, places, and events are products of the author's imagination, and any resemblance to actual events or places or persons, living or dead, is entirely coincidental.

Copyright © 2016 by Laurent Linn

All rights reserved, including the right of reproduction in whole or in part in any form.

MARGARET K. McELDERRY BOOKS is a trademark of Simon & Schuster, Inc.

For information about special discounts for bulk purchases, please contact Simon & Schuster Special Sales at 1-866-506-1949 or business@simonandschuster.com.

The Simon & Schuster Speakers Bureau can bring authors to your live event. For more information or to book an event, contact the Simon & Schuster Speakers Bureau at 1-866-248-3049 or visit our website at www.simonspeakers.com.

Book design by Sonia Chaghatzbanian and Irene Metaxatos

The text for this book is set in Aldine 401 BT Std.

The illustrations for this book are rendered in Prismacolor pencil on vellum paper with digital shading.

Manufactured in the United States of America

First Edition

10 9 8 7 6 5 4 3 2 1

Library of Congress Cataloging-in-Publication Data

Names: Linn, Laurent, author.

Title: Draw the line / Laurent Linn.

Description: New York : Margaret K. McElderry Books, [2016] | Summary: "A teen boy survives a hate crime against another gay student through his art"— Provided by publisher.

Identifiers: LCCN 2015029314| ISBN 9781481452809 (hardback) | ISBN 9781481452823 (ebook)

Subjects: | CYAC: Gays—Fiction. | Artists—Fiction. | Hate crimes—Fiction. | High schools—Fiction. | Schools—Fiction. | BISAC: JUVENILE FICTION / Social Issues / Violence. | JUVENILE FICTION / Art & Architecture.

Classification: LCC PZ7.L66295 Dr 2016 | DDC [Fic]—dc23

LC record available at http://lccn.loc.gov/2015029314

For my parents, with their dazzling
superpowers of unconditional love

And for Chris, whose superhuman
strength carries me through the darkest
clouds into the brightest sun

"He who fights with monsters might take
care lest he thereby become a monster."
—FRIEDRICH NIETZSCHE

"Every line tells its own story,
even the very tentative ones."
—GILLIAN REDWOOD

"These aren't the droids you're looking for."
—OBI-WAN KENOBI

One

I SHOULD HAVE BEEN BORN WITH AN OWNER'S MANUAL.

You know the WARNING page at the beginning that mentions all the dangers? This morning I've got a new one to add to the growing list that would come with mine: *Don't let nerd boy cut his own hair.* I could add: *at 3 freakin' a.m. on a school night*, but really, any time would have been a bad idea.

They say that everything always looks better in the morning. Well, they lie. As I blink through this 7:something a.m. sunlight blaring through my bathroom window, all I see in the mirror is irreparable damage and, over on my drawing table, the art inspiration for my hair massacre.

When it's late at night and the world finally leaves me alone, I shut my bedroom door, settle down, and draw. People talk about how when they smoke pot or take some other crap or whatever, they go somewhere else in their head. Well, the feel of a 3B pencil skimming across the paper's surface, trying to control that tiny resistance to the graphite leaving its mark, lifts *me* up . . . to a world *I* create. That's my zone.

I completely escape.

So there I was last night with my best pencils and inking pens all lined up, an epic video game soundtrack in my headphones, plenty of Dr Pepper at the ready, and my calico cat, Harley Quinn, asleep under my drawing table lamp. She was kinda curled up right smack in the way, but that's okay. We understand each other.

I started sketching and, after a couple hours, was speeding along on drawing a new comic panel of my secret superhero creation: Graphite.

I set up a website for him a couple years ago, which has a nice little following out there. But it's anonymous. Just two people on earth know the site's *mine*, and my only two friends would never tell a soul.

Crafting the details of my world takes time, so I don't update the site very often. But when I do finish a comic sequence it's cause for whoopin' it up or, it seems, grabbing the nearest scissors.

I was so loving how I'd drawn Graphite's hair to flip up in such a perfect way that, in my caffeinated, sugared-up, sleep-deprived stupor, I lost it. Possessed by this delusional superhero side of me, I just knew I could re-create that hair on myself . . . with craft scissors. Actually, with slightly-rusted-and-gummed-up-with-bits-of-tape craft scissors (even though my good pair was just a drawer away).

Starting with my bangs, I was soon snipping along, moving around the sides. I may be a good artist, but hair is a tricky material, especially when one is being an *idiot*. It went scary wrong. So in my continued brilliance I set out to "fix" what I'd already done by tiptoeing around and searching for Dad's electric hair buzzer. I found it. My repair job didn't quite work out how I'd hoped.

So basically, in the middle of the night I became a toddler.

And here I am now, applying globs of hair goop from every container I have and that I could sneak out of Mom's bathroom after she left for work. But all this stuff only darkens my copper-brown hair more, making the missing chunks scream out.

I need hair cement, but I got nothin'! What's thick and sticky . . . maybe toothpaste? Stupid, I know, but I'm desperate. Hey, yeah, it kinda works. *Oh, god*, no it doesn't. It just adds glittery blue sparkles.

CRAP!

From my bed, C-3PO's muffled voice moans, *"We're doomed!"* Digging through the sheets, I find my phone.

Text from Audrey: Hey boy, just seeing ur text from ... 3AM!?! U = certifiable. WTF!?!?! Howz the new do?

I roll my shoulders, which pop, then type: I'm very talented. Wait till u see in person.

Audrey: Lordy. I'm scared. ☺ Those selfies u sent would wake the dead - which you look like.

Me: YOU'RE scared?!

Audrey: What were u thinking, Adrian? You're 16, not 6.

Shoulda consulted with me first. You need a fashion chaperone.

Me: If u say so

Audrey: Chill. Maybe not so bad in person? & after all, you're the superhero, Graphite Boy.

Yeah, right.

I type: See you before first period?

Audrey: If i can apply my face in time!

Me: ok

Well, what did I expect from her? She's never even had one strand of hair out of place, much less sculpted a topographical map on her own head.

How'd it get to be almost time to go? I've gotta hurry.

Dammit, I'm better than this! I'm so careful about blending into the background—how'd I slip up like this?

I dump my whole shirt drawer on the bed and apply what I know about color psychology. Blue is true, white is pure, red is angry or sexy. Purple is regal and commanding. Maybe I still have that purple T-shirt? Here it is. . . . Oh, yeah. With Super Grover crashing into a streetlamp printed on it. Not so commanding. I toss it to the floor.

The mound-o-shirts moves and a pair of jade eyes peers at me from between the folds.

"Comfy?" I say. Harley Quinn blinks at me.

That's it: camouflage. I don't mean the army kind, too aggressive. I need the animal kind that blends into its surroundings to avoid predators. The school lockers are taxi yellow, the hallway tile is navy blue, the cafeteria is eggshell white, so, what . . . plaid? This is insane.

I go for my usual smoky gray, psychologically meaning death, depression, and nothingness.

To a gray T-shirt, I add faded jeans, cheap old sneakers, and a gray hoodie . . . my almost-perfect cloak of high school invisibility. Like any good freak superhero wannabe, I'm an expert at fading into the background. However, I'm neither super nor hero. Just freak.

My drawing table is piled up like a crime scene, so I shove everything into my mess-of-a-desk. Oh, god, not this? In the bottom drawer I uncover the piece I entered in that Freshman Art Show two years ago. It was my best work way back then. I called it *Renaissance Hero*. I worked so freakin' hard on it, but it didn't win anything. Instead, some a-hole vandalized it, scrawling across it what other kids always thought of my art. I never showed anything at school again.

In fact, that was the last time I signed my name on my art.

And now I'm about to waltz into school with my latest masterpiece . . . attached to the top of my head.

I put my old, defaced drawing back, cover it up with stuff, and shut the desk drawer. Then I tuck away last night's Graphite drawing between pages sixty-six and sixty-seven of *Michelangelo at the Louvre*. My parents wouldn't think to look at my art books. Not that they'd even bother to come in here, but you never know.

Why did I hang this *Power to the Geek* poster so high on the back of my bedroom door? Whenever I leave, *Geek* stares me right in the face. Like I need reminding.

I replace Mom's hair goop, and then up goes my hood and

I hustle down the hall, past the gallery of old framed photos of little-kid me. My stomach still gets queasy seeing the one of me squealing with Mom and Dad, taken as we plummeted down the big drop of that massive Six Flags roller coaster. Back then—when Dad used to be Dad and, well, we did things—we actually took family pictures.

I stop and try to straighten the photo frame, but it just wants to hang crooked.

So I dash to the front door, grab the knob, and yell, "Bye, Dad."

"Yup." Dad twists in his recliner to glance at me from the living room, giving me his half-assed wave. I step outside and shut the door.

Here we go.

It may be October, but in Rock Hollow, this hometown slice-o-heaven, it's still hot, and this hoodie over my head doesn't help. Even though it's a quick walk to school, I slip my backpack off my shoulders and carry it to avoid a lovely bag-shaped sweat stain.

In picturesque places I've never been to, a few leaves on the ground at the beginning of fall probably mean a gorgeous, colorful autumn is on the way. But here, the horrific Texas summer drought has pretty much killed everything, so the dead leaves are just dead leaves, all starting to texture the front yards of sickly pea-green grass.

One last corner to turn and . . . this is it. Glorious Rock Hollow High.

Two

I SQUINT AT THE STEEL-GRAY SKY. HELP ME, OBI-WAN KENOBI, YOU'RE my only hope. Oh, yes, I pray to Obi-Wan. If people knew, they might laugh, but *he* may actually listen to me. Unlike certain other divine beings . . . you know who you are.

Passing a parked car in the school driveway, I catch a glimpse of myself in the window. It's a faint reflection, but enough to see a sleep-deprived nerd in a drooped hoodie staring back.

I take a deep breath and walk toward the main doors at my practiced don't-notice-me pace as others zoom past. A couple guys greet each other with a "Whatup?" and a hefty arm punch.

I. Do. Not. Understand. This. Species. Why would you hit someone to say hi?

I check that my hood is up and join the flow as I climb the steps, scanning for a friendly face, not seeing any. Only two of those exist, really, but Audrey's in front of a mirror somewhere, and Trent, my other friend, is the master of tardy.

Once through the doors, I navigate the noisy crowd toward my locker and notice all the guys with "professionally" cut hair. No one else looks like some deranged five-year-old randomly attacked him in the night with a Weedwacker. Even though you get in trouble if you wear hats or hoodies in school, I gotta keep this hood up as long as I can.

Ow! Someone bumps me in the elbow with their backpack.

"Huh?" A girl I don't know turns around. "Oh, sorry. Didn't see you."

Good.

"No prob—," I say, but she's already moved on.

I keep going.

Like a giant sponge, Rock Hollow High absorbs kids from three suburbs, so every day I see faces I don't know, and who don't know me. Though I doubt even some kids I've gone to school with since birth would know my name.

Oh, boy, I sure know these two faces, though. Doug is cruising in this direction, his telltale keychain jangling from his belt loop. Even with shoe squeaks and locker slams bouncing off the walls, those keys have a distinct pitch. And Buddy, his suck-up lackey, trails right behind.

Not only is Doug Richter massive—he's so solid it's like he has no neck, with his head sitting right on his shoulders—he's a super-talented football player. Evidently. I wouldn't really know since I've never been forced to go to a game, praise Obi-Wan.

People veer out of his way, except for some giggling girls

and the school security guard, who does a fist bump with Doug as he passes. It's hard to tell where Doug's looking with that raggedy red trucker cap he always wears pulled down so low over his eyes. Of course, he can wear whatever the hell he wants. At Rock Hollow, when you're big on the football team you're about as big as Jesus. And in these parts, nothing is bigger than that.

Doug's little leech is on "the team" too, but Buddy is a sucky player. He hasn't been kicked off only because he's fearless and will go after anyone or anything to get the ball. And once he has it, he protects it as viciously as Gollum guards his *precious*. Or so I've heard.

Doug lumbers by me as Buddy, in his usual Rock Hollow Saber Cats jacket, yaps away. They don't even glance in my direction.

Good. This hoodie seems to work—my own cloaking device.

I make it to my locker. Someone's taped up orange flyers all over saying:

Don't Forget: HALLOWEEN HOEDOWN, Oct 29th!!!
See a member of the Pep Club to volunteer.
COSTUMES ENCOURAGED, Y'ALL!

Good to know where I *won't* be on October 29th. But if it were now instead of a few weeks away, I could just blend in with the zombies.

A couple of teachers head my way, so I ease down my hood. As far as I can tell, no one notices my hair.

Seven minutes to class. As soon as the teachers pass and turn the corner, I pull my hood up again. Taking my time, I put things away, grab what I need for French, and shut my locker door. As the five-minute bell rings, I survey the hall, but it's clear I'm still invisible as usual.

I have just enough time to check my site.

You're not supposed to use phones in the hall, blah blah blah, but I go to my Graphite website. I'm a little obsessive—I check my comments all the time—but hey. I'd much rather be in Graphite's world.

Someone behind me laughs. Just some loud girls walking by.

I face the lockers and drop my backpack on the floor between my feet. Come on, "global network." This crap phone's so slow. I look over my shoulder, but no one's even remotely looking my way.

I got some new posts. One's from BigGreenBro, who always likes my stuff, asking, *How do you draw muscles so good?* I almost reply, *You can learn a lot on porn sites*, but instead type, *You just have to study the body and how it moves.*

BigGreenBro always has positive comments. I figure he must draw too. Or she? Well, a girl wouldn't call herself Bro, but what do I know?

A comment from Anonymous says *what's up with the lame-ass costume? what are those ribbony things? welcome to the 21st century.* Real sweet. Delete. And then one from phaserstud, who always thinks it necessary to say I should draw tits, which is so annoying since Graphite's *gay*.

Bam!

I clutch my phone to my chest. Just someone slamming a locker.

Breathe, Adrian.

Now that I have muscles on my mind, I hunch over even more and scan my gallery page for my favorite drawing, which I still can't believe I posted, even though my name is nowhere on my site. Graphite, kneeling in the Trevi Fountain, is shirtless and, well, wet. Very. That was fun to draw. And research. It may be time for another inspired work like—"*Hey!*"

Someone plows into my left side. My phone flies out of my hand and hits the wall with a *crack!* I spin around. "What—"

"Sorry! Not my fault!" It's that senior drama kid, Kobe, his spiky bleached-out hair at full attention.

Behind him is Doug's pet asswipe, Buddy, gangly and wiry and always switched on. He kicks at Kobe's pointy purple boots. "Hey, homo, don't go shovin' people like that. Ain't ladylike." Buddy motions to push him into someone else, then smirks as Kobe flinches.

Backed against the lockers, Kobe glares. "Really? This is how you ask me on a date? Roses work better, ya know."

"What'd you say, faggot?" Buddy spits out the words.

I step to the side. Rubbing my shoulder, I glance at the floor and spot my phone. Crap. Between it and me is Doug, arms crossed. He doesn't look at me, though, and no one seems to notice my phone.

From under that dirty red cap, Doug eyes Buddy, then glances around. Even with everyone rushing to first period, a few people hang back and watch the scene. How come there's no teacher in sight?

Kobe turns to go, but Buddy grabs his arm and swings him. Kobe trips and falls into Doug's chest.

"What the—" Doug shoves him off. I jump out of the way as Kobe hits the floor hard.

He scrambles to get up and screams at Doug, "Get away, you damn cow pussy."

Buddy gapes at Doug. "Holy shit! Did he just call you a damn *cow* pussy?"

Some guy nearby goes, "Whoa, dude said that to *Doug*?"

"Is that even a thing?" someone asks.

"Oh, man." Buddy shakes his head and smiles at Kobe. "So much for you, little bitch." He steps aside to give Doug room. More kids gather around.

Another guy next to me says, "This oughta be good."

Good?

I try to blend in with the lockers. I check around but can't just slink away or pick up my phone.

With all eyes on him, Doug scans up and down the hall, inhales, and steps toward Kobe. "You need to shut your fuckin' mouth."

Kobe's eyes dart from Doug to Buddy. Then to me. I freeze. The fear in Kobe's eyes stops my breath.

Buddy looks at me. "Ha!" He barks out a laugh and points at my head. "What the fuck happened to you?"

Crap! My hoodie fell back. "Nothing," I try to say, but my throat won't work.

Doug turns his focus to me.

With quick strokes, I smooth down my hair as best as I can. My face is on fire.

Using the moment, Kobe dashes down the hall through the crowd. Buddy spins and takes off after him.

As Doug turns to follow them, I eye my phone, a few feet away by the heating vent. He notices and, with his stupid keychain clanking against his hip, walks toward it.

"Hey," I mumble, "that's mine—" and I trip over my backpack and fall on my ass. A few gawkers laugh.

Doug reaches for my phone.

Out of nowhere, big black leather boots stomp over and kick my phone. It slides under the heating vent, into the wall. Gone.

Only one person wears boots like that. All six foot three inches of him, skinny, dressed head to toe in goth black, cascades of silver chains jangling from his belt, and looking bored. Trent. Man, am I glad to see him.

"What the hell's your deal?" Doug draws out the words. But Trent just stares down at him, his face blank.

Doug grunts. "Freak." Then he heads off in Buddy's direction.

Trent helps me stand.

"I can get up," I say.

He hands me my backpack. "El haircut-o no work-o, I take it?" he says.

Turning my back to the dispersing crowd, I say, "Trent, why the hell did you kick my phone into the vent?"

"Favor, dude."

"Favor? Really?"

He rolls his eyes. "No time to reach it. At least piss brain doesn't have it, does he?" He motions down the hall where Doug went.

"Well, neither do I." I attempt to flatten my hair and peer under the vent but can't see a thing except clumps of dust.

I jump as the final bell rings. "Damn! Look, meet me here after first period. I'll bring a ruler and tape, or whatever. I need my phone."

Trent salutes me. "*Bueno*, dude." He clomps down the hall. As he turns the corner, he half-smiles. "By the way, your hair looks like crap. It's *awesome*."

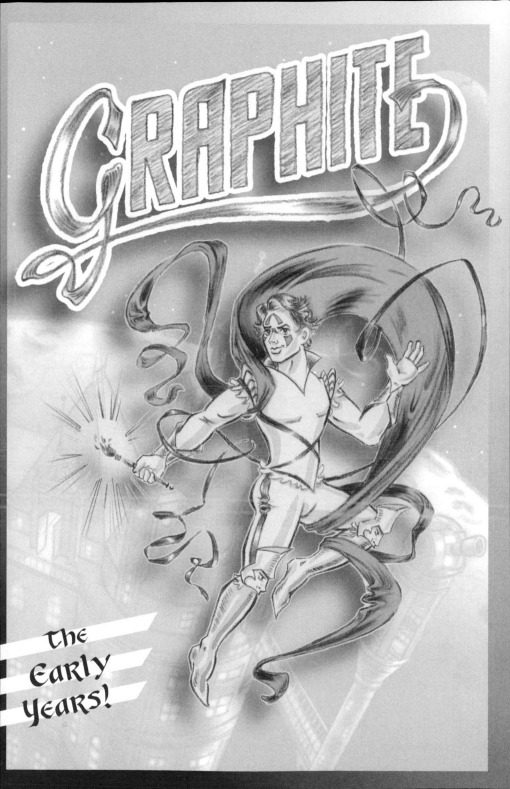

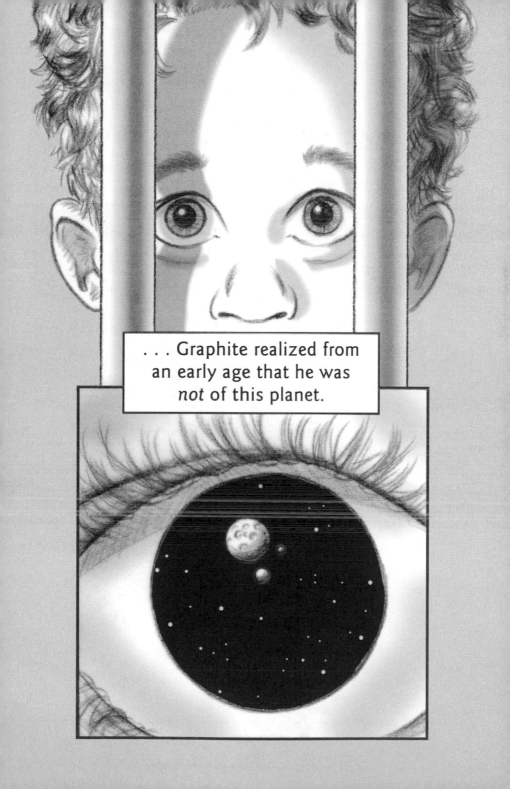

. . . Graphite realized from an early age that he was *not* of this planet.

Without any clue as to his roots, he created his own identity, mapped the skies, and searched the universe for his home world . . .

. . . but to no avail.

Now a recluse in his hidden palace on the dark side of the moon, he is all but forgotten. This is as he wishes. He finds peace in his secluded domain.

Using his powers, he can create any nonliving thing he desires. Whether an addition to his realm or a feast for a king, it becomes real.

In the material world, Graphite wants for nothing. Yet . . .

. . . he longs for companionship,
of a certain nature.
Alas, it seems not to be.

Three

EVEN WITH ALL THE CAFETERIA CLANGS AND BABBLES ECHOING OFF
the cinder block walls, I speak in a low voice.

I hold up my poor, cracked used-to-be phone. "You see?
This is why I'm not gay."

Clutching his half-eaten burrito, Trent tilts his head, like
dogs do. "Dude, you *are* gay."

Ugh. "I'm gay, but I'm not *gay*!"

"Okay. That hurts my brain."

I roll my eyes. "You know exactly what I mean. I'm outwardly gay on the inside, but inwardly gay on the outside.
Now, if I were outwardly gay on the outside, well, I'd probably end up like this phone."

"Ow!" Trent says. "Stop. My brain!"

"BOYS." Audrey pushes her empty chili bowl to the side
and says in her I'm-a-senior-and-you-guys-are-not tone,

"Are we really going through this again? And, Adrian, pull that damn hood off your head. I swear."

This thing's hot, anyway. And we three are pretty much removed here in the corner at our usual table—our little Nerd Island. No surprise, we always get it to ourselves. Down goes my hoodie. It's like lowering my shields.

"Good god!" Trent covers his eyes. "Put it back! Put it back!"

Audrey snorts. "Trent! Stop." Eyeing my hair, she says, "Really, it's not so baaa—" More cracking up.

I grit my teeth. "Guys! Not. Funny. All right?"

Trent sits up straight. "Got it. Jokes aside, your hair looks even better." I think he means it. "And, oddly, smells minty fresh."

Audrey purses her lips, then says, "Adrian, you white boys do some crazy-ass stuff with your hair. But what possessed you to do *that*?"

I smirk at her. "You guys are a real comfort." Then I pop open my can of Dr Pepper and take a swig.

She adjusts her chunky baubled necklace (every day a different one—"to keep one's eyes from looking at the rest of me," she says). "Everybody's gay now, Adrian. Look at all these sports figures and celebrities. Gay marriage all over the place? And all these gay teens going to dances together? Poll numbers show that—"

"Why, thank you, Professor." Trent salutes her with a tortilla chip. "I'm sure your findings are elucidating on the matter. But, ya know, your point?"

She gives him the Audrey Eye. "'Elucidating'? That your word of the day?"

"Indubitably." He rolls up his gauzy black sleeve to reveal where he wrote *elucidating* on his forearm. Each day he has a new word to drop into conversation, a whole advanced vocabulary in various stages of smears covering his skin.

I lower my voice. "Audrey, maybe coming out is magically easy for people somewhere else. So they want us to think. But I happen to live in the *real* world. Besides, my life is no one's business. And it's not as if I'll ever have someone to take to a dance, anyway."

"I'm just saying—"

"*You* don't understand what it's like to be gay."

She crosses her arms. "You think that's hard? You don't understand what it's like to be a plus-size black girl."

"Oh no no no." Trent tosses tortilla chips at us. "Stop right there. Put down your weapons. How'd we get here? Weren't we just talking about hair?"

Audrey sighs. "I only—"

Trent holds up his hands. "Hey, you don't hear me going on about all the you-must-play-basketball, how's-the-weather-up-there, sit-down-cuz-you're-casting-a-shadow-across-North-America crap I get, just because I'm as freakishly tall as the Eiffel Tower?"

Audrey blinks. "Well, we just did."

Trent turns to me. "Changing subjects. So . . . do you know what happened to that guy Kobe after this morning?"

I shake my head. Those scared eyes appear in my mind.

"Hope he doesn't look like this." I pick up my was-phone. "Guess this counts as collateral damage."

"If I were in Doug's sights," Audrey says, "it's *after* school I'd be worried about. I doubt he'd go too far on school property."

Trent grunts. "Harder to get away with crap when Daddy's not around."

Everyone knows Doug's father was Mr. Hotshit Football Dude here back when he was in high school. Family legacy. But more than that, now he's a top cop.

And with Doug and Buddy together it's like two chemicals that, when mixed the wrong way, could explode.

Doug and I have gone to the same schools since first grade, even a lot of the same classes, and I suppose we're used to each other after all these years. I'm used to avoiding him, and he's used to not seeing me. I'm like the lockers to him, always there but who gives a crap. At least I guess—hard to really know since Doug barely says a word to anyone. Of course, he doesn't have to. Who's going to mess with *him*?

But now it seems he and Buddy are on a Homo Hunt and, after having a front-row seat this morning . . . I don't know. Only Audrey and Trent know about *me*, and I aim to keep it that way.

All day I've been dashing from class to class, head down and hood up when possible, getting some crap during classes for the postmodern sculpture that is my hair. But no one ever takes me seriously anyway, if they notice me at all.

Doug, Buddy, and their Saber Cats football friends have the other lunch period so are in class now—or football practice, or jackass homeroom, or whatever the hell they do. Still, I survey the cafeteria in case but only spy the predictable pods of look-alikes in their little clusters.

I lift my soft drink for a sip but catch someone glaring at me so intensely I freeze. He looks away, then right back.

"Hey, be careful!" Audrey grabs the Dr Pepper from my hand. "You trying to get me wet? This cardigan ain't cheap."

"Good save, there, Audrey." Trent tosses her a few napkins.

"Huh?" I say. How'd I spill that?

"Dude, you really need some sleep," Trent says. "You're losing your grip. Literally."

I look back at the glaring guy, but he's turned to his friends, talking like nothing happened.

"Sorry, Audrey." I help sop up the last drops. "Listen, over by the column with the clock, who's that guy? With the curly black hair and Saber Cats shirt?"

They turn to see. Trent shrugs.

"Oh, god." Audrey rolls her eyes. "He's in my AP history and is *so* annoying. He sits next to me, but all I know is he's on the wrestling team and won't shut up about it."

"Wrestling? Well, he was just, like, staring *through* me. Did you see?"

"Nope," Trent says with a mouthful of bean burrito. "Prob'ly just in awe of your new hair-hat."

"People *are* staring at you, Adrian, so just drop it," Audrey says, still dabbing at her sweater.

Right. Audrey and Trent may give me crap, but I can't imagine having to fend for myself without them, not even among the geeky fanboys—the least alarming group here—all huddled at their table over there against the wall. I'm a sci-fi/fantasy fanboy myself, of course, but they're a bit *too* geeky for me. I'm less fan and more *creator*. Besides, all they want to do is draw big tits on almost-clad babes shooting guns and crap. Not my world.

"Audrey," I say, "if you had to go sit with another group here, right now, which table would you go to?"

She arches an eyebrow. "Why? You tryin' to tell me somethin'?"

"No," I say. "Just curious."

She eyes me, then crosses her arms and surveys the room. "Since I don't see a table of fellow glamorous, intelligent single ladies in here . . . I'd have to say I'd be with the teachers. Although maybe not that creepy science teacher with the comb-over. Yeek."

"Teachers?"

"You asked! And think about it," she says. "That's where you'd get the *real* scoop on this place."

"C'mon," Trent says. "You don't care about all that bullshit."

"Hey, it's always good to know what's truly going on. Fewer surprises that way."

Trent swallows half a brownie, then says, "I'll tell you what's going on around here." He shapes his black-nail-polished fingers into a big zero.

"Well, at least caffeine is going on now." Audrey dramatically holds up her latte and takes a sip. Ever since the coffee bar appeared in the cafeteria this semester, she's been downing lattes like it's the sustenance of life itself.

I check out the staring Wrestler Guy again, but he's focused on his friends. It must have been like Trent said. I tuck my phone in my backpack, then slip farther down in my chair. "How am I gonna tell Mom about this? After the last phone—"

Trent holds up a peace sign. "Two."

I roll my eyes. "Okay okay. After the last *two* phones, she said this was *it*. And she doesn't mess around."

Audrey and Trent glance at each other. They know money trees don't grow at my house.

The whole screen is cracked. Power button does nothing. "When I get home I'll put it in a bowl of rice."

"Say what?" Audrey says.

"Dude, that's only if you get a phone *wet*," Trent says, "which is one of the many hazards of toilet texting, I'm afraid."

Audrey's eyes pop. "Wow, that's way TMI, there, Trent."

He smiles. "I speak from experience."

She turns her full body to face him. "Please. Never. Text. Me. Again."

Great. *I* won't be texting *anyone* again.

Trent eyes my untouched burrito. "Go for it," I say. "And don't look at me like that, Audrey. I'm not gonna faint. I'm just not hungry." My stomach's so knotted up it's almost like I'm gonna puke, in fact.

She shakes her head. "I swear, a strong wind's gonna come along one day and scoop up your skinny ass."

I snort a little Dr Pepper through my nose.

"Oh," Audrey says, "you *can* smile!"

High-pitched squeals bounce over from the drama kids' table.

"There's Kobe," Trent says. "Looks okay from here."

Where? Oh, good. He seems to be unscathed, and lucky . . . for now. The drama kids are howling at whatever tidbit Kobe is revealing as he holds court. Other than him, I don't know the names of any of the kids at that table. Even though there are a couple guys, it's mostly girls, all making asses of themselves. Whatever.

With jazz hands in the air (not kidding), Kobe belts out some song about everything coming up roses as one of the girls falls out of her seat onto the floor. The cafeteria floor! Repulsive. The whole room turns for a second, and then the hoots and slurs commence, which just make Kobe go up an octave.

Not only is he the sole out gay kid I know of, but he's also so cliché gay it's no wonder there's a huge freakin' target on his back.

It's amazing he doesn't seem to care after what happened to that guy a couple years ago. I was just a freshman so didn't have any classes with him, but this junior came out as gay to his whole English class. Then it began: the names, the horrible crap they spread online and scrawled on his locker, and worse. One day after school he got jumped—they broke his arm in three places. He never came back to school. They said it was a couple seniors who did it, but no one got punished.

People don't talk about it anymore, like it never happened.

Oh, god, is Kobe actually tap-dancing now?

"Behold," I say to Audrey and Trent. "Yet another reason *I'm not gay.*"

Trent stares at the dramatics. "Words of wisdom, my friend. Words of wisdom. Even though you *are.*"

Audrey points at Trent's face. "Crazy." Then me. "Super-crazy." Then herself. "Outta here." She stands. "I've got a test on el imperfecto de subjuntivo next in español, and I gotta get there early."

Trent nods. "Allow moi to el help-o you-o to el study-o."

Audrey scoops up her purse, books, and tray in one swoop. "Oh, *hell-*o *no-*o, Señor Wack-o."

I crack up.

She stops. "Ooh! I forgot. Adrian, I'm taking you to my girl Patricia—she'll fix you up. I already texted her about your hair 911. And wipe that look off your face. She's done men's hair before. Least I think. Appointment scheduled for six p.m. Today. I'm picking you up."

"*What?*" Now I may really throw up.

"You're welcome." She strides away.

From Trent's expression, I must be extra pale at this news. "That'll be a treat," he says.

I flip up my hood and pull the cord around my face. Tight. Then I notice the staring Wrestler Guy leaving the cafeteria, peering right at me.

Four

ETERNALISM IS A PHILOSOPHICAL APPROACH TO EXPLORING THE
relative pace of time or, to be specific, in what circumstances
it moves fast versus slow. Time is, indeed, relative. I know
this, not only due to my *Slaughterhouse-Five* essay last year,
but because when you hack up your own hair, have your sole
means of mobile communication destroyed in redneck cross-
fire, and have scary guys staring at you all day, each minute
feels like a freakin' *eternity*.

You'd think being home would be a relief, but Mom works
her night job at the Holiday Inn desk tonight so it's up to me
to prep Dad's dinner. Because of when he takes his meds, he
has to eat early, which is why I'm here chopping lettuce in the
kitchen after school instead of drawing in my room.

As I attempt to open the utensil drawer, the handle pulls
off again. Dad should at least be able to fix a freakin' handle

in his condition. I mean, he designed and built this whole kitchen, for god's sake. It used to be nice.

I grab a screwdriver from the miscellaneous crap drawer and try to fix the handle myself. "Hey, Dad?" I call.

"Yup?" he yells from the living room, ESPN blaring.

"I got everything set. Salad and sandwich are all made and in the fridge. Whenever you want 'em." I try to tighten the damn screws, but they're both stripped.

He says something, but I can't make it out over the TV.

"What?" I say as the stupid handle just slips off and clangs on the floor. "Oh, come on!" I slam the drawer shut.

"Huh?" he says.

Take a breath, Adrian. I close my eyes. "What was that, Dad?"

"What kind of dressing did you put on the salad?"

Now I have no way to open the damn drawer. I wedge the screwdriver between the cabinet and the drawer front and wiggle it around.

"Ranch!" I say.

"Ranch?" he says. "Oh, well."

Really?

I grip the screwdriver and pry the drawer open. Maybe there are some screws in the garage I can use, but later. I just want to finish cleaning up and get to my drawing table.

"Hey, Ade?" Dad calls. I *hate* that nickname, but after a life of it at home, no choice. "Coors. D'ya mind?"

Mind? Let's see, besides Dad Duty, what the hell else would I want to be doing right now? But like the trained robot I am, I already have my hand in the fridge. So he won't holler for me again later, I bring two Coors and plop them down by his weekly meds container on the folding tray at his side. Hard to tell at this point where his body stops and the recliner begins.

He grunts but doesn't take his eyes away from the armored hulks on the screen trying to brain-damage each other to get that little ball. Again, I marvel how I could be the same species as these people. Although I do like it when they slap each other's butts. In super-tight pants. With those bulges.

"No! You're so slow. Hustle, hustle!" he yells.

It's been two and a half years since Dad's car wreck. It wasn't his fault and is beyond unfair. The crash broke his back. But after physical therapy ended, he stopped trying, slowed down, and got bigger. It's been only a couple years, but it feels like he's been home "recovering" a lot longer than that.

It all sucks so much, more for him than anyone. I get that, of course. I know he didn't ask for this.

But neither did Mom, having to work night and day for crap money.

And neither did I.

Focused on the game, he says, "Did ya see that? The ball was right there! That guy is completely blind. Blind!" He pops open a beer. "Thanks, son." He doesn't even glance at me.

I tape a BROKEN sign on the stupid drawer, finish up in the kitchen, then retreat to my room, followed by Harley Quinn.

I shut my door, go online, and scan for any new website comments. Nothing. It's not like a ton of people stumble upon my site, but at this point some do check in, so there's traffic.

But no one actually *gets* Graphite. No one. I shouldn't be

surprised, considering art imitates life. Or is it life imitates art? Either way. When I do find comments there are always *way* more negative ones than positive. Lots of ranting about what sucks, what *they'd* do different, what defies their narrow logic . . . the haters lecturing me on what a freaking superhero is supposed to be.

Of course, some are outraged that he's gay and have to spew various versions of digital hate. Thank god for the gay geeks who at least think Graphite's hot, although they seem bewildered too. Some say he doesn't do anything, doesn't kick anyone's ass, doesn't have sex, even that he's not queer *enough*.

And *forget* the Renaissance part. Everyone's all baffled why Graphite's world is filled with Renaissance beauty and design. 'Cause I freakin' like it and it's cool. Okay, you hating Internet a-holes?

Graphite isn't here to save the world, especially not for you. He's here for me.

I know all the mainstream gay characters, scan all the queer fan forums, see a lot of other fanboy character creations . . . but gay or straight, it's all about shootin' and screwin'. Graphite's about creating, not killing. I never got why superheroes need to destroy to make a difference.

At least Audrey and Trent understand Graphite's world some, but that's because I explain it to them. They like how I draw, but on their own, I bet they'd never look. And I have a whole bunch of drawings even they haven't seen.

They have no idea I've created superhero versions of *them*. Maybe I'll share those, someday, but I bet it'd freak them out.

The only way to see someone, truly see someone, is to draw them. Drawing makes you study every aspect . . . understand a person's essence.

But they might not like what I see in them.

Hey, a new comment pops up. From BigGreenBro: *Really like your latest comics and how you draw. What's next?*

Wow. That's the first time anyone's asked for more. Awesome. I reply. Graphite: *Thanks for asking. More coming soon!*

BigGreenBro: *Cool.*

I've tried in the past to find out who BigGreenBro could be, since he's one of the few who leaves positive comments. He's anonymous but has a page of his own on the DeviantArt site. But nothing's posted—no art, no bio, no photo, no comments. Just a lurker, I guess.

Graphite: *You an artist too?*

BigGreenBro: *Kinda. Don't draw so good. And still in high school.*

Graphite: *Yeah? Me too.*

Damn. Why'd I post that? Stupid! And my comments page is public so anyone can see.

BigGreenBro: *Cool. Thought so.*

Really? Gotta end this.

Graphite: *Later*

Why the hell did I do that? I get up and pace. Sure, he could be a teen, but he could also be some sixty-year-old pervert.

Harley paws my leg. "Maow!"

"Okay okay." I twirl her ribbon and she pounces.

I go ahead and delete the conversation, then log off.

No harm done, I guess. I list no personal info anywhere

on my site. I could be in Australia for all anyone knows. And maybe he really is just another teen?

All right, enough of the outside world. Time to draw.

I put on a *Little Big Planet* game soundtrack and kiss Harley on her tiny head.

For inspiration, I like to look at my boyfriend. He's Italian and his name is Bindo Altoviti. He's hot, mysterious, and much older than me. Oh, and he's dead. Pulling out *Renaissance Portraits: The Bold and the Beautiful*, I find him. Page forty-four. My Renaissance Hottie. So he died in the 1500s, big deal. A guy can dream. Raphael painted him to look so gorgeous, with those full lips, intense gaze, cascading hair—

Hair. Oh, yeah. Don't need the reminder of how drawing hair started this whole suck of a day. I flip the book shut and pull out my reference photos of my favorite palace, the Château de Chambord in France. A. Freakin. Maze. Ing. It has the craziest roof, filled with towers and spires like a whole little city in the sky. So, of course, Graphite's Moon Palace already has a lot of that, but I think it's time for a few *more* towers.

As soon as I switch on my drawing lamp, Harley leaps up to her spot on my table and becomes a purring ball-o-fur. I pin my reference printouts to my corkboard in front of me and start to sketch. My ancient, taped-together pencil sharpener sounds like an airplane taking off, but that doesn't disturb Harley. Her little ears do that radar turn thing, but she's already in her zone.

These new towers will be tricky. To get perspective right, you have to put yourself there in your mind and look at it from different angles. This is why I don't sketch on the computer. With paper you can literally scratch the surface. Dig in. And when you erase something the paper still shows what you tried.

I sketch it like you're walking along one of the garden paths, spires and monoliths towering above. No, not like that. Ugh. This eraser's almost down to the end.

I used to trace other people's art, and sometimes I still do. You can learn so much by copying something amazing. I once got a library book with every figure in the Sistine Chapel blown up big and spent an entire week tracing each page, over and over. Wow. Michelangelo sure knew how to draw smokin'-hot guys! Holy crap. With flowing fabric. And those faces, so intense. And the hands. And muscles. Mind-blowing. *Those* are some superheroes!

I keep trying to draw muscles and bodies like he did. Once in a while I find Graphite starts looking like a hot floating saint.

Uh-oh, now these roof spires are starting to look like Michelangelo's arms and legs. Or other body parts. Oh, my god. I've pretty much just sketched an entire roof garden of penises.

Hmmm . . . I don't think Graphite's palace needs a garden like *that*. I turn to a blank page and start—

BEEEP! BEEEP!

Harley lifts her head and yawns. Some annoying car horn. It must be the neighbor's dog in the street again, blocking the way.

BEEEEEEP!

Oh, come on. Fine. I get up and pull open the curtain to see what's the fuss and—

Huh? It's Audrey.

Oh, man! Six p.m. Haircut.

Crap!

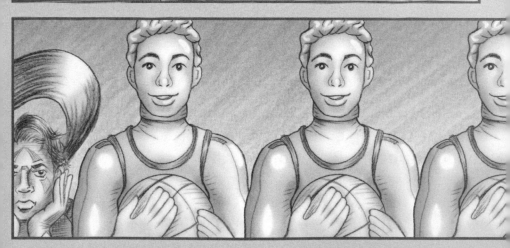

On Earth, Graphite was enlisted into a human conformist camp.

During a training exercise, he was able to hide using his Power of Invisibility.

A fellow Outsider, **Willow** saw those things that others could not. Surrounded by his Bubble of Calm, Willow used his keen X-Ray Vision to observe all.

On Earth, Graphite relieved his boredom by observing humans undetected. But it just left him feeling more alien than before . . .
Z Z Z Z Z
TAKE COVER! A TITANIC TWISTER IS A-COMIN'! AHHHHHHH!
SLAM!!!

The stranger's Powers of Telepathy gave Graphite away. Not only could **Sultry** read others' thoughts, but she did it with *style*. In an instant, Graphite recognized another fellow Outsider.

A second Outsider came into his world, but Graphite has yet to encounter another.

Five

BEEEP! BEEEEEP!

Okay okay! I wave at Audrey through the window to stop her laying on the horn.

I tuck away my sketchpad and art stuff, throw water on my face, grab my wallet and my phone (oh, yeah—never mind), reach the front door—then freeze. Why did I agree to this haircut? Not too late to back out, right?

But another horn blast gets me outside and now I'm in the world again.

A few dead leaves blow around in the gutter from the exhaust of Audrey's purring black Beemer, named Athena, after the Greek goddess of wisdom and courage—her favorite. As I drag myself toward the car, Audrey looks over from the driver's seat and her eyes get wide. Like she's shooing flies, she flaps her hands at me, knocking the tiny toy high heels that dangle from the rearview mirror. She then turns off the car, flings open the door, and leaps out.

"No, no, no! Step away from the vehicle!" She strides around the front of the car to face me on the sidewalk. "Turn." She rotates her finger.

"You've got to be kidding."

I get a hands-on-hips I-ain't-budging-till-you-do-as-I-say glare.

"This is idiotic," I say, but spin around.

"What am I gonna do with you? I'm takin' you to a nice salon, ya know. Did you get dressed in the dark again?"

I look to the heavens. "Can we just go?"

She surveys me up and down, glaring at the clothes I changed into after school. "Raggedy ol' sweatpants? Ripped concert T-shirt? You wear this in public?"

"First of all," I explain, "this is not a concert T-shirt. It says 'Trust Me, I'm a Jedi'—that's not a band. Secondly, this is Rock Hollow, Texas, not Milan, Italy."

I should comment on how *over*dressed she is in her purple cashmere sweater, satiny charcoal pants, glittery black pumps, and ever-present bling. But I know better. She may have the opposite of a model's body, but she sure knows how to look good.

"Adrian, underneath that frightening hair and all the nerdy, uh . . . well, *that*"—she gestures at my clothes—"you're actually cute. Where's your fashion gene? What kinda gay boy *are* you?"

"Shut up! People can hear you." I glance around at the neighbors' empty front yards. My stomach tightens.

She opens her arms. "Who? There isn't anyone out here

but us and the squirrels gatherin' up their winter nuts." She looks up at the oak tree by the sidewalk and points over to me. "Do *you* care if he's gay?"

"I said *shut up!*" I look back at my house and lower my voice. "You *never* know who's around." I head for the car and jump in.

Settling back in the driver's seat, she closes her door and gives me the Audrey Eye.

I scan the neighbors' houses. "Just because I like guys doesn't mean I have to be all fashiony fabulous."

"I take it you're not gonna change," she says.

I glare at her. "You know how I feel. I'm not a cliché. I am who I am."

She rolls her eyes. "I know *that*. I meant your clothes."

I buckle my seat belt. "Maybe I should consult your little squirrel friends on what to wear from now on."

"Worth a try." She pulls away from the curb and we head up the street.

With Audrey so stylish and me so, well . . . *not*, at first glance you wouldn't think we'd even know each other, much less be friends. But ever since a tornado drill back in fourth grade, we've clicked.

During a drill, you're supposed to sit along the hallway walls and tuck your head between your knees. I remember being in "the position" and looking up at this girl ranting about how there was "no way" she'd sit on "that filthy lino-leum in this Gucci skirt!" Mrs. Caruth informed her, "Better to sit down and get a little dirty than have some funnel cloud come down and snatch up you *and* that little skirt." The appalled look on Audrey's face cracked me up. But when she replied, "Sorry, Gucci's worth it," I laughed so hard I started snorting. Once the all clear sounded we got hauled off to the principal's office. No better way to bond than that.

"Why are you staring at me?" Audrey says. We're stopped at a red light.

"Huh? Ohmygod!" I say. "Trent!"

"Oh your god Trent *what*?"

"We have to pick him up. I asked him to come too."

MEEEEEEEEP! The car behind us lays on its horn.

"Simmer down! I see it's green!" Audrey zooms ahead. "Wish you'd told me. You're tryin' my nerves, Adrian. We can't be late—Patricia's squeezing you in as a favor."

A favor? This wasn't my idea.

But in a few minutes we're waiting outside Trent's house. You'd think it wouldn't take that long to get ready when your entire wardrobe is black. Applying eyeliner in a perfect goth way takes time, I know, but it's dealing with his mom that holds him up. Audrey knows better than to honk here. Same with ringing the doorbell. So we wait.

Audrey's purple-manicured nails tap the steering wheel while she eyes me and the dashboard clock.

"Fine." I slip out of the car, and just as I'm tiptoeing up the front walk, Trent appears in the doorway.

He nods at me. "'Sup?"

Inside the house the TV blasts way too loud.

"What's your mom doing?" I say.

"Screwing with my SOUL!" he yells, slamming the front door with a *BAM!*

As we hustle down the front walk, I ask, "What did God tell her to do this time?"

"Doesn't matter," he says. "She'll be passed out soon."

I reach out to pat him on the back, but he doesn't notice and glides by.

I glance back at his house. It's so long now since I've been inside. Must be over a year, just after his sister went to college, his dad dumped them all, and his mom got remarried to Jesus . . . and bourbon. Freaky to think his psycho mom's the same woman who was my gung-ho Cub Scout den mother when we were little. Cub Scouts. Makes me shiver. At least Trent and I became friends before we both dropped out. Never joined a group since. Obi-Wan be praised.

The front door opens and his mom steps out. Wow, I almost don't recognize her. Eyelids half-mast and hair all jumbled, she clutches the front of her nightgown. Then she spots me. In slow motion, her face goes from pinched to fierce. She points right at me and spits out, "Not today, Satan. *Not today!*"

I back up against the car.

"Mom!" Trent says through gritted teeth. He glances at the neighbors' quiet houses and dashes up to her, puts his hands on her shoulders. She knocks them away.

"Mom, calm down. You're tired."

Glaring at me, she says, "You will *not* go anywhere with that queer!"

Trent stands to his full height, tilts his head down, and

whispers in her ear. His mom scans the street and the neighbors' yards, then slinks back inside. Trent follows.

I jump into the backseat of the car and gape at wide-eyed Audrey. "What the hell?"

She just shakes her head.

Trent reappears in the doorway, alone. He pulls the front door shut with a soft click. Then he hurries to the car and folds himself into the front seat, shutting the car door. Audrey and I share a glance in the rearview mirror.

Audrey accelerates and we zip along the street, the setting sun flashing with a strobe-light rhythm through the gaps between houses.

Trent grips his knees and breaks the silence with "Welcome to my very own personal Kingdom on Earth."

Audrey shakes her head. "Lordy."

I lean forward, holding the back of Trent's seat. "What was that about me and Satan?"

He sighs. "She thinks you'll turn me gay."

"You told her I'm gay?"

"No. She figured it out for herself." He swallows. "Sorry."

I touch his shoulder. "Trent, *I'm* sorry. I had no idea you—"

"Can we just drop it?" He grabs Audrey's phone from the cup holder and scans through her music. "Let's move on, all right?"

I sit back and try to wrap my head around what just happened.

Unable to find any morose music, Trent shuts his eyes and taps Audrey's screen at random. We're jolted by some vapid, poppy, dancy tune that I know everyone's supposed to love. But, as with most things, I'm hardly the target audience.

Glancing sideways at Trent, Audrey attempts to lighten the mood and shimmies in her seat to the beat. *"Now* we're talkin'!"

Trent cracks a smile, breathes in deep, then exhales long and slow. How does he live with a mom like that?

Although there's no way I'm gonna shimmy, there is something pretty awesome about speeding along in a BMW with a kick-ass sound system, no matter what the music.

After a while, Audrey's phone dings. Trent lowers the music volume and says, "Hey, you got a text from the famous Patricia."

"Oh?" Audrey says. "Read it for me."

"'Did your friend sign the death waiver? Can't be sued again for accidental ear chopping.'"

Audrey groans.

"Ha, freakin', ha," I say.

"Uh-oh, dude. Listen up: 'SOOOOO sorry, but I'm swamped! Can't cut your friend's hair now, and weekend not looking good. SORRY!!!' Then she put about a hundred little sad faces and pink hearts."

"No way!" I say. "Let me see."

He holds up the phone for me to read as Audrey pulls into a parking lot to stop and see for herself.

"This sucks," I say. "What am I gonna do?"

Audrey texts her friend back, then tosses the phone to Trent. Squinting at my hair in the rearview mirror, she says, "We'll figure out something."

"Like what?"

Giving me a thumbs-up, Trent says, "Don't change a thing, looks awesome."

Rolling her eyes, Audrey slaps his hand away and gets us onto Settlement Street again.

Trent goes back to scanning Audrey's music. "So . . . what now?"

Although my drawing table pops into my head, my stomach has a different idea. "What's for dinner at your house, Audrey?"

"Parents' Methodist church group and Bible study," she says.

"Noooooo thankee," Trent says, playing another too-peppy song.

Audrey eases to a stop at a red light. "We're right near the mall. If Chili's is too crowded there we could do the food court."

I jump. "I can't go into the mall with my hair like this!"

"Maybe Tito's Taco Truck?" Trent says.

I shake my head. "Not in the mood to eat outside."

Audrey sighs. "C'mon, now, it's getting later and I'm in no mood to get pulled over for 'Driving While Black.'"

With no other easy eating options left—not at my or Trent's house, for sure—I suggest Boo, our usual place. Happily, they agree. Not only is the food good and cheap, but Boo is laid-back and pretty dark inside.

This is not at all the night I'd hoped for, but here we are—a badly dressed gay boy, a fashionable black girl, and a moody vampire—all out for fun on a Texas Friday night.

Yee-ha!

Six

AS TRENT ATTEMPTS IN DESPERATION TO FIND A NONBOUNCY TUNE on Audrey's phone, Boo's purple neon sign comes into view. Boo isn't fancy, being part of a strip mall and all, but there's no place like it. Its actual name is La Boulangerie, which means bakery in French. But, of course, it's impossible for most people to pronounce, so it's been called all sorts of different things, like Bowl Angry and, my personal favorite, Blue Laundry. Somehow, though, it has simply become Boo.

The only downside is the too-close-for-comfort redneck hangout next door, Bubba's. No joke, that's really its name.

We turn into the parking lot and, wow, there are already tons of cars here. Big-ass pickups, too: bubbamobiles. Just great. As we circle to find a parking spot, we glide past a couple of guys in well-worn cowboy hats ambling toward

Bubba's. They eye us through the windshield, do a double take, then glare like we're sideshow freaks.

"Park as close to Boo as possible, please," I say to Audrey, my fingers checking the door lock. Trent just ignores them.

Audrey mumbles to the rolled-up window, "Keep starin' at me like that and I'll shove those hats where the sun don't shine."

We find a close spot.

Trent unfolds himself from the front seat, always an amazing sight.

"Six hundred and nine days, my friends," he says. "Six hundred and nine." His daily Countdown Clock to Graduation helps him somehow but only makes escaping high school seem further away than ever for me.

As we walk to Boo's entrance, he turns to Audrey. "Just two hundred and forty-four for you. Sure you don't want to flunk out and keep us company next year?"

She arches an eyebrow. "Not a chance, funny boy. UT Austin, here I come!"

As soon as we step inside Boo, Audrey's shoulders slump. "Damn, wish those fries didn't smell so good." She pulls the bottom of her sweater down over her hips.

My eyes adjust as I survey the maze of mismatched old couches, chairs, and tables in dim pools of light, all divided by columns wallpapered with overlapping flyers, like a giant work in progress. I can relate.

Over the din of voices I just make out a classic Rolling Stones song. "Finally!" Trent says. "Actual music."

Here and there are some usual faces from both our and our

"rival" high school, and it looks like some community college kids, too. We're surrounded by the ever-present black clothes, splashes of bright neon here and there, blue and/or pink hair, the skinny-jeaned scruffy crowd . . . and no bubbas. To find anywhere else like Boo near Rock Hollow suburbia, you'd have to drive all the way to the cool parts of Dallas.

Still, I just want to eat and get out of here.

I follow Trent and Audrey to an open table and plop down on a lumpy old couch. You can scrawl anything you want on the walls here, and people do. Audrey's always bugging me to let loose with Graphite, but *no* way that's ever gonna happen.

"Hey," I say to Trent, "virgin territory." Our wall right here is one of the few he hasn't practiced his symbol on, some math formula he created called Infinite Radical. Since he's the math genius—as well as infinitely radical—I leave that to him. It'll be his first tattoo, he claims, once the design is perfect.

"Look," Audrey says, "there they go." We watch the vam pirey goth kids from school head out to the parking lot. A couple of them glance our way. Audrey turns to Trent. "I bet they still can't figure out why you won't even talk to them."

"Tough," he says.

"They're still the same people you used to hang out with," she says.

"That was a while ago. You know how I feel."

Trent and addiction don't go well together. Not a mystery why, considering his mom.

Audrey rolls her eyes. "They can't *all* be stoners, or meth addicts, or whatever else they do."

"You think they're heading outside to catch the last rays of the day?" I say.

She laughs. "If only! Still can't figure out why they don't disintegrate in the sun."

Trent smirks in spite of himself. I smile too, and exhale. I didn't realize I was holding my breath.

"Hey, don't look now," I say, "but guess who's working tables tonight." Of course, they both look now, and there he is. Loudly gossiping with some girl, drama queen Kobe reclines against the coffee bar. This morning was intense, but like at lunch, he now seems back to his normal everyone-look-at-me self.

"Okay, boys," Audrey says, "this girl needs to eat!" The melted cheddar cheese and sautéed mushrooms at the table behind us do smell good. She waves and gets Kobe's attention.

Great. No doubt he'll burst into song about what we order, jazz hands all aflutter.

Instead, he saunters over to our table and does his diva thing of facing you but looking away into the distance, like he's waiting for far more exciting people to appear, while pushing up that spiky bleached-out hair. As if gravity could possibly affect it with all the crap that must be in there. Well, today, *I'm* hardly one to talk.

Dropping one beat-up menu on our table—which, of course, we don't need—he says in a flat voice, "Hey, y'all."

When Audrey's annoyed, she has this way of talking real fast without breathing, all with a big smile. "I'll have a Morocco Wrap French fries and Diet Coke thank you very much." She's so good at returning attitude. I sometimes feel like I'm her Attitude Padawan, learning from the Master.

Trent speaks up next. "Veggie burger. Iced tea."

Still staring into space and not writing any of this down, Kobe quips, "How original."

Trent sits up taller and fidgets with the prongs of his fork.

I say, "Hey. I'll have the BBQ turkey burger? And a Dr Pepper. Please."

Kobe puts his hand on his chest and gasps at my hair. "Ohmygod! Who did *that* to you?"

Ah. The familiar burning sensation returns to my face. Didn't he already see my hair this morning in the hall? I guess he must've been too focused on getting the hell away.

"Uh, how was your day today?" I say. "All okay?"

Kobe tilts his head. "Um . . . what?"

I swallow. "Just, uh, wanna be sure everything's fine."

"What are you, my mommy?" He puts his hand on his hip. "Yeah, all's dandy." One last scowl, and then he leaves.

Trent looks from Audrey to me, then sings, "Awkward."

"What was *that*?" Audrey says.

I blink. "Just came out. With the crap he got this morning, thought I'd ask." That was weird.

"Smooth move, Samson," Trent says. "Stopped him ragging on your hair."

"Samson?"

With his fingers, he motions cutting his hair. Oh, that Samson. When Samson's hair was cut, he lost his strength. Wonder what I lost? Didn't have much to start with. All I know is I need to keep my damn mouth shut. I may have deflected Kobe's focus from my hair, but I just made an ass out of myself.

Audrey studies me. "Well, since his usual attitude is fully intact, everything must be all right."

"Guess so," I say.

I stare out the big windows at the parking lot, almost blinded by car windshields reflecting the last flash of sunlight.

Trent asks Audrey for a pen, then starts drawing his Infinite Radical equation and supposed future tattoo in a space on the wall between a sucky cartoon of Bart Simpson and where someone wrote *Living scares me to death.*

Audrey starts lecturing him about the evils of permanently mutilating one's body, but I can barely hear her over the blare of turned-up music and turned-up talking. More people pack the place, including the returning goth kids.

At last, Kobe appears with our food. After two trips of avoiding eye contact and basically plopping everything down in the middle of the table, he leaves without a word. Guess he's done with me and my hair. No complaints here.

After our mandatory rubbing of the hands with Purell (thank you, Mom—I mean, Audrey), we jump into eating. I'm hungry and want to make this quick so we can go.

As soon as I pick up my barbecue turkey burger, it starts dripping sauce, so I angle it toward my mouth to—

Splat!!!

"CRAP!" A warm, gooey mass slides down the front of my

T-shirt. I grab every napkin in sight, scoop the contents of the burger from my chest and lap, and dump it on my plate. "Aw, man!" *So* greasy and goopy.

I wipe off the remaining globs of turkey, tomato, and melted cheddar cheese glued together with Boo's special BBQ sauce.

Since Kobe didn't bring any water, that's the best I can do. Lumpy red smears cover my shirt, sticking to my skin.

"Unfortunate bun malfunction, there, Jedi," Trent says.

Audrey's grossed out. "You'd better wash that off right away. Cold water."

"It's fine, I don't care." No way I'm parading to the men's room like this.

"Uh-uh." Audrey points toward the back of the place. "That shirt is not getting in my car and dripping on my leather seats. Go!"

Fine. I stand and survey the quickest path to the bathroom. No sign of Kobe—don't need more loud shrieks of shock—but it's hard to see with just these old lamps scattered here and there. With my head down and hands covering my chest, I channel my inner Graphite and make myself as invisible as possible. I weave my way through the chairs and the noise and the smells, keeping my eyes on the floor. Almost there. I only have to squeeze by this one little—ouch! I bump my knee hard into a table leg.

"Uh, you okay?"

I look up—it's Lev. Holy god. Hot guy from French class. He's holding his spaghetti-wrapped fork in midbite. He exchanges a weird look with his girlfriend, Kathleen, sitting across from him.

"What . . ." Kathleen scans me up and down, from hair to shirt to hand rubbing knee. "What happened?"

I cough. "It's, well, I didn't see . . . the table leg. Doesn't hurt too bad, not broken. My knee! Not the table, heh, heh, heh." Holy crap. Lev's looking right at me. Wow. With his deep, dark amber eyes. He clenches his jaw—those hot neck muscles. Okay. That's not such a good expression. His eyes are bigger. Now he's kinda weirded out . . . by me. Look away, Adrian. Now.

"Are you really all right?" Kathleen says.

"Huh?" I breathe in. "Uh, no, it's fine. I just . . ."

I realize I'm clutching my chest, fabric splattered in dark-red barbecue sauce.

"Oh! No, no. It's not blood." I grab my shirt and pull it forward, all gooey as the fabric peels away from my skin. "See? Tomato! Tomato sauce! BBQ. You know, the special one!"

They gape at me like I'm a shrieking monkey.

I babble faster. "You know. Slipped out! The bread . . . it slid! Like, *gravity*!" Stop talking, Adrian, stop talking.

They look from my shirt to my face to each other. Dropping his fork on the plate, Lev busts out laughing, shoulders shaking, his long, dark curly hair falling in his face. Kathleen puts her hand over her mouth and tries to stop giggling, which doesn't work.

I let go of my shirt, which resticks to my skin in baggy folds. Then I turn toward the bathroom and limp away.

Seven

THANK GOD, THE MEN'S ROOM IS EMPTY. WELL, ALMOST. THERE IN the old, funky mirror is a derailed social experiment basted in BBQ sauce (not so special, though). Had no idea I look *this* pathetic.

As if I needed more proof that the superhero side of me is pure fantasy.

Praying no one walks through that door, I grab wads and wads of wet paper towels and do my best to clean up. It sort of works—T-shirt looks better than before, I guess. Later I'll check out the bruise I'm sure is spreading across my knee.

At least splashing water on my face feels good. That's the only thing.

I want to disappear from the planet but need to leave the bathroom first. With a deep breath, I open the door and make a beeline to our table, not even glancing at Lev or Kathleen or anyone.

As I slide in next to Trent on the beat-up couch, Audrey sees my T-shirt and says, "Oh, good, much better. Sorry about your dinner. And your shirt." She pauses. "Well, maybe not *that* shirt."

Ha. Ha.

"Another benefit of wearing black, my friends," Trent says. "Spills don't show. Less laundry."

Audrey shakes her head. "Lordy."

I face the pile of gross napkins and turkey burger remnants. While I was gone, Trent finished off his sandwich, but Audrey's still going on hers.

With me eyeing her plate, she says, "I have some fries. You want to order something else?"

I shake my head, then glance over my shoulder. Here near the front of the place, I thankfully can't see Lev or Kathleen at all.

"I just made a total *ass* of myself in front of that guy Lev Cohen, from my French class? And his girlfriend. They're sitting back there."

Trent checks behind us. "Do tell."

I cover my face with my hands. "I'm such a . . . ugghhhhh!"

He blinks. "I see."

Audrey pushes her plate of fries toward me.

"Guys," I say, "you didn't see how Lev gawked at me when I walked into class today. He sits right behind me, so basically he was forced to stare at every gap in my scalp for almost a full hour. I couldn't even look at him when class was done. And now I just babbled at them both about gravity while dripping puddles of barbecue sauce and looking like a mental ward refugee!"

"Is this the guy you think is hot?" Audrey asks.

I nod. "With the long wavy Renaissance hair. Full lips. Chiseled chin. Amber eyes."

"The hot *straight* guy?" she says.

Trent reaches for one of Audrey's fries but gets his hand slapped.

"What does it matter?" I say. "Not like I'm ever gonna meet anyone."

"Honey, especially not if you look at straight guys—"

"Okay okay, I get it. It's just that I gave him and Kathleen one hell of a story to spread around about pathetic Adrian," I say. "Besides, Audrey, you're hardly one to give advice on guys." I stuff four fries in my mouth.

She flashes me the Audrey Eye so fast it practically throws me back. "Just because I haven't yet found *man material* worthy of Ms. Audrey Hill doesn't mean I don't live in this world. You do remember what happened to Jacquie, right?"

I swallow. Beyond horrible. Her older sister, Jacquie, was date-raped two years ago, the night of her prom. By her "boyfriend."

Audrey straightens out the overlapping layers of sparkly bracelets on her left wrist. "You never know who to trust. Why do you think I'm so picky?"

Trent sneaks some fries, then says, "Picky? Have you, like, even been on a date?"

She glares at him. "Now, don't *you* start."

He opens his mouth to talk but chomps down on some fries instead and slumps down lower in his seat. Ever since last year when his goth girlfriend broke up with him (after all of three months), Trent claims to be asexual. Since when is a teen boy asexual?

Well, what the hell do *I* know?

When it comes to dating, or anything resembling sex, none of us can actually talk.

"Audrey," I say, "at school, guys check you out all the time."

She crosses her arms over her stomach. "Don't think so. Not with these swerves and curves."

I roll my eyes. "Oh, come on. Of course they do. I keep telling you, you're hot."

"Didn't your mother ever teach you not to lie?"

"Audrey, you have amazing style and a body to go with it. You've got classic Renaissance beauty."

"Yeah, I know. You've showed me all those paintings. So they liked fat girls back in the Dark Ages. Guess what? Welcome to the twenty-first century, Graphite Boy!"

I eye the tables next to us. "Don't call me that in public."

"Nobody heard me," she mumbles.

"Listen," Trent says, "dudes *do* check you out in the halls. One of them must be 'worthy' of a date."

She sits up straight and takes a sip of her Diet Coke. "You kiddin'? Our school? Slim pickin's there. And here? Well, I don't happen to have a thing for chewin' tobacco and boots."

I follow her gaze out the windows and, lit by the yellow parking lot lights, see a few rednecks from next door. Since people get carded at Bubba's sometimes, they take the party outside and swarm between their pickup trucks like orcs prowling around the Tower of Saruman. Even with reflections in the window making it hard to see, I recognize a few of them out there from school.

"Guys," I say, "can we get the check and go now? We're done, right?"

Audrey waves at Kobe, who's sitting at a table yapping.

Trent watches the parking lot. "Starting earlier than usual."

Hard to tell exactly what's going on out there, but it's pretty clear the bubbas are spreading over onto our side of the lot, like a virus.

"Oh, joy," Trent says. "Guess there's no football game tonight. Leaning on that silver car, isn't that Buddy?"

"Where?" My stomach drops. "Not only him. There's Doug, with that damn red cap." I can just make out his massive figure in the bubba cluster. I scoot closer to the wall. Hard to tell how well they can see us inside. It's almost darker in here than out there with those big parking lot lights kicking on and the sky filled with that just-past-sunset glow. But you never know.

"Dude." Trent taps my arm. "Stop gripping the table. They'd sooner go to the ballet than come in here. So chill."

Audrey finally gets Kobe's attention and makes the *check please* sign. "It's only Doug out there," she says. "Okay, and Buddy and whoever. But just because they made you drop your phone and laughed at your crazy hair doesn't mean they're out to get you."

"Yeah," I say, leaning back a little. "You're right." All around us, people continue to talk and eat and all. No big deal. I guess.

Kobe's tapping on the computer screen, so hopefully it's our check. I turn to the windows. "What's Doug doing now?"

"Listing to starboard," Trent says. "Man, he's trashed."

"Shocking," Audrey says, raising an eyebrow.

"Hey, Kobe!" yells one of the waitresses, standing near the front door. "You need to see this."

"Relax, honey," Kobe says from behind us, still at the computer. "I don't go for those big beefy types. Whoever he is, you can have him."

Some girls near him laugh.

"No, really," the waitress says. "Come look."

Well, of course everyone wants to look, so I sit up taller to get a better view out the window.

All around us there's a collective "Gross!"

"Ugh!" Audrey says. "Thank God we parked Athena in the side lot."

Can't tell which drunk bubba it was, but about two parking rows away, one of them just threw up all over the back of a pale blue Mustang. Outside, pushing through the bubba crowd, Doug wobbles over to see the car. Buddy doubles over laughing.

Kobe glides past our table, then stops in his tracks. "What the hell? That's my car! My *Mustang*!"

Some jerk says, "Doesn't barf burn through car paint?"

Kobe stares out the window for a moment, then quickly

grabs a roll of paper towels from the coffee bar. The waitress tries to stop him, but he strides to the door, pauses with his fist on the handle, stares down at the towels for a second, then pushes out the door. What does he think he's doing?

I stand for a better view and see Kobe head right into the pack of bubbas around his Mustang. The back windshield and trunk are kinda gross—really disgusting, actually—but dealing with some puke on your car isn't worth going out *there*.

Kobe's arrival brings more guys over. Of course, Doug's smack in the middle, checking out the scene. Is Kobe really . . . ? He rips off some towels and starts wiping the trunk. You're being so stupid!

Boo's manager zips past us to the window. "What's going on out there?" He runs outside.

While the door is open we can just hear Buddy holler, "Look! He wants to make it pretty!"

"Kobe, get out of there," I say. "It's just a car."

"He can't hear you," some genius near me says.

By this time, everyone in Boo is glued to the front windows, making it hard to see. I push to the front, Audrey beside me. Trent stays back at the table. All around us, people are jabbering, even laughing. What's wrong with them? This isn't funny.

Someone gasps as Buddy trips Kobe, but he recovers. I lean into the window to cut the glare from these inside lights.

Now the crowd out there is moving around. . . . What's happening? Wait, the manager steps between Kobe and the bubba rabble. Holds up his hands in an everybody-calm-down way.

Okay, good. A couple of the waiters go outside. Kobe looks pissed, but at least he's stopped trying to clean the damn car.

"Oh, well," some wise-ass says next to Audrey. "Thought it was gonna get exciting there for a minute."

"What's your problem?" she says. "This is way too exciting already, all right?"

Some electric guitar riff still blasts through the speakers above us—makes everything even more surreal.

"Hey, they're coming back inside." Trent's now standing right behind me.

The two brave waiters who went outside hurry back in. Craning my neck, I can just make out Kobe and the manager turning away from the car. With a cell phone to his ear, the manager hustles back. But I can't see Kobe anymore. Who's that in his way? My chest is tight.

As others return to their tables, I move closer to the door for a better view.

"Where you going?" Audrey says.

"I can't see what's happening," I say. "Can anyone see?"

The manager is back inside now, rapidly talking on his phone. Kobe is nowhere. My heart pounds in my ears.

There's too much of a reflection, too many people out there.

What's . . . ? If that guy would just move I could see. Move. Move! Okay, there's—Kobe's trapped. But he's screaming at Doug, pointing in his face.

"Hey!" I slap the window with my hands. Doug's twice his size! Why is he . . . ?

I push my way out the door and stop by the first row of cars.

"Back off!" Kobe pushes Doug.

The bubbas go "Oooooh!"

"Shit, the fag touched you?" Buddy says. "Fuck knows whose dick's been in that hand."

I take a few steps closer but stay between cars.

Squinting at Kobe, Doug slurs his words. "What the hell's *your* problem? Ain't my puke."

"The problem is *you*, asshole." Kobe's voice cracks. He's shaking.

Some guy yells at Doug, "This the dude who called you a cow pussy?" He busts out laughing.

The other guys crack up.

Doug scowls at Kobe. "You ain't worth my time."

"C'mon, Doug," some bubba says. "You gonna let this homo make a pussy outta *you*?"

Doug eyes the guy, then steps closer to Kobe, bumping him with his chest.

"Get away from me!" Eyes wild, Kobe shoves Doug back with both hands.

"Shit!" Doug's so drunk he stumbles a little.

Kobe, what the hell?

"*Whaaaat?* Faggot's in deep shit now!" Buddy yells, a grin cutting across his face.

"Dang!" someone says. "He's messin' with the wrong dude."

Glaring, Doug checks out all the bubbas yelling at him to *"Kick his ass!"*

Everyone starts chanting, "Doug, Doug, Doug, Doug . . ."

He nods. "Fuck this shit." Turns his whole body and rams Kobe, who slips but gets up. Kobe, don't push him back!

Doug pins Kobe against the car, hard.

I gasp and run forward. "No no no."

Doug spins Kobe around and garbles out, "God hates fags." He grabs the back of Kobe's skull, then smashes his face against the trunk with a loud *THUD!*

"NO! Leave him alone! STOP!" I yell.

The crowd's whoops and hollers drown me out.

Doug pummels Kobe's head against the vomit-covered trunk. Again and again. Kobe doesn't move, his skinny, limp arms flopping by his sides.

Waving my hands, I dash to the car. To Kobe.

"Stop it! STOP IT!" I shriek.

Everyone turns.

Oh, god. Oh, my god.

Buddy jumps behind me. "What's wrong, that your boyfriend?"

Others circle around.

I freeze.

Can't breathe.

Still gripping Kobe, Doug looks down at me, his face red and sweaty. He tries to focus his eyes. "Huh? You? Why are . . . ?"

Blood drips from Kobe's mouth. Maybe his eye? Can't tell—bloody saliva hangs down his chin.

I shake.

Doug drops Kobe on the car and moves toward me. He slurs, "What the hell?"

Oh, god.

More people close in.

What the fuck have I done?

Eight

I JUMP AS SOMEONE GRABS MY SHOULDERS AND YANKS ME BACK. It's Audrey.

Doug steps away, his cap crooked, eyes locked on mine.

Kobe's sprawled on the car.

"Good Lord!" Audrey's voice sounds distant. But she's right next to me, one hand covering her mouth.

Someone snatches my left arm. "Come on."

"Lemme go!" I pull away. "Stop—"

"Whoa!" Trent holds up his hands. "Just me."

I inhale. "Where's—" I turn around, dizzy. Doug's gone. Kobe's limp on the trunk of the car. Just lying there. "Trent, did you see?"

He hooks my arm, spins me around, and looks me over. "You hurt?"

I shake my head. "No. But—"

Audrey grips my other arm. "C'mon," she says. "We need to . . ."

A car revs up, headlights blinding. I slip. They steady me.

Buddy blocks our way, almost a shadow backlit by the headlights. He glares at me, then spits in my face.

Trent gasps. "What the hell?"

I try to wipe spit and chewing tobacco away as Buddy takes off into the mass of people. Gooey stink gets in my eye. I clean my face with my sleeve.

Trent and Audrey hurry me along.

We head through the parking lot. People blur past in all directions. Some run to get away, but some head to see what's happening.

I keep wiping at my face.

The manager appears. "Out of my way!"

"Kobe's messed up bad," someone says.

"Police are on the way. I'll . . . I'll call an ambulance, too." He pulls out his cell as he hurries on.

A guy right in front of us elbows his friend. "Outta here, dude. Ditch the beer. Let's go."

"Crap." The other guy tosses his beer can to the ground and splatters our shoes.

It's like the world is moving in slow motion.

I stumble as we step sideways between two parked cars. Everything's tilted. "Is Doug following us?" My pulse races.

"Lift your feet, Adrian." Trent balances me. "You need to walk."

"But . . . Doug?" I twist to look back.

Trent says, "C'mon, Audrey, let's just get him inside Boo."

Sounds of loud talking and engines starting and cars honking surround me. Can't breathe.

Behind us a girl screams, "Kobe!"

I gasp. "What now?"

"Come on, Adrian." Audrey tightens her grip on my arm. She's shaking. Or is it me?

Cars drive around us, or try to.

We make it to the door. Two girls ask, "What's happening?" People bunch around the doorway.

Trent guides me by my shoulders around scattered chairs and tables with half-eaten food.

"Here, sit." He angles me toward a chair near the wall.

I grab the armrests to steady myself, my palms slippery with sweat and Buddy's spit. "Are we safe?"

Audrey sits next to me, eyes wide. Alert. "Better here than out there."

Trent shakes my arm. "Hey! Adrian! You're panting." He inhales deeply. "Breeeathe."

I gulp air and look around. "We need to go!"

Trent squats down in front of me, his hands on my shoulders. "Okay, you *really* need to calm down. It's over. All right?"

"But—"

"It's *over*." He stares right into my eyes.

The voices from outside quiet down as faint sirens cut through. They get louder. Blue and red lights flash through the windows onto the walls all around.

Two police cars.

And an ambulance.

My knee. I forgot I banged my knee on that table—how long ago was that? It hurts again.

"Please, will you stop pacing?" Audrey says.

I didn't know I was. "Why won't they *tell* us anything? What time is it, even?" I ask again of no one in particular.

I reach for my phone but feel my empty pocket and remember that, too.

Trent holds up his phone: 7:42. "Been about twenty minutes since the ambulance left." He stands and stretches. "Bunch of bullshit."

Unconscious but breathing. That's all we overheard. That's not enough. At least Kobe must be at the hospital by now.

Thank goodness this Officer Storch is leaning in the doorway, between us and the outside. Protection. Here inside Boo the music's finally off, but the silence just turns up the pummeling in my head. Bright fluorescent lights are on full blast. Two weary waiters keep moving around, cleaning tables.

I can't wrap my head around *any* of this.

The police have been talking to people one by one, at least the ones that didn't hightail it out of here right away. We and about five others in here are the last few. Guess the drunk "witnesses" are being interviewed next door at Bubba's? Did they arrest Doug? No one's telling us a damn thing.

I hug my arms around myself. Hate this shivering.

What the hell possessed me? I barely know Kobe! And what

could *I* possibly do? I've never seen anybody beaten like . . . No! I shake my head and push out the images. Just have to inhale deep, like Trent says.

So. Wrong.

Unconscious but breathing.

Is that gonna be me? What am I going to do?

"I can't take this." I go to the window, stare at the cops around Kobe's car.

Audrey comes over and wraps her arm around me.

Another police car pulls up and glides to a stop. The headlights cut off and a bulky cop steps out of the driver's side; Officer Storch leaves us and hustles over to greet him. All the other police gather around him too.

Audrey inhales. "Looks just like him, doesn't he?"

"Who?" Trent asks, squinting through the window's mirrorlike reflection.

"Doug," she says. "That one must be his father."

My stomach flips.

"I was wondering when he'd show up," Trent says. He leans over to me. "Remember. *You* didn't do anything. Okay?" His voice quivers a little. "Just take it slow."

"What's gonna happen?" I ask.

Even with our own faces reflected in the glass, I can tell Doug's father is staring right at us. I turn away.

After a couple minutes, Officer Storch hurries back to us. "All right, folks, our sergeant just arrived and wants to wrap this up."

I glance at Audrey, who mouths, *Sergeant?*

Storch steps over to me. Looks me up and down, studying my chopped hair and stained shirt. He has a slight sneer. "You're Adrian Piper, right?"

My mouth tastes like chalk. "Yes, sir."

"Come with me."

My feet move like I'm pushing through sand as I make my way out the door.

"This way," Officer Storch says.

I follow, leaving Trent and Audrey inside Boo. The air is dry and warm out here, but my skin is cold. Storch heads through the parking lot toward a police car parked away from the others. What's happening? Why are we—oh, okay. We're not getting in. He goes around to the far side and leans against the hood. I stop and stand a few feet away, facing him.

The car blocks our view of Boo's windows, preventing everyone inside there from seeing us. But clustered around Kobe's car, Doug's father and the other cops have a clear view of us. At least we're out of earshot—I hope.

On the street, just a few yards away, traffic zooms by.

Another cop comes over and pulls out a note pad. Her face is square and pale, with a mouth like a tiny, pinched line. She squints at me, trying to figure out my hair and all, I guess. I look down. My heart hammers.

"This is Officer Perry," says Storch. "She and I are going to ask you some questions."

I clasp my hands in front of me and nod. The buzzing yellow streetlight casts greenish shadows under their noses and eyebrows, making their eyes almost disappear.

"Your name?" Officer Perry says.

I swallow. "Adrian Piper."

"Age?"

"Sixteen."

She scribbles. "Got any ID?"

Storch cuts her off. "How 'bout we get all that after we talk a bit?" Still leaning against the hood, he crosses his arms and peers at me. "So, I understand you claim to have witnessed part of the incident?"

"Is he okay?" I say before I even realize the voice is mine.

"Who?" Storch asks.

I'm all queasy. "Kobe."

"Kobe Saito?" Officer Perry says. "The boy who was taken to the hospital. That right?"

I nod.

"Listen up," Storch says. "We're asking the questions now, all right?"

"Okay," I say.

"Excuse me?" Storch says louder.

"Yes, sir." I glare at the ground, my face hopefully in shadow.

Officer Perry holds her pen, ready to write. "What exactly did you witness?"

I take a breath and tell them every detail, plain and clear. My own voice sounds distant.

I need to know if they caught Doug. But I don't dare ask.

Officer Storch frowns. He and Perry exchange looks. "What you claim doesn't quite square with others' accounts. You absolutely sure that's what you witnessed?"

I gape at them. "Yes. Absolutely."

Perry writes for a moment, then says, "The others we've spoken to have a different story."

"But how could they? I was right there! I saw it!"

Storch straightens up. "What exactly is your relationship with the injured boy?"

My throat starts closing. "We go to the same school. Don't really know him."

"That a fact?" Storch turns to Perry, who flips through her note pad, scanning the pages.

Oh, god—what have people told them? Lied about? Kobe being my boyfriend? That's what Buddy yelled out. These cops won't believe *me*.

I clear my throat. "Does it matter how I know him? *I* wasn't a part of what happened. I just saw it."

"But it sounds like you *were* a part of it," he says. "You inserted yourself into the altercation and provoked Doug Richter. Just like this boy Kobe did."

"But I told you, Kobe didn't start it."

Storch sighs. "Just how would you know that? As you stated yourself, you joined the fight after it had already begun. You were in the restaurant, with no clear line of vision, when the episode began. Correct?"

"Yes, but—"

"So how could you possibly have seen who initiated it?" he says.

Perry closes her note pad. "We have many witnesses who

were at the car *before* the fight took place, and during, who independently tell us that Kobe Saito came out of the restaurant, went directly to Doug Richter, and verbally and physically provoked him. It seems pretty clear that Kobe Saito, with intent, attacked Mr. Richter, who simply defended himself."

"What?" This is insane. "Who's in the hospital? Doug's fifty times bigger than Kobe, and Doug was drunk!"

"Son, you might wanna calm down." Storch steps right up to me. "You're making accusations here that you have no way of knowing are true. In fact"—he grimaces—"you smell like beer yourself."

"Look at that shirt," Perry says. "You're a mess."

"I wasn't drinking! Some guy in the parking lot threw his beer down and it . . . it splattered me. *I* didn't drink it!"

He looks sideways at Perry, then back at me. "That may be true. May be false."

What the hell is this? "It's true! I'll take a Breathalyzer test. I can prove it."

Storch holds up his hand. "You better take it easy. One thing at a time."

Officer Perry tilts her head. "Best to stick with what you know, all right?"

Storch glances over at Doug's father and the other cops, who watch us from a distance, then steps back and leans against the car, crossing his arms.

I try to catch my breath.

Storch looks at the ground, then up at me. He smiles. "Look, we're the good guys, remember? We're not here to place blame—that's not our job. We're here to gather facts. And you have to remember, what you *think* happened isn't necessarily what *did* happen."

My brain is upside down. How, how can they do this? I open my mouth, but—I don't know what to say.

Officer Perry clicks her pen and slips it into her shirt pocket. "Sounds to me like your friend started a fight, and you saw it in progress and simply wanted to jump in and help him out. I understand. It's hard to think clearly in those situations." She tucks her note pad into a pouch on her belt. "I'm sorry your friend was injured, but luckily, others stopped the fight before you became physically involved."

"I'd say that about sums it up," says Storch. "Don't you think, son?"

I blink. I want to scream *NO!* But before I can even take a breath, they turn and walk away, as if I've suddenly disappeared.

Or never existed at all.

Nine

LIKE BLOOD, INK IS MIRACULOUS. WHETHER CONFINED IN A PEN OR free on a brush, it spreads and builds, giving my drawings life. It always has.

Until now.

I used to feel the ink flow from me as I drew, as if it were connected to my bloodstream, feeding Graphite and making him strong. My life gave him life.

It was circular. As the energy flowed from me and I watched what came out, it flowed back. My art gave *me* life too.

But now there's paper in front of me, I'm poised with a pen, but . . . nothing.

Nothing.

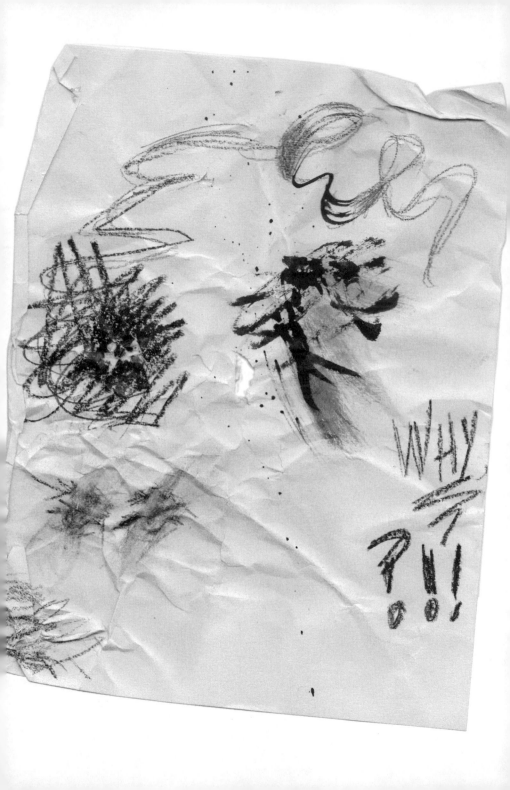

Ten

I ALWAYS THOUGHT MY BEDROOM CARPET WAS SIMPLY BEIGE. I WAS wrong. Up close, as I lie here on my side, face resting on the rug, these thin beams of sunlight coming through the window make the carpet fibers glow, reflecting so many hidden colors. Golden highlights, iridescent blues and purples, even an alien sort of green.

You see a lot when you lie on the floor, eyes wide open. But nothing helps. Nothing stops this repeating loop of panic in my brain. Reliving every bloody image, every brutal detail. Your body is supposed to take care of you, purge sickness, heal itself. Is reliving Kobe's beating really going to flush this nightmare from my head? Watching Doug slam Kobe's head into the car over and over and over? Feeling Buddy's spit on my skin?

It's Sunday morning. Boo was just Friday night, not even

two days now, but it could've been weeks ago. Or minutes. The time warp comes and goes.

The rest of the world seems to continue. The same crap is on TV, I have to make the same stuff for dinner, and the same neighbor's dog keeps barking at cars driving by.

After screwing with my head, the police didn't interrogate anyone else Friday night. They said we should just go home. So we did, Audrey and Trent grilling me in the car about what the cops wanted.

With Mom working her night job and Dad asleep in front of the TV, it was easy to come straight to my room. I never quite got it before, but now I do. You actually *can* cry yourself to sleep.

Then yesterday somehow went by. Like a movie, I just watched. And this morning . . . watching.

The doorbell rings. My stomach drops.

I push up on my knees and peer out the window. Athena's parked at the curb. I exhale . . . just Audrey.

All weekend, every freaking car door slam had me on alert. But the police were done with me, right? What do I know?

I stand and try not to disturb Harley, who stays curled in a little cozy ball on the carpet.

There's talk coming from the hall. Since Mom's still at her church, Dad must have let Audrey in. Then I hear Trent's voice say, "You should—"

"Knock?" Audrey says, opening my door. "Why? See, he's up and dressed."

Harley slinks past my legs into the closet. She doesn't get Audrey.

Trent plops down on my bed, silver belt chains jingling, as Audrey closes the door.

I blink. "Did I know you were coming?"

"No," she says. "But it's time—*wow!*"

Trent points at my head. "Lookin' slick, there, Graphite Boy. Literally."

"Oh, yeah." I reach up and pat my hair, newly cut, flattened, and smoothed back.

When Mom forced me out of bed yesterday afternoon, she freaked over my hair. I told her the truth, or the basic truth, that I'd tried cutting it myself.

Of course, I didn't say *anything* about what happened at Boo. The fewer pieces they have of the "your son is gay" puzzle, the better.

"Mom hauled me off to Dad's barber, and he did his best," I say. "He evened out the long parts so I can almost cover up the gaps with hair cement."

"Least your head's protected now," Trent says. "Looks solid."

Audrey smiles. "I think it's cute."

"Yeah," I say, "like a first grader on class photo day."

Doorbell again. I spin and look out the window. Just Dad's friend Pete. Dad calls down the hall that he's off to watch the game. I yell, "Okay!" *The game.* As if I'd know what the hell game he means. Through the window, I watch him limp with his cane to the car and off they go. Guess I'm off Dad Duty for a while.

It's so sunny outside. How can it be sunny? I shut the curtains and sink into my desk chair. From my X-Men action figures lined up along the bookshelf, I pick up Angel and fiddle with his wings.

Audrey opens the bedroom door again, all the way. "Now that we're alone, d'ya mind?" She eyes my dirty clothes and crap on the floor. "Stuffy in here." Even on a Sunday she's all blingy with her hair straightened and everything. Oh, right, it's after church.

She perches on the edge of the bed. "I haven't heard anything more since I messaged you yesterday. I've been scanning local news, websites, whatever I can think of. Nothing."

Trent shoots her a look.

"Well," she says, "some BS online and all, of course, but nothing I care to repeat."

"Don't have to," I say. "I saw it."

Trent blows his hair from his eyes. "Doug got away with it, free and easy. Of course. Damn prick. 'Self-defense' my ass."

I stare at my hands. "As soon as his father showed up that night, I just knew it." And then, of course, after what the cops said . . . or *didn't*.

I take a breath and turn to my computer. "Let me show you something. Everything's going to be okay. He sent me this a couple hours ago."

They peer at the screen.

"Who?" Audrey says.

I open the message. "Kobe."

hey A—

im at hospital. all painkillered. very banged up. nothing permanent they say. lots of horrible healing

i remember a little. that asshole doug for sure. thank god for drugs cuz I don't know what id do. wouldnt be pretty. not pretty. pretty. funny word.

my momz raising hell with police and everyone

i heard you tried to save me like damsel in distress. none of my stupid socalled friends did shit. no one did. my hero. too bad you didnl get there sooner.

-K

I stare at my Angel action figure as they read Kobe's message over again.

"Oh, my." Audrey breathes in deep. "Thank God. When I think of what he looked like, just . . ." She shakes her head.

Trent lies back on the bed, which squeaks. "Good news there. Freaky message, though. I'd be careful. How're you holdin' up?"

"I'm not," I say.

Audrey turns to me. "That was amazing what you did, Adrian. Going to help Kobe like that."

"What? It was the stupidest thing I've ever done in my life."

"Okay," she says, "yes, it was stupid. But it was also amazing. Brave."

"No. It wasn't."

Trent studies me for a moment, eyeing my hair, then says, "Hey, can I see it?"

"See what?" I ask.

"Exhibit A, the drawing so powerful it drove you to attack your own head."

"Really? It's just a sketch."

"Oooh, this oughta be good," Audrey says.

I sigh, then slip my art out from the Michelangelo book where I hid it Friday morning. Should have destroyed this.

"It's not finished." I hand it to Trent.

"Dude!" He pores over it. "Whoa. How do you *do* this? Check it out."

"You don't have to try to make me feel good."

Audrey takes it and shakes her head. "No, really, it's true. I will say, though, his hair's not *that* inspiring." She glances at my hair. "But Graphite does seem alive."

"Well, he's not anymore," I say. "Yesterday I took down the site."

They both pipe up. "What! Why?"

"You kidding?" I sink into the chair. "Too dangerous. And who cares, anyway? Other than me."

"*I* check out your site," Trent says.

Audrey nods. "And no one knows it's yours."

Trent smiles. "Wish you'd conjure up a palace for me. But farther away from here than the moon, like in the Andromeda Galaxy."

My stomach flips. "Guys, can I show you something? Promise you won't get upset."

Audrey places my sketch on the drawing table and squints at me. "That depends. . . ."

I pull down *Maxfield Parrish, Master of Illustration* from my bookshelf and take out a bunch of my art hidden in the pages.

I hold my drawings to my chest so they can't see. "Okay. Don't be mad I never showed you these before."

They exchange looks.

"No one's ever seen these," I say, "so you don't have to worry."

Trent grunts. "Just show us already."

I inhale. "Oh, boy." I hand Audrey the comic panels of my superhero versions of them. Trent scoots over next to her and they study the pages.

Silence.

Oh, god, they hate it.

Trent blows the hair from his eyes and pulls a page close to his face. "Whoa. Dude."

Audrey gasps. She looks up at me, then back at the pages, then up at me again. She holds out the page of Sultry after the tornado. "That supposed to be *me*?"

I swallow. "Uh-huh."

"Sultry? *Sultry!* Were you on drugs or something when you did this?"

I can't help but smile. "No."

Trent blinks at me, mouth wide open.

There goes my smile. "Uh, what do you think?"

He blinks again. "Dude. This is awesome. I got X-Ray Vision! Look how you drew my hair. Cool."

Audrey taps one of the pages. "He drew me like a hoochie mama!"

Trent and I crack up.

He points at her. "Did she just say 'hoochie mama'?"

She stifles a smile. "And you made me all bossy-like! I'm not bossy."

Trent laughs harder and falls back on the bed.

"Sultry's assertive, not bossy," I say.

She looks down at the pages. "Sorry, but this ain't me. I'll take those boots, though, and those legs you gave me. But otherwise, nuh-uh." She shakes her head.

Trent rolls to his side and scans the pages. "So why am I called *Willow*? Because I'm freakishly tall as a tree? Might as well call me Sequoia."

"*No.*" I get up and look at the page he's holding. "You're Willow because you're so grounded that you don't snap when a big wind comes along. You flow with the breeze."

He sits up all the way, hair falling back in his face. "Yeah, right. Don't think so."

They keep looking through the papers a little longer but don't say much else. Then Audrey gathers the pages up and hands them to me.

Trent chuckles. "Least you didn't make me a hoochie mama."

Audrey slaps his knee. "You better not call me that ever again if you value your life."

I place the pages back in the book and put it away. Least now they know.

She gives me a hopeful smile. "They're beautiful drawings, though."

I slump in my chair. "Thanks."

Awkward silence.

"All right." She sits up straight. "Time to take action."

"Huh?"

"Adrian, this is now an official intervention. For two days you don't return my calls. You barely respond when I send you messages. You don't leave your house. Enough hiding out and hoping it all goes away."

Trent reclines and fluffs a pillow under his head. "Always works for me."

In the corner of my eye I notice Harley peeking around the closet door, but she stays put.

Audrey straightens out her cascading gold necklace so it lies perfectly on her chest, like armor. "All right, we have to focus—"

"I know you mean well," I say, "but I just can't . . . I dunno. I just can't."

"We need to plan. You don't know what you'll be walking into tomorrow morning. So before first period, you should go to the assistant principal's office and see Mr. McConnell and explain—"

"Whaaaa?" Trent springs to life.

"Why would I do that?" My voice cracks.

"Why wouldn't you?" she says. "He needs to know what really happened from—"

"Yeah, right," Trent says. "That won't do jack. It'll only make it worse."

She rolls her eyes. "It wouldn't hurt."

"Yes, it would. No way am I getting interrogated again."
I pick up my Angel figure from the drawing table and pace.
"And if Doug found out I blabbed to the school? That's as
good as signing my own death certificate."

"You've got to let them know your side—"

"No! I've done enough damage."

"Fine." Audrey holds up her hands. "Have it your way."

"Look, it's already better," I say. "Kobe's okay. Well, not
okay, obviously, but not, like, in a coma. He's messaging and
stuff. And his mom's raising hell, so why should I?"

Audrey grunts. "Still, you should—"

"Why don't *you* tell the school, then?" I say. "If it's gonna
make everything so much better."

"I'm not going to play messenger for you. You're the one
who saw how it happened," she says. "And you're the one
who confronted Doug."

"You guys," Trent says, "Doug was shitfaced. He won't
remember crap. And even though he got away with it, he
probably got his fat wrist slapped—he did pummel a dude,
you know—so he'll be on good behavior. Least for a while.
And it's not like Adrian actually did anything. Why make it so
much worse?"

I nod. "Yeah, you're right."

"No, you're not." Audrey turns to me. "Look. Buddy spat
in your face! And I heard what he said when you ran out there,
that you were Kobe's 'boyfriend.' That may not be true, but
now the worst possible people *think* it is. No, hold on! Let me
finish! You can't just pretend everything's all right, because,

no matter what, they think you're gay now. You don't know *what* they'll do."

"Ow!" I gripped Angel too hard and pinched my palm. It broke off his wings. "Dammit!" I throw the pieces to the floor.

"Audrey," Trent says, "you're just upsetting him more."

I flex and rub my hand. "I know you're only trying to help. But Trent's right. Yes he is! I just gotta lie low. What else can I do?"

She folds her arms and fixes me with a stare. "Plenty. I'm only looking out for you."

"What," Trent says, "and I'm not?"

I kick the broken action figure pieces to the side. "Look, I just gotta think about this some more."

Qapla'! Qapla'!

"Your computer," Trent says. "It's speaking in tongues."

"It's just Klingon." My *new message* sound. What now? "Hey, it's from Kobe."

going around. thought you shuld see . . .

"There's a link that says 'funny fag.' Huh?"

Trent shakes his head. "Don't open it."

Too late. It's a short phone video.

Some freaked-out kid in a parking lot, wide-eyed and shrieking.

It's me.

Eleven

THEY SAY IF YOU WERE TO MEET YOURSELF ON THE STREET YOU
wouldn't recognize yourself. That there's no way to know
how other people see you.

But now I think I do know.

Watching that video on Sunday of me screaming at Doug
was like plummeting through cracked ice into frigid water. At
first you panic, but eventually you freeze.

Audrey and Trent finally gave up on their intervention and
left me alone, which was good. I needed quiet.

I have no clue who took the video. It doesn't matter since
there's absolutely nothing I can do about it—nothing. Except
watch it again. And again.

Most kids from school don't care who sees what they put
online, and some of them wrote a lot about Doug and Kobe,
and a little about me. They posted a few blurry phone pictures

too . . . and that video. The way they describe me could be true: Faggot. Wuss. Freak. Clueless. Little girl. Unbelievably stupid. Screwed up. So dead.

Maybe I would recognize myself on the street after all.

When your parents pay more attention to themselves than you, it doesn't take a lot to convince them you're sick and need to stay home. And when you actually feel sick—sick to your soul—well, it's true.

Audrey attempted another intervention Monday night but finally gave up. I'm not the best company anymore. I did agree to talk to her and Trent on the phone, though, so I heard more than I want to know about what people are saying at school. Otherwise, I've blocked out the world.

Even Graphite doesn't help. I try to sketch, but . . . nothing.

I never replied to Kobe's message with that video. Probably why he hasn't contacted me again. Well, he *is* in the hospital, after all, and busy recovering. I hope.

My staying home sick worked for the past two days, until lack of any fever, vomiting, diarrhea—or the truth—convinced Mom it's just teen hormones. She doesn't tolerate "laziness" in people. Except Dad, of course, but not much she can do there.

So this cold Wednesday morning I'm plastering back the remnants of my hair with the thickest gunk Mom bought me and am dressed all in black, but I don't bother with a hoodie. It doesn't really hide you, just feels like it. Or felt like it. Before.

I check my computer one last time, but still nothing from Kobe. This is driving me crazy. I type a quick message.

Hey ~ sorry so silent. How are you? I hope much better.
~Adrian

I hover the cursor over Send, then just finally click it.
Maybe that was stupid and I shouldn't get more involved, like
Trent says, but I want to know.

Tap-tap-tap.

Mom knocks on my bedroom door. "Ade, I'm fixin' to
leave."

I shut down the computer. "You can come in."

I need to finally tell her about my phone. Oh, boy.

She steps into my room, decked out in her too-tight
power-red skirt and jacket, hair straight and highlights
gleaming. All set for her day job. Must be showing one
of her few expensive houses to expensive people today.
"Now, you won't be late for school, correct?"

"I'm all ready, see?"

She looks me up and down. "Good. Now, what's today?
Wednesday? Can't keep track. I'll take care of your dad's dinner tonight."

I follow her to the front hall through a cloud of that citrus
perfume she wears on Important Days. Dad's not in the living
room, so he must still be in bed. This is my chance.

"You look great, Mom. I'd buy a house from you."

She and her reflection frown at each other in the wall mirror as she fiddles with her bangs. "Sweet of you to say, but
tell that to these buyers. Been trying to sell that home for
months."

"You will."

Okay. It's now or never.

"Uh, Mom?"

She twists open her magenta lipstick, which clashes with her outfit, and leans close to the mirror. "Yeah, honey?"

I steady my breath. "Something bad happened."

The mirror Mom's eyes look into mine. "What?"

"I still can't believe it. But you know that old phone of yours you gave me?"

She turns from the mirror. "Now, do not tell me you lost a phone *again*."

"No! Not lost." From my pocket I pull out my busted phone. "It wasn't my fault! These guys were bumping people at school and this old phone hit the floor. There wasn't anything I could—"

"Adrian." Mom closes her eyes and presses her forehead. "I don't need this right now."

"I know that. I had nothing to do with it!"

She takes the phone, inspects it, and hands it back. "You'll just have to make do."

"It's, uh, well, dead. Completely. I tried everything, but it won't—"

"That's it." She applies her lipstick in quick strokes. "You have to pay for your next phone, Adrian. I can't."

"How am I supposed—"

"You can get a job, like we've talked about," she says, twisting her lipstick closed. "It would sure help."

"Well, *like we've talked about*, when would I be able to work with all my chores here? And you always have the car—"

"Excuse me? I happen to own the car—"

"—and so how am I supposed to get *to* this magical job—"

"—because *someone* has to keep us in this house!"

"It's not—"

"Enough!" She shoves the cap on the lipstick with a *snap* and tosses it in her purse. "Look at me."

She's wearing heels today, so we're at the same eye level. I grip the phone tight.

Mom takes a breath. "Honey, I do the best I can. Until your dad gets better—now, hush. Listen to me. Until then, we have to make do. We cannot afford extras. You know that."

I look in her eyes. "Mom, it's not extra. I really need a phone."

She glances at her watch, pulls her jangly keys out of her purse, and zips it shut. "Not every teenager needs a phone."

"I do." My heart speeds up. "For *safety*."

She checks her lips and teeth in the mirror, then grabs her briefcase from the hall table. "I don't have time to go through this again."

I clear my throat. "But I'm . . . well, there's stuff happening, and . . . I don't know." My chest tightens. "Last Friday night—"

"Adrian, I am not buying you a new phone. Period." She opens the front door. The sunlight floods in, making me squint. "Now, hurry up and get yourself to school."

In the bright light, Mom's makeup looks like she's wearing a mask.

"Good luck," I say, "with that home." For other people.

"Thanks." She heads to the car. "I'll need it."

I slowly push my body against the door to close it, then look in the mirror at the pathetic kid clutching a dead phone. How the hell am I supposed to buy a new one?

"Ade?" Dad's shuffling from their bedroom.

What now?

"In here." I don't need to be grilled on what just happened.

With his cane, he limps into the hall, barely dressed in that saggy old robe. "Has your mom left yet?"

How'd he not hear all that?

"Yeah, and I'm about to head out too."

He starts toward the living room. "Before you go, son, I need some breakfast."

I walk to school, fast and hard. It got cold out. Bizarre being in the world again after four days. Like I've just been ejected from a space-time continuum.

The school security guard is outside the front doors, laughing with some senior. I focus on the concrete as I pass by.

"Such a crappy play," the guard says. "Referee got it straight, though, when . . ." He stops.

I glance up and he's squinting at me. Then his face hardens. He turns back to the senior. "Yeah, so, game got sloppy there at the end. But our guys pulled it out."

As I push through the front doors, my head pounds as if my heart has moved in between my ears. That guard is a retired cop. He must—oh, god. He must know Doug's father. What has he been told?

The halls are deafening with lockers and laughing and babbling. I need to keep my head down and just move along.

BAM! I'm slammed against the lockers. Pain shoots through my left arm.

"Dude—whoops!" It's a sophomore football kid with a big grin on his face. He holds up his hands. "Accident."

I don't move a muscle.

His buddy looks around, then rips down a Halloween Hoedown flyer taped to the wall and balls it up. "Quit shovin' the homo, bro!" he says, beaning his friend with the wadded paper. "He might squeal at you." They elbow each other down the hall, laughing.

People stare. I keep going and act like I'm not hurt. I want to reach over and massage my shoulder, but I can't show any weakness.

A teacher strolls out of her classroom. Where were you a minute ago?

On full alert, I navigate through these rat tunnel–like halls and reach my locker. I spin the lock back and forth so fast I can't get the combination right.

"There you are!" Audrey's at my side.

I practically leap to the ceiling. "God! Don't do that!"

"Do what?"

"Sneak up on me!"

"Really?" she says. "Two days of recuperating and you're still this jumpy? I was hoping a break would make you more focused."

"Focused?" I scan the hallway, rub my shoulder, and lower

my voice. "I've already been sideswiped. And Doug's prowling around here somewhere, he and Buddy both. I'm wearing a target, remember?" I try my combination again.

She crosses her arms over the notebooks she carries. "Listen. I've been thinking more about this, and I have a plan for how you should proceed."

Oh, god, really? "Let's not go through this again."

I pop my lock at last and yank open my locker. Something falls to the floor. I reach down and it's a folded paper with my name on it. I don't recognize the handwriting. Besides, no one writes notes to me. I look around, but everyone's rushing to class. What the hell?

"Who's that from?" Audrey says.

"No clue."

"Well, open it."

Two girls pass by, one saying, "Oh, yeah, that's definitely him. Check out the hair."

I slip the note in my pocket. "Not here."

"Don't pay any attention to them," Audrey says. "Give it to me. I can be subtle."

"No," I say. "Let's take it outside."

Since I've missed homework in every class, I load practically all my books and folders into my beat-up backpack. It's heavy as hell now.

"What are you . . . ? Why are you doing that?" Audrey asks.

I zip my bag closed as much as I can. "No way I'm coming back here until the end of the day. Just gonna cruise from one class to the next." I close my locker and heave my backpack onto my unhurt shoulder. Without making eye contact with anyone, I survey the hall. "Where's Trent?"

She shrugs. "Haven't heard from him yet today."

I inhale. "C'mon."

My first-period French class is just across the outside courtyard, not far from Audrey's AP English. We head for the door, but as we get there, the staring Wrestler Guy comes through it. Audrey looks straight ahead and picks up speed, catching the door before it shuts and flinging it open again. I follow as Staring Guy squints at Audrey, then does a double take at me. I hustle outside.

"Don't rush ahead of me like that! Did you see the way he—"

"Just ignore him," Audrey says. "He's obnoxious and people arc noticing you today, okay?"

"No. Not okay." I check over my shoulder. He doesn't come back out. "They're more than just 'noticing.'"

Even though a few groups hang out in the courtyard before class, being outside is slightly safer, less trapped. But about forty classroom windows surround us, and you can see right through the big glass cafeteria doors where people cluster.

I lead us over the crunchy dead grass to one of the sad, skinny trees planted off to the side. It's a good vantage point to view all around. I slip my backpack off my shoulder and drop it on the ground.

"Well?" Cradling her notebooks, Audrey loops her purse on her arm.

The note. I check around again to be sure no one's watching, then pull it out of my pocket. It's just a square of folded lined paper with *Adrian* in blue ink. I subtly hold it away from us and unfold it. "You don't know what could be inside," I say.

Audrey rolls her eyes. "What, like anthrax?"

Nothing falls out.

Scrawled in blue ink, in letters so sloppy it has to be someone disguising their handwriting, is this:

You know me but you dont know me.
Is your friend ok? I saw what
happened. I was there.
He ok?

Huh?

I reread it.

And again.

Audrey puts her hand on my arm. "Hold it steady. I can't read it."

"Is this a joke?"

I flip the paper over, looking again for a name. "I don't get it. What does this mean?"

I check around us. No! I freeze. It's Doug, inside the cafeteria doors. "We gotta go." My chest tightens as I crumple the note and shove it in my pocket.

"Hey, I wasn't done yet."

I bend down for my backpack. "Turn slowly." My voice cracks. "Doug, over there, in the cafeteria with that group." I struggle to lift my bag onto my shoulder, my head dizzy.

She eyes him, then me. "All right. Let's get to class."

Without drawing attention, we make our way through the far door and inside. "Listen," she says. "I'll fill you in on my plan at lunch. I've got it all figured out. Text me if you . . . oh, yeah."

"Exactly."

She gives me a little hug, then leaves.

I hightail it to French and arrive just after the bell rings. Hoping to quietly slip in, I instead bang the door with this stupid backpack as everyone, including hot Lev, turns to me.

Twelve

THANK OBI-WAN, BUBBAS DON'T TAKE FRENCH.

After a bit of muttering and gawking, everyone quiets down as I ease into my chair-desk. Has the whole freaking school heard about idiot Adrian already, or seen that video? I don't even glance at Lev, though I feel his eyes staring at the back of my plastered-down helmet hair. Oh, god, he and Kathleen must've seen everything Friday night.

Other than getting out my notebook and pen, I keep still and focus on the desk.

I'm so screwed. Audrey had better have a *real* plan, not like what she said at my house.

Fifteen minutes into this class and I'm just now calm enough to breathe normally. Or try to. It's hard when you have to repeat *Je voudrais me promener sur les grands boulevards de Paris* a hundred times. It takes a lot of breath.

"Tray bee-yayn, class," Madame Pauline says. "Tray bee-yayn."

Yes, indeed. Madame Pauline. My grasp of this amazing language has already been seriously jeopardized by this woman's horrendous accent. I mean, I've lived in Texas all my life but I don't have too strong a drawl. But with Madame Pauline, dang!

She says her name like "Muh-dayum Paw-leeen." I swear, if I hadn't taken French last year from a different teacher, I'd probably think this was how French people really talked. Like farm-raised Texans. Madame Pauline says she's been to France a few times. As soon as she opened her mouth, they must have thought she was having a seizure.

At least everyone's focused on her now and not me.

"On-cohwer," she says.

What she's trying to say is *encore*. So we repeat that same long sentence again. It means *I would like to walk along the boulevards of Paris*. Can you imagine? Wandering the streets where the Renaissance got its name? Seeing Michelangelo's masterpieces at the Louvre? I've studied these posters she has on the walls so many times, even copying some of them in my sketchbook, that I feel like I know Paris already. But what would Paris think of me?

Well, dreaming of getting away from Rock Hollow is like dreaming Graphite is more than a stupid cartoon. I used to think . . . Oh, hell. Who cares what I used to think?

Madame Pauline picks up the textbook and leans on her desk. "Everyone open to chapter fourteen."

I shift in my seat to get my book and feel that note wedged

in my pocket. Who the hell wrote it? I so need to text Audrey and Trent right now. I hate this. And what does that mean, *You know me but you don't know me?* Who the hell are you?

Has to be a joke, someone screwing with me, trying to scare me even more. Confreakingratulations, jackass. It's working.

But they ask if "my friend" is okay. Oh, god, now everyone thinks Kobe is my—

"Adrian?" Madame Pauline stares at me.

"Uh . . . *oui, Madame?*"

Am I supposed to say something? What did I miss?

"Page one thirty-seven, please."

All eyes are on me again. Guess I'm supposed to read from the text. So I do. It seems to be the right thing. Gotta keep my voice steady. Madame Pauline continues to amble through the rows of desks, here and there correcting my pronunciation from across the room. Some nerve, *her* correcting *me*.

I finish at last and she calls on the next reader. Lev.

Damn I love his voice. Kinda gravelly. I twist just a teeny bit to get a glimpse of him. Oh. He's looking right at me.

"Sorry," he says, "can I borrow your book? Left mine in my locker."

My face burns. Holy crap, he's so freakin' cute. Those eyes.

"Adrian?" Madame Pauline says. "Lev needs your *leever*."

"My liver?" I squint at her. People laugh. Oh, *livre*. "Ah, my book, my book."

Her mouth pinches, holding back a smile.

I hurriedly grab the textbook and, without thinking, close it. Oops. I lost our place.

As I turn to Lev, I try a friendly little laugh.

HaAA-a-aww!

My throat's so dry. A raspy squawk comes from my mouth like a loud donkey in pain. What the hell was *that*?

Lev jerks back, eyes big. He gapes at me like, well, I just imitated a farm animal. I catch his eyes and we both start laughing. The book slips from my hands and hits the floor with a *thud*.

The whole class cracks up. Just makes me lose it more. And more.

I bend down to get the book as I gasp for air. Then I really let loose. Oh, man. What's happening?

"Okay, Adrian, enough," Madame Pauline says.

Can't control it. I fumble with the book.

"Here." Lev reaches out. "I'll take it." He puts his hand on my shoulder.

It's just a slight pressure.

I'm still sore from that locker slam. But instead of pain, a warm streak shoots through me. Deep inside.

I can't breathe.

I'm not laughing now—I'm crying.

He pulls back his hand.

"Adrian?" Madame Pauline is next to me.

Why can't I stop? My chest heaves. I cover my face—it's wet.

"You all right?" she says softly.

Her voice makes me cry more. Stop it, Adrian! Stop. This.

I tame my breath, slow down, and stuff it in. Wiping tears from my face, I glance up at Madame Pauline.

The room is silent.

"Sorry." I wipe my hands on my jeans.

She leans down. "What do you need? Should we go out in the hall for a minute?"

I shake my head and stare at my desk.

Then I swallow. "Well, maybe I'll get some water."

She nods.

Reaching back without looking at him, I put my book on Lev's desk. Then I slide out of my chair and, staring at the floor tiles, make it out the door.

The hall is empty. I lean against the wall, cover my face, and exhale a few more silent sobs.

What just happened?

I still feel where Lev touched me, the same shoulder that hit the lockers. It's the only part of me that isn't numb.

What the hell is happening to me? I fall apart right in the middle of class? I *have* to be more careful. Get it together, Adrian! Don't be such a wimp.

I gotta try to shake off this freak-out and come back to earth. The water fountain isn't far, so I dash over in case anyone comes around. The squeaks from my shoes echo off the walls. At the fountain, the cold water burns my throat.

Come on, pull it together.

Okay. Here we go. I make it back to the door, put my hand on the handle, and inhale. Heart thumping, I slip in and ease into my seat. My book is back on my desk in front of me.

Breath by breath, I come down to earth. It's not until after three more people have read out loud that I risk glancing around. Everyone's focused on their own stuff again, but they eye me from time to time. Especially Madame Pauline. But she doesn't ask me any more questions.

I always thought most kids in this class seemed pretty cool, but what do I know? Maybe someone already texted the world about me losing it, about how weak I am. Easy prey.

Graphite Boy my ass.

Near the end of the period, Lev taps me on the arm. I tense up and look over my shoulder.

"Thanks for loaning me your book," he whispers.

All I can do is nod.

As Madame Pauline writes our assignment on the board, I realize I'll have to hang back and talk about whatever homework I missed the past two days. So when the bell rings I stay in my seat and slowly pack up.

Lev stands and puts away his stuff, including a huge pile of Halloween Hoedown flyers he passed around during class.

"Your knee okay?" he says.

"My knee?" Oh, from running into his table at Boo. Like a moron. My face flames up again. "Wow. Sorry about that. I was . . . uh, yeah. Fine." Voice squeaks.

We kind of half-look at each other for a moment.

"So," he says. "Did you see my note?"

Thirteen

I BLINK. DID LEV JUST . . . NO. MUST NOT HAVE HEARD HIM RIGHT.
"Did you say *your* note?" I ask.

"Yeah. Did you see it?" He's acting so calm. Even smiling. At *me*.

He shifts his bag. "Well?" he says.

"Um, I think so?" Still in my seat, I check around to see if anyone's listening. "That note was from *you*?"

He scrunches his forehead. "Who else?"

"I . . . I don't know. I wasn't sure." I swallow.

He steps back a little. "Why are you acting so weird? I thought you'd laugh."

"It was a joke?"

"Of course!"

"This note you slipped in my locker?" I rest my hand on my pocket.

"Huh? What do you mean?" he says.

"You didn't put that note in my locker?"

"Locker? I'm talking about the note I just put in your *book!*" He points to my French book on the desk. I flip open the cover and see an orange Halloween Hoedown flyer folded in half with *Monsieur Adrian Piper* written on it.

"Oh," I say, wiping sweat from my palms. "No . . . I didn't see this."

"What did you think I was talking about?"

"Nothing. There was this other note. Sorry. Got confused."

His face is bright red. "Well, I meant this one." He turns. "You can look at it later. I, uh, gotta talk French Club stuff with Madame Pauline."

Instead of walking past me, he goes around the next row of desks.

I open his note, written on the back of the flyer. It's a drawing of a Paris street corner with a big road sign that says INTERDIT DE RIRE, which means NO LAUGHING ALLOWED. And is that a stick-figure Madame Pauline in a French police uniform? It is—Lev's labeled everything. Oh, my god, she's shaking a baguette in the air and chasing after a stick-figure *me*. Why would he do this?

Lev finally takes off while the next class starts coming in, so I put the note back in my book and approach Madame Pauline at her desk. She turns to me and puts her papers down.

I can't look her in the eyes. "Um, sorry about my meltdown earlier. I don't know what happened."

"Don't wanna pry, so I won't," she says. "But you look like you're feelin' so low your feet would dangle off a dime."

Makes me grin.

She winks. "Listen, everybody has days that suck."

"Guess so." Did she just say *suck*?

"Hope your day gets better." She smiles and gives me a look that's more mom than teacher. "Anything I can do to help?"

I shake my head.

"You sure?" she asks.

"I'm fine," I say.

"All right, then. You can turn in the homework on *vown-dr-dee*." That's her way of saying Friday in French.

"*Merci,*" I say, and move on. Only one class down but I swear this backpack is heavier, even though it's got the same crap in it.

I take a deep breath and step into the hall. I can do this. But I keep my eyes on everyone zipping around, ready for any sudden movement . . . especially Doug. I try strutting like some macho straight guy, moving my shoulders but not my hips. Almost topple back with my two-ton bag and it only makes people shoot weirder looks at me.

Picking up my pace, I barely make it to algebra in time but can't focus at all. It seems people watch every move I make. But I'm not gonna have a repeat of what happened in French. What the hell was *that*? I was laughing like a maniac and then weeping like a freakin' baby?

I *really* need to get a grip. Really.

For the next two periods I stuff all emotion deep inside, keep my head down, and stay out of the way. Between periods I ready myself to run into a classroom, any classroom, at the first sign of trouble. That's the best plan I can think of.

But I've had no more bubba sightings—so far.

In my classes, I take secret peeks at the locker note when I can, and Lev's cartoon, but that just screws with my head even more. Plus, it reminds me of my big mouth and what a certifiable psycho Lev thinks I am.

Lunch period finally arrives. As my shoulders relax a bit at the sight of Audrey and Trent, my muscles scream from the backpack and, well, everything. When I relax is when I feel the pain.

I'm shaky telling Audrey and Trent about my freak-out in French. It's mortifying to go through it again, even if it's just words. I'm so dazed it sounds like I'm describing someone else. I don't mention Lev touching my shoulder, though.

"I still get flashes in my head, too, of Kobe on that car," Audrey says. "But you've got to keep it together."

Trent nods. "I'm gettin' all sorts of new attention myself this week." He checks over his shoulder, then looks at me. "Especially since you're back today. No offense. We got six hundred and four days on the Countdown Clock, so we just gotta suck it up."

Suck seems to be the word of the day.

Now that they're with me and I can actually calm down a bit, I pull out Lev's cartoon.

"Funny!" Trent holds Lev's note. "Even though it's cartoony, it does look like you."

"This is sweet," Audrey says. "Though unintentionally cruel."

"Huh?" I say.

"Clearly he has no idea you have a crush on him."

I grit my teeth and whisper, "Not so loud!" We're spaced apart from other tables, but her voice carries, even with the high-decibel chatter bouncing around. I don't think anyone heard.

"Sorry." She lowers her voice. "Anyway, straight guys are clueless about crushes." She frowns at a chipped fingernail. "If he knew how you feel, well, I'm sure he wouldn't have given you that note. It could create false hope."

"Thanks, Audrey," I say. "Just made my day worse."

"Not trying to. Just sayin' it like it is."

"So why'd he draw this, then?" Trent says.

"He must've just felt sorry for me." That makes sense after the ass I made of myself in front of him and Kathleen Friday night. Well, in front of everyone.

Though I'll take pity over getting slammed into the wall.

"Okay okay," Audrey says, pushing her tray aside to make room. "Where's that note from your locker?"

I put away Lev's cartoon and take a deep breath. Having no clue who wrote this, I don't want to draw attention, so I casually pull the mysterious paper from my pocket. I explain to Trent how it fell from my locker as we study the intentionally bad handwriting.

You know me but you dont know me. Is your friend ok? I saw what happened. I was there. He ok?

"It's obvious." Trent starts in on his second chili dog. "Someone's screwing with you."

"I'm not so sure." Audrey untangles a few strands of hair caught in one of her dangly silver earrings. "That second line about 'is your friend okay' sounds genuine."

"My *friend*," I say. "Great. So everyone thinks Kobe and I are friends and, thanks to freakin' Buddy, maybe even boyfriends."

Of course, I know all the stares and locker slams aren't just about me being gay. Even more, it's that I stood up to Doug, and no one *ever* does that.

Trent leans back and blows his bangs from his eyes, but they just fall back in his face. "You know, in times like this I ponder Gandhi's immortal words: 'When the shit storm hits, get yourself a big-ass umbrella.'"

"Huh?" I squint. "Did he really say that?"

Audrey snorts and rolls her eyes.

He grins. "Made it up. Just tryin' to inject some"—he checks his forearm—"sagacity."

"Thanks, Willow." I smirk.

He tilts his head, blinks at me, then gets it. "Oh, right. Superhero me." Shakes his head. "Don't think so, muchacho."

"Anyhoo . . . ," Audrey says, "back to the note?"

Trent licks chili off his fingers. "Any clues who wrote it?"

"No," I say. "Well, almost no. I thought it was from Lev for a minute, but it's not."

"Huh?" Audrey listens but keeps studying the piece of paper. "Let me see his drawing again."

"Long story," I say, handing her Lev's cartoon. "Main point is he didn't know about this locker note. Unless he was faking it really well."

"Hard to tell." Audrey compares the notes. "We know he was at Boo that night with Kathleen."

"So were a million other people," I say. All day I've tried to picture everyone from school who was there, but the place was packed.

"It's like I'm being stalked," I say. "That line, 'You know me but you don't know me'? Scary, right?"

"Definitely has to be a sick joke," Trent says. "What guy would ask a question without any way for you to answer?" He wipes his mouth, then balls up the napkin.

Audrey grunts. "This could be from a girl, you know." She points to the paper. "Nothing here is specific to boys."

"Great. So it really *could* be anyone."

"You're way overanalyzing it, guys." Trent makes a little trash sculpture on his plate. "It's just a little note. Think about it. If someone were really wondering if Kobe was dead or alive, why wouldn't they just say who they are? Ignore it."

Good point.

A pack of skater guys get up from a nearby table and head our way.

"Quick, Audrey, give 'em to me." I grab both notes and cover them with her tray.

As they pass, I jump as one of the guys throws up his hands and squeals, "Leave him alone! Don't hurt him! Stop it! Stop it!" They crack up and bump into each other, turning back to smirk at me as they go.

"Oh, my god." My insides turn cold. "Does this . . . Has *everyone* seen that video of Adrian the asshole?"

Trent sits up straight and glares at them. "*You're* not the asshole."

People at other tables laugh or whisper or look annoyed.

Audrey turns to me. "I know how you feel, Adrian, but you should definitely report this. Don't let them get away with it."

"They just did," Trent says.

"And when those 'dudes' find out I reported them?" I stand and pack up my stuff. "It won't be just Doug out to kill me."

She exhales. "I don't get you, Adrian."

Join the club.

We go to dump our trash. Audrey and Trent move toward the doors, but, spotting the drama table, I hang back. They're a whole lot quieter than usual over there. No wonder. But they must know the latest about Kobe. My legs move before my brain kicks in and I walk right toward them.

I pause, but I'm only a table away from them. Their conversation stops dead. I can't just spin and leave at this point with heads all around turning my way, so I go up to them.

"Hey," I mumble, pulse speeding up.

The drama kids look at each other, then me.

"Uh, how's Kobe?" I say.

"Home," a girl with big neon-orange glasses says. "Like, he's home now. Well, Sunday, actually."

"Have you seen him?" I ask.

She shakes her head. "He doesn't want to see anyone." Another girl puts her arm around her and squeezes her shoulder.

A short blond guy at the table shrugs. "Guess I don't blame him."

No one says anything else. They just kinda look at me.

My face gets hot. "Well, see ya."

As I turn, the girl in the orange glasses says softly, "Adrian, thank you."

The staring faces from nearby tables blur away for a second.

I look back at her and clear my throat. "What's your name?"

"Carmen."

I blink, do a little wave at Carmen, then catch up to Audrey and Trent, who hang by the doors.

Audrey's face might as well be a question mark and Trent's an exclamation point.

"I dunno," I say, heading into the hall. "Just had to find out, I guess."

"What?" question mark Audrey asks.

"That Kobe's home. Since Sunday."

Audrey glances at Trent. "That's good to know, at least. What else?"

I navigate to the courtyard doors, step outside into the glare of the pale-gray overcast sky, and breathe in damp, clammy air. Only small groups of non-bubbas are out here.

When we're away from the crowds I say, "What possessed me to do that? So freakin' stupid, exposing myself in front of everyone."

"Slow down there, Graphite Boy—uh, Adrian," Trent says, glancing around. "Oops, just slipped. Sorry."

I flash him a look.

We stop next to a wall and I toss my damn backpack on the brittle grass.

Trent plops down cross-legged.

I rub my temples. "I wouldn't have done that if I had my phone."

"What do you mean?" Audrey tests a spot of grass with her palm, decides it won't swallow her whole, then eases down on the ground.

"I would have used my phone to find out how Kobe is doing," I say. "Just asked him myself. Not go and waltz over to the drama kids! In front of the whole cafeteria!" I kick the ground, sending a chunk of sod to disintegrate against the brick wall.

"Hey, now!" Audrey holds up her hands. "Don't be sendin' dirt all over the place!" She scowls and brushes bits of dirt and grass from her charcoal-gray skirt.

I breathe in deep and sink to the ground. "Sorry." I almost call her Sultry.

"No matter what you do," Trent says, "assholes will think what assholes will think."

Audrey aims her camera phone at herself and checks her makeup. "So what else did they say about Kobe?"

"Just that he doesn't want visitors." But what does that mean? "Hey, Audrey, can I see your phone?"

"In a sec."

"Here." Trent hands me his and I log on to my account. I look twice to be sure, but it's there: a message from Kobe. I tap the screen and read it.

Huh?

Holy crap. This isn't good.

Fourteen

"HEY, GUYS?" I SAY TO TRENT AND AUDREY. "I GOT A SCARY message from Kobe." I picture his bloody face. Eyes shut. Mouth hanging open.

"Meaning?" Trent says.

I scan the courtyard where we sit in our own little circle on the grass.

"This morning I messaged Kobe just to see if he was better," I say. "And now listen to this: 'better? better than? my life is screwed. face is screwed. brain is screwed. you have no idea. but no one will see. ever. i'll be gone.' What does that mean?"

Trent raises his eyebrows. "Dude is majorly medicated, I surmise."

"It's good you reached out," Audrey says. "Sounds like he needs some positive reinforcement and response."

"Is that your official opinion, Doctor?" Trent says, plucking the few healthy blades of grass from the ground around him, leaving the dead ones alone.

"Think we should worry?" I say. "I mean, that sounds suicidal, right?"

"I dunno, it's probably the meds talking. Besides, Kobe never struck me as the type to feel sorry for himself," Trent says, tossing shredded blades of grass into the wind.

Audrey takes the phone, reads the message, then hands it back to me.

She purses her lips. "Hmm . . . he could mean all sorts of things. Didn't his other message talk about his mom being on top of it? I'm sure his family is taking care of him."

"But he even told his friends not to visit," I say. "This is freaking me out."

I read his message again.

"He's not *your* freak show, Adrian," Trent says. "I don't think you should get mixed up with him more than you already are. It could stoke the rumors."

"I know, but still." I can't think of what to write back, so I log out and hand Trent his phone. "'No one will see. Ever. I'll be *gone*'? That doesn't sound right."

"Look," Trent says, "I just want to protect you. And this is drama queen Kobe we're talkin' about, remember? He probably just wants more attention from you."

"But he—"

"Why don't you send him a message after school? He's probably fine, but you could make sure." Audrey rummages in her bag and pulls out a pink folder. "Besides, don't you think you have enough to worry about? Speaking of which, you ready for my plan?"

I sigh. Oh, yeah. Her "plan."

I glance at Trent. He holds up his hands in a not-part-of-whatever-this-is way.

"I don't want what happened to Kobe happening to you," she says.

"Uh, yeah!" I say. "That makes two of us!"

"I've been doing all sorts of research, and, well, I have an idea for what you should do. Hear me out. First step, like I already said, is you should tell your side of the story."

I look up at the sky. "We've already been through this, Audrey."

"Just listen, okay?" She tugs at her skirt, smoothing the hem down over her knees. "Once you tell Assistant Principal McConnell what really happened—let me finish!—then ideally that'll get the ball rolling so you can step out of it and they'll start investigating."

"You're delusional," Trent says. "If the cops could turn Doug kicking Kobe's ass into 'self defense,' no one here's gonna do squat."

"But," she says, shooting Trent a look, "if they do nothing, then you've tried that route." She places the folder in front of her on the grass. "Then you can go to the next step."

She eyes me, but I watch her without speaking.

She continues. "I've looked into what other gay teens around the country have done in similar—"

"Oh, come on," Trent says.

"—in similar situations, and it can help!"

The wind flips her folder, so she slaps it against the ground with her palm.

I cross my arms. "Like what?"

"You could contact the news, or spread the truth on social media, or start a petition calling for Doug's father to be censured—"

"Wha—wha . . . ? Hold on!" I straighten up on my knees. "What the hell are you talking about?"

"Uh, Audrey," Trent says, "have you met my friend, here? His name is Adrian—you know, the guy who'd *never* freakin' do anything like that?"

"These are just ideas, guys," she says. "I'm trying to figure out how to keep you safe, Adrian." She sticks the folder under her knee.

I glare at her. "More like the opposite. First, are you insane? Second, are you insane? Third, how could me threatening everyone *else* keep me safe?"

The wind gusts and kicks up dirt and leaves. I shut my eyes and turn my head until it calms down.

Audrey smooths her hair back in place. "What deterrent does Doug have now to hurting you?"

"Adrian keeping out of his way and not rockin' the boat!" Trent says. "Let that doomed cruise ship just sail away."

I nod.

A few groups on the other side of the courtyard head back in.

Audrey continues. "Taking action could actually bring justice, you know. And at the least, if anything happened to you, everyone would know it was Doug."

"Oh! So I'd basically just be letting everyone know who to go thank when I get killed?"

"You're completely missing my point!" she says.

I stand. "Why don't *you* go start a petition or a sit-in or whatever the hell you want me to do?"

She shakes her head. "*You* were there. I didn't see it up close like you."

"So?" I scan around, but no one's in earshot.

"Besides, I think it would have the most impact—and highlight that Kobe's beating was a hate crime—if it came from another gay teen." She picks up the pink folder and holds it out to me.

"That's *so* not true," I say.

"Un. Freakin'. Believable." Trent gets up.

"What am I, Audrey? Your senior project?"

Still on the grass, with one hand on her hip and the other clutching the folder, she says, "Adrian, you're my friend. Will you at least think about what I'm saying? Please?"

I stretch my arms way up and twist my spine back and forth. Almost every joint pops.

Eyeing her, I take the folder. "What's in here? And does it have to be *pink*?"

Audrey shifts her knees. "I just printed out info about different cases from schools all over the place. Plus some other stuff. Some could apply, some not, but it's all good reference."

With his back to us, Trent watches people amble back

inside. "Do not rock the boat. Choppy waters out there."

"Will you stop it with the boat stuff? Jeez, we got it." Audrey pushes herself up from the ground and brushes herself off.

I stick the folder deep in my stupid backpack and heave it onto my shoulder. What was I thinking, bringing every damn book and folder I have? I've hardly used any of it.

Audrey puts her hand on my arm. "Think about what I said, all right?"

I want to tell her to leave me the hell alone, but instead I say, "I honestly don't think my brain can handle anything else today."

She nods.

We go back inside, head our separate ways, and I hustle to chemistry.

I know she cares, but that girl needs to get a life and worry about her own crap. And with Kobe possibly teetering on the edge, he doesn't need me doing anything stupid and pushing us *both* off the cliff. Kobe's in danger too, but maybe more from himself than—

Slam! I plow right into a wall of guys, who say, "Watch it!"

I almost stagger off-balance but catch myself.

Crap. It's the staring Wrestler Guy with two others.

"Look where you're going, douchebag," says the shortest one, who's stocky but shorter than me.

"Sorry" is all I manage to squeak. I spot a teacher way down the hall.

Wrestler Guy looks around us, then at me. "Piper, right?"

I swallow. I hate that using-my-last-name crap. "Uh, yeah?"

The short guy points at me. "You know this wuss, Calderón?"

"Nah," Wrestler Guy says, "just seen him around." He locks eyes with me and his face turns bright red.

Huh?

"C'mon." With the back of his hand, the other friend pops Calderón on the shoulder. "Can't be late."

"Yeah," Calderón says, scanning me up and down. He locks eyes with me again and blushes even more.

He turns and they move on.

What was *that*? What did he mean, he's "seen" me around? In the video? Or at Boo? And why was he so embarrassed and looking at me like that?

No. It couldn't be. Did Calderón write the note? Is there even more to it, like *he's* gay?

Now I'm delusional.

I make it to chemistry as the bell rings. It's easier to ignore the few odd looks I get right now, with what just happened. I rack my brain to remember if he was there Friday night. He would have been with the bubbas, though. Okay, this is *way* too much.

I can't do this. I gotta pay attention here, focus.

I take a long, deep breath, then pull out my books.

Lev's girlfriend, Kathleen, is in this class, and I catch her checking me out a lot. It's like I'm some sort of experiment gone wrong. I'm sure Lev filled her in on what a freak I was in French. She's probably just waiting for me to melt down here, too. No way that's gonna happen.

Catching up after missing two days helps refocus my head. Chemistry isn't my thing in any case, so I have no choice but to really concentrate. The class goes by pretty quickly. When the bell rings I'm the first out the door.

To avoid the bathrooms all day, I've practically had nothing to drink. But now I majorly gotta go. So, on my way to sixth period, I enter the boys' room on the second floor by the entrance to the auditorium balcony. This one's always the least crowded. There are just four guys in here now, and they don't look at me as I head right to the stalls, which are all empty.

I slip into the one stall with the door that stays shut. It's criminal they took off the latches, but at least there are doors. I can barely wedge in here and close it with my stupid backpack.

I unzip and let loose. Whew. That's sooo much better.

Ugh. Someone's scratched a really bad drawing of a spread-eagled girl onto the wall divider. I could do way better. Well, drawing a guy, of course, and in a *far* less repulsive and demeaning pose. I would draw Graphite.

Graphite. Weird. Haven't thought much about him today.

I hear all the guys leave. Then someone else enters and a loud voice bounces around the tiles. "You're so fulla shit."

What?

Then I hear a deeper voice. "I swear, this one'll kick your ass."

NO! Buddy. Doug.

I freeze.

There's no sound of Doug's keys—clanking like a dog's

tags, always hanging from his side—but I'd know their voices anywhere.

"No way," Buddy says. "Gimme your worst, I can handle it."

"Not this batch," Doug says. "You're too much of a pussy."

I silently zip up and turn, careful not to bump the door or walls. Gripping my backpack straps, I peer through the narrow opening between the stall door and divider. I face the sink and mirrors.

They go to the urinals, off to the left. I can't see them and there are no other sounds. I'm in here alone . . . with them.

I'm trapped! I should make a run for it. Now. Right now.

My backpack's so huge. This stall's too tight.

And my legs won't move.

DAMMIT!

"What's your famous 'secret ingredient' this time?" Buddy asks. "You always talk about your ohhhh-so-secret ingredient. What the hell is it?"

"It's a half cup of none of your damn business."

Their voices bring back everything. My mind races.

"Hey, don't splash me, faggot," Doug says. A urinal flushes and he comes into my view.

What do I do? If I had my damn phone, I could text for help.

I pull back so Doug can't see me peering through. Bending my knees, I pretend to sit so he'll think it's just some guy doing his business. He must notice my feet under the stall door. But my shoes could be anyone's. He doesn't know.

Just gotta wait this out.

They have no idea it's me. No idea.

Through my narrow view I can spy Doug checking himself in the mirror. He glances in Buddy's direction, then takes off the red cap, his dull brown hair molded in a bowl shape. Odd to see his whole face, even though it's more of a glimpse from here.

I think of what his eyes looked like that night. Bloodshot. Coming at me.

Doug spikes up his hair. He styles it to one side and smiles at his reflection. Freakin' weird. Like a different person.

I hear Buddy finish and zip up. Doug fits his cap back on his head in one quick motion, smile gone.

I pull back even more in case they can see part of my face. Buddy comes into view.

"Just wait, Bud," Doug says. "One drop'll turn your nuts inside out. This batch's a *twenty*-alarmer."

What the hell are they talking about?

"Twenty? No such thing. And, bro, real men don't *cook*." Buddy flops his hand with a limp wrist.

"Screw you. You're just a wuss."

"I've tried all your lame-ass hot sauces. Guess what? Your shit ain't so hot."

"Watch it, dickhead," Doug says. "My sauces are better than anything you'll ever do. Even hotter, like me."

Buddy cackles.

Doug checks his reflection in the mirror and adjusts his hat. "I'm *too* hot. Ladies just line up to get burned."

"That why they never stick around?"

Doug kicks at the back of Buddy's knee. "They can't handle it."

"Oh, yeah? So what's your secret ingredient?"

Doug pops him on the chest. "It's called secret for a reason."

"Bro, the wimpiest baby could handle you or any hot sauce you make. Even that little homo Piper."

What? Oh, my god.

"Hey, that little fag's here, ya know," Buddy says. My heart hammers. "Back at school. I saw him this morning."

Doug sniffs. "I know. I saw him."

I put my palm to my chest. My heartbeat's so loud they must hear.

Doug turns a faucet on and off and flicks water at Buddy.

"Come off it!" Buddy says.

"Wimp," Doug says. "Okay, let's move."

"Hear that guy in there?" Buddy takes a step toward my stall. "Gross. He's panting. What's he doing?"

I hold my breath.

Buddy punches the hand dryers on, noise bouncing off the tiles. I can't see where they went. Did they leave?

The stall door next to me opens. Shoes squeak. What's happening?

Above me I hear, "Holy shit!" Buddy gapes at me over the divider, then pounds it with his knee.

Oh, my god! I scramble, claw at the door, open and slam it against the divider. I wedge out of the stall. Doug blocks me.

He squints at me, confused.

Buddy bolts out of the other stall. "You? What the fuck you doin' in there? Jackin' off watchin' me pee?"

There's no one else here and I can't get to the door.

Buddy grabs his crotch. "Tryin' to see my dick?" He shoves me toward the urinals.

"Hey!" I barely steady myself.

"*No.*" Doug grabs Buddy's arm. "You fuckin' nuts? Not here."

The bell rings.

Doug steps right to me, stares down in my face.

I don't move a muscle.

Hand dryers stop, leaving silence.

"Piper." Doug's spittle lands in my eye. He glances at Buddy, then back at me. He studies my face. "I'm watching you, every step. Everything you do."

He looks down at my shaking hands, then turns to go.

Buddy kicks me. "Ow!"

Doug whips around, grabs the front of Buddy's shirt, and pulls him up. "I. Said. Not. Here." He practically tosses him toward the door.

Buddy glares back at me. Then they're gone.

My breathing echoes all around the empty room.

I rub my shin where Buddy kicked me. It burns. I hold back a moment, then open the bathroom door, ready to run, or scream. But the halls are almost empty and classroom doors are closing. Wait—there, all the way at the end of the hall. Doug and Buddy turn the corner. They're gone.

I can't stay here, and there's no way I'm ready for class.

With no one around now, I try the auditorium balcony door. It's not locked. Checking over my shoulder, I slip in and close the door with a soft *click*. As if smothered by a pillow, the echo and brightness of the hall disappear and are replaced by cool darkness. It's practically pitch-black.

I'm in a little side hall that wraps around the balcony level. I lean against the scratchy carpeted wall and let my eyes get used to the faint glow of red from the exit sign above my head. My shin stings. I grope my way along the wall to one of the two archways that lead to the seats.

I peek around the corner. Rows of dark-purple seats fan down from where I stand at the top of an aisle. A couple dimmed lights faintly shine from the ceiling, making soft glowing pools between here and the railing. Everything else is in shadow.

Without making a sound, I descend one step.

All the way down below, beyond the railing, only the stage curtain has any light on it, casting stark shadows in the deep folds of the golden fabric.

I stand perfectly still and scan all the seats, listening for any sound. My eyes adjust more and, with the faint light from the ceiling and red exit signs above both archways, it's clear I'm alone. I only hear my heart, pounding through my ribs.

In the top row, I slide over to the far corner. My back and shoulders throb as I take off my backpack and place it on the floor. Springs creak as I ease into a seat and pull my knees up against my chest. Then there's only heavy silence.

What do I do? What the hell do I do?

I am so screwed.

Fifteen

I WALK RIGHT INTO CLASS AND UP TO THE TEACHER, WHISPER SO only he can hear, "Sorry I'm late, but I needed extra time in the bathroom," and then sit down. It's the best excuse I could come up with to cover my ten (fifteen?) minutes of hiding in the balcony. I must look bad enough that he believes me. He doesn't ask questions so must think I'm still "sick" from being out for two days.

Well, I am.

Everyone's still watching me, of course, but it's better to be in this class than out in the hall, exposed. Plus, I don't need the school calling my parents to say I disappeared.

It's last period—almost the hell out of here.

Well, for today.

¤ ¤ ¤

"Those assholes." Through the car window, Trent glares into the distance.

Audrey drives with her usual finesse as we zip by parked cars in the shopping mall lot. I grab the seat as she spots an open space, whips into it, and comes to a quick stop.

"Harassing you in the bathroom? Why didn't you go straight to the assistant principal?" she says, shutting off the engine. "What were you thinking?"

"About not getting killed, okay?" Leaving my backpack on the floor, I hop out on the passenger side and a raindrop hits my face. Sporadic dark dots pepper the pavement. I close the door. I've got a massive headache.

Trent extracts himself from the car and shuts his door.

Audrey slams hers. "Adrian, this is serious."

"*Really?*" Trent says. "Wow, I'm sure he didn't notice that."

"Audrey, you weren't there!" I scan the lot. No one is nearby. "Like I told you, Doug's watching every step I take. He's got eyes everywhere."

Audrey, hands on hips, ignores the raindrops and stares at me across the hood. "Then maybe Doug would be more careful if he knew *he* was being watched by—"

"The school?" Trent says. "Oh, come on. What are they gonna do? Doug is God, remember? Football rules and he rules football. Where do you think you live, Norway?"

I start toward the mall. "Besides, he made it clear with Buddy. It's not at school that worries me most."

Trent easily catches up to me with those long legs, his

black boots clomping along. "Then why'd you want to come to the mall?" he says. "Little exposed, don't you think?"

"Safety in numbers," I say. Well, numbers that aren't drunk bubbas. "Besides, Doug and Buddy have football practice after school, right?"

After a few steps I stop and look back at Audrey, trailing us.

"I get where you're coming from," I say to her. "In a perfect world I'd run to the authorities and all would be la-di-da happy. But you saw how the cops closed ranks around Doug. His dad's a sergeant, remember? And anyway, around here, no one's gonna side with the *gay* kid."

Huffing, she marches past us.

"I'm only looking out for you," she says. "This incident is the perfect example of what I was telling you earlier. You've got to do something to protect yourself. I'm not being some naïve dreamer here—the only option is to let the school know. Okay? Done."

I grit my teeth and keep my thoughts to myself. She's not listening anyway.

We enter the mall through Neiman Marcus, the only worthy entrance according to you-can-guess-who. Overpriced luxury stores aren't my thing, but the tinkling music and pricey perfume samples seem to calm Audrey. Trent and I keep going, zigzagging around the glittering glass cases, and wait for her outside the store in the actual mall.

It's not too crowded—just the usual mix of parents with strollers, old people "power-walking," business types, and after-school kids. Some I recognize, but at least there's no one

I'm worried about. And here, everyone's more interested in looking in mirrors than looking at me.

Trent's belt chains jangle as we sit on one of the benches sandwiched between towering potted plants. I lean back and let my muscles go limp. Comforting mall sounds echo all around. I want to close my eyes, but I'd probably just pass out. "Can we get some coffee?" I say. My headache's worse.

"Better wait for Her Highness," he says.

I spot Audrey over in Neiman's, drooling over the rainbow of lipsticks.

Trent blows his jet-black hair from his eyes. "Just ignore her. I don't get what planet she thinks she's living on."

"More like what solar system," I say.

I watch her banter with the big-haired saleslady.

An old couple strolls by, but when they see Trent in his goth finery, their faces harden and they pick up their pace. He slumps lower on the bench, curving his back into a C shape.

"Why's Audrey ragging on you so much?" he says. "What's the deal with that pink 'research folder' crap?"

"I think I actually get it," I say. "She got picked on a lot in elementary school. *Really* cruel stuff about her weight. And for being black. Back then, she'd always go to the teachers and they'd take care of it. She must think that'll magically work for me." Of course, I can't imagine that would even work for her now—not at Rock Hollow High—but she doesn't need the teachers anymore. She can take care of herself.

I rub my shoulders, which is like massaging granite, then tilt my head from side to side.

Trent watches. He stretches his arms and pops his knuckles. "Dude, gotta hunker down and don't let it get to you. You can't control the volcano, so just keep to your path."

"And don't rock the boat?"

He nods. "You got it."

Easy for him to say. Maybe if I were over six feet tall and looked like Jack Skellington, *I* wouldn't worry so much either. Except that I know he does, somewhere inside there.

I ask for his phone again, log on to my account, and check messages. "Nothing more from Kobe."

"Listen, he's probably just being a drama queen," Trent says.

"He's home from the hospital after getting beat up! Give him a break."

He nods. "You're right."

A tiny girl toddles over and waves at us. As her mom calls her back, I smile and return the wave.

"But listen, Graphite Boy," he says. "You're already too connected with him. Doug's watching. Only digs your grave deeper."

"But what if Kobe *is* suicidal?"

Trent shakes his head. "Some people just like to scare you. Believe me, I live with the Queen of Give Me Attention. Remember when my mom threatened to set the house on fire because she thought no one loved her? Well, she never did."

I sigh. Instead of *Yeah, well, your mom's not a kid who just got his face bashed in for being gay,* I say, "Guess she felt someone cared after all."

I know he and Audrey are just looking out for me, but why can't they see what *I* see?

I give back his phone since I can't think of what I'd say to Kobe anyway. *Don't hurt yourself any more than Doug did? Don't worry, it'll be okay?* What the hell do I know?

With a teensy shopping bag in hand, Audrey strides over. "No better therapy than retail therapy. This mall is *sanctuary*."

Hmm, maybe for *some* people. But I bet that lipstick cost as much as a cell phone. Must be nice to have that kind of pocket change.

Trent pats me on the back. "Dude here needs Starbucks therapy."

We amble off to the food court as Audrey babbles about, well . . . I've tuned out. It's all about her, anyway.

We pass store after store with mirror-windows and I look like crap. I'd avoid walking by the cute blond guy who works the sunglasses cart, but he never looks at me anyway. He really is hot. Which makes me think of Lev, and then the notes, still in my pocket. And Kobe's scary message won't leave my brain.

Enough!

I splurge on a venti latte and hope to hell this helps. Trent gets some Amazon-jungle-friendly soy thing while Audrey grabs her latte first and finds a table. Of course, it's *her* choice where to sit. Like everything.

We plop down off to the side of the food court by the windows, rain softly thunking against the glass, which reflects the glaring theme park palette of neon lights and signs in here. I stare out the window into the flat, cold, gray world of Rock

Hollow. Where out there is *my* place, *my* sanctuary? Certainly not the school. Paris, maybe? Yeah, right, like that's in the realm of possibility. My house? Yes, but it's really just my cramped little room . . . not much. I've never wished Graphite's world were real more than I do now.

"So, back to the hot sauce," Trent says.

I turn to him. "Huh?"

"Doug freakin' makes hot sauce? You sure that's what he and dickhead Buddy were talking about?"

"So insane, right?" I say.

"My friends: That. Is. Hysterical," he says. "Can you imagine him in his apron, little bottles of spices all lined up? Ha!"

"'Hot sauce'?" Audrey whips out her phone and taps away. "Must be slang for drugs. I'll Google it. Doesn't meth have a million other names?"

I glare at her. "Look, they were talking about his twenty-alarm hot sauce. People don't rate drugs by 'alarms,'" I say. "I was there. He was talking about cooking. Trust me."

She keeps searching on her phone. Trent sips his coffee and raises his eyebrows.

"You don't believe me?" I say.

She doesn't even look up.

I blurt out, "Okay, Audrey. You're pissed because I won't go crying to the principal like you want. I get it."

Her nostrils flare, but she keeps her eyes on the phone. "You don't have to listen to reason if you don't want to. That's your business."

I stare at my napkin and rip it into shreds.

"Sooo," Trent says, pulling out his phone. "Movie? I can see what's about to start."

I exhale. "Cavernous dark room? Deafening sound system? Mindless fluff to make me forget my crappy life?" I say. "Yes, please."

"Can't. My parents expect me for dinner tonight." Audrey clicks off her phone and tosses it in her purse. "Sorry."

Trent slumps back.

"You know what? I need to get home." I pick up my cup and stand.

Trent glares at Audrey and gets up. Turns to me. "You sure?"

"I just need to get home. Be alone."

Audrey looks from me to Trent. "Whatever," she says.

We walk back in silence past the stores and mirrors and squealing little kids and posing teens. But my pounding headache doesn't stay behind. I toss out what's left of my coffee. Caffeine's only made me more jittery.

It's pouring rain now, so we dash to the car. I get in the back as usual. Audrey stays quiet and doesn't make even one comment about her upholstery getting wet.

Rush-hour traffic slows us down. Trent attempts to lighten the mood and starts telling us what crazy Hawaiian shirt one of his teachers wore today, but neither Audrey nor I say anything so he trails off. He tries again with another story but soon gives up, leaving only the patter of the rain and annoying squeaks of the windshield wipers.

We ease forward inch by inch as we near the big intersection with Mission Road.

Audrey sighs and catches my eyes in the rearview mirror. "Adrian, I'm sorry. I don't want you mad at me."

"Yeah?" I say.

"Look, I could call my parents and see if I can skip dinner. We could still go to a movie."

I sigh. "It's all right. I think I'll just go home and sleep. Plus, I do have three days' worth of homework I should at least look at." Like that's gonna happen. I glimpse my backpack on the floor. Audrey's stupid pink folder peeks out through the zipper.

We make it through the intersection and traffic clears up. We're almost to Trent's house now.

"Hey, guys," I say. "Remember that Wrestler Guy that keeps staring at me? I literally ran into him today, with two of his friends. It was freaky. His name is Calderón."

"Ugh," Audrey says. "Yes, I know. Manuel Calderón. Sits right next to me in AP history, remember? Self-centered jerk. Never shuts up."

I loosen my seat belt and scoot forward to lean on Trent's seat. "He was acting really weird, though. Sounds stupid, maybe, but he might have written the locker note."

"Him?" Audrey laughs. "No way. His world revolves only around him."

Trent looks over his shoulder at me. "What'd he do that was weird?"

"Well, he—"

"Nuh-uh," Audrey says. "That guy?"

"Again, Audrey," I say, "you weren't there. I saw his face. He actually—"

"With *his* macho self? I'm tellin' you, not possible."

I push back into my seat, the seat belt clicking tight. "Well, I guess you know everything, then, Audrey. Don't you?"

The damn seat belt is locked. It won't budge.

"All I mean," she says, "is I see him every—"

"Oh, don't explain. Your word is gospel." I hit the button and the seat belt retracts with a *thwack*. "You know all about him, you know all about everyone. You know all about *me*."

"Guys," Trent says. "Let's maybe chill?"

She slows to turn onto Trent's street, then glances back at me. "Adrian, you don't understand. I'm only—"

"No," I say, gripping the door handle. "I completely understand. You've got *all* the answers, filed neatly in your little pink folders."

"Oh, come on." She pulls the car to the curb. "Trent, you understood what I meant."

He holds up his hands. "Keep me outta this."

I glance out the window. We're at Trent's house.

Shifting into park, Audrey says, "Listen, maybe it's just that I can see things a bit more clearly."

"Actually," I say, "maybe *you* should listen. How could you possibly see things more clearly? You don't know what my life is like, Audrey. You're not me."

She turns and glares at me, silent and seething.

I grab my backpack, fling open the door, and step right in a puddle. Dirty water seeps into my shoe. I shut the door and stand on the curb.

Trent gets out and looks at the sky. The rain has stopped.

Out of her view, he motions toward Audrey in the car and mouths, *What the?* Then, stooping down to grab his bag from the seat, he says to Audrey, "Thanks for the fun time." He holds the door open for me to get in front so she can drop me off at home next.

I don't move.

"Well?" The car interior muffles Audrey's voice.

The air smells fresh out here. Chilly but crisp.

"Don't have all day, Adrian," she says.

Leaning down to look at her, I say, "I'm gonna walk."

I slam the door.

Audrey rolls down the passenger window and yells, "Adrian, get in the damn car."

I grit my teeth. "Just leave me alone."

"You are unbelievable," she says, then zooms off, tires crunching on the wet pavement.

Sixteen

TRENT SHAKES HIS HAIR, STILL DAMP FROM THE DOWNPOUR IN THE mall parking lot. His gothy eyeliner is all smudged. "Audrey needs a puppy."

I squint at him. "What?"

"Or a boyfriend," he says, "or a philanthropic foundation or some crap to focus on other than you."

"She just won't let up!"

"Don't waste brain energy on it." He stares down the street as she and Athena disappear from view. "Wanna come in? Mom won't be home for another few hours. At least."

"Really? You sure that's a good idea?"

"My damn house too."

It's stopped raining, but sporadic heavy drops fall on me from tree branches above. Exhaling deeply, I roll my neck, then heft my backpack onto my shoulder. "Okay, but your mom probably wouldn't be too pleased to see Satan in your house. I'll only come in if you're *positive* she won't come back early."

"She won't. Her insanity is predictable. Usually."

I follow all black-clad, chain-jangling six foot three inches of him toward the house that his mom didn't set on fire.

What do I do? Audrey wants me to freakin' become a political movement and Trent wants me to hide under the covers until the storm passes?

No one gets what I'm going through. *No one.*

Well, actually . . . no, what am I thinking? That's stupid, right?

As we get to the front door, I stop. "Ya know, I should probably get home after all. I'm wiped and, well, I can't remember if I'm on Dad Duty tonight," I say, knowing full well I'm not.

"Oh, right. That." He glances at the house. "Babysitting parents rocks, don't it?"

"Hey," I say. "Can I use your phone?"

He tilts his head and looks down at me from his lofty elevation. "Be careful how involved you get with Kobe."

"Lay off it, all right? It's not like Doug's monitoring my communications."

That makes him smile. "Bet the only thing Doug monitors online involves big tits or touchdowns. So, yeah, you have nothing to worry about there."

He hands me his phone. Then, from the box on the door, he gets the mail and flips through it.

I tap my password and—no new Kobe message.

I log out, close my eyes, and think.

The neighborhood is quiet, with just a few faint sounds of kid voices from some backyard nearby and the dull engine of an airplane far above.

Keeping the screen out of Trent's view, I Google Kobe's address and scroll through.

There.

I know that street. Not too far to walk.

"Bunch of religious crap. Big surprise." Trent scowls at the mail he's holding, then turns to me. "So, any more freaky messages?"

I take a breath. "Nope."

"See? That's good," he says. "Best to stay away from that mess."

Sorry, too late.

I quickly erase the search history and hand back his phone. "Thanks."

He slips it in his pocket and pulls out his keys. "Dude, I know it's never been your thing, but just go home and play some violent, bloody, killing video game to exorcise the demons from your head. That's what I'll be doing."

It's never been my thing before and never will be. I shift my backpack onto both shoulders. "Have fun with that." I turn and give a little wave.

"May the Force be with you." He bows and closes the door.

I start down the sidewalk. Once I'm out of view of Trent's house, I cut through the alley and head in the opposite direction, passing one block, then another. Dogs bark at me from behind their fences. My footsteps and my breath form a rhythm. The air tastes like dead, wet leaves.

This neighborhood kinda looks like mine—how can Kobe afford his own Mustang?

It's still chilly, but I'm sweating from walking so fast.

There it is. I spot Kobe's powder-blue car—all cleaned up. His house is just a regular house: tan brick, brown roof, little yard with a few oak trees letting go of their leaves. Weird. I was imagining something more, well, dramatic. Like a circus tent.

Should I be here? He doesn't want visitors, and hell, I don't even know these people.

Oh, come on, just freakin' do it!

I half-walk, half-tiptoe to the front door. My hand shakes as I press the bell.

"Who is it?" It's a little girl's voice.

"Is—" My throat rasps. "Is Kobe home? I go to school with him. It's, uh, Adrian Piper?"

The door jostles like she's jumping up to look through the peephole. Then, "Koooobaaaay! Someone to seeee yooouu!"

It seems a minute goes by. Then, through the door, "Adrian? Why the hell are you here?"

"Kobe? Is that you?"

"What do you want?"

Relieved, I smile at the peephole. "Just to say hi and see how you're doing."

Nothing.

"All right," I say, "guess I'll—"

The locks click and the door opens a crack. "You shouldn't have come," he says from behind the door.

"Well. Here I am."

"You alone?" he says.

Very. "Just me."

The door inches open wider and he peers around.

"Ohmygod," I say.

He turns away, then sighs and looks right at me. "You don't have to call me God." He scans the street.

Horrible. I recognize the voice, but the face . . . The skin that's not bandaged is bruised and yellow. Puffy, deep-purple bags are under his eyes. His nose must have been broken. "Kobe, I'm so sorry." I try not to stare.

"Don't worry, feels worse than it looks." He slurs his words a little.

A weird pause, and then he says, "I'm gonna close the door. Are you coming in or what?"

So I enter. He locks the door and, with a slightly tilted walk, leads me past a staircase and through a little hall. It's kinda otherworldly to see him barefoot, wearing just a T-shirt and baggy shorts, like spying an actor in the dressing room before a performance.

We enter a kitchen about as small as mine. But wow, this is nice. The black granite counters and pale wood cabinets are lit with tiny halogen lights, like a cozy art gallery.

"Come to see the freak?" he says.

"No," I say. "Came to see you."

"Same thing."

He sinks into a chair at a glass table along the wall, so I take off my bag and sit across from him. Like a little audience of medication, pill bottles are lined up next to us. A hand-drawn schedule is tucked under a big orange bottle.

"That's a lot of drugs," I blurt out.

He glances at them. "Not enough."

Is this for real or just melodrama, like Trent thinks? I can't tell.

"I know it's hard to look at me," he says. "Just pretend I'm recovering from a full face-lift and that I'll be even more gorgeous than before."

The words are Kobe but the voice is flat, dull. It must be the meds . . . and, well, having your face bashed. Though it makes me queasy, I can't stop staring.

He was cute, not like a model, but people always looked.

"How does it—how do you feel?" I ask.

He lifts his hand to rub his eye but stops himself. "Beyond. Hell. What do you think?"

His little sister—she looks to be ten—glides in on squeaky pink shoes, opens the refrigerator, and moves things around. Her hands are in the fridge but her eyes are on me. I guess I'm the new art on display.

"Hi," I say.

Her eyes get wide and shift to Kobe.

"It's okay," Kobe says to her. "He's not one of the bad guys."

She stares at me, then pulls some yogurt thing from the fridge.

Kobe checks out the wall clock, scans the pill chart, grabs one of the bottles, and glances at his sister.

"C'mon," he says to me.

He stands awkwardly and leads me through a sliding glass door to the backyard. We walk in silence to an old play set. Like it's a chair, Kobe eases onto the bottom of the slide and lets out a sigh. "Make yourself comfortable."

The grass is spongy wet, so I take the seat of a swing, flip it over to the dry side, and sit. The chains squeak.

Focusing on the bottle label, he opens the cap, pushes a pill into his mouth, and swallows. Even that looks painful.

The back of the house has two angled attic windows, like staring eyes. "Your parents home?"

"Not yet." He recaps the little bottle. "Adrian, why are you here?"

"Your message weirded me out." There. I said it.

He turns the closed pill bottle upside down and back in a slow rhythm, pills sounding like a tiny maraca.

I wipe my sweaty palms on my jeans. "What did you mean by . . . well, you said 'no one will see, ever'?"

He doesn't answer.

"You were talking about your face," I say, "about you. It sounded like, well, you might do something." I look at the pill bottle in his hand.

"Oh." He shakes the pills faster, like a gambler about to roll the dice. "You'd think these things would help. They kinda do, but not enough." He stops, considers the bottle, and drops it in the grass at his side.

Almost as if he's moving in slow motion, he leans back against the slide and rests his head. He mumbles, "Outside of this house, who would miss me? Everyone might just be relieved."

I twist toward him in the swing, crisscrossing the chains. I can see it in his face, behind his unintended mask. This *isn't* empty drama. "Holy crap, Kobe. That's not true. At lunch, you should see how that whole table of your friends just sit there, worried. *They* miss you."

"No, they don't. Where the hell have they been? No one visited me in the hospital. No one even sent a damn flower. No one."

"Really?"

Wincing, he sits up and reaches for the pill bottle. Opening it, he looks right at me and takes another pill.

I stare.

He holds the bottle out. "Want one? They're hydrocodone flavored."

"Uh, didn't you just take one?"

"You're not my mommy, all right? This is my damn life." He closes the bottle and sticks it in his pocket. "Besides, in my message I *wasn't* talking about killing myself, okay?"

"What do you mean?"

"I'm changing schools."

"Oh! *That's* what you meant?" I exhale and slowly spin back to face forward, uncrossing the chains of the swing. "But it's the middle of the school year. You're a senior. Would you even graduate on time?"

"Graduate? Who gives a crap about graduating, Adrian? Wake up! Look at me. You think Doug doesn't want to finish the job? No way I'm steppin' foot in that school again. Ever."

I kick the ground and rock back and forth in the swing. "Maybe I should change schools too."

"Why? Gonna follow me? Please don't say you have a crush on me, Adrian. Although I know this face must be hard to resist." He looks down at his hands.

I lift my feet off the ground, let the momentum pull me forward and back. "No, Kobe. You've never, like, been my type. No offense."

"But you are gay, yes?" he says. "I mean, come on, girl."

As I swing back and forth, reflections of the sky shift on the house windows, like they're blinking eyes. "Yes, I am. Gay." My throat catches. "Takes one to know one, I guess?"

"Oh, no, not always. You'd be surprised," he says. "But I did wonder about you."

I kick my feet and swing faster. "Well, no more wondering, seems everyone knows now. You're the one who sent me that video going around. Of me shrieking? 'Funny fag,' remember?"

He looks up. "Oh, crap. Right."

"That's why *I* should change schools too."

"Is Doug . . . ?"

I nod.

He sighs, deep. "Got it."

I stop kicking and let the swing carry me back and forth. "How do you do it?" I ask. "How do you be so out and proud and not care what people think? Get through it all?"

"Uh, clearly I *don't.*" He carefully shifts his legs over the side of the slide to face me. "I'm stupid, Adrian. I do stupid things. But you seem smart. Horrendously dressed with a hideous haircut, but smart. You'll do better than me."

"Huh? How?"

He shrugs. "I don't really know you, but seems to me you look at things, figure things out. I mean, you're here, right? If the tables were turned, I probably wouldn't have come to see you." He smiles. "No offense."

Skidding my shoes against the little patch of dirt under the swing, I slow to a stop. But my brain keeps going, turning over his words.

He grunts. "You'd probably even be a better actor than me. You watch people. I only want to be watched . . . well . . . wanted."

One of the bandages barely clings to his cheek, exposing a few stitches. I point to it. "Should you put on a new one?"

He peels it off and flings it on the ground. "Doesn't matter. They come off all the time."

The wind picks up, tossing fallen leaves against the backyard fence.

I stand, lift one leg over the seat, and straddle it to face him. "What do you remember? From Friday night at Boo, I mean."

"Not much. My car, all those assholes. Doug. I was so—" He clears his throat. "They say you came running out. Tried to stop . . ." He blinks hard. "Shit! Crying hurts. I can't even effin' touch my eyes!"

He bends over and, taking part of his sleeve, gently dabs his face.

"Why did you do it?" he asks.

I lean forward and grip the chain, swallow back my own tears. "It's just that you were all alone. It was you against all of them. Against Doug."

Wincing, he sits up. "Doug."

I wipe my eyes. "Your first message said your mom was raising hell with the cops. What happened?"

"Nothing. Haven't you heard? I'm a tough bitch. So tough that poor little Doug had to defend himself from *me* attacking *him*."

"Damn fucker," I say.

His eyes pop. "You're full of surprises, little Adrian."

Tell me about it.

Reaching into his pocket, he pulls out the pill bottle.

"Just don't," I say.

"What is it with you? Stop trying to 'save' me." He looks me up and down. "You sure you're not hot for me?"

"Quite sure," I say. "No—"

"—offense?" he says. "Yeah yeah."

He stands in a woozy way and blinks. "Whoa. Maybe you're right, Nurse Piper. These pills are wicked. I think I need a nap."

We head back into the house, I grab my backpack from the kitchen, and he leads me to the entry hall.

"Hold up," he says. "I have something for you." Grasping the railing, he goes upstairs, one slow step at a time.

I'm full of surprises? What's he doing?

After a minute he appears at the top of the stairs. Gliding down, one hand on the railing and the other behind his back, he says in a whispery voice, "There's nothing else, just us. And the cameras. And those wonderful people out there in the dark."

Oh, man. Now he's hallucinating. What was in those pills? "Uh, there aren't any cameras. Do you need help?"

He rolls his eyes. "Oh, come on—Norma Desmond? *Sunset Boulevard*? You *do* know the movie, right?"

I tilt my head. "Huh? I don't think so."

"What kind of homo are you?" He finishes his descent and, keeping one arm behind him, sits on the bottom step. "Doesn't matter, anyway. I'm seriously not ready for my close-up."

I shrug. "If you say so."

"Okay, listen. They found these in my hand. You know, when I was unconscious?" He looks up at me. "Must have grabbed hold of whatever I could in the moment. The paramedics assumed they were mine. Hold out your hand."

I do.

"Let's call this your reward, for chivalry." From behind his back, he brings around a set of clinking keys attached to a car fob and drops them in my palm.

I squint at him.

"They're not mine," he says. "They're Doug's."

Seventeen

I TAKE THE KEYS.

They're always hanging off Doug's belt loop, jangling as he walks like a warning signal. But now they're silent, in my palm. "Why give them to me?"

"You earned 'em," Kobe says. "Besides, I don't want any part of that asshole in my house. I think of him enough when I look in the mirror."

"But—"

"Do whatever you want with them, I don't care." He yawns wide, then grimaces. I can't imagine what it must be like when a simple yawn hurts. "Sorry, Adrian, I gotta lie down." He goes to the front door.

"Um, okay." Holding the keys, I slip my backpack onto both shoulders.

As he opens the door, Kobe clutches the handle to

steady himself. "Whoa, world's tilting."

I step outside. "Well, take care of yourself. And feel better. I mean it."

"I know you do, Nurse Piper." He smiles and shuts the door.

I exhale deeply and head down the block. He's all right, just changing schools. Still, all those pills . . .

I study Doug's keys as I walk. Feels like I'm holding something toxic. What the hell am I supposed to do with them, waltz into his house or steal his pickup truck? There's a car remote fob, a few keys that must be to his house, and a dangling keychain. Wait. The keychain is the Hulk, bare chest and arms open wide. Don't tell me Doug reads comics? Must be the movies he likes, the limitless destruction. I can't imagine him actually reading anything or looking at *art* . . . or understanding what it is to be a mutant.

Anyone who could do what he did to Kobe doesn't have a soul.

I stick the keys in my backpack and continue the long walk home, sorting and filing everything Kobe said. At least he was honest and didn't dictate how I should solve the woes of the world—or avoid them all. Strange how someone I barely know could understand me more than my friends do.

As I get closer to my house the streetlights flicker on.

I arrive home and have a fun exchange with Mom, her asking, "Why are you so late for dinner?" and me saying, "If I had a phone I would have called you."

For most of dinner we eat in silence. But, hoping she'll

perk up and maybe even have money soon for a new phone, I ask, "Hey, Mom, how'd the house showing go today?"

She doesn't perk but slumps. "They barely spent five minutes at the showing. The kitchen wasn't *big* enough for them. That kitchen's as big as this house!" She glances toward our kitchen. "And completely renovated. Sub-Zero and everything."

"Someone will want to buy it," Dad says. "You'll see."

"Yeah," I say.

Mom reaches for her wineglass and the silence resumes.

As soon as I finish I head to my room. Harley helps me find a good hiding spot for Doug's keys in the recesses of my closet. I tuck them in one of those bright-red sneakers I never wear.

As I get into comfy clothes, I empty my jeans pockets and—oh, yeah—find the notes.

I shove the locker note in the back of my desk drawer. Out of sight, out of mind. I hope.

Lev's cartoon is luckier. It goes between a couple pages in *Symbolism in Renaissance Masterworks* on my bookshelf.

Harley stretches, then hops on the drawing table. I click on the lamp and she curls up in her warm spot. She's always so carefree, needing only food, toys, and a place to nap to be happy. Must be nice.

I extract Audrey's bright-pink folder from my bag. She's un-freakin'-believable. Inside are all these articles, websites, stories . . . gay kids on a crusade for justice, Gay-Straight Alliances to the rescue. Well, at Rock Hollow High, not only are Gay and Straight hardly allied, but they have yet to be formally introduced.

Everyone talked about how Kobe tried to start a GSA last year. But evidently only he and a couple straight sponsor teachers showed up for the first and only meeting. Big fail.

And why is there crap in this folder about gay celebrities getting married? What does she think a lesbian rock star's wedding in *People* magazine has to do with me?

Thanks, but no thanks. In the drawer goes the pink folder.

I need better resources, better inspiration. It takes a little while, but I pull out every graphic novel, comic, whatever I have with a gay character. From Northstar and Midnighter to some indie comics, I dig up everything I have. Piling them on the drawing table, I explore. Then I go online and pore over site after site, seeing how comic creators deal with this freakin' world that thinks I shouldn't exist.

I know these superheroes inside and out, straight or gay. They battle oppression and evil. They hide their identities with their masks and costumes, then speed off to destroy the enemy. They call in their masked friends and destroy some more.

Well, my mask got torn off. And I don't destroy.

Knock, knock. "Ade, it's me."

"Dad?" I jump up and crack the door enough to look out but not enough for him to look in. "Yeah?"

"I'm off to bed," he says.

Huh? He never tells me when he turns in. "Do you need something?"

"Naw, just thought I'd say good night." He angles his head to get a peek into my room. I close the door a bit more.

"Just reading. Homework."

"That's good. Keepin' up with your studies." He nods. "Everything all right?"

"Uh, yeah? Why?"

"Oh, dinner was a little quiet, that's all."

I want to say: *Probably because you shut off the TV for once.* But instead I say, "Just tired."

He nods. "All right then, son. 'Night."

"Good night."

Lit by the sliver of light coming from my room, he shuffles down the hall, his cane taking much of his weight.

I shut my door. What was *that* about? He must've had one beer too many tonight or something. It's nice of him, but like I'm gonna tell him anything?

Whatever. I put the pile of superhero books and comics aside and get out Michelangelo, my unwavering Renaissance friend, always there to inspire. When he lived, you could be executed just for being gay like he was. Yet he filled churches and palaces with hot naked guys and got praised to high heaven. How did he get away with that?

I pull out my sketchpads. Just seeing Graphite is like plugging into a power socket. Damn, I've missed you.

I sketch so fast I zip through one pad of paper and start another, drawing line after curve after line. It's better than words, better than plotting and planning—or doing nothing at all.

And it's far better than playing bloody video games.

Graphite has a lot to express tonight.

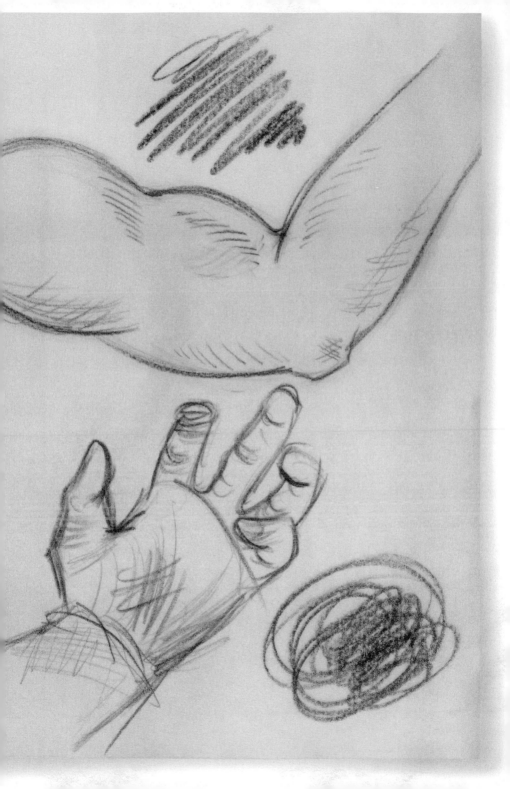

Eighteen

CHILLY WIND WRAPS AROUND ME THIS MORNING ON MY MARCH TO
school. I'm determined, though. No more meltdowns, no
more getting caught off guard, and no more empty bathrooms.

I turn the corner and—uh-oh. On the opposite side of the
street from me a police car slows to a stop at the edge of the
school's front lawn. I hang by a tree in someone's yard.

The black-and-white car's front passenger door opens
and—*What?*—Doug steps out. Oh. He's getting a ride from
Daddy. I can make out his father's profile in the driver's seat.

This has nothing to do with me at all.

I exhale and slip behind the tree, leaning into the rough
bark. But I don't move a muscle since the tree's not wide
enough to cover me. I cup my hand, ready to tap on my palm
as if I'm absorbed in a nonexistent phone and not watching

him in case he looks over. It's lame, but it's all I got.

Doug scans the schoolyard but no one's nearby. He doesn't even look in my direction. Good.

I can't hear the words, but his dad's yelling from inside the car.

Standing by the open passenger door, Doug puffs up to his full bulk and puts his arms out to the sides. His voice is clear. "Don't worry, I get how it makes you look!"

More muffled dad yelling comes from within, but I can't make it out.

"God, it's like—I got it!" Doug grips the edge of the car door. "Really. I'm not some wuss kid."

Whatever his dad responds is lower, more muted.

Doug's shoulders slump. "I know I'm *your* kid. Whose else?" He grabs his duffel bag from the backseat. "Okay, fine."

His dad barks out something.

Doug inhales. "Fine, *sir*. Yes, sir."

As he shuts the door, the car pulls away down the street. He just stands there a moment watching it disappear.

Glancing around again (and not noticing me, thank god), Doug flips off where his dad's cop car was, shooting his middle finger straight in the air. Then he drops his bag and looks at the ground. Taking off his red cap, he ruffles his hair and growls.

Please don't look over here.

A couple cars zoom by, so he fits his cap back on tight and his expression goes blank, forming his usual mask. He hefts his duffel bag over a shoulder and puffs out his chest, stands tall, then cuts across the lawn away from me and toward the school.

Holy crap. What the hell was *that*?

I wipe my sweaty palms on my jeans.

So things aren't so great at home . . . good! But his dad couldn't have been giving him crap about beating up Kobe. It probably made him proud. Plus, that was almost a week ago, so maybe all this was about "losing" his pickup truck keys? Or maybe it was about having to drive Doug to school?

Well, whatever it was, I hope it gets worse for him. Much.

Unless that means he'll just turn around and take it out on somebody else.

Like me.

Oh, man.

Doug gets smaller and smaller as he heads off in the distance. As soon as he's through the front doors I step away from the tree and slowly make my way across the street and over the lawn. I give him lots of time to get to wherever the hell he goes first thing.

On full alert, I enter the school and snake through the halls. Taped along the walls, the Halloween Hoedown flyers are now joined by ones saying PEP RALLY TOMORROW!!!

Obi-Wan, help.

All seems clear at my locker. There's no new note and no Audrey. Maybe they'll both leave me alone.

No sign of Doug, either.

I make it to French without trouble. When I sit down I mumble, "Thanks for the cartoon," to Lev so he won't hate me. How is it possible a simple taupe T-shirt can look so hot? V-neck. His smooth little muscles show through the tight sleeves. It makes other things tight . . . like a certain pair of pants. Boy, it's hard to get through class. This is a bit of self-torture (hots for straight dude = doom, right?) but a nice distraction.

He doesn't talk to me or draw more cartoons, though. All through class, he splits his attention between Madame Pauline and frantically writing some article for *Claws*, our regrettably named school paper. What organization *isn't* he in?

As I go through my morning classes, I get a few funny looks here and there. In addition to what I did at Boo, news of my meltdown must have spread too.

But I have no more Doug sightings so far. Or Buddy. How do I keep that going?

After third period I spot three jock pricks heading toward me. Whether they're set to plaster me against the lockers or simply walking down the hall, I duck into a classroom and act confused with the teacher. "Whoops, wrong class." They're gone when I step back in the hall.

I zip though the courtyard and into the cafeteria, braced for a different kind of assault. The Audrey kind.

I exhale. Just Trent at the table, all set with two sloppy joes.

As I sit across from him, he looks me up and down. "No more bathroom brawls, I take it?"

"Not yet," I say, glancing around. "Any sign of Audrey?"

"Passed her in the hall this morning. She grunted at me. I took it as a positive step."

From my backpack, I pull out my lame turkey sandwich

and banana. When I made Dad's lunch this morning I made one for me, too. Need to save every cent of allowance if I have to buy my own phone. It'll only take thirty-seven years.

"Well," I say, "since seniors can lunch off campus, Audrey's probably venting her aggression at Tito's Taco Truck."

"Poor, poor Tito."

"Or she's holed up in the library."

"Poor, poor literature."

The usual babbling and laughing and clanking bounce off the walls, but it's still quiet over there at the drama kids' table. They left an empty chair where Kobe would usually be.

"I can't do it," I say.

Through a mouthful of sloppy joe, Trent says, "Whaa?"

"Pretend. Not rock the boat. The boat's already capsized, Trent. I need to swim to shore."

He swallows and squints at me. "No comprenday, amigo."

"Just using your favorite cliché." I sit up and take a quick breath. "Listen. After I saw you yesterday I went to Kobe's house, okay?"

He blinks. "What are you . . . huh?"

I lean forward, elbows on the table, and tell him—not about Doug's keys, but the rest. I describe Kobe's face, the pills, and relay everything he said. Audrey can't handle me, but maybe Trent can?

I'm tired of dancing around everyone's damn comfort zones.

Arms crossed over his chest, and peering at me, he says, "Holy crap."

"So, yeah," I say.

He's quiet for a while. Looking around the room, he eyes the skater dudes and the drama kids and all the other clusters. "You should've just left him alone. Not what I would have done." He blows his bangs from his eyes. "But hell, what do I know?"

"Seriously, Trent, what do you think I should do? *Other* than nothing."

He lowers his voice. "Listen, if you wanna know how to barely handle a born-again alcoholic forty-two-year-old woman who talks to Jesus and is so deep in a hole of terror that she has no love left, I'm your man. But homophobic ass-holes? Beat-up, pill-popping queens and mysterious notes?" He sits back. "Dude, outta my league."

"Well, I've been frickin' drafted into this league."

"Wow. You know a sports term."

I sigh.

He hunches over his tray and picks up sloppy joe number two. "Sorry I don't have a little pink folder for you. Or much of anything else."

For the rest of lunch, Trent avoids talking about Kobe or anything real.

Thanks, Willow.

At least Audrey doesn't show up, so I get to have a full period of near peace.

I eat a few bites of my sandwich here and there. From across the cafeteria, Manuel Calderón keeps checking me out, weirdly looking around the room and then back at me.

What the hell does he want, to kill me or kiss me?

I can't stop looking over at Kobe's empty chair; the sound of a shaking pill bottle rattles in my head.

Just a few minutes left before next period, so I stand and gather my stuff. "I'm gonna head on, all right?"

Trent shrugs. "Have a"—he eyes his markered forearm—"prosaic day."

I grin and go dump my trash. Then take a deep breath and make my way around tables to the drama kids.

"Mind if I sit for a second?" I say to the startled group in mid-cleanup.

"Uh, okay?" Carmen, the girl with the neon-orange glasses, glances at her friends.

My stomach flips as I ease into the open chair where Kobe sat. They watch me, wide-eyed.

"Um . . . okay." I clear my throat. "So you need to go see Kobe."

Carmen does a double take. "What are you talking about?"

Chairs scrape the floor and trays clatter at tables around us. People are on the move and it seems no one's listening in.

Here goes. "So last night I went to see him. He's not doing well."

"You what?" Another girl turns her whole body to me.

The blond guy says, "But he doesn't *want* to see anyone!"

"Look," I say, "you know him much better than I do and I'm pretty sure he'll be pissed I said anything. But, well, he *needs* you guys, all right?" God, that sounds stupid.

I keep my voice down. "He's majorly in a bad way. Just go, don't wait for an invitation. Trust me."

Carmen shakes her head. "But . . . but what'd he say?"

Bell rings. I stand and push the chair back under the table. "Sorry, I gotta go. Just ask Kobe, he'll tell you. Okay?"

"I guess?"

I catch Trent's eyes as he passes. He looks away and moves through the doors. Thanks for the support. Friend.

I take one last look at the drama group and say, "Trust me." Then I blend with the crowd, senses back on alert.

Maybe Kobe wouldn't have done that for me, but maybe he would have. I don't know. At least that pill bottle has stopped rattling in my head . . . for now.

I can't avoid my locker anymore since I left my chemistry book in there, so I ease along the—ugh! Why do freshman girls have to squeal so freakin' loud? My heart almost busts through my chest.

I stay close to the wall. My locker's down the next hall, if I could just get by. Move it, people. I turn the corner.

No! No no no! Doug. He's walking my way, right in my path.

People are everywhere. I stop and hold my ground, stare right at him.

His eyes are wide under that red cap. He looks over his shoulder toward my locker, then right back at me. People get quiet around us. There's no sign of Buddy.

I clench my jaw. You damn son of a bitch.

Graphite's face flashes in my mind, eyes on fire.

Doug comes closer. "You better watch your back, Piper."

I glance down at his hip—his belt loop is empty.

I look back in his face and grunt. My throat won't work. The words are stuck.

He surveys the little crowd around us. Then, keeping his eyes on mine, he walks past. "Watchin' you." He heads off down the hall.

Some guy laughs. "Ooooooh! Wouldn't wanna be you!"

"Leave the homo alone," another says. "Must be hard enough having AIDS."

"Haaaaa!"

A girl steps toward them. "C'mon, *that's not funny*." It's Lev's girlfriend, Kathleen.

"Ha!" One of them laughs in her face. But they move on.

She looks at me. "They're just idiots."

"Yeah, I know."

She smiles. I nod at her and turn.

Just walk, Adrian. Keep your eyes in front and don't look weak. I make it to my locker and check over my shoulder. She's gone, and so is Doug. I unclench my fists.

Watchin' you, he says? Yeah, I kinda knew that already.

The usual buzz surrounds me now. Okay, gotta make this quick.

Huh? My locker's completely covered in pep rally flyers, layers of them. Is this why Doug looked over this way? Making one last check of his handiwork? Asshole.

My hand shakes so much I can't turn the lock. It's stuck.

No. It's freakin' *glued*.

DAMMIT!

I slam my palm against the locker and rip down the flyers.

What? What's . . . ? I don't . . .

Oh, my god. I rip them all down.

Someone's written underneath, in thick red marker, in huge letters—

GOD HATES FAGS

Nineteen

BEHIND THE COUNTER, THE OFFICE SECRETARY POPS OUT OF HER chair. "Slow down, honey, I can't understand what you're saying."

My mouth is dry. I swallow. "I said, someone defaced my locker. And they glued it shut."

She puts a hand on her chest and lets out a breath. "Oh. The way you ran in here you had me all worried, thinking it was an emergency."

"But it is! They wrote something, well, *horrible*." I can't stop panting.

She purses her lips. "All right, I'll see if Mr. McConnell is busy. Wait right there." She steps into the assistant principal's office.

What? Oh no. I'm so stupid. Of course she'd tell *him*. What was I thinking?

I wipe sweat from my forehead.

After a moment she comes out and waves me in.

Mr. McConnell's office is small and cramped, which makes him seem even wider than he usually looks. Rows of sports trophies gleam from the top of his bookshelves.

He sits behind a pile of folders on his desk, backlit by a tall window behind him, and holds a coffee mug emblazoned with DON'T MESS WITH TEXAS. "So what's this about? You found graffiti?"

"Yes, sir." I take a breath. "On my locker. And they glued the lock."

He sighs and puts down the mug.

"Don't think I know your name." He smiles. "That's actually a good sign, means you haven't been sent to me before." He laughs at his own joke.

"Adrian Piper."

His smile doesn't falter, but his eyes narrow. He pushes himself out of his chair, which squeaks in relief. Coming around the side of the desk, he leans against it and crosses his arms. "Adrian Piper. So, tell me what happened."

I describe the glued lock, the layered pep rally flyers, and the scrawled red words. "It says 'God hates fags.'"

His eyebrows go up.

"And I know who did it," I say. My stomach flips.

He nods at the chair across from his desk. "Take a seat." Then he closes the door.

Backpack still on my shoulders, I perch on the edge of the chair.

Leaning against the desk again, he straightens his dark-red tie and looks at me.

Here goes. "It was . . . I think it was Doug Richter."

"What?" Wide smile. "Our Doug? That boy's head is on the game tomorrow, not gluin' and writin' on lockers."

I gape at him. "But he was right there! Before I even got to my locker he looked back at it, checking."

"Did you actually see him do anything?"

"No, but it was clear he knew about it and was coming from that direction."

He stares down at me and grins. "Son, just looking at something doesn't mean much. He probably just thought someone had extra spirit, puttin' all those pep rally posters on their locker, the way you described it."

"Well, can't you check the security cameras?"

His eyebrows pop up again. "What cameras?"

"Aren't there hidden cameras everywhere?"

He grunts. "Is that what you think? I wish. Sure would make my life easier."

"But I've seen them outside. . . ."

"Oh, sure, we have 'em on the exterior, but not inside. Yet. But if you happen to have an extra hundred and seventy-nine thousand dollars to install them, the school board would sure like to hear from you." He checks his watch.

"Mr. McConnell, Doug's out to hurt me. He threatened me today, and yesterday. Him and his friend Buddy."

He crosses his arms again and tilts his head. "Hurt you?"

I grip my knees. "Because of what happened last Friday

night. I'm sure you know about what Doug did."

He gazes out the window for a moment, then walks around the desk and eases into his chair. "Yes, I'm aware. Bad incident. The police gave us their full report and I've spoken with all the parents. But I don't follow what that has to do with you."

Sure you don't. The full police report? The parents? Crap.

I sit up and look him right in the eyes. "When he was beating Kobe, I tried to stop Doug and he threatened me. Buddy did too."

He shakes his head, opens his mouth to speak.

"That's not all," I add. "What he wrote on my locker? That's exactly what he said when he smashed Kobe's face—"

"Hang on there, son." Holds his palm in the air. "Now, let me just tell ya. We're not gonna get into a 'he said this and I said that' kinda thing. The fight happened off campus, in the evening, and law enforcement has the final say. *Period.* It's not a school matter. Besides, a lot of you kids were drinking and I'm sure a lot of things were said. The police—"

"*I* wasn't—"

"Excuse me, young man. I'm speaking." He pauses, then leans back in his chair. "Doug was trying to defend himself, so I bet he was pretty ticked off in general. I know I would be if someone came at me the week before a big game. And, like you with *your* friend, I'm sure Buddy was just freaked out his guy was hurt."

Holy. Crap.

"Now listen." The smile returns. "I can imagine how upsetting that whole thing must have been, but we gotta move on. It's wrapped up. Focus on school. Get past it. Yes?"

Not waiting for an answer, he stands. Reaches behind a shelf and pulls out a huge pair of pliers. He holds them up and grins. "Your locker ain't the first to get glued. Come on, let's go see the damage."

Dammit, Adrian! Why'd you open your big mouth?

I grit my teeth and get up from the chair.

Thank god the halls are empty with everyone in fifth period, so no one's around to see this walk of shame. As we go, he blabbers on about lessons he learned in *his* high school days. Boys will be boys and bullshit like that.

And Audrey thought going to the "authorities" would help? I *knew* this would happen. What possessed me to run to the assistant principal's office like a little kid?

The ripped-down flyers litter the floor around my locker, those vicious words on full display.

McConnell scowls. "That is just wrong. I can see why you're so upset."

Huh? "You can?"

"Of course. Taking the Lord's name in vain. Disgusting."

Ah. I see. I take a deep breath and keep my mouth shut. I've done enough damage.

In one motion, he grips the combination lock dial with the pliers and twists. It loosens and turns.

"See, not so bad," he says. "Get what you need and I'll walk

you to class and let your teacher know it's okay you're tardy."
He winks.

What the hell? Like, now we're *buds*?

He pulls out his phone and starts texting. "We'll get this
cleaned off right away."

I step to the locker, stare at the bright-red words, and sear
this image into my brain.

I spin the combination dial, crunchy with bits of glue, and
open the locker. Okay, what books did I—

No.

A folded paper hits the floor.

Written in blue ink, the same bad handwriting as before:
Adrian.

After school, I dash home. With Harley curled on my drawing
table, I reread the note. Again.

Glad you're *back*. You look wiped.
How's your friend? He home now?
Maybe he's ok?
What's he going to do?
Write *back*. There's a *brick*
missing in the wall *by* cafeteria
Dumpster. Put your note in there.

Who *are* you? And what is this, some kind of lame TV spy
movie? At least he—or she—gives me a way to respond. Not
a very creative way, but it's something.

But how do I write on a piece of paper what shape Kobe's in? And now I don't even really know. Plus, like Trent says, it could be a trap.

Man, this makes my brain hurt.

I run my hand over Harley's little head. "What do you think?"

She just yawns and recurls into a fluff ball, unconcerned with our effed-up human ways. I stick the note in the back of my drawer with the first one.

I need to focus on Doug.

During the last two periods of school I kept repeating words in my head. Over and over. *God hates fags. Boys will be boys. Watchin' you, Piper. Watchin'.*

Then it hit me, like a crash in the dark that instantly puts you on full alert.

Unlike Michelangelo, I may not have church ceilings and museum walls to hang art on, to show what I need the world to see. But I do have lockers.

And I have the Internet.

Doug says he's watching *me?* Well, he's not the only one with eyes.

Time to kick into action.

Doesn't take long to put up my Graphite site again.

I sketch until dinner. It's a Mom work night so I have to make a huge salad for Dad and me. We eat in front of the TV. I wolf it down, but Dad's in a weirdly talkative mood, actually asking about homework and stuff. I don't have time for this! I give him a quick summary of what I'm doing in French and algebra, clean up, then grab a few Dr

Peppers for the night and hightail it to my room.

Here we go. I close my door, put on a *Lord of the Rings* film soundtrack, flip on my scanner and printer, line up my best pencils and inking pens, take a swig of Dr Pepper, and get to it.

I've got a lot to unleash.

One night, when Kerosene happened to glance at his chariot . . .
WOOO!
BLECH!
HA HA!
HEY! THAT'S MY CAR!

OH, YEAH? *YOU* DON'T HAVE A CHOICE.
Part monster, part mechanical beast, and part unknown, ***Thug*** spread ripples of fear throughout the land.
Always at his master's side was ***Bootlicker***, a hideous hybrid of rattlesnake and wiener dog.
HEH HEH HEH . . . KILL HIM, THUG!

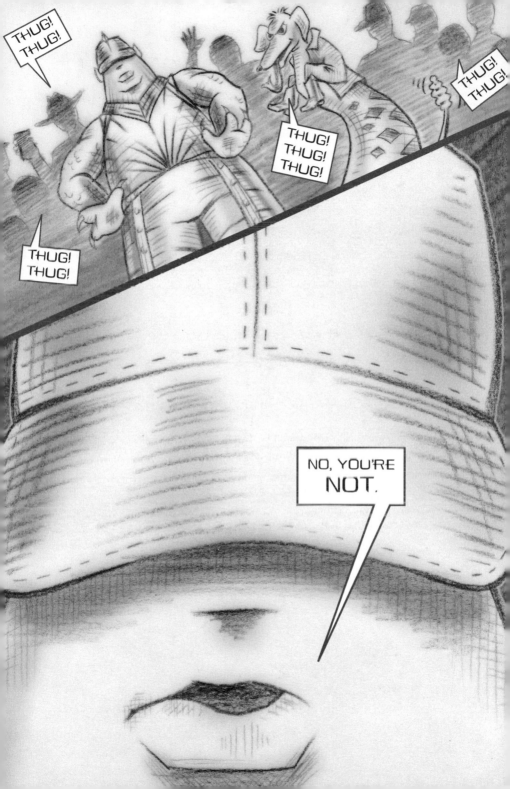

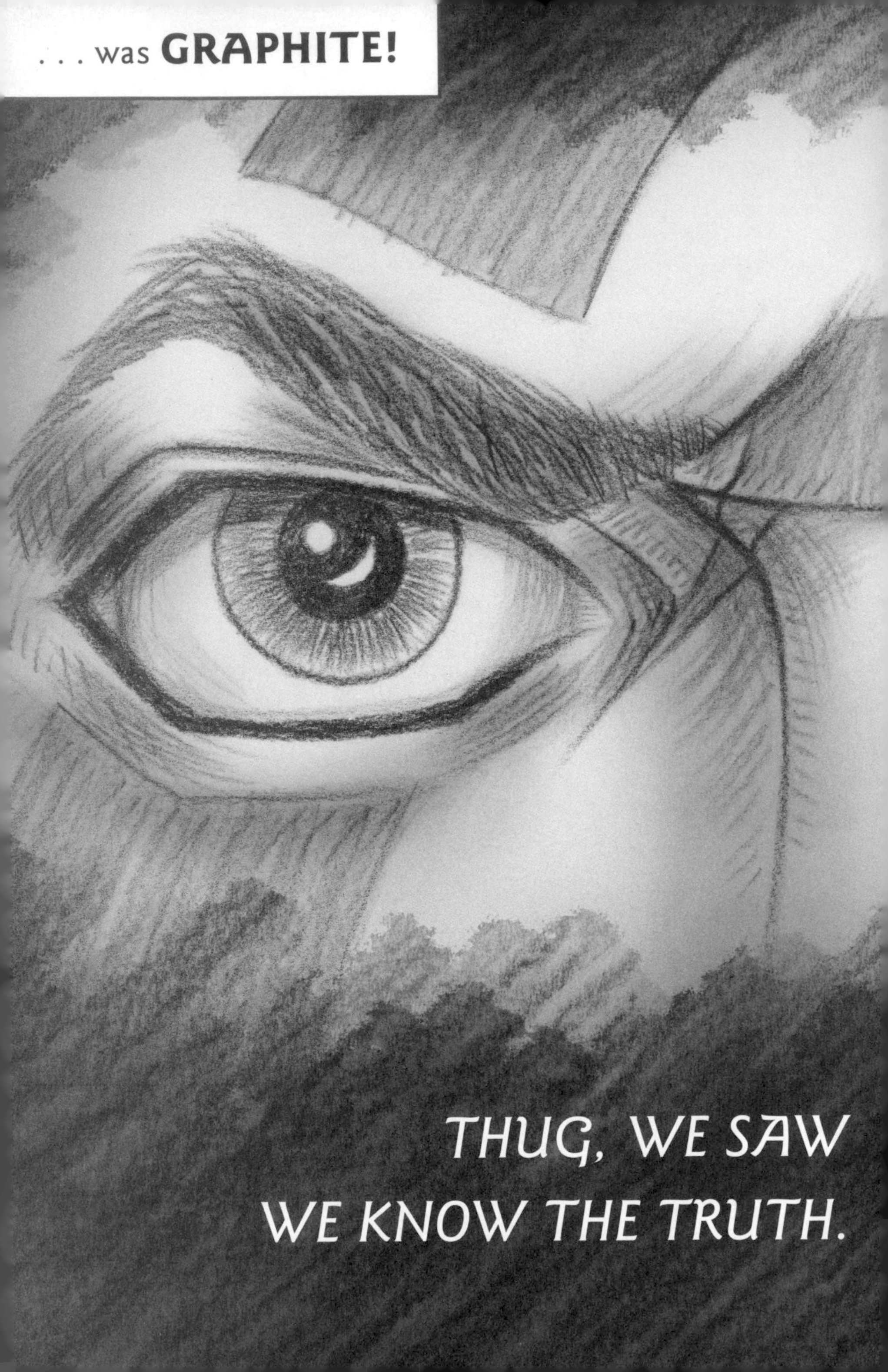
. . . was GRAPHITE!
THUG, WE SAW
WE KNOW THE TRUTH.

WHAT YOU DID.
WE'RE WATCHING **YOU**.

Twenty

FROM THE CHURCHYARD ACROSS THE STREET FROM THE SCHOOL, I
have the perfect view of the whole student parking lot. I'm
perched out of the way behind a little brick wall in front of the
big church sign. This week it says, YUP, YOU GOT NOWHERE
TO HIDE. APPLY FOR GOD'S LOVE INSIDE. So God automatically
hates me *and* I have to apply to get love? Doesn't seem quite
worth it.

Jedi deities don't discriminate.

I haven't written a note yet to place behind the cafeteria Dumpster, but even from here it's obvious it has to be
the worst-possible place for delivering secret messages. This
note writer is either an idiot or is truly setting me up. Maybe
both. The Dumpster just happens to be right by the cafeteria
side doors that open onto the biggest student lot, so it's in
plain sight this time of morning. Any time of day, really. But

it's a freakin' pep rally day, so people are hanging out shoe polishing each other's windshields.

It also happens to be right next to Doug's parking spot.

Well, the Dumpster isn't my main concern. I'm on a different mission. Something I need to know.

So I hang back.

While I wait, I unzip my backpack yet again—I can't stop checking. The inside pouch holds a red Sharpie marker and a roll of clear tape. And safely tucked between my French folder and my algebra homework is the stack of papers I printed out this morning. I made about twenty-five copies of the same art, the last comic image I posted on my site last night: just Graphite's eyes. Livid. Intense. But instead of *Thug*, these say *Doug, we saw what you did. We know the truth. We're watching YOU.*

So what if the *we* is only me? If I pull this off, that could change. How many others know the truth about what really happened at Boo but are too scared to speak up?

Hopefully my plan will change that. Send a signal it's all right to stand up and be heard. And really freak Doug out at the same time.

I check something else, too. Still there, zipped in my jacket pocket. Doug's keys.

His dad drove him to school yesterday, but maybe he got another set of keys to his truck for today? The football guys don't have official parking spaces, but no one else would dare park in that front-row end spot by the cafeteria doors.

But it's empty. No big red bubbamobile yet.

A shiny black Beemer zips by and into the lot. Crap. Did she see me? Audrey parks kinda far away, so my view is slightly blocked. She's not getting out. What's she doing? Looks like . . . oh, applying makeup. Shocking. I haven't heard a peep from her since two days ago in front of Trent's house, when I basically told her where she could shove that pink folder. I still can't believe she—

Wait!

Okay, here we go. Doug's pickup rolls past and guns into the lot like a fiery tank. Windows are tinted, but it's definitely his. The truck's bigger than I remember.

I freeze and hunch over. Looking down at my hand again, I pretend like I'm focused on my nonexistent phone, just in case. But dressed in my usual gray neutrals, I'm sure I blend in with the tan brick church wall and dead grass around me.

He pulls right into "his" parking spot and cuts the engine, which is audible even all the way over here.

The passenger door flings open and Bootlicker Buddy hops down. As Doug steps out of the driver's side, the whole truck shifts. They're both dressed in their red-and-white football crap, ready to be the superstars of the day.

Well, Doug, you'll get some attention, all right.

They shut the doors. I hold my breath, keeping my eyes and ears on alert. Doug lifts his hand and with a *bwoop-bwoop!* locks the truck.

He must have a backup set of keys and remote he just couldn't use yesterday. Or could he get new locks that fast? Guess we'll find out.

They strut toward the main entrance and disappear around the corner.

Like I'm in no hurry, I cross the road and walk through the lot, dodging the steady stream of arriving cars. I'm a couple rows away from Doug's pickup. I look over at Audrey's car, but from what I can make out, she's still obsessed with her rearview mirror. She wouldn't really notice me over here anyway.

There's no one near Doug's truck. Just act normal, Adrian. Don't freak.

I duck between a narrow row of parked cars, fumbling with the key fob in my pocket. Morning sun blinding off the windshields. With my thumb I feel for the door lock button. I have to be sure to press the right—

"*Ahhh!*" Oh, god! I grab my crotch. Pain shoots through me like electricity.

I turn and limp away, quick. Can't be trapped between cars.

"Ohmygod! You okay?" asks whoever just opened his car door into my nuts.

I know that voice. I look back and—

Lev.

Knees bent, I hop from one foot to the other. *Shiiit!* I gotta wait out the intense *pain*.

"Sorry!" He leaps from the driver's seat and gawks at me. "I didn't see you! Honestly."

Snorting laughter bursts from inside the car. Kathleen.

Lev shoots her a look. "Not funny." He steps toward me. "I *so* didn't notice you. Oh, my god, I'm sorry. Really bad timing, there."

"Ya think?" I grimace and gasp. Maybe I can stand up straight, the pain's easing now. Oooh, no, not really. I just have to breathe into it.

Now that I can kinda limp, I gotta get out of here.

"Wait!" Lev says. "Don't be mad. Didn't mean to get you in the doodads."

Kathleen steps out from the passenger side, grinning at Lev and me both. *"Doodads?* I'm sorry, but guys are so weird."

"Understatement of the century, sister" comes from a few feet behind me.

Audrey. She shakes her head, hikes her purse strap over her shoulder, and keeps walking. She doesn't even glance at me.

Dammit. Did she see the whole thing?

"What's up with your friend?" Lev says.

"Don't ask," I say between deep breaths.

Still eyeing me, he grabs his bag and shuts the door with a soft *thwump*. He drives a lemon-yellow Beetle—guess he doesn't care about getting lots of attention.

Kathleen pulls out a huge pile of poster board from the backseat and closes her door. "C'mon, Lev. We've got to drop off your extremely lightweight and not-at-all-insanely-heavy pep rally signs. All five million of them."

He locks his car, grabs the signs, and says to me, "They all right now?"

"Huh?"

"Ya know." He makes a pained face and glances toward my crotch.

My face burns. I nod and croak, "See ya," and head in the opposite direction.

From behind comes "Bye. And really sorry!"

I limp to the edge of the lot and pretend to gaze around like I'm waiting for someone. There's just a faint tingle now from the aftermath of throbbing pain between my legs.

Audrey saw me get slammed by a car door in the "doo-dads" and Lev just asked about my banged-up balls! Can this day get any worse?

Lev and Kathleen disappear around the corner. It's close to the first bell and crowds are thinning out. And the pain has left my nuts at last.

Okay, Adrian. Focus! Now's the time.

Doug's pickup is just two rows away. Barely moving, I reach in my jacket pocket, feel the car fob lock button, and look *away* from the truck.

Here goes.

Bwoop!

I jump. A muffled sound, but the locks definitely clicked open.

It works.

I hit it twice and *bwoop-bwoop!* Locked again.

Check over my shoulder. No one noticed. I exhale.

Hand shaking, I tuck the keys in my backpack.

Hold on. Where exactly are those exterior security cameras McConnell talked about? I scan around. There's one, sticking out from the front corner of the building. And another, right above the cafeteria doors. Crap.

But maybe . . . I pretend to give up on whoever I'm waiting for and head through the lot toward Doug's truck. Where he parks, there's a little awning covering the stairs leading to the cafeteria side doors. I pass his truck and casually look up. Yes! Both cameras are blocked by the awning.

Thank you, Obi-Wan.

One last look at his pickup. That's weird. His vanity plate says INEBG. What the hell does that mean? Inebriated, but with a G? I Need Every . . . Beer . . . something? I don't get it.

The first bell rings, so I hustle along.

Gotta stay sharp. Today I'm on a mission.

Thankfully, Lev walks into first period late. "Setting up for the pep rally," he tells Madame Pauline. He really *is* in every school group.

She nods and keeps conjugating to us. I stare down at my book as he takes his seat behind me. How can I ever look at him again?

A few minutes later the loudspeaker crackles. I sit back, waiting for some too-peppy babble to come spilling forth about Saber Cat spirit.

"Teachers and students, please excuse this interruption."

My stomach flips. Assistant Principal McConnell.

Madame Pauline sighs, leans on her desk, and crosses her arms.

"Due to recent incidents, I must make this announcement. This is a reminder to all students that graffiti of any kind will not be tolerated. Vandalism to school property is a crime."

The stoner guy two seats away from me laughs. "Guess he finally had to go in a boys' bathroom."

Madame Pauline shushes him.

That voice booms again. "School property is for everyone to enjoy. You should treat it like your own home. Okay, hold up. Forget I said that, heh, heh."

Laughs all around.

"You should treat it *better*. Now, back to work, and Go Saber Cats!!!"

I catch Madame Pauline rolling her eyes. She quickly quiets everyone down and jumps back into the lesson.

But it's all I can do to not scream.

All right, McConnell. Think you've dealt with the hate scrawled on my locker? Think that's all you have to do to wash your hands of it? Fine.

I've got my own message to spread.

After class, we file through the hall leading to the gym for the pep rally and my insides do the dance they always have when approaching this torture chamber. I don't give a crap how "character-building" gym class is supposed to be. My character isn't constructed that way.

I hang back and let people pass. Seems all the bubbas must be inside already since I don't see any of them here. Veering off to the wall, I check my bag yet again. Sharpie, tape roll, and twenty-five pairs of Graphite's eyes, all in their place.

I scan the hallway—can't let Trent or Audrey see me. We've

always suffered through pep rallies together, sitting next to each other and making fun of, well, everything. Audrey's especially good at that.

But not today.

No one's watching me. Do I dare? Just a test?

Putting my bag on the floor, I reach in, rip off a piece of tape, and prep one of my printouts inside my backpack. Casually looking around, pretending to scratch between my shoulder blades like I have an itch, I bring the paper behind me and stick it to the wall in a flash. I then lean back, covering the paper.

I wait until there's almost no one left in the hall and step away. Ambling along with the last stragglers, I check behind me. It makes me catch my breath. My art stands out from the wall like a gallery painting, demanding attention, just as I planned.

This could work.

I enter the gym, the air thick with talking and yelling and drums and cymbals. The blazing lights are on full wattage. It's suffocating. Both sides of the bleachers are packed with every student, teacher, and whatever, all in red and white. Well, almost. The cluster of black-draped goth kids huddles off to one edge near the back. And here and there, a few small groups of unspirited people dare to wear other colors of the rainbow.

I search for another kid in black. There. Trent is across the gym with Audrey, seated at the top of the bleachers, far away. Good.

A teacher motions at us few kids standing by the doors.

"C'mon. Everyone, take a seat!" she yells over the band as it kicks into high gear with a *boom boom boom!*

I slip into a nearby second-row seat and perch on the very end.

Crossing my arms, I slump down as much as I can to stay hidden behind the row in front of me.

"Helllooooooooooo, Rock Hollow High!" the coach's voice echoes.

With his humongo beer belly, he's holding court at the microphone at the other end of the gym. Lined up on each side of him are the bouncy bouncy cheerleaders holding up a huge paper banner scrawled with human-sized letters spelling GO SABER CATS! KILL! KILL! KILL!

Obi-Wan, give me strength.

I search the crowd. The security guard's gotta be here. Yes. He's sitting behind the coach with a grin across his bubba face. With a primo spot like that, he's not going anywhere.

The coach blathers on for way too long, his sentences punctuated by drums and horns from the band. Kids holler all around me and I'm surrounded by smells of sweat mixing with perfume.

I need to get out of here but have to wait for just the right moment. This is taking too long.

All these faces. How many of you are hiding secrets? Which one of you is writing those notes? I scan for Manuel Calderón. There are too many faces.

"Are you ready?" the coach yells. "What? I can't hear you!"

"Yeeeeeees! *WOOOOO!*" scream the hordes of drones all around me.

This insane call-and-response goes on and on.

Then, "RHH, please welcome our champions. *The Saber Cats!!!*"

I sit up as the force of the screams and the band practically blow out the sides of the building. Football players bust through the paper banner, then run onto the court one by one as the coach growls their names into the mic.

The engulfing energy is like hysteria. I hug my arms around myself. What the hell am I thinking? Me and my stupid drawings against *this*?

I channel my inner Jedi and close my eyes, let the noise pass through me.

It can't be *only* me who feels this way—it can't. There's no way I'm the only one sitting in these bleachers who's had enough, who's fed up, who feels like their only choices are either to hide who they are or be punished for simply stepping into the light.

But where are they and why aren't they saying something, *doing* something? Even my friends aren't taking action. Audrey *talks* about it, but has she actually done anything? And Trent just harps on not rocking the damn boat. Even Kobe's hiding at home.

It has to be me.

I have to do something. Have to.

I inhale and open my eyes—the light seems harsher than before. Here comes Buddy through the ripped paper banner, frantically waving at the bleachers like he's won some kind of prize. But he's near the beginning with the other unimportant players.

It doesn't take long to get to the big guys. I slide to the edge of the bleacher seat and position myself.

Here it comes.

"Give it up for our giant of the gridiron, Doug Richter!"

A pause, then Doug jogs out into the center of the court in full uniform armor. All around, people stand and hoot and howl. Barking out "Whuh!WhuhWhuh!Whuh!" like a bunch of gorillas in heat.

Then it starts, and builds, and builds. "Doug, Doug, Doug, Doug . . ." Much louder, many more voices, but it's the same chant I heard just before Doug smashed Kobe's face.

I slip off the edge of the seat and survey the scene one last time. All eyes are focused on their "warriors" right now.

Pushing my back against the hard metal door, I open it and slip out.

I don't have much time.

Twenty-one

THE METAL DOOR CLICKS SHUT BEHIND ME, BUT THE BOOMS OF THE
drums and the screams of the crowd are barely muffled.

There's no one out here in the hall.

I go right to the water fountain and hang for a minute.
Getting a quick drink is an easy enough excuse in case anyone
follows me out.

No one does.

I've mapped and timed my route over and over in my head.
I have two main targets and only fifteen minutes max. The
hall clock says 11:00 on the dot.

Let's go.

I glance at the gym doors. Nothing. Time's a-wasting.
C'mon, Adrian, *go!*

I dash down the hall and turn the corner. There's no roam-
ing security guard and no hall cameras, so relax. Hugging the

wall, I walk as calmly as I can and turn down the first hallway. I don't encounter a soul. I have to conquer my shaking hands and get to work. The sound of ripping tape off the plastic dispenser echoes around the hall tiles and lockers. I tape up three printouts. This is taking too long, but wow, that looks cool. Graphite's eyes hanging across the lockers.

It's not Michelangelo in the Louvre, but I'm displaying my art again at last.

Yes, Doug's watching me. And now *he's* gonna get a taste of what that's like.

Doug, we saw what you did. We know the truth. We're watching YOU.

Audrey's gonna freak when she sees. Well, so the hell what? Trent'll think it's cool. Maybe.

I peek around the corner but that hall is empty too, which is so freaky to see.

Crap, 11:03!

The cafeteria doors are wide open, so I make a beeline there, slip inside, and head to mission number one.

I stop cold—people are talking. Where are they? I sneak along the wall. The voices are coming from within the kitchen, behind the serving counters. No one's in view. But I have to slip past the counters to get to the parking lot side door. I can't stop now. A last look all around and here I go, step by quiet step, slinking by like a shadow. I crouch down under the counters and practically crawl past. The talking doesn't stop. No one saw.

I make it to the doors—damn! Why didn't I check this out first?

EMERGENCY EXIT ONLY. ALARM WILL SOUND.

Through the window I spot Doug's pickup just at the bottom of the steps. So close!

Wait, I've seen the smoker kids sneak out through these doors at lunch, right? Well, hell, here goes. I push the handle and . . . it opens. No alarm. Just the pulse of my heart trying to thump its way out of my ribs.

I step outside, and crap! Door's gonna lock behind me. How come I didn't think about—oh, got it. I reach in my bag, ball up one of the papers, and wedge it between the frame and door so it won't shut.

From the top of the little steps, the Dumpster is to my left and Doug's truck is at the bottom of the stairs.

The coast looks clear, so I reach in my pocket and *bwoop!* unlock his truck.

Not a soul out here.

I still can't figure out what the hell INEBG means on his license plate. Maybe it stands for a sports term. No wonder I don't get it.

Pulling my sleeve over my hand (I mustn't leave fingerprints), I approach and open the driver's door. I almost choke on the stink of old beer and—gross! In the cup holders on Buddy's side I spot a couple Snapple bottles filled with chewing tobacco spit. The memory of it in my face makes me want to gag.

Littering the floor are crumpled junk food containers, stained socks, sports magazines . . . and cookbooks? *Dish It Up Like a Dude*? *Put Some Balls In It: Barbeque for Real Men*? He must be serious about that hot sauce crap.

Okay, I don't have time for this, not in my plans.

Hold on, something's wedged beneath his seat. I wiggle it out—

What? This isn't possible. It's a sketchbook, filled with the Hulk? No way. *He draws comic characters?*

I check over my shoulder, then flip through page after page of the Hulk. A bunch of sketches of Hulk's alter ego, Bruce Banner, a few X-Men here and there, but *what the hell?*

Wait a minute, where did I see . . . ? Oh, yeah, I check Doug's keys. A Hulk keychain. What's the deal?

I don't have a freakin' phone to snap any pictures. Do I take the sketchbook?

No. Remember the mission. You're being sloppy.

I thumb through the pages one last time. This is some serious sketching, even if it's really amateur. I close it, but . . . wait.

From my backpack, I take one printout. Just one. Before I place the sketchbook back exactly like it was, I slip Graphite's eyes right in the middle, the paper edge sticking out just a bit.

I was going to tape it to the inside of the windshield. But this'll really screw with his head.

Shut the door, look around, and *bwoop-bwoop!* Locked.

Done.

He has no clue I draw, no clue I have his keys. Yes, he said he's "watching" me. So a couple synapses may connect in that dim brain of his and make him suspect me. But hopefully, despite his father's cover-up of the truth, it will freak Doug out to know people saw what he *really* did to Kobe—and that we're watching *him.*

As I dash up the steps to the doors, I scan the wall behind the Dumpster for the missing brick that note mentioned, but I don't see—oh, there. Way down low there's an empty hole. Well, good to know about, I guess.

Back in the cafeteria, I pick up my wadded-paper wedge, put it in my backpack, softly click the door shut, and sneak unnoticed past the counters again. I slip into the almost-hidden side alcove with the snack and drink machines and tape a printout to the one that says SNACK ATTACK.

From the gym, faint cheers punctuated by drumbeats filter through the building. It's 11:09! I'm almost out of time. Gotta forget about taping up any more eyes. I hustle up the stairs, tossing a few printouts on the ground. Thank god the second floor's a ghost town too.

Do I dare? I ease open a girls' bathroom door, ready to bolt. "Hello?"

My voice echoes, then silence.

So weird in here without urinals. And pink tile? Freakin' sexist. Whoa, they have candy machines in here? Oh. Not candy. Tampons. Focus!

I toss a couple printouts on the floor and leave, bolting down the hall toward the auditorium.

I've been avoiding that boys' bathroom where Buddy clearly wanted to beat the crap out of me. But here I am, and I toss more watching eyes around.

Good job, Graphite. Looks awesome. Keep going.

This is freakin' wild! Got the whole school to myself.

Now for mission number two, my main task.

Over the last couple months, I've passed Doug holding court at his locker enough to know exactly where to avoid going. Now I need to haul ass to get there in time.

I shouldn't have left his locker for last, but no choice with my route. So I book it.

I couldn't sleep last night, deciding what I should write on his locker. They have to be words to sting, words to penetrate. Like *GOD HATES FAGS*, they need to be words to hurt, deep.

But the words never came.

Spewing hate is a talent I don't possess.

But while taping up these printouts, it hit me. On his locker, I'll write something simple and to the point: *We saw what you did. You can't hide. You will PAY.*

I'm not sure what that really means, but it sounds good. And it goes with Graphite's eyes.

Two halls to go and I keep randomly tossing around printouts as I barrel ahead. And here I am.

Red and white balloons and a DESTROY 'EM, DOUG! OFF THE RICHTER SCALE! sign are slapped on his locker, as if marking it just for me. I yank off the balloons and pop the bastards. *Damn*, that was loud! I freeze.

The only sound is the muffled buzz from the pep rally echoing up the stairs; otherwise, nothing.

Still okay.

I rip down the sign and toss it on the floor.

Time for *my* graffiti love note.

I plop my backpack on the floor.

No. Come on. Where the hell is my red marker? I just had it! It's gotta be here.

Nowhere.

Dammit. Must've fallen along the way when I was pulling out my art. Gotta find it quick.

I grab my bag and dash down the hall, then round the corner and—

"*There* you are, Adrian."

Holy crap.

Twenty-two

I STOP IN MY TRACKS.

Coming right to me, black boots clomping along, is Trent.

"Been lookin' for you," he says, and halts in front of me.

I check down the empty hall behind him. "Why are you here?" I whisper.

"Why am *I* here?" He points at one of my Graphite eyes pages on the floor. "Dude, what the hell? What are you doing?"

Echoing up the stairway, pep rally screams grow louder from below. They must've opened the doors.

He eyes the stairs.

I glance back toward Doug's locker. I'm out of time.

"Dammit!" I walk past Trent. "C'mon."

I lead him to the nearest boys' room. It's empty. We shut the door and stop in front of the sinks.

Trent stares down at me. "What's up with these signs?

Doug's gonna kill you for this—these drawings are like suicide notes. You get that, right?"

I open my bag and toss the tape roll and my few remaining printouts in the trash, ditching the evidence.

"Trent, no one knows my art."

"You delusional? Who else would it be? You're the one who got in his face. Dude, he's gonna hunt you down. Why are you risking your life?"

The bell rings and I jump. "I had to do *something*. And not just for me. It's for Kobe as well, and who knows who else." Maybe for that note writer, too.

I catch myself in the mirror. My hair is flipped up at weird angles, like a manic Graphite. Not a bad look.

The buzz of talking and a locker slam come from outside.

"Quick," I say, "let's go."

We step out as more voices and people fill the hall. No one bothers to look our way more than usual, so we join the flow and head toward the cafeteria. Being next to Trent usually gives me a sense of protection, but I've also got Graphite with me today.

I tug at Trent's sleeve. "No, not those stairs. Everyone's going up, not down. We'll stand out. This way."

He lowers his voice. "Dude, where'd this criminal mind come from? You're flippin' me out."

We backtrack and pass Graphite's eyes here and there. Someone snaps a photo of one.

In the stairwell, some girl picks up one of my pages and says to her friend, "That's creepy. I don't get it."

Damn, so I tossed a few printouts around? Doug's locker was my main target. Screwed that up. But at least he'll see what I left in his locked truck.

My stomach flips.

The cafeteria is no longer a ghost town but filling with pepped-up kids screaming and laughing. We plop down at our usual table, facing each other.

"All right, Trent, how'd you find me?"

"Wasn't easy." He leans forward, elbows on the table. "Had to pee and saw one of your masterpieces right there on the wall. So obvious it was Graphite—"

"To you."

"Yes, to me! I checked down the hall and saw a little trail. I figured you had to be stupidly running around trying to get your ass expelled. And exactly *why* did you do this?"

I slouch. "No one saw me. No one."

He blows the hair from his eyes. "*I* saw you."

"C'mon. You know what I mean."

He opens his mouth to speak but pauses, then rises to his full height. "Hungry." Stalks away to the food line.

I take a deep, deep breath, then exhale nice and slow. I won't let him ruin this for me.

He may be hungry, but I'm freakin' starving.

Gathering and checking my materials and then getting to school so early, I didn't have time to make my lunch this morning. So I'll have to break my bring-lunch-from-home-to-save-moolah-to-buy-a-phone rule. But today I deserve to treat myself—I've earned it.

As I make my way to the line, I eye the closed doors to the parking lot. It feels like that was hours ago. I can't see past that column to the tucked-away drink machine alcove, but my handiwork is there for sure.

I glance over toward Manuel Calderón. Whoa. He's holding a flyer of Graphite's eyes over his face like a mask as another guy takes his picture. I speed to the line before he notices me staring.

Does that mean he thinks it's cool? Hope so. He's being so blatant about it.

Trent's already wolfing his lunch by the time I return with my tray full of pizza and a massive hot chocolate.

We eat in silence for a couple minutes. So good to have a moment to—

Oh, god, no. Here we go.

Trent stops chewing. He notices Audrey too, storming right toward me like a sound wave about to blow my eardrums.

I hold up my hands. "Before you start—"

She slaps the table, so I grab my hot chocolate before it topples over.

Then she lifts her hand to reveal a wadded-up ball of paper. I can tell it's one of my flyers. I snatch it out of sight.

Her eyes practically flame. "What the hell do you think you're doing? Are you *that* stupid?" She reaches across the table and bops me on the side of my head.

I jump up. "Do *not* hit me. Do you understand?" I say through my teeth.

"Woooo!" comes from a nearby table, then lots of laughing.

Trent points at Audrey. "Cool it." Then he points at me. "Sit."

I shove the paper wad in my pocket, ease back in my chair, and glare at her. "*Never* touch me again."

She sits and crosses her arms, then lowers her voice. "And this little stunt of yours is supposed to do *what?*"

"A most excellent question." Trent clasps his hands and leans forward on the table.

I sigh. Checking around, I keep my voice low. "I got another note in my locker. It asked how Kobe is again, but also asked what he's going to do. There are others out there who saw what Doug did, who know the truth. Maybe this will help them stand up too. And make Doug paranoid, instead of me."

Audrey and Trent look at each other.

Trent shakes his head. "Sorry, but that makes no sense. All's gonna happen is Doug'll be one pissed-off mofo."

"Got that right," Audrey says. "And how's anyone gonna connect your little drawings to what happened at Boo? Talk about vague. Might as well start writin' what I'm gonna say at your funeral."

Well, I definitely won't be telling them about getting into Doug's truck.

I sneer. "Thanks for being such a supportive friend. Good to know you guys have my back."

"Dude, I'm tryin'." Trent slouches in his seat. "What do you call me going to find you just now?"

Audrey grips the table. "A supportive friend? Adrian, you

think I did all that research for *me*? Spent all that time figuring out how to handle this the *smart* way? Unbelievable."

"Is it the smart way or is it just *your* way?" I lean over the table, in her face. "Friends listen to each other. All you do is talk talk talk."

Her jaw drops and she looks to Trent. "Do you believe this?"

His eyes dart back and forth from her to me. "Actually, Adrian, I think you're in over your head here. With, like, everything? You're gonna get burned."

I look at the ceiling. "I know what I'm doing."

Audrey stands. "Honey, you don't have a clue."

I keep my voice down. "I tried it your way, Audrey. I went to McConnell just like you wanted. Guess what? Doug might as well be McConnell's own kid, the way he protects him. *Your* plan didn't work. I got this!"

"Uh-huh." She adjusts her gargantuan sparkly necklace. "I'm done talking *and* listening to you!"

She shoves her chair into the table, which almost jostles my cup again. I snatch it up. She stomps away.

I ignore the hoots from around us and turn to Trent. "Think she'll tell anyone it was me?"

"Hard to predict where Hurricane Audrey will hit next."

"She'd better mind her own damn business."

I haven't even touched this stupid hot chocolate. It's cold now. I plunk it onto the tray, which pops the top right off, spilling it on my pants.

"Dammit!" I push away from the table, then grab a bunch of napkins and wipe my crotch, glaring at people laughing even harder nearby. The tables around us are getting a real show today.

Trent hands me his napkins. "*Again?* Gravity sure doesn't like you."

Damn, the stain is so dark against my faded jeans.

"Dude," he says, peering at my pants. "I hate to tell ya, but you spilled just the right amount."

"What?"

"Maybe you should add more, so it looks like you really spilled something. Right now it just looks like—"

"Yeah yeah, I get it." I sit and try to act normal, but it's hard to when your underwear's all clammy. First my nuts get slammed by a car door, and now *this*.

Obi-Wan, why is the universe targeting my junk?

"You'd better wipe that stain with peanut butter to get it out."

"Ooh, that's it!" I toss a wad of soaked napkins on the table. "I think I'll just spread a jar of peanut butter all over the front of my freakin' pants!"

He frowns and slumps farther down in his seat. "Only tryin' to make a joke."

"Sorry, Trent, it's not you. Just a bad day for my balls." I sigh and rub my forehead. "You do know peanut butter is for getting out gum, not stains, right?"

"Yes, thus my levity." He tries a grin. "That'd be fun to see, though. Peanut butter."

Can't go through the day looking like I peed my pants. "Guess I'll try using 7UP. I'll be back."

I head toward the drink machines, looking at the floor as I go. My shirt's not long enough to pull down that far, so I clasp my hands in front of my pants. Might as well hold a sign with an arrow.

I look at the drama kids' table but they're engrossed in themselves. Carmen seems perky. I wonder if she talked to Kobe. I'll have to find out. Later.

Almost there. I make it and duck into the little alcove with the drink machines, hidden from view.

No one here except for Graphite's eyes hanging crooked from the SNACK ATTACK machine.

I fumble with a chocolaty wet dollar bill in the drink machine slot, which keeps spitting it back. Just take it! It finally slides in.

I punch the 7UP button and the can plops down, but it gets wedged in the opening.

"Really? Oh, come on!"

"What's wrong?"

I jump. Holy crap. It's Lev.

I stand and clasp my hands in front of me. "Where'd you come from?"

He looks over his shoulder. "Um, the cafeteria? Didn't mean to startle you."

"But you don't have this lunch period."

He smiles, then shrugs. "I do today. Pep rally screwed up my schedule."

I stare at him.

"Saw you come in here and just wanna apologize again. . . ."

His cheeks flush. "Look, about this morning when I nailed you in the, well, you know. God, what can I say? So sorry. *Complete accident.*"

My throat tightens, so I just nod.

He glances at my hands crossed over my pants. "You *still* in pain?"

"Uh, no, no, fine. All fine." Gotta get out of here. I reach down to try to loosen the can. Still stuck.

Crap, I moved my hands. Without thinking, I glance down at the stain, which, of course, makes Lev notice. It *so* looks like I peed my pants. He's staring right at the spot.

"Oh, nn-not what it, uh, looks like," I stammer. "It's just— spilled my hot chocolate. I mean, it didn't burn, so I'm gonna use 7UP. Not peanut butter."

He stares at me like I'm unhinged. Then glances back down at my crotch.

So I look at his.

Tight jeans. Wow. Nice. Images pop in my head. Of him. And me.

We look up at each other. His eyes are wide. My face is on fire. All of me, actually. Now there's a little tent in my pants.

He sees.

My eyes wander over his body. Can't help it. He's standing so close. Okay, not anymore. He's backing up.

I turn to the drink machine, covering myself again with my hands. "I've got to get it out," I babble.

"*What?*"

"Oh, no!" I say. "I don't mean *that*! The 7UP! That'll do it. My pants. The spot the spot!"

He cracks up. "You are freakin' hysterical! Wow."

I cross my arms and shrink away from him. Graphite's eyes stare at me. Like I need reminding I'm no superhero.

I rip down the printout, ball it up, and throw it on the floor.

"Hey," he says, "don't be mad."

"Go ahead, laugh all you want. Just leave me alone."

"What? *No!*" He holds up his hands. "No, I didn't mean . . . Oh, god, I don't want you to . . . Look, it's just that you're funny."

I sigh. "Yeah, ha-ha."

He shakes his head. "What I mean is—ugh. I'm not saying it right." He checks over his shoulder. No one else is in view. We're all alone. He steps closer. "I think you're funny. And cute."

"Huh?"

"Very," he whispers.

Then he kisses me.

Twenty-three

KISS?

That's the best word they can come up with for this? Are you effin' kidding me?

NO. More like haawaaHOOOOOOOmaahaaHOLY-FREAKING*CRAAAAAAAAP!*

What? Was? *THAT?!*

"Adrian? You okay?" Lev comes back into focus. Kinda.

I blink.

He backs away. "Oh, man, I'm so sorry."

I just gape at him. His cheeks turn redder by the second. I look down at my crotch. Oh, god. The painful fabric tent is bigger. Straining. I don't dare adjust myself.

He giggles as his blush spreads up his face and down his neck. "Okay, don't freak on me. . . ." He checks over his shoulder.

"Um, I'm confused?" I'm plastered back against one of the drink machines, hands splayed out, covering my crotch.

He rubs his face. Wavy strands of his crazy gorgeous hair fall and hang down to his chin. "Wow, not how I planned this *at all*."

"You planned this?"

Two girls zip around the corner, almost running right into Lev. "Whoops! Sorry," one says.

I spin to face the wall.

Lev jumps. "Huh? Oh, nothing. I mean, we're leaving. Just need to grab it."

I keep my hands firmly blocking my crotch.

He glances at the girls and points to the stuck 7UP can. "It's stuck." He bends down and wrestles with the can.

"Yeah," I say, too loud. "It got stuck. Stupid can."

"Stupid can." Lev's voice cracks.

I point. "It got stuck."

The other girl shoots us a look. "Yeah, you, like, said that." She rolls her eyes. She glides a couple dollars into the juice machine next to us and takes her drink, and they scoot away.

Lev frees the 7UP and holds it out. "I'd wait to open it. It's all shook up now." He nervous-giggles again. "Heh-heh-heh. And not just the can."

My body parts move like they're acting independently. (And not only below the belt.) My hand takes the can, and then my feet start to walk.

"Look," Lev says, his voice as wobbly as my legs. "Didn't mean to freak you out. Honest."

Holding the can in front of me like it's a time bomb, I exit the alcove before someone else can come in. "Gotta go," I squeak.

He nods, his lips in an uncertain smile.

My pants tent goes down as I zombie-walk back to the table.

"Yikes." Trent eyes my pants. "So it didn't come out?"

"God, no!" I check behind me. "We're in public. But—hey, you didn't see anything, did you?"

He notices the can. "What are you talking about? Where've you been all this time?"

"Oh." I glance at my crotch. "You meant did the *stain* come out. Right." I slump into the chair.

He pries the can from my hand and puts it on the table. "Dude, what's up with you?"

"Exactly."

He squints at me, then says, "Okay, freakazoid, you've got, like, six minutes to deal with that hot chocolate mess before the bell." He gathers his stuff and lowers his voice. "And considering your morning activities, the less attention you draw to yourself the better. El comprenday, muchacho?"

I pretend to tip an invisible hat to him.

Standing, he says, "Freakin' me out, dude." He starts to leave, turns back with one more "Freakin' me out, dude," and then he's off.

I scan the cafeteria, surveying what feels like an alien landscape. Lighting seems odd. Faces are weird. Sounds are too clear.

Did all that really just happen? Like, *really?*
I touch my lips.
Lev. Kissed. Me!

The past ten minutes is all a humongo whoosh in my spin-cycle head: boys' bathroom, soaking my crotch in 7UP (how often do ya get to say *that?*), not giving a rat's ass who saw me (again, how often do ya get to say that?), drying said crotch under hand dryer attached to wall (ditto), then somehow arriving on time for chemistry.

Chemistry. I've just discovered a WHOLE new meaning to that word.

Yes, I'm sixteen, and yes, I'm pathetic. I have no kissing experience to compare to Lev's.

Lev's freakin' KISS!

Kathleen's in this class. Oh, god, don't look over here. Is it written all over me?

It's impossible to sit here and study atomic fusion when actual atoms are actually fusing in my head. My brain keeps churning out questions. Is Lev really gay? Just messing with me? A sick joke? Maybe he's straight but just curious? Bi? Does Kathleen know? Could he actually, possibly even like me? Does any of it matter since Doug's gonna bash my face in anyway?

In the bathroom and the halls I overhear a few theories about what my Graphite eyes could mean: kids from the other high school snuck in and put them up; our cheerleaders were just being funny; the work of a jealous teammate.

At least there's some buzz.

McConnell hasn't come after me yet, which I take as a very good sign no one saw me. But it's sinking in now, what could happen if Doug finally figures it out. Then, when he finds the printout I left in his pickup?

It'll be harsh. No, much worse.

But I *had* to do something.

And at least I'll die having been kissed. Right?

The bell rings. Probably stupid, but on my way to last period, I retrace my graffiti path and head upstairs to Doug's locker. I haven't encountered him yet and really want to see his reaction . . . from a distance.

I keep my eyes open for bubbas. And Audrey. And now, even Lev. The chances of encountering land mines keep increasing. But unlike a video game, in this life I can't respawn if I step on the wrong one.

As I approach Doug's locker my pulse picks up. Maybe I won't see him, but it's worth a try? I blend with the flow. It's hard to see through everyone crowding, but . . . he's not there. I exhale and keep going, hugging the wall opposite his locker in case—

"Wooo!" comes from behind me. I turn. A guy pumps his fist in the air as Doug and Buddy and a couple other jocks round the corner.

Oh, man.

"Dooouuug!" The guy keeps pumping his fist and chants, "We're-watching-you! We're-watching-you!"

What?

Two girls start chanting the same thing. What *I* wrote! *My* phrase! *No-no-no-no-no!* You got it wrong!

I keep close to the wall.

Doug slows and, eyes narrowed, stares at the chanting guy. Then he grins and nods. They bump fists.

Buddy points his finger in a number one sign and holds it over his head. "That's right!" He goes to fist-bump the same guy, who only does it half-assed. The dude is clearly not so enthused about Buddy.

Scowling, Buddy turns, puts his hand on Doug's shoulder, and says loud enough for everyone to hear, "No homo, but you know who's *really* watching your back. Right, bro?" Bootlicker keeps a grip on Doug's shoulder.

Doug spots me. I freeze.

He squints and locks eyes on me.

I stare back, my expression blank.

Then he looks away and down the hall. Shaking off Buddy's hand, he picks up his pace and passes me by. There's that sound again. Hooked to Doug's belt loop is his backup set of keys, clanking along with his stride.

Following behind, Buddy checks out the general scene, hovering in Doug's glow. He grins at someone and holds up his palm. "Yo, bro!"

It's Manuel Calderón. "Hey, Bud," he says, and high-fives him as they pass.

Manuel sees me. His eyes widen and he starts to wave but stops himself. Dropping his hand, he moves on.

What the hell?

"Ooo, looky!" Buddy notices me.

I back up against a locker.

In a flash he makes a fist and comes right at my face. He's too fast!

He swings. I shut my eyes, brace for—

Nothing.

I peek—his fist hovers an inch from my nose. He keeps it there a split second more, then pulls it away. "HAAAAAAAA!" he screams in my face. "You're such a freakin' pussy."

People step away from us.

He turns to Doug, then points at me. "Look, it's the homo! Bet he crapped himself."

"Bud." Doug glares at him. "Hello? Game day? Focus, asswipe." He turns and heads to his locker, not even glancing at me.

The other bubbas laugh.

Buddy scowls at the other guys, turns his head toward me, clears his throat.

But I'm ready. In a millisecond I raise my hand as he spits at my face. I catch his slimy loogie and reach out to wipe it on him.

He jumps back, lands on a girl's foot.

"*Ow!*" she screams. "Watch it!"

Buddy thumps my chest. "His fault." He sneers, says, "Faggot," then turns away.

Balancing on one foot while holding the other, the girl grimaces at my hand holding his spit.

"Ewww! God, that's gross."

"You have no freakin' idea," I say.

Making sure no one follows, I keep my hand at my side and hightail it in the opposite direction from Buddy and Doug to find a bathroom sink. I turn the corner—

"Hey!" Someone grabs my shoulder.

I jerk free and spin around.

Manuel puts up his hands and checks over his shoulder. "It's okay. Just wanted to see if you're all right." His face turns red and he glances at my disgusting spit hand. He lowers his voice. "Sorry I didn't help ya out back there. Buddy's such a *pendejo*, right?"

I stare at him. "Pendayho?"

"Sorry. Means he's a dick." He swallows. "Listen, somethin' I wanted to ask . . ." A couple bubbas round the corner. He stiffens and turns away as they pass. "Actually, it's cool. Never mind." He takes off.

What. The. Hell. Is. Going. *On?*

Twenty-four

WHEN THE FINAL BELL RINGS I'M AT MY LOCKER IN A FLASH. NOT EVEN a trace of *god, hates*, or *fags* on it. I spin the lock and fling open the door, ready for another note. Nothing.

It has to be Manuel, after that weird-ass stuff today. With his embarrassed expression and what those notes say, it's just gotta be him. Maybe because he's friends with Doug the beating really freaked him out. Maybe he needs my help. Or maybe he likes me? No way. But crap, what the hell do I know? After freakin' *Lev* kissed me! Who knows who's next!

I need to write back and see if it's him.

I'm unloading most of my backpack crap when Trent peers over the open locker door from the other side. "Dude, you are so effin' lucky."

"Huh?" How'd he find out about Lev kissing me?

He glances around, lowers his voice. "Everyone thinks the

Pep Club is behind your clandestine handiwork."

Oh. The flyers. "Yeah, so it seems." I shove the last book inside and slam the door shut. He jumps back.

"Sorry! Didn't mean to . . . Let's just get out of here," I say.

With Trent in tow, I bust out of the front doors and into fresh air at last.

As soon as we're clear of crowds I say, "People are such freakin' *idiots*! How could they not get it? The Pep Club? Oh, come on. No one in that club can draw worth crap."

"Better let people think it. You dodged a major bullet there. For once I'm glad people are stupid. Saves your ass."

I rub my eyes. "You know, I almost put my website on those flyers. Should have. *That* would've made it crystal clear. Morons."

He stops walking. "What do you mean? You took down your site."

"Back up again, and with new art." I face him. "It's still anonymous, of course, but check it out and you'll see."

"See what?"

"*My* version of Doug's crime."

He puts his arms out to the sides. "You're already in it deep. Why are you asking for more?"

"I'm only asking for people to open their eyes."

"Doug and Buddy are some serious shit. I don't know how else to put this, but are you really tough enough to face them? And survive it? I don't think so."

"Trent, I know the risks. I had a front-row seat to Kobe's beating, remember? I'm not giving up."

His voice is low. "You should."

"How can you say that to me?" I grunt, spin around, and keep walking.

From the corner of my eye I catch him heading toward the parking lot. No thanks for the confidence there. Friend.

I get some distance between me and the school, then slow my pace. I make it past the lawn, almost to the sidewalk.

"Hey, Adrian, wait up!" comes from behind.

I turn. "Oh!"

Lev comes running over. He slows and stops a few feet away. "I was hoping to see you after . . . I . . . really . . . oh, man."

I make sure no one's in earshot. "Uh, why aren't you setting up for the game? You're in the Pep Club, right?"

"Well, I do have to get back." He looks at the ground. "You hate me, don't you?"

"Hate you?"

He tucks his hair behind his ears and crosses his arms. Tight jean jacket stretches over his wide shoulders. He's even cuter in the afternoon sunlight. "Well, you seem not happy. About me, uh"—he clears his throat—"you know, kissing you?"

Now it's my turn to have a face on fire. "I'm not pissed at you. Just royally confused. I mean, well . . ." I sigh.

We both study the nearby holly bush. Then the sidewalk. A couple birds chirp away in a distant tree.

"Um," he says at last, "I . . . okay. Can I ask you a question?"

"I guess."

He takes a breath. "You don't have to answer."

I nod and grip my backpack straps.

He steps a tiny bit closer and uncrosses, then recrosses his arms, then lowers his voice. "Are you and Trent, like, together?"

"What? No. No, he's just a friend." Or so I thought.

"But you two are always together and stuff, so I—"

"We're not. Really. Okay?"

After a second he lifts his eyes to mine. Those sexy amber eyes.

Insides. Bubbling.

"Are you and *Kobe*, like . . . ?"

"NO!" I say. "Is that what people are saying? No way."

"So, then." He exhales. "Are you, like, seeing anyone?"

My hands are clammy. *"Me?"*

He bites his lower lip. "Damn, I'm really bad at this. Oh, boy, I'll just say it. I like you? I mean, wow, that sounded like a question. It's a statement. I like you." He scratches the back of his head. "I'm *so* screwing this up."

My pulse pounds and it's all I can do not to reach out and touch him. Instead, I nervous-giggle.

"What's so funny?"

"You're so hot." Did I just say that? I take a deep breath. "What I mean is . . . oh, god. I thought you were straight. Does Kathleen know?"

Big grin. Big, cute grin. "Of course. She's, like, my Trent. Or my Audrey. Did you think—"

"Well, *you* thought—"

"Well, yeah." Curls of hair fall back in his face. "Guess I did. But I thought, maybe to you, I was pretty obvious."

"And I'm pretty clueless."

"I'd be happy to clue you in." He swallows. "So . . . you wanna go out with me?"

Ohmygodohmygodohmygodohmygod.

Am I doing a freak-out happy dance? Oh, wow, I am. At least I'm at home and my bedroom door is closed and I only have an audience of one, and she's a cat.

Why did I say yes to him? Okay, I know why I said yes.

"Yes," I said, and then he said, "Great," then "How about tomorrow night?" and I said, "Sure," like I have anything else to do and holy crap how did it get to be tomorrow night already? And just half an hour until he's here!

Yoga breathing, Adrian, calm yoga breathing. Like I've ever done yoga. Maybe I should start right now.

I have no memory of how I floated home yesterday. I do remember deflecting Dad's questions about why I was smiling so big. "Got an A on my French test" was all I came up with. I couldn't eat dinner, couldn't focus on drawing, and couldn't get to sleep. All of me was way too excited, in *so* many ways. But after some necessary, um, activity (no computer visuals needed this time—remembering that kiss was *plenty* to go by), I fell asleep at last.

I woke up knowing it all had to have been a dream, but then I saw Lev's message this morning confirming we're on.

Hell, YES, we're on! But I don't know where we're going or what we're doing. It's a surprise, he wrote.

Okay, that part's a little disconcerting.

With him being in the Pep Club and all, it has crossed my mind that this may be a trap. Like he's on Doug's side or something. But no. He *kissed* me. That's pretty extreme for a bubba. And he seems so sweet.

Plus, it seems he's in every club and on every committee, not just the sports ones. But still . . .

I look (for the gazillionth time) at the drawing he made for me in French. For me. He can't be faking this, right?

I. Cannot. Believe. Lev. Is. GAY! Freakin' hot Lev! And he asked *me* out!

Ohmygodohmygodohmygod.

I turn to the full-length mirror on the back of my closet door. "Harley, what do you think? Are these jeans all right?" From her pillowy perch on my bed, she yawns.

"Yeah, you're right. All my jeans are identical. Baggy and blah." I pull them off and toss them on the growing pile-o-pants on the floor. Next to the big pile-o-shirts.

Audrey would know what to wear. How many times have we talked about that "someday" when I'd go on a date? What I'd wear (her concern) and who it'd be with (mine). Well, forget her. Don't need more of her advice.

Lev sees me every day, so what's the big deal? I mean, he knows what I look like.

Qapla'! Qapla'! comes my Klingon new-message alert from the computer.

Maybe another from . . . No. It's Audrey. Seems she's not quite done with me yet. The message only says Serves you right. Oh, god, what now? There's a link. I click.

What? No way.

It's a Tumblr page. At the top is *my* art of Graphite's eyes! With *DOUG, WE'RE WATCHING YOU* all in huge letters.

What the hell?

There are tons of photos and gifs of last night's game, with Doug front and center. *The unstoppable Doug kills it off the Richter Scale for a major win!* Video loop of the whole crowd chanting *my damn phrase*!

They stole my art and my words and created a Doug *fan page*?

I slam the desk and pace. Harley's now on alert.

Those assholes.

Okay, fine. Fine! So my attempt to actually do something on my own damn terms was a big fail. I'm so glad freakin' Audrey is so freakin' happy about it.

Qapla'! Qapla'!

Come on. I can't take any more.

Oh—a new message from Kobe: You got some nerve talkin behind my back to my friends. They just showed up outta nowhere yesterday. Nurse Piper strikes again. What am I gonna do with you?

I blink. I think he means that in a good way. Carmen must have gone to see him. Finally some good news.

I reply: Watch it or it may happen again. Send.

That's one less thing to worry about. I hope.

Shoot! Lev'll be here in fifteen minutes.

Okay, I gotta clear my head. I scoop up Harley and calm her after my little freak-out. Just cuddling her calms me, too.

No it doesn't. I'm about to go *on my first date*!

I put her down, brush my teeth, then put on my best-fitting pair of jeans and paw through the shirt pile.

Stripes. Lev wears stripes, right? He must like them. I slip on my blue-and-yellow-striped shirt with the white collar. I look over my beat-up shoes, but none of them say "date." Wait. From the back of my closet I pull out the red sneakers, my hiding place for Doug's keys. With a clanky *thud*, I toss those in the back of the closet, then put on the shoes and check myself in the mirror. Between the blue-and-yellow shirt and red shoes I'm all the primary colors.

"Harley, what do you think?"

From her pillow, she lifts her back leg and licks herself.

"That good, huh? You're a big help."

AHH! The doorbell. Why didn't he just honk?

"I got it! I'll answer!" I scream.

Shoving my wallet and keys in my pockets, I hustle down the hall, then slow up so Dad thinks it's probably just Audrey or Trent. I'm sure "freaked-out-and-going-on-a-date" is written all over my face and I'm *not* going to hand him a "Hey, I'm gay" clue.

I get to the door and peer through the peephole. There he is. Damn, Lev's crazy handsome even through this little eye tunnel.

"Who's at the door?" Dad says from his chair.

Shoot. "It's all right, it's for me. Just a friend."

One last check in the hall mirror. Crap. My hair is sticking up all over.

I grip the doorknob with my shaky hand.

Well, here we go.

Twenty-five

I EASE OPEN THE DOOR. RIGHT HERE OUTSIDE MY OWN HOUSE, BACKED by the softest peachy-orange sunset: Lev.

Hands clasped in front of him, he shrugs. "Hi!"

How can a simple shrug be so freakin' adorable? I lean on the doorframe. His wavy Renaissance hair falls to his shoulders. Deep-purple V-neck shirt with one slim pale-blue line traveling across his chest. Ironed (!) khakis. Blue Nikes. Stunning, head to toe.

Sloppy-dressed me is *so* not worthy of that much hotness. He must think I'm such a geek. Well, guess I am. Too late to change now. Can't help the huge grin spreading over my face. "Hi."

I turn to tell Dad I'm—ahh! He's right behind me.

"Who is it, Ade?"

Heart palpitating, I squeeze between the open door and frame. "Just a friend. Off to study."

He peers around the door. "Don't know this one, do I?"

I sigh, then open the door wider and try to sound casual. "Lev, this is my dad. Dad, this is Lev. From my French class. We're gonna study."

Dad nods at Lev, but Lev reaches past me to shake hands. "Hi, Mr. Piper. Lev Cohen."

Since Dad uses his right hand for his cane, he shakes with his left. "Do you want to come in for a minute? Got a great game on."

What?

"No, Dad, we really need to go." And I'm glad Mom is at work. She'd probably ask us to stay for milk and cookies.

Dad looks from me to Lev. "French class. Never had an ear for languages, myself. Apart from speaking Texan, heh-heh."

Obi-Wan, help.

Lev polite-laughs. "My grandmother was born in New York and she really does think Texan is its own language."

Smiling, Dad steps into the doorway more. "Guess it's the only one I know."

Lev pulls his hair behind his ears. "Other than some not-so-good French, me too."

I step next to Lev. "See ya later, Dad!"

"Where're you guys studying tonight?"

Whoa—where's all this I'm-so-interested-in-what-you're-up-to coming from?

Lev looks at me, then says, "Probably just at a Starbucks or something."

Good answer.

I'm already halfway across the front yard when Dad waves. "Have fun, guys. *Bon voyage* and *à la mode!*" He hobbles inside and shuts the door.

I roll my eyes at Lev. "Sorry about that."

"No, your dad's funny."

Mortifying is the word I'd use.

He goes to open my door for me.

"That's okay, I got it," I say, checking to be sure Dad's not watching from the window.

Lev zips around to the driver's side and gets in. We both buckle up. He clears his throat. "Ready?"

I glance at my house. "Please!"

He accelerates down my street. I check the neighbors' yards but not a soul in sight. I forgot that his car is a lemon-yellow Beetle. Might as well be in a clown car with a neon sign saying LOOK AT ME!

Wow. So near him, so enclosed in this little car. Alone. Just us.

It's getting hard to breathe.

"Is your—" His voice cracks. "Is your dad, like, okay?"

I swallow. "He doesn't know about me. Neither of my parents do."

"What I meant is, he has a cane. . . . You don't have to talk about it."

"Oh. It's okay. Bad car wreck, couple years ago."

"Must be, well, anyway . . ." He glances at me. "I kinda figured you aren't out to your dad from the way you freaked." Hopeful smile. "Sorry about ringing the bell—"

"Oh, no," I say, "I should have said to honk. If I hadn't just broken my phone, like, just a few days ago, I would've texted. Need to pick up a new one a-sap."

He stops at the red light at the end of my street. "My grandmother doesn't know about me, thank god, but my parents are cool with me being gay and all. Hope I didn't say anything to, you know, make it weird for you?"

"No, he was just being nosey. Good save there with the studying-at-Starbucks line, though."

His cologne is spicy. And this car is spotless. This can't just be for me, right?

"Um"—I turn to him—"we're not really going to Starbucks, are we?"

He cracks up, then exhales deep like he was storing up his breath. "No. That'd be pretty lame, wouldn't it?"

I nod. "Hashtag Truth."

Oh, god, that sounded stupid.

He smiles. "That's cute."

I point ahead. "Light's green."

"Oops," he says, and we're off, engine humming like a toy car.

I run my palm over the smooth yellow metal doorframe by my shoulder. "I was wondering what your car would be like inside. Guess the one time I had the chance to look I was slightly distracted." I eye him. "Being in excruciating pain between my legs and all."

His face goes red.

I hold up my hand. "Oh, god, didn't mean to—wasn't your

fault! Well, kinda was, but . . . mine, too." I nervous-laugh. "The pain did go away. All's okay there . . . now . . ." Just shut up, Adrian.

I stare out the window.

He makes a complete stop at the stop sign before turning, unlike Audrey, who practically rolls right through.

The longer neither of us talks, the harder it is to think of what to say. Did I just screw it all up?

I'm so dying to know where we're going but have no clue when's the right time to ask. I'm not breathing. Gotta calm down, here. I catch my reflection in the side mirror and my hair is terrifying. Casually, I attempt to smooth it down.

We zoom down Mission Road. I scan the cars we pass to see if there's anyone I recognize—or anyone who recognizes me. People definitely stare at this car.

He puts on a song and the speakers blare. "Whoops!" He spins the volume button and it quiets down. "Sorry."

Jazz. Least I think it is. The beat is fast-paced, boppy and peppy. It's just instruments, no vocals.

"Is this music all right?" he says. "I can change it."

"No, it's fun." I smile. "And it's your car."

He smiles back. "You're here too."

Out of the corner of my eye, I watch his amazing jawline . . . those sexy hands gripping the wheel . . . his wide shoulders bopping to the beat.

Crap, why are these jeans so tight? They're getting tighter . . . again. Now they're *way* too tight. I know I'm a teen guy and all, but this is almost becoming a recurring medical condition.

"Uh, what music is this?" My voice cracks. I pretend to adjust my seat belt as I shift things around. Oh, man, that's better. Too obvious?

"It's Django Reinhardt," he says. "Know him? From the 1930s and '40s. It's like stepping back in time. Something about the rhythms is so calming. I'm always running and running . . ." He shakes his head. "Anyway, not important . . ."

"I really like it." And you.

We stop again at a red light. He faces me. "What do you listen to?"

I cross my arms. "Well, you probably wouldn't like what I like. Do you play video games?"

"Uh, not so much. Why?"

Crap. I inhale. "You'll probably think it's stupid, but my favorite music is video game soundtracks. And movie soundtracks, but epic, sweeping, transformative stuff. I can't handle the violent, killing, bloody, gory games. Too much of all that in real life."

He glances at me, then grins. "To quote your friend, 'Understatement of the century, sister.'"

I smile but cringe inside. I don't want to talk about Audrey right now.

"The music I like is dreamy," I say. "Powerful. It's mysterious and strong and takes me places. In my head, I mean. Guess that's kinda obvious. Heh-heh." I check out his reaction, but he just listens. "It's not like I actually go somewhere. You know, like physically . . ." God, I'm babbling. My face is on fire. Just shut up, Adrian.

He tilts his head at me. "No, I get it. And I like how you talk about it."

Beeeep!

"Oh!" I grab the door handle.

"Sorry!" he yells through the window at the car he almost sideswiped in the next lane. He stares ahead. "Guess I should keep my eyes on the road. Instead of on, well . . . I'm not so good at this. Date thing, I mean. Driving I'm good at, but not—oh, boy." He sighs.

Date thing. Wow. I like the sound of that.

Me. On a date thing.

He reaches out to steady the mess of badges and pendants swinging from his rearview mirror.

I talk over the new song that just came on with a fun, fast guitar sound. "What's this one?" I point to a dangling plastic badge that says NFTY SUMMER RETREAT.

Barely taking his eyes off the road, he glances at it. "Oh. From my temple youth group last summer. It was okay."

I scan the other pendants and stuff. Pep Club, Poetry Club, Key Club, French Club . . . so many. "You sure do a lot of clubbing."

He rolls his eyes. "*Way* too much. Those are all tangled, aren't they?"

I lift up one shaped like a piece of pie. "Wait, there's a Baking Club?"

"That's a fun one. You like cupcakes? I make a mean pumpkin spice cupcake."

"When do you find the time?"

He frowns.

I'm ruining this again. I have to change the subject, quick. "We're coming up on my favorite tree." I point out the window to the right.

He slows down. "Where?"

The one car behind us lays on its horn and swerves around.

"Sorry!" He signals and pulls into a parking lot. Stops. "Think I need to get off the road for a minute."

Damn. I'm so screwing this up. "I didn't mean to almost get us in a wreck."

"Wasn't you. It's just, well . . ." A big smile spreads across his face. "You are so friggin' cute."

I swallow.

He reaches over, touches my cheek. As he leans in, his lips get close to mine.

"Not here." I pull back and scan around. We're in a Taco Bueno lot and a group of people are heading our way.

He glances out the window and nods. Then, trying to not be too obvious, he adjusts *him*self.

Seems we share the same medical condition.

Clearing his throat, he says, "So, you have a favorite tree?"

"Over there, in front of the library."

He drives through the lot, which connects all the stores on this block; he parks in front of the library and turns off the car.

"Show me."

Wow. "Okay."

Good, barely anyone here. Just a few old people going inside and a mom leaving with a kid.

We get out and I lead him to the most wonderful old elm tree in the big grassy area off to the side. We stop underneath it and I put my palm against the rough, ridged bark. My shoulders relax.

He cranes his neck. "So tall. Never noticed it before."

I run my fingers through the bumpy bark ridges. "I used to ride my bike here when I was little. I'd check out books and sit right there in the shade to read. See how all those massive branches up there are like these wild, dancing arms? So free and strong, going wherever the hell they want to, finding the sunlight."

He steps closer to me, leans on the trunk, and gazes up.

I pick up a fallen leaf. "They can be the most vibrant gold this time of year. Even if it's been a dry summer. I love this transition of pale green into bright yellow."

He takes it and smiles. "Mind if I keep it?"

I look around, but no one is nearby. "Sure?"

He opens his wallet and slides the leaf next to his license.

"Does your tree have a name?" he asks.

"How did you know?"

"Well, if I had a favorite tree, I'd name it."

Damn he's sweet. "Promise not to tell? Or laugh?"

He touches the trunk. "Promise."

"You're gonna think it's weird. But I was, like, ten years old, okay? His name is Roald Dahl."

Big smile. "Me like." He pulls out his phone for a selfie,

puts his arm around me and pulls close. My insides heat up. He angles the phone so we'll be in the photo with the twisting branches above.

I clear my throat. "Um, you won't post this photo, right? Like, anywhere. And I mean *anywhere*."

"No. Just for me. And you, of course. Really." He squeezes my shoulder. "Here we are. You, me, and Roald Dahl."

He taps the button and captures us.

Then turns to me and says, "So, do you like drag queens?"

Twenty-six

WITH WIND WHIPPING THROUGH THE OPEN WINDOWS AND ROARING IN my ears, we speed toward Dallas. Headlights glow from cars in the opposite lanes as the last shades of sunset melt away.

"Okay," I say, "let me get this straight."

"Straight?" Lev grins.

"You're taking me to something called Teen Drag Queen Bingo? This really exists?"

Enough of this wind. I roll up the window.

He rolls his up too and turns down the jazz music some. "We don't have to go if you don't want to. It was just an idea I wanted to surprise you with."

Well, bingo, you did.

"Like I said," he continues, "I've been before and we're really gonna have fun." He reaches over and squeezes my knee. "Trust me?"

Two days ago I didn't even suspect Lev was gay and now he's setting my knee on fire and taking me to play bingo with a drag queen at an LGBT community center?

He glances at me with a hopeful expression. My brain wants to say, *Don't hate me, but holy crap, this is* so *not my thing*, but my knee and the rest of my body win out and I actually say, "Okay, why not?"

"Good! Ohmygod, just wait till you meet LaTrina. She's the drag hostess with the mostest. She's not, like, RuPaul level or anything, but she's hysterical. Just hope she doesn't pick on you, though. LaTrina can be fierce." He grins.

I gaze at the clear purple sky. Obi-Wan, oh, why hast thou forsaken me?

The dials and monitors in the dashboard glow a futuristic blue, which should be calming but makes me think of being abducted in an alien ship. At least it's a gay one.

Lev looks over his shoulder, then changes lanes when it's clear. I look over *my* shoulder to be sure some hidden reality show van isn't trailing us.

As we drive on to what surely will be certain doom, Lev asks me about Kobe and what really happened at Boo. He says he and Kathleen couldn't see from where they stood that night and he's been dying to know the truth.

At last, someone wants the truth. So I tell him about that night, the cops, and even when I visited Kobe at home.

He interrupts with questions and a lot of *no way!*s but wants to hear it all.

I leave out some details, like Doug's keys and, of course, Graphite's eyes, but I spill a lot.

It's a relief—speaking the truth.

We've been driving for almost half an hour now. I sit back and sink into the seat. It's bliss to have some distance from Rock Hollow.

"After a while," Lev says, "you would think you'd get used to it, right? Staying under the radar, I mean. As far as I know, no one at school knows *I'm* gay, thank goodness, at least not Doug or his crew."

"Is that why you're in the Pep Club, to throw them off since you do stuff for football games?"

He gives me a sideways glance. "No! I actually *like* being a part of that—it's fun. Maybe they assume Kathleen's my girlfriend like you did, or something. But they must think I'm straight. Otherwise I'd definitely get all the homophobic crap too. Well, *far* worse than 'crap.'"

"Yeah, tell me about it."

Lev sighs. "Adrian, what you did at Boo was fucking incredible. Beyond amazing. *Freaked* me out, though, the whole thing. Of course. And when you didn't come back to school for a few days, that weirded me out even more."

"Really?"

"Yes. But you going to help Kobe that night blew me away. You're a hero."

Wow.

Lev turns at the next intersection. "Almost there!"

My stomach spins. I've never been to the gay neighborhood,

but from what I've seen of it online, it's all party party party, going shirtless and getting smashed. Lev isn't really some secret party boy, is he? Please, no. But you never know who someone is under their mask. Hell, I thought he was straight.

We turn off the highway and, well, we're here. Rainbow flags are practically everywhere and lots of people are out, ready for a big Saturday night. I check out the cars driving by and the people on the street. Little clusters of men and some women amble down the sidewalks.

Lev notices me sitting back from the window and says, "If you're worried about seeing anyone we know, I can't imagine they'd be around here."

"What about at bingo?"

"Ha! Not from our school. Although I did see Kobe there one time."

"Really? He knows about you?"

He nods. "Doesn't know much—it's not like we have anything in common. But he knows I'm gay. And that I've played bingo." Cute smile.

Looking closer at people on the sidewalk, I spot some nerdy guys here and there. Everyone seems to be having fun. Just regular people. No wasted shirtless clichés yet, but the night is young.

Lev turns a corner onto a more residential street. We get farther away from the crowds and enter the parking lot of a low, spread-out building. Oh, boy, here we go. It's kinda old but with lots of windows and white brick lit by floodlights mounted on the walls. Seems like a normal building. Maybe a bit too normal. "You're not secretly taking me to some Bible class, are you?" I say.

"Ha! That'd be a fun first date for two guys."

My ears hum hearing him say those words. *First date for two guys.*

I spot a subtle lit-up sign by the entrance that says ROBERT SESSIONS LGBT COMMUNITY CENTER.

So it's for real.

A few teen guys hang by some cars but no one dressed in drag.

This tiny lot is already full, so we have to park on the side street. We get out and he locks the car with a *beep-beep.*

We're right under a streetlamp, so Lev's car almost glows neon yellow.

A man in a hoodie walks toward us from the shadowy sidewalk, hands in his pockets, squinting at the yellow Beetle. I hold my breath, but he doesn't stop. Keeps walking. Then he turns back, looks right at us, and says, "Love your car! It's adorable."

"Thanks!" Lev says a bit too loud. Watching the man move on down the street, Lev says to me, "At school I only hear the opposite. Every freakin' day."

I exhale and say, "I bet."

Already this neighborhood is full of surprises.

As we approach the building and my pulse speeds up, I scan the faces of the other teens arriving. No one I've ever seen.

Lev stops and leans into me. "It's okay. Everyone's cool here." He tilts his head, looking right into my eyes, but I pull back. Can't do a public kiss, as amazing as those lips look. He's clearly disappointed but nods and keeps walking, so I follow.

The LGBT community center. While I vaguely knew it existed, I've never had the urge to even look up this place online. Never felt part of this community, but now I'm walking right into its literal center. *And* I'm about to play bingo. All so this hot and sweet and adorable guy will like me.

We head through the front doors and my eyes have to adjust to the brightly lit little lobby. The walls are covered with colorful posters and flyers. One bulletin board says HAPPY LGBT HISTORY MONTH! across the top in rainbow-colored letters, with photos tacked below of famous gays and lesbians through history. A lot I don't know, but some I do.

"Hey!" I point at the board. "They've got Ian McKellen as both Gandalf *and* Magneto. Very cool."

"And there's Cole Porter. I'll play you his music."

All sorts of posters layer another wall. Speed dating, suicide prevention hotline, lesbian poetry readings, Coming Out Day . . . and Teen Drag Queen Bingo. The design is horrendous and it's not a great photo, but there's LaTrina. Just her face, but she looks intriguing, like a cross between a Barbie doll and a clown. Still, I'm not ready to get picked on by her yet.

Behind a tiny circular desk in the middle of the room sits a large woman in a lime-green polo shirt.

Her face lights up when she sees Lev. "Hey, hon!"

He waves at her. "Hey, Maria."

We continue past and down a hall.

"How often do you come to this?" I ask.

"Oh, I've only been to bingo three times. I know Maria from the summer I volunteered here. Mailing flyers, making posters, stuff like that."

He notices my eyebrows shooting up and sighs. "Yeah, I have trouble saying no."

"Oh?"

His face turns red. "To volunteer work, I mean. Not, uh, to other things."

I squeeze his shoulder and whisper, "You're cute."

Little kids' squeals come from an open door ahead and bounce off the brick walls around us.

"Gay kindergarteners?" I ask.

Lev cracks up. "No, they have classes here for little kids of gay *parents*."

My cheeks heat up. Should've figured that one out.

A tiny boy runs into the hall and holds up a painting. "Looky!" he squeals. He's filled every inch of a piece of construction paper with a scene, using purple crayons and green tempera paint.

"Wow," I say, "that's a cool unigiraffe."

He beams. "I know. It's like a regular giraffe but *magic*."

Lev studies the art. "Where's a unigiraffe? How'd you see that so fast?"

A teacher with bright-red hair piled on top of her head comes out of the room. "Come along, Jimmy, let's not bother anyone."

Jimmy points at me. "He likes my unigiraffe." He dashes back into the room to join some other kids.

I peer in. Little art tables are grouped in the center and big drawing tables line the walls. Art hangs all over. "There's a studio here?"

"Yep," says the teacher. "Teen drawing classes are Tuesday nights, if you're interested. They meet—Jimmy, leave her alone!" She turns from us.

A few easels hold some serious paintings in one corner, and on a wall above a big craft sink, someone's started to stencil a mural of the castle from *Spirited Away*.

"This is awesome," I say to Lev.

"Hold on. How did you see that unigiraffe? It looked like a mess of color to me."

"Well, I like to draw. A lot. I'm actually . . ." I swallow. "I'm an artist." I glance at him. It's scary but a relief all at the same time, telling him at last.

"You're an artist? How come I haven't seen anything?" His eyes get wide. "No wonder you acted so weird in French when I gave you *my* lame drawing."

"Your drawing wasn't lame!"

"It so definitely was. What kind of stuff do you draw? When can I see?"

"Sorry, I . . . I *will* show you sometime." Not sure if I trust him enough to share Graphite yet.

Little Jimmy bounces back over. "Here!" He holds up his art.

The red-haired teacher smiles. "He wants to give it to you to keep. Feel free to say no."

"Oh, but I'd love to have your unigiraffe, Jimmy." I take it. "Thank you."

"Uh-huh." He runs off squealing, the teacher trailing after him.

"Wow," I say. "This place isn't anything like I expected."

Lev tilts his head. "What did you expect?"

"I don't know, but not all this. I bet the teachers don't make fun of what kids draw *here*."

"What do you mean?"

"Well, this sure ain't no Rock Hollow High."

Lev holds up his hand and says, "Halleloo to that!"

We make our way down the hall, where about five guys are lined up and laughing with each other. At a folding table set up along the wall with a sign saying TEEN DRAG QUEEN BINGO IS 15 TO 19 ONLY, a college-looking guy with purple hair checks our IDs and collects the money.

"No no, my treat," Lev says, waving my money away and paying for us. "I dragged you here, after all."

Following buttery popcorn smells, we step into a big, colorfully lit room with Beyoncé blasting from speakers along the walls. Long pieces of red velvet hang crooked on either side of a small platform, and Mylar streamers are taped up here and there around the room, kinda haphazard-like. About seven round tables with mismatched folding chairs are clustered in the center.

I speak loudly into Lev's ear so he can hear me over the music. "This place was decorated by *gays*?"

He busts out laughing. "Gays who definitely don't watch

do-it-yourself decorating shows. Still, A-plus for effort."

Three mirror balls spin from the ceiling. Little stars of light dance across his face, making his eyes sparkle.

Those eyes almost make blaring pop music and mirror balls okay.

Two muscle boys, wearing sweaters so tight they might as well not wear them at all, push past us. Looks like thirty or so people are here. Except for a couple of adults standing around keeping their eyes on things, all teens. It's mainly guys but a few girls, too, with everyone's chatter competing with the music.

At a table right in the middle sit three guys in various states of drag. One is so pretty he could almost pass for a girl, but the other two, no way. I elbow Lev. "Is one of them LaTrina?"

He cranes his neck to see. "No. Haven't seen them before." He smiles at me. "Fun already, right?"

Uh . . . jury's still in deliberation.

I follow Lev to the drinks table, which has a popcorn machine next to it. He pays for one massive bag of popcorn and two cans of 7UP. "Guess this is our official drink, huh?"

I cover my face. "Least this time we don't have to wrestle it out of a machine."

We scan the tables, which have four chairs each and are all pretty full.

Lev points. "There—two seats together."

"Right up front? We'll practically be onstage."

He shrugs. "No other choice."

There are two guys about our age already at the table. I

grab a fistful of popcorn—salty, buttery comfort food.

Okay, Obi-Wan, we can do this.

Everyone's taking their seats, so, cradling his drink and the popcorn bag in one hand, Lev grabs my hand with the other. "C'mon."

His hand squeeze wins and we make our way through the tables. Some of these guys look like they could be college freshmen, but most are definitely high school. I don't spot anyone I recognize. A few are funkily dressed, others not. Some are super-cute. If I were to see most of these guys anywhere else, I'd never guess they were gay.

I'm right in the middle of—

Holy crap. I stop.

Almost everyone here is gay.

Practically everyone in the whole building.

So this is what it's like to be in a room—an entire building—of people like me.

Wow.

"You all right?"

I blink at Lev. "Uh, yeah. Just taking it in." The mirror ball reflections swirl in unison, jumping from face to face, body to body, making the room spin.

People are checking us out, so I look down and keep walking to the table.

"These taken?" Lev asks the two guys seated there. They shake their heads, so we put down our drinks and popcorn. So it doesn't get bent, I place Jimmy's rolled-up paper next to me. The banged-up metal chairs squeak as we sit. We're right up against the little stage platform. Oh, boy.

The kid next to me has a bowl cut, bleached almost white but with dark roots, bangs practically covering his eyes. Even with really bad acne he's cute.

The other guy wears a black T-shirt that says SHANTAY YOU STAY in bright-pink letters that glow in the colored lights. He's got close-cropped, tight, curly black hair and at least two earrings in each ear.

Silver sequins are sprinkled all over the purple plastic tablecloth. In the center is a stack of bingo cards and, whoa, I'm guessing those are bingo markers?

Seeing my expression, Lev laughs.

The guy next to me says, "I know. They look like multicolored, shiny-topped dildos, don't they?"

I smile even as my face gets hot.

The guy in the T-shirt rolls his eyes. "Everything looks like a dick to you."

"But it's true!" Bleached-hair guy reaches over and rubs the back of his friend's head, keeping his hand there.

Under the table, Lev squeezes my knee.

Okay, wow.

"What color do you want?" he asks me.

"Huh?"

He takes his hand off my leg to grab us a few bingo cards. "What marker color?"

"Oh," I squeak. I go for the red, but holy crap, it really is so phallic it's like grabbing a, well, yeah. I fumble with it, sending silver sequins into my lap and onto the linoleum floor.

I glance at the two guys, expecting another joke, but they're only paying attention to each other now. They kiss. At the tables around us, if anyone notices, they don't care. Other guy couples have their arms around each other here and there. Cuddling. Laughing. Everyone acts like it's normal, like nothing bad is going to happen.

This is . . . I don't know. I stare down at zooming spots of light glittering off the sequins. It's like floating in space.

"What is it?" Lev says.

I look up, bringing his sweet face into focus. Then I put my hand in his and smile.

He leans in to kiss me, but all at once the music stops and the lights go off.

Showtime.

Twenty-seven

"WILLKOMMEN, BIENVENUE, WELCOME," BOOMS A VOICE FROM THE speakers in the dark. "The crappy old rec room at the gay center brings you . . . *Teen Drag Queen Bingo!*"

Everyone claps and whoops, and I scoot my chair closer to Lev.

Except for the mirror balls, the lights come back on, but the little stage is still empty.

The speakers crackle. "Here she is, our hostess with the leastest, our lady of lame, our mistress of, well, no one—"

"Cut the bullshit, honey!" From out in the hall comes another voice, loud and gravelly. "These tits are already startin' to sag."

"Please welcome . . . *LaTrina!*"

Framed by the doorway, a tall figure backs into the room, then spins to face us. Her eyes go wide and she covers her mouth with her hands, pretending she's shocked we're here.

Across the room I can only see her from the shoulders up, but already it's quite a sight. Surveying the crowd, she bats what must be many layers of fake eyelashes, surrounded by dense black eyeliner, sparkly green eye shadow, and arched eyebrows penciled on her forehead. Her red overly painted lips stand out, but it's the massive fiery copper wig that really pops. And defies gravity.

She wouldn't pass for a girl, but she is pretty . . . in a beauty-pageant-meets-circus kinda way.

Blowing kisses all around, her emerald-green dress flowing, she makes her way through the tables to the platform. Right where I'm sitting.

Holy wow, she's tall. As a guy he must be big already, but with those six-inch-heeled boots and the massive wig, she's a giant.

Lev rubs my back. "Don't look so freaked."

I nod and take a breath. As LaTrina steps onto the platform I hunch over and put my hands in my lap, like when you don't want a teacher to call on you.

Audience participation and I have never gotten along.

Everyone is laughing, so I look up to see why. Towering over us, she's in profile, rubbing her weirdly round belly—the front of her dress is stuffed to make her look pregnant. She shrugs. "Who knew? Incubation for baby drag queens is only a month."

Scanning the crowd, she says, "Hmmm, wonder which one of you is the daddy?"

Please don't notice me please don't notice me.

She puts her hands on her hips. "Y'all are babies yourself. Such a young group tonight."

"You're only twenty, bitch, so don't get sassy," one of the drag queens at that center table yells. Giggles spread around the room.

LaTrina smirks. "Some of my drag sisters came to harass—I mean support—me tonight. Don't pay attention to any of those hos."

She pats around all over herself, layers of silver bracelets jangling. "Have any of you good people seen my balls? Where are my—oh, *here* they are!" She reaches down under her skirt and, now no longer "pregnant," pulls out a clear plastic globe filled with little numbered balls. A bingo baby.

"Can't do bingo without my balls, you know." She flips back her hair. "In fact, can't think of *anything* I'd do without my balls."

Lev laughs and bumps my shoulder. "So funny, right?"

I realize I'm smiling.

She clutches the plastic globe to her padded chest. "Oh, such dirty minds! I meant these bingo balls." Then, looking right at Lev, she says, "You don't wanna know where the other ones are tucked away."

Lev laughs so freely, so relaxed. It's kinda contagious.

Laughter comes from all around. I'm in a room full of gay guys . . . still trying to wrap my head around this.

LaTrina reaches behind one of the crooked red velvet drapes taped to the wall and reveals a big shopping bag, explaining it's filled with "a few trinkets for tonight's lucky winners." Then she starts the game.

I'm so distracted hoping she doesn't pick on me that it takes a while to focus. Tossing out funny one-liners here and there, she announces number after number and it seems forever until someone hollers "Bingo!" at last. It's a guy at the back of the room.

LaTrina peers at him over the crowd. "Congrats! What's your name, honey?"

"It's Curtis—"

"LIAR!" she screams, then slaps her hands over her mouth, pretending to be shocked.

Everyone cracks up.

The poor guy turns bright red.

Eyes wide, she says, "I am so sorry, y'all. But I was born with a condition called Honesty Tourette's. Instead of cussing, I yell my inner truth."

I smile at Lev.

"I apologize, dear," LaTrina says. "Now, what's your name again?"

He laughs and shakes his head. "You sure you're okay?"

She nods and mouths, *Fine.*

He inhales. "All right. It's Curt—"

"*LIAR!*" she screams, then covers her mouth again.

I bust out laughing.

Tossing her hands in the air, she says, "Oh, screw it." She reaches in the shopping bag, pulls out a tiny baby bib that says WHOSE BOOB DO I HAVE TO SUCK TO GET A DRINK

AROUND HERE?, and tosses it across the room at the guy.

This. Is. Hysterical.

She goes back to her balls and we speed along through the next game.

Up close, LaTrina's emerald satin dress is so impressive, made of a tight-fitting corset and flowing skirt that's short in front but long in back. With a shiny silver belt, noisy silver bracelets, and those dangerous-looking black boots, it's almost like a superhero outfit—but with even more flair, which is saying a lot.

Drag queens could definitely give serious cosplayers a run for their money. Hmm . . . drag queens and superheroes. Seems like LaTrina needs to make an appearance in Graphite's world. That'll be fun to draw.

Gripping Lev's shoulder, I whisper in his ear, "Thanks for bringing me."

He wraps his arm around me. "I knew you'd have fun."

I shut my eyes for just a moment, letting his arm make the room and the chatter fall away. Then I open my eyes again.

It's almost like I'm outside myself looking down at us, seeing a guy holding me. And all of me, inside and outside, is amazed.

One last squeeze and he lets go.

Glancing up, I catch the guy seated next to me watching us, smiling.

This may not be the "real" world, but it's pretty damn real for me.

After many games of not winning, Lev and I finish one

bag of popcorn, then start on another. My bingo cards have sucked all night and I haven't even come close until the card I have now. But the other guys at our table have done all right. Their prizes, a solar-powered toy hula girl and a Pope-shaped soap-on-a-rope, are proudly displayed in the center of the table.

"Here we go . . . another spin of my orb!" LaTrina twirls her plastic globe, opens the top, and reaches in.

I look down at my bingo card. Finally, I just need two more numbers to win.

Having almost won three times so far, Lev's poised with his green marker. "I'm so close! G seven. Just need that."

Each time LaTrina announces a letter, she makes it stand for something. "G," she says, "for . . . ?"

People yell out various things all at once: "Gay?" "Gaga?" "Gluteus maximus?"

"G," she says, "for Gird Your Loins . . . three! G-three, anyone?"

From around the room comes a massive "Awwwww."

"Shoot!" says Lev.

"Yesssss!" says the guy next to me as he whips the cap off his marker and stamps his card.

Lev bumps my arm. "Hey, you have it too! Hurry! Mark it, mark it!"

How'd I miss that? I fumble with my marker and stamp a red blob on the G-3 square. There's one possibility now I could get bingo, if she calls I-40.

LaTrina wiggles her fingers. "Okay, I'm goin' in."

Lev chants under his breath, "G-seven, G-seven, G-seven. Pleeease!"

She pulls out another ball. "*I* . . . for I am so ready to get outta these damn heels."

She called I! My turn to chant under my breath. "I-forty, I-forty, I-forty, I-forty."

LaTrina hears—she's so close by she could reach out and touch me. She bats her lashes at me. "I recognize your face. What's your name?"

I clear my throat and squeak, "Uh, Adrian."

"UhAdrian, now that's a unique na—" Her smile fades and she stares at me. "Are you *the* Adrian?"

What? My stomach drops and I glance at Lev, who just looks at me wide-eyed.

I shrug. "I don't know?" Who does she think I am?

"Call out the number!" someone yells from across the room.

Her smirk and composure snap back as LaTrina puts her hands on her hips. "Calm your nerves, honey." Pretending to check out the ball in her hand, she peers over at my card on the table. Then she holds the ball up in the air, waving it and blocking the number with her fingers. "I-forty!" She quickly drops the ball back in the plastic globe.

What? "*BINGO!*" I yell, quickly stamping the square and knocking sequins all over the place.

"Woo-hoo!" Lev says.

"Bingo!" a girl screams at another table.

"Sorry, dear." LaTrina points to me. "This cutie said it first."

Lev and the guys at my table clap and say, "Yaaay!"

LaTrina puts out her palm. "Verification!"

I hand her my card. In one motion she glances at it and tosses it over her shoulder. "Looks good!" She reaches into her shopping bag but bites her lower lip. "Oh, dear. We're out of prizes."

I stare at her empty bag. Oh, well. At least I won, even if she did fake the number.

"Hold on," she says, "you ain't leavin' empty-handed." Fingering her bracelets, she chooses one and slips it off. "For our last prize of the night, something near and dear to a queen's heart: tacky plastic jewelry."

She hands me a thin silver band with little stars etched around the outside.

"Think of it as protection, like Wonder Woman's magic bracelets. I always do." She twists her forearms back and forth, making her jewelry clink and tinkle.

I slip the bracelet onto my left wrist.

A *boom-boom-boom* comes over the speakers, like someone tapping the mic.

LaTrina rolls her eyes. "I hear ya, I hear ya! Well, boys and girls, not only have we run outta prizes, but we've run outta time. Hope you've had fun, and thanks for having me!" She opens her arms wide and curtsies.

"Ladies and gentlemen," says the voice over the speakers, who I now see is a guy standing by the doorway. "The ever-lovely, and *long-winded*, LaTrina!"

We all applaud as LaTrina flips off the microphone guy, then saunters over to her table of friends. The chatter starts up again. All at once, the fluorescent lights flick on and the solar-powered hula dancer twitches her hips, making the sequins on the table jump.

Blinking in the garish light, I say, "There goes the magic."

Lev snaps the cap on his marker with a *pop* and turns to me. "How does she know you?"

"I have no clue."

"She totally gave you that last number," the guy next to me with the bleached-blond hair says.

"You noticed that too?" I say. "I have no idea why she'd do that."

The other guy grabs the hula girl and Pope soap from the table. "I think she likes you." Both guys get up.

Lev loops his arm through mine. "She'd better not."

"I bet she was just giving me crap," I say. "All a part of her act, right?"

The guys smile and wave as they turn to go.

We say bye to them and I sink back in my chair. "That was a trip!"

Lev checks out his phone. "It's after nine o'clock. That hour sure whooshed by. My face *so* hurts from laughing."

I rub my cheeks. "Mine too."

People are heading out, so I stand and pick up little Jimmy's painting from the table. From my lap, glittery sequins tumble to the floor. Lev gets up and spins in place, raining more sequins around our feet.

As we head to the door LaTrina waves me over to where she and about five of her friends still sit.

"Uh-oh, what now?" I whisper to Lev.

"I knew it." She nods, her rhinestone earrings swinging against her neck. "You *are* the Adrian."

"Sorry?"

A skinny guy in a turtleneck sitting next to LaTrina gestures to the group at their table. "We all know Kobe."

Oh.

LaTrina eyes me. "I recognize you from that video he sent. You were screaming at the guy bashing him."

I freeze. They're all staring at me.

That horrible phone video from Boo.

LaTrina puts her hands on the table. "He told me about you."

I swallow. "What did he say?"

Even through her mask of makeup her expression is serious. "He said if it wasn't for you he'd probably be dead."

I look at a surprised Lev, then back at her. "He did?"

"You came to his rescue."

One of her drag friends snaps her fingers. "You must have the balls of a drag queen. Fierce!"

I shake my head. "I—I don't know about that. It was kinda terrifying."

The skinny guy says to Lev, "You've got a brave friend, there."

Lev puts his arm around me. "He's pretty awesome."

People clear the tables around us, folding and banging the chairs.

I fiddle with my new bracelet and say to LaTrina, "So, have you seen Kobe in person?"

She shakes her head.

"You should," I say. "Just go see him no matter what he tells you. He's in bad shape but really needs to laugh."

Someone flicks the lights on and off.

LaTrina stands and says, "Jeez! We get the hint." Then she grabs my wrist. "Okay, I'll go see him. But maybe out of drag. Don't wanna frighten any children. Or small animals."

I smile.

She lets go. "See ya round, *the* Adrian."

Lev and I make our way through the building and out the front door into the chilly night. An almost-full moon peeks over the trees and a few people hang out talking by their cars.

I inhale a deep, deep breath. "Okay. Mind officially blown!"

He takes my hand and laces his fingers through mine. "She's right, just like I told you in the car. You are a hero."

"Well, I don't know about *that*."

"No one else did anything that night," he says. "I sure didn't."

"But—"

"You're special." With his free hand, he brushes his hair out of his face. "Can I tell you something?"

My heart pounds faster. "What?"

"I've liked you ever since I first saw you last year."

Three guys bust out of the lobby, laughing and chatting, and walk around us into the lot.

"C'mere." I pull him around the side of the building, away

from the floodlights and into the shadows, and lean against the wall. "I've liked you for a long time too."

"Really?"

"Yes, *way* really." I take his other hand. "So what made you, ya know, kiss me in the cafeteria?"

"Between what you did at Boo and that cute hair, I was finally pretty sure you were gay. And when you walked into my car door—"

"Hey, you opened it in—"

"*Anyway*, I just couldn't take it anymore and had to let you know how I felt."

"You need to shut up now."

He blinks. "Why?"

"Because it's my turn." Spinning us so his back is to the wall, I focus on the glints of moonlight in his eyes. Then I kiss him, as only *the* Adrian could.

Twenty-eight

THE MORNING LIGHT SLIPS THROUGH GAPS IN THE CURTAINS AND makes a soft shadow pattern across my bedroom ceiling. It's like a work of art, transforming with the sunrise. I can't see the bedside clock, so I lift my head to peer over Harley, curled up in a ball next to my pillow. This is a first—I'm wide awake even before my alarm goes off. On a *Monday morning*.

Sitting up, I scratch Harley behind her ears. She stretches and yawns, tilting her head at me.

"I know, you've never seen me excited to get to school before, have you?"

She puts her paw over her tiny face and shuts her eyes. Clearly, she doesn't care that I get to see Lev this morning.

I hop up and go to my drawing table. Nothing like seeing your art fresh the next day after you've created it. Especially first thing, when your brain is blank and you can almost look at your creation like it's not yours.

Wow, that's even better than I remember. I spent so much of yesterday sketching Oasis, my superhero version of Lev, getting his hair and costume and face just right, but no drawing could compare to the real thing.

Still wrapping my brain around that I'm, well, not *boyfriends*, but something-romantic-I-don't-know-the-word-for, with Lev. *Lev!*

Saturday night, we finally peeled ourselves away from the wall of the LGBT center—*that* was mind-blowing—and drove back, my body buzzing and both of us talking like crazy. We were starving, so we stopped in a Taco Bueno. But we were instantly reminded we weren't surrounded by people like us anymore and were thrust back into the effin' real world. A table of jocks hanging out there decided to announce to the whole place that we had some silver sequins stuck in our hair and, wow, isn't that pretty. Like fairy dust. So we took our burritos and ate in the car.

As Lev drove me home, I told him all about the mysterious locker notes. When I mentioned I thought it could be Manuel Calderón writing them, Lev said he doubts it because Manuel's a wrestler. Wouldn't he be on Doug's side?

But I explained about Manuel thinking Buddy's a dick, so maybe he thinks worse of Doug? Plus, he seems so awkward and shy. I told Lev how he gets all weird and blushes when he talks to me.

Lev said he'd better not have a crush on me, or else.

"Or else what?" I asked.

He smiled. "Or else I'll get LaTrina on his ass."

That'd be a sight.

Thinking about these notes got me fed up, so last night I wrote my response at last. I'm going to leave it in that brick wall this morning:

I think I know who you are.
Why won't you just talk to me?

I'm sick of stupid games.

Blasting the soundtrack to *Star Wars Episode IV*, I zip around and get ready for school.

While we're having our granola in the kitchen, Mom says she likes that I'm finally wearing this white button-down shirt she bought me a while ago. When I tell her it suits my mood today, she smiles.

I can't help smiling myself.

I speed-walk to school to meet Lev early at his car in the parking lot like we planned. There he is, leaning on his trunk. As soon as he sees me approach, his face turns into one big grin.

Maybe I'll melt right here on the asphalt.

Or I'll just wave, which I do, and say, "Hey!"

He steps forward but reconsiders and leans back against the car again. "Hi!"

I get it, I want to throw my arms around him, too. But obviously, that ain't happenin' here.

He points to my wrist. "You're wearing it."

I twist LaTrina's bracelet. "Yeah. Haven't taken it off."

He looks down at the ground, wavy strands of hair blowing over his face. "Does that mean you're still glad you went with me on Saturday?"

I reach my foot forward and tap the tip of his shoe with mine. "Definitely. Are you?"

He taps my foot even harder. "Absofreakinlutely."

We lock eyes, then look away.

My insides tingle.

"Thanks for coming so super-early." When I told Lev my plan on the phone last night about writing a note back, he offered to be my lookout.

Surveying the lot, I say, "You got a good spot. We can see everything from here."

He pulls his hair back behind his ears. "Did you write the note?"

Some car arrives and parks in the row behind us.

"Yeah, all set." I pull my French folder out of my backpack and hand it to him so it'll look like we're just talking about homework. I placed my note inside.

He opens the folder and reads my note, gripping it so it doesn't blow away—it's such a windy morning.

He nods. "That's great, short and to the point."

I glance over at the Dumpster by the cafeteria, but no one's near it.

As soon as the girl behind us locks her car and moves on, I crumple the note into a tiny wad and slip it into my front pocket. Putting the folder back inside, I hand my bag to Lev and take a deep breath. "Guess it's now or never."

He scans around. "Coast looks clear."

At a slow and casual pace, I make my way to the Dumpster about two rows away. Next to it, Doug's parking space is empty, so I need to act fast in case he pulls up.

Ugh—the stench is beyond nasty back here.

Stepping behind the Dumpster, I spot the missing brick and cram my note as far inside the gap as I can. Little pieces of mortar crunch as I twist so it stays in place.

When I get away from the gross wall, I take a quick look back—you can only see a tiny bit of white poking out.

Across the rows of cars, Lev gives me an all-clear thumbs-up. My pulse going a mile a minute, I hustle back to Lev's car. A few more people walk through the lot, but they're paying more attention to their phones than to me.

Lev hands me my backpack and says under his breath, "Success?"

I exhale and say, "Yes. Disgusting place to leave a stupid note. Maybe it is someone's idea of a joke after all. Did anyone see me?"

"No, you were very stealth. Much calmer than I'd be."

I wouldn't call this calm.

He grabs his bag from the backseat, shuts the door, and locks his car. "Didn't see anyone lurking, either."

"Maybe I'll watch just a bit in case Mystery Guy decides to come by and take a look."

"Okay." He hefts his backpack on his shoulders. "Let me

know what happens. See ya in French, *the* Adrian."

As he leaves for some Pep Club meeting, I find a lookout point along the side of the building and plop down on the grass by a little group of trees. I inhale, then slowly let it out.

Note delivered.

I lean back against a tree and, squinting with the sun right in my eyes, watch Lev disappear around the corner that leads to the main entrance. Not only is he an *amazing* kisser, but he's an awesome accomplice, too. Neither Audrey nor Trent ever offered to be my lookout . . . for anything. Of course, I never asked them. But if they knew I'd replied and written my own note, Audrey would rewrite it entirely and send it out to the global media, and Trent would just tell me to stop wasting trees.

How nice to have someone trust me for a change.

The wind whips around. Some brown leaves rain down and dance across the lawn.

Sitting here, I'm halfway between the parking lot and the corner of the building near the entrance. The Dumpster is slightly hidden behind the cafeteria steps about, what, fifty feet away? But I'll be able to see if anyone goes there, espe-cially since Doug's bubbamobile isn't here yet to block my view. His bright-red tank is hard to miss, so I'll be up and out of here before he even shuts off the engine.

After ten or more minutes of hanging out, avoiding eye contact with the parade of kids that walk past, I'm tired of watching a very boring Dumpster. This time has been con-structive in one way: I've discovered all sorts of crap in my backpack I forgot was there. I've been wondering where this gummy eraser—

Bwoop-bwoop!

Crap. I know that sound.

How'd I not hear Doug's pickup arrive? He and Buddy are already heading my way.

I toss everything in my bag and zip it. Shifting my legs, I get ready to jump up and run but hold my breath and wait.

Tapping Doug's arm with the back of his hand, Buddy nods his chin in the opposite direction from me toward a blond girl crossing the street. "Yo, look."

Doug shakes his head. "Dude, never gonna happen. How many times has she told you to go screw yourself?"

"Catch ya later." Buddy dashes across the lawn to her.

Doug rolls his eyes and keeps walking.

Not moving a muscle, I stare at the ground and keep him in my periphery. Coming this way, he must have the sun in his eyes at least.

His heavy steps crunch in the dead grass and pass me by.

Okay, good.

Then he stops.

I lift my head and blink in the sunlight. He's looking down, right at me.

Don't mess with me, Doug.

He scrunches his forehead and scans around. Suddenly, he stiffens and takes one look toward his truck, then stares at the ground for a second.

Oh, god.

The wind kicks up, so he grabs the brim of his cap and pulls it down farther over his face. He gives me one last hard stare, turns away, and walks around the corner.

Could he possibly have figured out *I* drew those flyers, like Trent and Audrey said he would? I don't see how. Maybe he's just paranoid now about people getting in his truck, or he's annoyed I'm watching him. Still, that was weird.

I get up and slip my backpack onto both shoulders. Eyeing Buddy, who's over on the sidewalk annoying that girl, I ease along the side of the building and peek around the corner.

People are arriving and some hang out on the front steps.

High-fiving some guy who booms "Awesome win!," Doug heads through the doors. I need to wait just a couple minutes and get some space between us.

I check back where Buddy is. I'm out of earshot, but it's clear the girl doesn't like his hands on her shoulders. She shoves him away, hard. He cracks up but, looking around, mouths something to her and turns to come this way.

I wipe my sweaty palms on my jeans and slink back along the wall in the shadows to the trees, raising my shields and channeling my practiced Graphite invisibility moves.

Pissed off and muttering to himself as he makes a beeline to the entrance, he doesn't even look in my direction as he disappears around the building.

Asshole.

The girl runs over to a couple other girls and they hang together on the sidewalk, glaring at where Buddy went.

The first bell rings.

"Give it back!" someone yells. From around the corner, pieces of paper float by in the wind and tumble across the grass, casting long shadows.

I walk back and peer around again. Buddy's running in a big circle, holding a purple backpack, pulling out folders and tossing them in the air, papers flying in all directions. That drama girl Carmen is frantically gathering up what she can, screaming at Buddy to "Give it back!"

People just watch, some laughing.

Whipping around the corner, I take off after Buddy, pounding the ground with my feet.

He turns Carmen's backpack inside out and shakes what's left onto the ground.

I run harder, the lawn and everything bouncing and blurred in my periphery. I'm almost to Buddy now.

He sees and spins to face me. Slipping on a folder, he hits the ground.

Running past, I stoop and yank the bag from his fist, then stop and pant.

He jumps up, shaking out his fingers. "What the—"

"Leave her alone!" I yell. Gripping the bag tight, I take a step toward him.

Sun's behind me, so he holds up his hand to block it from his eyes. He gapes at me, then jerks his head around, scanning for, what? Doug? Backup?

My chest heaves.

It gets quiet. Lots of eyes watch us.

I try to catch my breath but don't look away from him.

He points right in my face. "You are *dead!*" He kicks one of Carmen's books and sends it flying. I jump out of the way. Then he stomps up the steps and through the doors.

Kids say "Oooooh!" and "Wouldn't wanna be you," but most people just look like they don't want any trouble and head inside. They only care about getting away from the scene.

"C'mon, help us pick up her stuff!" I say.

No one does.

Turning the backpack right side out again and scooping up the other books as I go, I dash over to Carmen and hold open her bag. "Here."

Shaking, she puts what she's gathered into it and takes it. "It had everything. All my homework. Everything."

I squeeze her shoulder. "Let's keep going."

We chase down more papers, which swirl around the grass.

By the sidewalk, the girl Buddy harassed and her two friends drop their bags on the ground and run to join us, trying to stop what they can from blowing into the street.

After picking up the rest of the pages and folders and pens and books, we all gather around Carmen and help her shove what we collected into her bag. Some pages blew away, past the street and beyond, but I think we caught most of it.

Half her hair has come loose from her ponytail and hangs over her face. She takes off her neon-orange glasses and, through tears, keeps repeating, "Thank you."

The blond girl tells her she's sorry and "Buddy's such a prick," and pats her shoulder. Then she and her friends scoot up the steps and go inside.

No, he's far worse than just a prick.

Second bell rings.

Eyes frantic, Carmen clutches her bag to her chest. "What do I do? All my homework. I'm screwed."

I force a grin. "I think we got most everything. Maybe not so bad once you sort through it all?"

I survey the now almost-empty front lawn and steps. No damn teachers. No damn security guard. Sure there are cameras outside, but so what? Buddy's got McConnell for protection. He'd probably say something about boys being boys and harmless pranks the Monday after a big game or some bullshit.

No. This has got to stop.

But taping art to lockers clearly doesn't work.

I need a real plan.

Twenty-nine

SLIPPING INTO FRENCH A MILLISECOND BEFORE THE FINAL BELL, I plop my bag on the floor by my desk, sink into my seat, and turn to Lev.

He leans forward. "What is it?"

Still catching my breath, I say, "Tell you later."

He gives me a confused look, but just seeing him again makes me smile.

I spin around before anyone can notice and get my books and stuff ready.

As Madame Pauline gets to the lesson and the minutes pass, my breath returns to normal and I stop sweating. At last, my brain slows down.

All right, a plan. Buddy's on Doug's leash even if he sometimes gets out of control. He licks Doug's boots and desperately needs his approval, so whatever I come up with still needs to focus on Doug. It has to be a plan to take care of both at the same time.

And it can't be majorly lame like my last attempt. So then . . . *what?*

"Ah-loers, cha-pee-tra deez-wheat see voo plahy," Madame Pauline says.

Thank god that, in addition to translating the French, we can also translate her accent. We flip to chapter eighteen in our books like she asked and I repeat the phrases I'm supposed to, but Lev keeps kicking at my shoes. Hard to not bust into a grin. I swing my feet under my seat as much as I can to kick back. Until I bump his desk, which scrapes on the floor tile, and people look at us. We stop.

I fiddle with my LaTrina bracelet and glance back at Lev once in a while to remind myself Saturday night wasn't just a fantasy. It's so weird being in this class for the first time knowing who Lev really is. And that he likes *me.*

After class he and I head down the hall together. Through chatter and locker slams bouncing all around, I tell Lev about what happened with Carmen and Buddy.

Lev stops in his tracks. "And you went for him?"

"Well, yeah. I mean, no, I went for the bag, not Buddy."

"What did he do?"

"Got pissed off." I look around us in case Buddy appears out of nowhere. "He sure wasn't expecting someone to ruin his fun, especially not me."

As I fill Lev in on the details, his eyes get wide.

He shakes his head. "I could never jump into the middle of something like that."

"I'm still amazed *I* did."

"I'm not." Leaning into me, he says under his breath, "Just be careful when you're out there saving the day."

It's all I can do to not kiss him right on those awesome lips. But, of course, no way that's *ever* gonna happen here.

In the corner of my eye I catch Audrey walking past. Seeing Lev and me whispering so close together, she does a double take and her eyeballs practically pop out of her head.

She and I lock eyes for a split second. Then she frowns and spins around, plowing right into a guy's big chest.

"Whoa!" he says.

Oh, boy, the big chest belongs to Manuel.

Straightening her blouse, Audrey looks up. "Didn't mean to—oh." Then she sees it's him. "Watch where you're going!"

He puts up his palms. "Oh, my god, I'm *so* sorry—"

She pushes past him and moves on.

Flustered, he notices me, then looks back at her. "Really sorry. Really!"

He takes one more look at me, sees Lev, and walks away, fast.

I turn to Lev. "That was so so freakin' weird."

"That's Manuel, right?"

I nod. "Talk about worlds colliding."

"You're right, he was weirded out. But he'd better find a *different* cute guy to freak out around—you're taken." He grins, then glances up at the wall clock. "Ooh, we should get going."

I give him a little wave. "See you later."

He waves back, and we part.

I'm still pissed at Audrey, but it's *so* bizarre she doesn't know about what's up with Lev and me. I bet they'd like each other if she knew . . . Oh, screw it.

I gotta get to algebra.

Lunchtime. Going between classes has been blissfully uneventful since this morning, but at this point I'm ready for whatever.

Navigating to the cafeteria, I spot Kathleen closing her locker so I look for Lev in case he's with her, but he's not here.

As I pass, she sees me and smiles big. "Hey! I heard you guys had fun Saturday night."

Uh-oh. How much did he tell her? My expression must be saying the same thing as my brain because she blushes and says, "The bingo game sounded awesome."

"It was."

We just kinda look at each other.

I grip my backpack straps. "Maybe we should all go sometime?"

"Oh! Great idea. I'd love to."

I nod. "Well, see ya later." Then I head for the cafeteria.

Oh, man, what else did he tell her? Of course, I would've too. Guess I did talk about it to Harley, but it's kind of a one-sided conversation with a cat.

Inside the cafeteria, I go by the drama table to check on Carmen, who's already there with her friends. She tells me she got most everything back but has to redo some massive project, which majorly screwed her grade, and she's really pissed off. She's also been getting crap all day, like a few guys lunging at her in the halls and pretending to grab her backpack. So many people saw what happened this morning that she can't escape it.

I tell her I know that feeling too freakin' well and that she's not alone.

As I start to leave, she stands and gives me a hug. I awkwardly pat her back and she lets go. These drama kids are always hugging. But of course I get why she hugged me, which is kind of amazing.

I tell her to hang in there and then I move on. As I zigzag through the bustling tables, I glance back. She notices and smiles, so I smile back.

And I don't give a crap who sees.

No Audrey at our usual spot—hardly a surprise—but no Trent yet either. I brought my lunch, but he's probably stuck in the line. At least, after all that weirdness on Friday after school, I hope he comes. He was being a jerk, but so was I.

There, he is paying for his lunch. Pretty easy to spot a giant vampire. He looks over toward me and I wave. He pauses for a split second but comes over and plops down his tray.

Seeing him makes me want to blurt out everything about my date with Lev. Not here, though.

"Howdy," I say.

He slides into a chair. "'Sup?"

I unwrap my turkey and Swiss sandwich as he starts in on burrito number one.

317

He's really quiet, so we eat in silence.

Digging my fingernail into my orange, I peel back the skin and squirt juice in my eyes. "*Ow!* That sucked."

He grins and hands me a napkin. "What is it with you and your War on Food? You always lose."

I wipe my eyes and face. "Sad but true."

He unwraps burrito number two. "Hey, so I looked at your website like you said I should."

No one's paying attention to us and there's the usual clatter and chatter. "What did you think?"

He slowly shakes his head and leans in. "Dude, if 'Thug' and . . . what's your name for Buddy? 'Bootlicker'? Oh, my god. If they ever see all that stuff, you're *so* dead."

"That actually wouldn't change much since they've told me that already. Even today."

His eyebrows go up.

"Long story. But what else did you think? I, well . . . kinda posted some other comics too."

"You mean of me? So I noticed." He leans back and smiles. "Willow's pretty kick-ass, isn't he? Still not sure about my name, but I love my outfit. Wish I really owned that jacket."

My shoulders relax. "Good, you're not pissed?" I bite into a section of my orange.

"I'm not, but can't speak for *Sultry* Audrey."

"Well, who can?"

He grins. "And even if those assholes ever see it—and they *will* kill you—that stuff you drew of Thug beating Kobe . . . freakin' awesome comics."

"You really think so? Probably the hardest thing I've ever drawn."

"Epic. But I wouldn't toss around any more stuff up and down the halls. Lucky misfire, there, dude." He downs more burrito.

I roll my eyes. "No, that won't happen again."

Not the flyers and especially not the misfire.

But what *is* my plan? It hurts my brain to think about it.

And right now I have someone else on my mind.

I finish my orange and slap my hands on the table. "Ohmygod!"

He jumps. "What?"

"Sorry. It's just, holy crap, I have so much to tell you!"

"Um, okay?"

No way I'm filling him in here, though, so we clean up our stuff and make a plan to meet after school.

I gotta talk to *someone* about Lev.

When I get to chemistry we have a new project and have to pick a partner. Even though we don't sit so close, Kathleen and I glance at each other and she gives me a little grin. I shrug and smile back because, well, why shouldn't we be partners?

We huddle at a lab table by the wall, and after we've divided our tasks for the project, she grills me about LaTrina and asks if I remember her best jokes. So I do the closest impersonation I can. When I scream "Liar!" I get in trouble for disrupting class for the first time . . . *ever*. Kinda awesome.

Following my usual routes from class to class, I avoid

anyone I don't want to see and make it through the rest of the day.

When the last bell rings I zip to Lev's locker and find him waiting for me.

"Hey!" I say.

"So, Kathleen told me you guys had way too much fun in chemistry."

I give him a confused look. "Really? What did she say?"

"Well, she said you were talking about—"

"*Liar!*" Feigning shock, I slap my hands to my mouth and open my eyes wide.

He busts out laughing. "Oh, man. My face *still* hurts from when she did that."

Chrrrp chrrrp comes from his pocket. He pulls out his phone and reads a text.

"Ooh, I gotta dash to a Pep Club meeting about the Halloween Hoedown. Wait till you see what we're planning. It's going to be sooooo awesome!" He waves and practically bounces off down the hall.

Even though I'm in a bouncing mood myself, I simply walk through the halls to my locker. I spin the combination, open the door with a *click*, and—

Another folded paper lands at my feet.

I scoop it up and check around, but no one is watching.

I don't want to wait, so, steadying my hands, I unfold the first flap. What's . . . ? It's written on the back of something this time, so I flip over the page.

I freeze.

No.

No way.

It's a printout of a website home page.

Mine.

Thirty

AS TRENT AND I WALK FROM SCHOOL TO HIS HOUSE, HE BUTTONS UP his flowing black coat against the chilly wind.

But I unzip my jacket. I'm boiling hot. "How did he find it? And how the hell did he know it's *my* site?" I kick a rock and send it skittering into the street.

Trent sighs. "You don't know it's Manuel. You're just guessing."

"But who else acts that wacko around me?"

"Um, *everyone*?"

In a yard to our right, a German shepherd barks and runs up to the chain link fence between it and us. I'm tempted to bark back.

"Now you're freaking out random dogs, Adrian. Chill."

We pass the house and cross the next street.

"You're right, I guess; still could be anyone." I unfold the note and shake the paper at Trent. "This is creepy, right?"

He shrugs. "You're the one who wrote back. What'd you expect?"

"Not for it to be on a printout of Graphite's home page!" I slow my pace and read it again.

You need to *be* way more careful.
Things you don't understand.
Ok let's talk in person.
Where's a good place to meet so we
can *be* in private?

"The end of that first line, 'Things you don't understand,' that's just plain creepy. Like what? And then 'You need to be way more careful,' sounds just like you and Audrey. You sure one of you didn't write this?"

"Ha. Ha."

I refold the note and stick it in my pocket. "Well, it's not just you guys. Lev wants me to be careful too, but he sure didn't write it."

"How do you know? And what do you mean he wants you to—"

I spin to face him. "OhmygodTrent now I can tell you!"

He stops. "Ohyourgod *what?*"

"Wow, where do I start? Do you remember on Friday—was it just Friday? feels like so long ago—when I spilled hot chocolate on my pants and went to that little alcove with the drink machines? Well, the 7UP got stuck and—"

"Adrian, whoa!" He grabs my arm. "You're hurtin' my synapses. Dial it down. Take a breath."

I inhale and let it out.

He starts walking again. "Okay, so you spilled crap on your crotch, disappeared for a long time, uh-huh?"

Trying not to literally bounce alongside him, I say, "So, who should walk in but . . . ?"

He groans. "Just freakin' tell me."

"Okay, so *Lev* comes in and, fast forward . . . he kisses me!"

Pausing in midstride, he turns his head and blinks. "Hold up. He *kissed* you?"

"Yes!"

He checks all around, but no one's in the yards of the big houses surrounding us. "Go on."

So I do. And as we walk, I talk. Tell him all about Lev actually being gay—"*Amazing*, right?"—riding in Lev's car, the LGBT center, and LaTrina. Okay, I don't tell him *everything*. Some details are just for me to know. And think about. A lot.

While I've recounted the (almost) whole date, we've covered a lot of ground and are practically to his house.

Saying it all out loud is almost like reliving it. "Can you believe it? My head's still spinning."

Trent stops on his corner and turns to me. "You sure you can trust him?"

"Huh? Well, of course. The woman at the LGBT center knows him. He volunteers there. Lev's not some spy for Doug, pretending to be gay, if that's what you're worried about."

"No." He rolls his eyes. "What I mean is you hang with

this guy once and you're falling fast and hard. I know you, Adrian. You always dive into everything headfirst—"

"Actually, you're wrong. My problem is I never dive in." I stomp on a few brittle leaves by my shoe with a *crunch*. "Why can't you just be happy for me?"

He sighs. "All I'm saying is it's best to test the water before you jump."

"Trent, the water's fine. Besides, you're no dating expert."

Shoulders slumping, he starts down the sidewalk.

"Listen." I catch up to him. "It's just that someone wants to go out with me instead of beat the crap out of me. Makes me happy."

He nods. "Okay."

We stop in front of his house and I say, "You still want me to come in?"

"Of course."

In the windows, all the curtains are closed. "And you're absolutely-beyond-a-shadow-of-a-doubt *sure* your mom's not home?"

"Positive. Like I told you, she's staying at my aunt's house tonight to help cook for some big work dinner thing. I even spoke with my aunt, so I know it's true. Mom's gone for the whole night. Praise be."

I take a breath. "All right, if you're *sure*."

As we approach his front door I'm braced for his mom to leap out and wail *Satan!* at me again. But Trent gets the mail, unlocks the door, and turns off the alarm without incident.

Still, it takes all my energy to move my legs and step into the front hall. To our right, the living room is gloomy with all the curtains shut. "It's been so long since I was inside your house."

He shuts and fastens the door. "Ain't my house anymore. My room's my room, but the rest . . . Well, see for yourself." He flicks on the living room lights.

I turn around to see what he's—"Jesus!"

"Oh, you know him?"

On the wall above the fireplace, smack in the center of the room, is a giant portrait of Jesus, his face twisted in pain. It's all lit up like a billboard, with an ornate gold frame that glints in the spotlights.

Around it hang a few small family photos and what look to be some Bible verses mounted on shiny, lacquered pieces of wood. But . . . "Wow."

Trent tosses the mail on the coffee table. "Each day, I never know who's gonna judge me the most, my mom or him."

Next to the portrait is a liquor cabinet. "Christ keeps it well stocked, I see."

He grunts.

Trent crosses the room to the staircase and starts up. "C'mon."

Retreating up the stairs, I survey the room below. Those eyes seem to follow me.

I take the last steps two at a time.

Sunlight spills into the hall as Trent pushes open his bedroom door and we enter. Nice and bright in here. He shuts the door, drops his backpack, and kicks off his boots. "Make yourself at home."

He slips out of his long coat and hangs it in his closet between organized hangers of shirts and pants. Almost all black, but not one out of place. Grabbing his boots, he sets them in a gap between pairs of shoes lined in a row along the wall.

"Wow, did you get a maid?"

"No, why?" He untucks the black T-shirt he's wearing and rolls up the bottoms of his skinny gray jeans.

"Everything's so clean and neat."

"I like it that way." He lights a stick of incense, sending a sweet, spicy smoke into the air.

I shake off my jacket and lay it on the corner of the bed, which is made up with a black-and-gold brocade bedspread and black pillowcases. Tidy shelves filled with books and Rubik's Cubes and other little puzzles stand on each side of his window.

He moves to his computer and logs on. "Wanna play a game?"

His desktop image is a comic panel of Willow from my site.

"Hey, cool," I say.

He grins. "Told you I like him. Well, his outfit."

We compromise on a puzzle game and he proceeds to whup me, again and again. When I'm sick of losing, we switch to racing supercharged cars through Tokyo and I kick his ass.

After a while the sun sets, filling the room with bright orange. Then our stomachs speak up.

The house is thankfully silent and still as we head down to the kitchen, Jesus watching our every move. We make sandwiches and bring them back upstairs with plenty of chips and Dr Pepper.

He shuts his door. It's almost dark outside now, so he flicks on the overhead light and his desk lamp. Floating across his computer screen is another drawing of Willow from my site—he made it his screen saver, too. Very cool.

I smile at Trent as we sit and face each other on the bed and spread out our picnic.

Just to be sure I don't get yelled at later, I borrow his phone to call Mom and say I'm eating at Trent's.

All is okay.

With the racing game soundtrack playing on a loop in the background, we take our time eating.

"Listen," Trent says, popping a chip into his mouth, "I *am* happy for you. You know, with Lev being into you and all. It's just . . ."

"What?" I take a sip of my drink.

He leans back against the headboard. "Audrey's off doing her, well, whatever the hell she's up to, and now you're all busy with Lev. Didn't hear from anyone all weekend. Nothing."

"I thought—"

He holds up his hand. "I get it, it's just a couple days. But school sucks, this place sucks, and, well . . . it's no fun being alone in my head all the time. Trust me."

I reach behind me and hit the Mute button on his keyboard. Silence. "Maybe this thing with Lev will keep being great, or maybe it won't. But come on, I'm not going to stop being your friend. I'm here now, right?"

He grins.

"Besides," I say, "you and Lev would like each other. In fact, his friend Kathleen wants to go with us to Teen Drag Queen Bingo. We could all go together."

His eyebrows shoot up. "I'm guessing that's more *your* thing than mine."

I laugh. "You don't *have* to be gay to go. It's not, like, a requirement."

A dull thump comes from outside in the hall.

Trent spins his head toward the closed door, then unfolds his legs and stands. Stepping over to the door, he quietly turns the tab in the knob, locking it.

I spring up.

Eyes wide, he listens at the door. Everything is silent. He glances at me, then at the knob. "Mom?"

Thirty-one

BAM! THE DOOR BUMPS.

He jumps back. My body jolts.

The knob jiggles.

He glares at the floor and whispers, "My aunt promised. Mom must have pissed her off or showed up drunk."

BAM! BAM! BAM! She pounds so hard the hinges squeak.

"I hear what you're saying in there!" she shrieks from the other side. "I know who it is. I know what he's trying to do."

Trent grits his teeth. "Mom!"

I scan the room, searching for—what?

"I won't allow it, Trenton! Not. In. My. HOUSE!"

He puts his hands on his head. "Mom. Stop it."

I stare at him. "What's happening?"

"Open this door! OPEN THIS DOOR!!!"

POP! POP! She kicks it, over and over.

Trent slams his fist and pounds back. *BAM!* "Stop it! This is *my* room! *Leave me the hell alone!"*

SMACK! He slaps it hard with his open palm, his eyes wide, chest heaving.

I look around. There's nowhere to go.

I glue my eyes on Trent. He scowls at the door.

It gets quiet.

"Trenton, honey," she says in a slurred voice. "God will forgive you, sweetie. He will. He does. Just don't listen to the lies. He's tryin' to turn you into one of *them.* Get that, that . . . get it out of here. You know how . . . how . . ."

Get *it* out of here? Me?

"Mom. You're drunk."

"Nooooo, not, that's not—"

"*Go to bed!"* he hollers.

Her voice is low, muffled. "My boy. My little boy."

Then nothing.

I whisper, "What do we do?"

Trent doesn't look me in the eye. "I'm sorry, you should go. I can handle her."

"No way. I'm not leaving you alone with—"

"It's not the first time she's been this drunk. Get your bag. It'll only get worse if you don't."

Is this for real?

I clench my jaw, then pull on my shoes and grab my back-pack.

Trent exhales.

His manner shifts. He stands tall.

"Mom, we need to talk." His voice is deeper. He turns the knob and eases open the door.

She's right there, blinking in the dark hallway. Her floral blouse is half untucked from her skirt. She looks him up and down, then scowls.

"This is *my* house," she hisses.

He inhales deeply. "Mom, breeeathe."

She squints, eyes darting around. Finding me, she locks her glazed eyes on me and points at my face. "Get that *homosexual* out of here."

I take a step toward them. *"What—"*

Trent throws his hand out to the side and shoots me a warning look. I stop.

"Mom, you're tired. You know how you get." He takes hold of her shoulders, like he's soothing a child. "Time for bed."

"God *hates* fags, Trenton." She moans. *"Why?* Why are you doing this to me?"

Huh? Why is *he* doing this to *you?*

He grips her upper arms. "Okay, you *really* need to calm down. All right?" He gently turns her around and into the hall. "Shhhhhh. Time to sleep, now. You're tired, right?"

She jerks her head in a nod, then whines, "My boy." She starts to cry.

Holding her up, he guides her down the hall toward her room.

I follow, but he turns his head to me and, his eyes begging, he mouths, *GO!*

I nod and dash down the stairs. The living room is dark now with the lights off. 7:42 PM glows red from the cable box across the room. It's so early.

I barely make out those portrait eyes, watching me.

I slip out the front door and gulp the night air. I'm panting.

Making it to the sidewalk, I turn and glare up at her second-floor window. There's a dim light behind the curtain.

She calls herself a *mother*? What kind of mother does this?

My fingernails dig into my palms, so I unclench my fists and stretch my fingers. Pulling my shoulders down and back, I slow my breath.

I wait. As I study the crisscross patterns of tree shadows cast by the streetlamp onto the sidewalk, I try to sort out the nightmare I just witnessed.

The air is moist and the wind is gone.

My ears almost buzz with the silence of the street, but her shrieking still bounces around in my skull.

After a couple minutes, the light goes off in the window. Then Trent appears in his and notices me down here. I hold up my palm in a shaky wave.

He puts his face in his hands, then looks up and gestures for me to go.

I turn and, with one last wave, move down the block. Hopefully she's passed out and he can get some peace.

Until tomorrow, or the next day, and the next . . .

No wonder he's counting down every moment until he graduates and is free.

My limbs are so jittery I pick up my pace and run. Except

for my shoes slapping the pavement and a few passing cars or voices from backyards here and there, it's quiet as I race home.

Those words. She said those exact words that keep getting hurled at me. *God hates fags.*

I don't know who the hell your God is. Not that portrait in your living room, that's for sure. No matter who you worship, how would you know what he thinks?

How would Doug know? Or anyone?

Blaming some deity for your own hate seems pretty messed up to me.

After a few blocks, my run turns into a stride, then into a regular walk. I'm still sweaty but breathing normally now.

God hates fags.

Fag. What a strange word. As if those three letters could contain the meaning of *me*.

Of Kobe . . . or Lev . . .

Of anyone.

Fag. I don't care who flings it at me.

I will not be contained.

No more screwing with *this* fag.

As I arrive at my block, I make out the glowing windows of my house. It's never looked so inviting.

I enter my brightly lit living room and let out a long breath.

Mom and Dad are at the table eating pasta and veggies. Not even taking off my backpack, I give them each a big hug, squeezing hard. They hug me back but look at me funny.

"Changed my mind about dinner at Trent's," I say. "I'll wash up and be right back."

Splashing water on my face and changing shirts helps, and cuddling Harley in my room for a minute calms me down even more. As I glance over at my drawing pencils, my fingers itch to dive in, but pasta sure sounds good right now.

At the dinner table I deflect my parents' questions about "Is everything okay?" I just tell them Trent forgot he had plans, and besides, I have a lot of homework.

I never think about that little gold cross Mom always wears around her neck. But I glance at it now. I wonder what *her* God would think of me.

Dad asks how French is going and says he thought my "new friend" was so polite. I nod and say, "He's cool to study with."

Well, and other things.

Dinner over, I scoop up Harley from the living room couch, bring her to my room, and shut the door.

I stare at the doorknob. Can't imagine never knowing if you're safe in your own damn room.

I message Trent, asking if he's okay.

His reply pops up right away: Yeah, she's out cold. Messed up, right? I'm OK. Sorry you had to see that.

I respond: Hang in there, Willow. See you tomorrow and we'll plan something FUN for this weekend. For real.

I stand and stretch tall, every muscle, and feel my body again.

Hold on a minute. I sit down again and check, make sure I didn't miss anything from Kobe. No, nothing. So I write a quick message and ask what's up. Does he want another visit? I hit Send and log out.

Hope he's not still screwing with those pills.

I put on the *Hobbit* soundtrack. Changing into comfy clothes, I find that note in my pocket, written on the back of Graphite's home page.

> You need to be way more careful.
> Things you don't understand.
> Ok let's talk in person.
> Where's a good place to meet so we can be in private?

From my drawer, I pull out the first two locker notes and reread them all. I still can't get a sense if this guy is for real or screwing with me. Either way, I'm sick of playing this game. It's time to take control.

I sit at my drawing table and pull out a blank piece of paper.

He wants to meet in person? Fine. Somewhere at school but hidden. Somewhere quiet to talk but easy to escape from . . . just in case.

Got it.

In the same scrawl I wrote my other note in, I scribble:

> OK
> Meet me before school Wednesday morning at 7:30 am in the auditorium balcony. You can get in from the hall upstairs. I'll be there.

I'll leave this note tomorrow. No matter who it is, I need to discover how they found my website.

If it is someone messing with me, either they won't show up or I'll finally find out who it is.

But if it's Manuel or someone who really does care, maybe I can help.

This last note says, *Things you don't understand.*

Time to get enlightened.

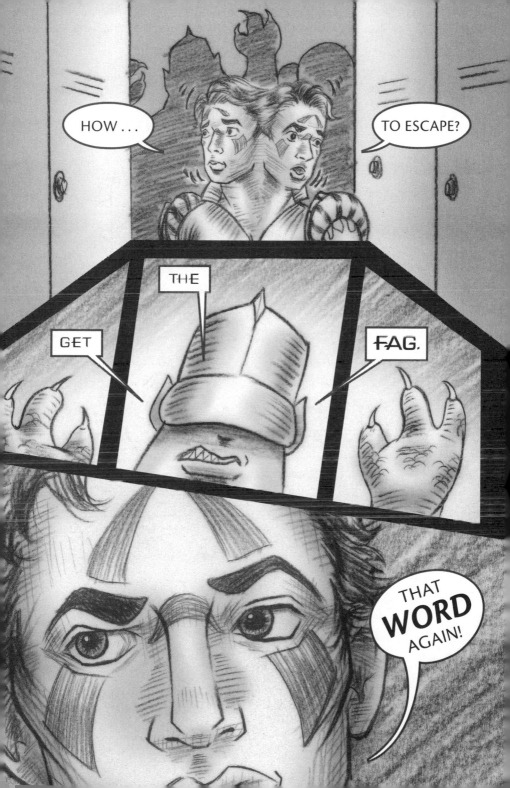

AHA! AN OPENING IN THE FENCE! IF I CAN JUST GET TO THAT TREE.
WAIT! THAT'S NO TREE . . .

IT'S ONE OF *THEM.* GET THAT, THAT . . . **GET *IT!***
"IT"? I'M NO **"IT"**! THE MONSTERS KEEP COMING AND COMING!

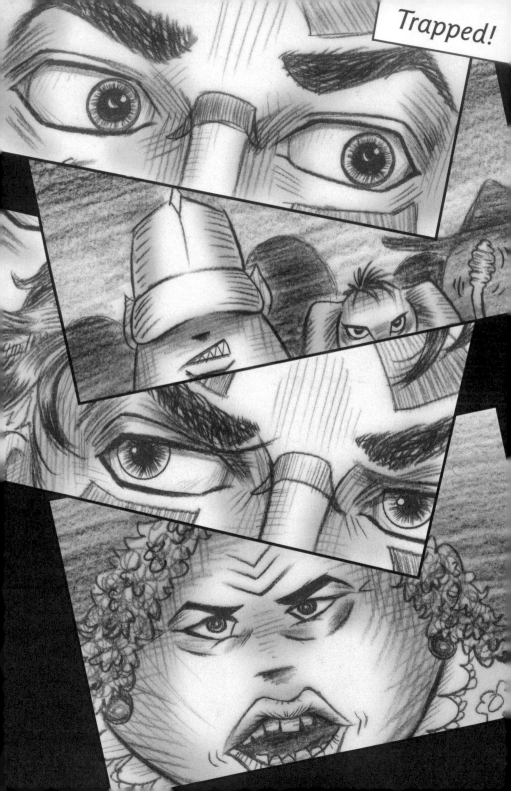

Thirty-two

I SWEAR, IF I'M EVER A SPY OR A SECRET AGENT I'LL NEVER CHOOSE a Dumpster for passing messages. So amateur and SO repulsive. What combination of cafeteria leftovers makes this stench? Actually, I don't want to know. And pulling my shirt collar up over my nose doesn't block out a thing.

Gross!

Get to school early: check.

Slip behind this hideous Dumpster unseen: check.

Shove the wadded-up note into the brick hole: check.

Slip out and away free as a bird: fail.

Why did every car known to man decide to arrive *right now*? It's like some never-ending stream of people flowing by right *here*.

Come on, come on. Okay, is it letting up? I peer around—good. Just these two girls in sight, aaaand . . . there they go.

Holding my breath, I step—NO! Doug's freakin' pickup zooms into the lot.

Dammit!

No way I'm getting trapped. Go, Adrian. Go!

I don't want to run, so I casually zip out and around the little cafeteria steps.

Doug pulls into his space just a few feet behind me. I move toward the main entrance and glance back—he's opened his door and stares right at me.

Crap.

I keep going.

Okay. Maybe he didn't see where I came from but only sees me walking. Act casual!

I turn the corner, out of his sight.

After a beat, I peek back around the corner. Still in the driver's seat with the door open and one foot out, he's turned away, grabbing something inside the truck.

The other seat is empty. No Buddy this morning.

Keeping my eyes glued on Doug, I dash over to a bunch of trees, then casually loop back into the parking lot. Ducking between parked cars, I block myself from his view a couple rows behind him.

He steps out of the truck, slinging his duffel bag over his shoulder. First staring at the corner where I turned, he then looks all around.

More people are arriving, but he just glances at them. He doesn't see me.

Shutting his door and locking it, he scans around again.

No! No no no! He steps next to the Dumpster and checks it out.

Oh, my god. He saw. He completely saw me come out from back there.

Is he—damn! He's going behind the Dumpster.

People walk past me, so I open my backpack and pretend to search for something. But I keep watching the Dumpster from the corner of my eye.

Doug comes out. Adjusting his cap, he pulls it down more over his eyes.

He leans against his pickup. What's he doing? Just hanging there. Now he . . .

I freeze.

No. This is not happening. This cannot be happening.

In his hand is my note. He opens it, flattens it out. Reads it.

Shit.

My insides flip.

Nothing I can do. Nothing.

He's reading it and knows it was me.

One last look around and he crumples it up. He shoves it in his pocket and takes off toward the entrance, disappearing around the corner.

I grip my bag to my chest. What do I do?

First bell rings. Taking slow steps, I head in, putting distance between us.

Think! What did I say in that note? Only a time and place to meet. Nothing more. No names. And it's not my real handwriting in case he shows it to anyone. That's good.

I go into the building. No sign of him. Lockers clang and laughter buzzes around me, but it's like I'm moving through water. Everything seems blurred, muffled, slow.

Focus, Adrian.

Maybe it's not so bad. So he knows I left a note for someone to meet me before school tomorrow morning. No big deal, right? I just don't show up and that's that.

I simply don't show up.

I take a deep breath and step into French. Lev's wearing a bright-green shirt, like a little oasis in the desert. My oasis. One smile from him helps bring me back to earth.

But then he tells me he can't get together after school until Thursday, he's so booked with club meetings and stuff. I say it's okay, even though it's not.

What about the Adrian Club?

I slump in my seat and get set for class.

At least getting through first period settles my brain.

All morning, going from class to class, I turn it over in my head. Maybe Doug just happened to see me and discovered that little white paper in the wall. Or—oh, god—maybe *he's* been writing the notes all along and it *is* a trap.

If so, he wrote them to lure me in, like bait.

And I took it.

But that doesn't make sense—that's too calculated for a thug like him. He must've just seen me there and found my note.

Maybe?

At lunch with Trent, I almost let it slip about Doug, but

I don't need a lecture. Besides, Trent doesn't need to hear about *my* problems today.

Boy, he looks wiped. He doesn't want to talk about last night, none of it. And I don't want to make him feel worse by telling him what I think of his mother. So I just say, "Let me know what you want to do this weekend. Anything you want. And you should stay over at my house." I dramatically look over each shoulder, then whisper, "I've got a stash of peanut butter peppermint pretzel ice cream. We'll whoop it up!"

He grins. "Yeah, that's pretty wild, there. Is it legal?"

"It's okay, my parents are my suppliers."

"In that case, how can I refuse?"

Lunch ends and we move on.

Like a little gerbil, I get back on the treadmill of school and spin through class after class.

My head keeps spinning too. There's got to be a way to use Doug finding the note to *my* advantage, whether he found it by chance or even whether it was a trap all along.

Wait a minute . . . if it was a trap . . .

My stomach drops.

I got it.

At seven thirty tomorrow morning, I'm showing up. And if Doug does too, I'll be ready.

Whether he wrote the notes or not doesn't matter. He'll walk right into *my* trap.

Time to draw the line.

Thirty-three

THE AUDITORIUM BALCONY IS PERFECT, AS IF I CHOSE THIS SETTING for confronting Doug all along: quiet, deserted, more than one exit, and right in the middle of the school.

I check my watch. 7:12 a.m. I still have eighteen minutes.

Last night I stayed up late forming this plan. Just like I would a work of art, I sketched it out, revised, and refined.

And now I'm ready—assuming he shows.

I arrived about twenty minutes ago and found the light switches. Way down below, beyond the balcony railing, the main auditorium is pitch-black and empty. But up here in the balcony I've dimmed the lights to the perfect glow. I need to keep it somewhat dark but still be able to see everything clearly.

I've checked out all the exits up here too. I can easily escape, assuming I can make it to one of them. If not, there's a fire alarm at the top of each of the two aisles. At least I'd get someone's attention.

Oh, my god.

What the hell am I thinking?

No. No freaking out. I *am* doing this.

And not just for me.

I shake out my hands. Focus. If I falter, I just need to picture *God Hates Fags* scrawled across my locker . . . or remember Kobe's face.

It calms me already, but also pisses me off.

Okay, time for one last check of the main part of my plan.

I scoot across this top row of seats to the back corner where I hid out last week, cowering.

On a little tripod covered in dull black tape, I've set up my old video camera and arranged the lens to just peek over the top of the back corner seat. It'll catch every sound, every image. Doug won't see it in the dark, but it will sure see him.

McConnell thinks there aren't any security cameras inside the school? There's one now.

And it's about to record Doug's confession.

I return to my position. These two aisle archways have deep-purple velvet curtains hanging on each side, meant for pure decoration. In this dim light you wouldn't notice if one was slightly fuller than the other. With me hiding behind it.

7:17. Still have—

Wait, what's that?

I slip into place behind one of the little curtains and the echo of the auditorium disappears. Silent and so dark. I pull back the curtain edge just enough to see down the little entry hall. A sliver of bright fluorescent light glows from the end of the hallway. Someone's opened the door, peers in.

He showed up.

That's Doug's silhouette for sure, with his duffel bag slung over his shoulder and that damn cap on his head.

I grip the curtain tight to keep my hand from shaking.

He glances behind, then comes through the door. Alone. He silently closes it, which shuts out the light.

I hold my breath.

He just hangs there.

Did he think he'd come early and get here before me?

He eases in my direction but stops at the first archway.

"Hello?" His whisper is loud.

He turns, goes down the aisle. His phone lights up, casting shadows on his face like a freak show mask. Using it as a flashlight, he holds out his phone and slowly sweeps its light over the rows of seats.

I ease the curtain edge against the wall, leaving just a tiny gap to see out. I stand perfectly still.

Oh, no, please don't—good. He looked right at the row with my camera but didn't see it.

I let out a silent breath.

He walks down the aisle, aiming his light all around. Stopping at the bottom row, he then comes across to my aisle. Before clicking off his phone, he takes one last survey.

Wiping his forehead, he sighs and leans back against the railing.

If he were to give the all clear to someone he'd do it now, wouldn't he? Let that prick Buddy know it's safe to sneak in and hide before I got here?

But Doug doesn't move.

He just waits.

We wait.

I inhale deeply. It's time. I'm going to get that confession, make him admit that beating Kobe wasn't self-defense, but a crime.

I sharpen my mind with Jedi focus, then pull back the curtain from my hiding spot at the top of the aisle. Stepping out, I stare down at him. "Why are you here?" My voice echoes.

He grips the railing. "Shit! Where'd you come from?"

"I said, why are you here?"

"Who's with you?"

I clear my throat. "I'm alone."

"You lying?"

"No. What about you?"

He lets go of the railing and straightens up. "Just me."

"So why—"

"How the fuck did you get in my truck?"

I steady my voice. "I have a better question, Doug. Why did you beat the crap out of Kobe? Because he's gay? You know what he did to *you*, right? NOTHING."

"Wha—what is this?"

I move a bit closer down the aisle so we're both in the camera's view. "Is that your plan for me now? Beat the crap out of another fag? Writing those notes to trap me?"

"I didn't write them to trap you!"

I stop. Oh, my god. He *did* write the notes.

"Then . . ." My voice catches. "Then why?"

He looks down. "Shit." He just stares at the floor.

I freeze. "What is it?"

"I shouldn't be here." Glancing at me, he moves sideways across the front row. His duffel bag thumps against the armrests as he goes.

I hold up my hand. "Wait. I'm not done. Wait!"

Now in the other aisle, he looks at me across the middle section of seats.

"Okay," I say, "I'll tell you how I got in your truck if you tell me why you wrote those notes."

He checks around us and says in a low voice, "You're talkin' too loud."

I nod.

Pushing up the sleeves of his varsity jacket, he puts his hands on his hips. Then he crosses his arms. "Shit."

"You already said that."

He shoots me a look. "So . . . how is he?"

"Who, Kobe? What, suddenly you care?"

Staring at the floor, he says, "How bad is it? Like, is he . . . anything permanent?"

"Permanent?" I glare. "You mean physically, emotionally, or mentally? I'm guessing all of the above. Happy?"

He sighs. "Look, this ain't easy for me."

"Easy for *you*?"

He stays in his aisle but leans against a seat back. It squeaks.

"I never . . . God. Guys get hurt in practice, but I've never hurt anyone like *that*. Never beat up a guy before. You gotta understand."

What? "All I *gotta* understand is—"

"Just tell me. Is he gonna be okay?" He shifts his duffel bag to the other shoulder.

"Of course not."

He closes his eyes, rubs his forehead. "So is he planning to do anything? I mean, like, you know—cause trouble?"

"What the hell is wrong with you?" I yell.

He points right at me. "I'm not a dumb-ass *Thug*, like in your stupid comic."

"Yes, you are. And my comics aren't stu—hold up. How *did* you find my website?"

He turns his head, stares out at the auditorium darkness. Then back at me. "Fine." Grips his bag strap tight. "I know you saw my sketchbook, since you broke into my truck."

"Hey, I—" Crap. Guess technically I did break in. I sigh. "Go on."

"Well, now you know, I like drawing comic stuff."

"So?"

"*You* may think it's no big fuckin' deal. But the one time the guys caught me drawing in my sketchbook . . . well, they still give me shit for that."

"Why?"

He shakes his head. "Wow, you really are clueless, aren't you?"

About the arcane ways of jocks? Yes, thank Obi-Wan. "So, about my website?"

"Dude, you always drew crazy shit in middle school, even back in elementary school. Fancy weird superhero shit. But you don't suck at it."

"Um, thanks?"

"I look at comic stuff online, and someone's page linked to your site. It was so obviously yours, looked just like what you always drew, so I kept checkin' back. Then you wrote you were in high school, so I knew for sure—"

"You read my comments?"

"Well, yeah." He tugs at the brim of his cap. "I'm, uh, well, I'm BigGreenBro."

I stare at him across the whole section of seats between us. He's lying. "You can't be. That guy likes my art and writes intelligent comments."

"You asshole. I'm not some dipshit moron, just 'cause I look like—*ugh!*" He punches at a seat with a *thunk*.

I jump but stand steady, heart pounding. "Wait. If it really is you, then what does BigGreenBro mean?"

He crosses his arms. "Really? Who's the moron now? You saw what I draw, think about it."

But his sketchbook was filled with . . . oh. I grip the back of a seat, fight the sensation of the floor tilting sideways. He's seen all the art I've posted. Holy crap, I've been writing back and forth with him all this time. Talking about art—with *Doug?*

Of course. Big green bro. He's obsessed with . . . "You're the Hulk."

"Guess you're not as dumb as *you* look, either." He smirks.

"But I'm *not* the Hulk. That side's the enemy. I'm not that guy."

"Well, you may not literally be green—"

"Screw you! So I'm a huge guy? So I love football? I'm damn good at it. But I'm no . . ." He drops his bag in a seat. "Shit."

Not taking my eyes off him, I lean against an armrest. This is too much.

Doug is BigGreenBro?

I shake my head. "I don't understand."

"I'm not some stereotype dumb jock bruiser. The tough guy, the bully . . . the *thug*, like you and everyone else thinks." He glares. "That's not *ME!*" He thumps his chest.

Even with this whole section of seats dividing us, I step farther back in my aisle.

"How can you say that?" My voice fills the empty auditorium. "You keep harassing me—"

"You're the one harassing *me* with that stupid 'We're watching you' crap you put all over."

"That's not harassment. That's justice. Besides, you were 'watching me' me first, every freakin' day. You wrote 'God Hates Fags' on my locker, remember?"

"Screw you! I've been protecting you, asshole."

Huh? "What the hell are you talking about? Protecting me?"

"Yes, idiot. You think *I* did that on your locker? No, I covered it up. Buddy wrote it. If it weren't for me, he'd have already kicked your ass. I saved you in that bathroom, too. You're lucky."

What? That can't be right. I search my memory. My head spins.

"Why?" I say. "Why would you protect *me?*"

"Well, you're an okay guy, even if you are a homo. And after what happened to your friend . . . if you got beat up, everyone would think *I* did it."

Oh. My. God.

His cap casts a dark shadow on his face. "Look, I'm in deep shit."

"Oh, really?" I turn and make sure the camera sees us both. Speaking clearly, I say, "You got your father to cover it all up. Admit it, you didn't beat Kobe in 'self-defense.'"

"You don't get it!" He glares at me. "Everyone rides my ass, expectin' me to be all this macho shit. Pushing, pushing. Coach, the team, frickin' Buddy. My *dad.*" He spits out the word. "To him, my drawin' and cookin' is for pussies and soooo freakin' gay." He points at my face. "And I ain't no homo."

"That's a relief. Wouldn't want *you* on my team."

He grunts. "And I ain't no thug."

"But you are, *asshole,*" I say. "You're the one who said 'God hates fags' when you smashed his skull. *You* put him in the hospital."

Pressing hard with his hands, he wipes sweat from his forehead and rubs it on his jeans.

We stare at each other.

"Look, I—" His words bounce around the balcony. He grimaces. Checking all around, he edges sideways across the row of seats toward me.

I back up the aisle. But he stops about ten seats away, in the middle of the row.

He speaks low. "I was drunk. And with everyone ridin' my ass, twenty-four seven . . . all those guys screamin' at me. I lost it."

"That's no excuse!" I hurl my words.

He balls his hands into tight fists and closes his eyes. "You don't *get it!*" He punches a seat. Then pushes into my aisle.

I hop backward, ready to run.

He looks at the ground. "SHIT!"

BAM! With his boot heel, he kicks the side of a seat.

His face contorts like it did at Boo.

I back away, quick. Putting distance between him and me, I eye the archway. It's not too far.

He kicks the seat again, hard. "This is such fucking"— *bash!*—"SHIT!" *BASH!*

He glares at me.

I've got to get out of here. I twist around fast.

Slip. Fall.

AHH! My face hits an armrest.

Oh, god! My nose!

I'm on the floor. Colors swirl in my eyes, in my head. I taste blood.

Doug steps over, looms above me. "What did you *do?*"

I push up, crawl up the aisle. "Don't touch me!"

"I didn't touch you!"

I try to stand. Ow! My nose throbs, blood dripping down.

Sitting back against the side of a seat, I squeeze my nose tight.

"Just keep away!" It comes out sounding like a Munchkin.

"Don't move." He stands over me. "I mean it, *don't move.*"

I gotta breathe—can't faint.

He steps away, grabs his duffel bag, and hauls it over to me. Mumbles, "Crap!" Then he unzips the bag.

What's he doing? I glance back at one of the fire alarms. I could reach it.

He squats down next to me with gray fabric in his hand. "Here, hold this to your nose. Squeeze. You hit the armrest pretty bad."

I blink. "What is it?"

"Just a jersey."

"Is it clean?"

He grunts. "Shit, you really are gay."

I grab it. *"Not funny."*

I gently let go of my nose. It's still bleeding but doesn't feel broken.

Press the shirt to my face. Ugh! It's sweaty. *So* gross.

He points down at me. "I did *not* do this. I didn't touch you."

He turns his back and steps away, then grunts and faces the row across from me.

Bash! He kicks a seat.

I push up, get up. My head is pounding.

Scrambling away across a row of seats, I cling to the armrests. My nose throbs.

In the aisle, he slumps down cross-legged and takes off his cap, burying his face in his hands.

I keep moving away and get to the opposite aisle, putting the center section between us.

What the hell is wrong with this freak?

He lifts his face; it's deep red. "What do I do?"

"What do *you* do?" My voice is muffled in the fabric.

I pull the shirt from my nose; it's soaked with blood. I sit on an armrest and hold my nose again.

He grits his teeth. "This is screwed up. So screwed up. I'm in such major shit."

Oh, my god. This is *insane.*

He sits there on the floor, panting, hunched over, staring at the carpet.

Keeping my eyes on him, I take deep breaths. I steady my pulse, clear my head.

I picture Audrey. Trent. Lev. Kobe. Even LaTrina.

Graphite.

In my mind, I populate this place with everyone I can so they're standing next to me.

I'm not alone.

My shoulders relax a bit, my eyes focus.

Doug just sits there.

My nose is bleeding less now, so I pull away his disgusting shirt.

"Okay." I break the silence. "You want to know what to do? How not to be a thug? I'll tell you. Number one, you call off Buddy. You both leave me alone, leave all my friends alone. Number two—"

"What the—"

"I'm not done!" I stand. "Number two, you fess up about Kobe. It wasn't 'self-defense.'"

He whips his cap back on his head and pushes himself up. "You don't get it."

"No, I get it. I *really* get it."

He glares at me. "You don't have a damn clue." Stepping to the side, he grabs his bag from the floor. Then heads up his aisle.

"I'm gonna keep going, Doug," I say. "I'm gonna keep being me. I have nothing left to prove. But you do. Can you *prove* you're not Thug?"

"Toss me my jersey."

Does he think it could be evidence? Well, I don't need it. I'll have more documentation of all of this than just a bloody shirt.

I throw it to him. He lets it hit the floor. Then, avoiding the bloody part, he picks it up and drops it in his bag.

He jabs his finger in my direction. "This never happened. You understand? I was never here." Then he starts up the aisle.

"They found them in his hand."

He scrunches his face. "Huh?"

"Your keys," I say. "Kobe must have grabbed hold of them. The paramedics pried them from his hand after you beat him unconscious."

He stops, stares at me.

My chest heaves. "You told me why you wrote the notes, so I'm telling you how I got in your truck. Kobe gave me your keys. I went to see him. Trust me, he's in *way* deeper shit than you."

One last glare and he strides through the archway, down the little hall. In a moment there's a muffled *click* from the door.

I dash up the aisle and check. Hall's empty. He's gone.

"Holy *shit!*" I yell into the empty space.

I touch my nose. Even though it stopped bleeding, it really hurts.

Steadying myself, I make it over to the camera. How long have I been in here? Did it shut off?

Shaking, I look in the viewfinder. Still recording.

I hit Stop and quickly rewind to see if—yes, I got everything.

Everything.

Thirty-four

I GRAB THE CAMERA AND COLLAPSE THE PORTABLE TRIPOD, QUICK.
It takes some effort with my shaky hands, but I'm just able to
squeeze everything into my huge backpack and zip it shut. I
can't leave any evidence of this, this . . . What the hell *was* this?

Checking my watch, I see it's almost time for the first bell.

I push open the balcony door and peer out into the hallway. The white fluorescent light practically blinds me.

There's no sign of Doug. I slip out and hustle down the
hall. People stare and gasp at my bloody nose and shirt.

I dash to the bathroom, the same one where Doug says he
"protected" me from Buddy.

A guy I don't know does a double take and almost jumps
away from me. "Whoa, man! You okay?"

Just a couple guys are in here, but they're not bubbas. I
ignore them and check in the mirror—ah! I look as scary and

banged up as I feel, nose all bloody and swollen. Kobe's face flashes in my mind. But I'm not as bad as him, not even close.

Still. This is SO screwed up!

Ow! I can't press too hard. Wet paper towels at least get the blood off my face. I swirl water around my mouth and spit it out to get rid of the metal taste.

As I clean up I keep checking behind me in the mirror. A few guys come in and out, but no one I know. I avoid their questions and mumble that I'm fine.

My face is clean now, but my nose is puffy and . . . damn! Bruises spread like ink through the skin under my eyes.

The throbbing in my head is almost unbearable.

In a stall, I gently take off my T-shirt, then put it on backward, the clean side now in front. I'll just have to wear my jacket all day to cover the rest, so I put that on too.

Back in the hall, I stare at the ground and slip past the comments that come at me.

That was freakin' *crazy*! Doug beat up Kobe because of what . . . peer pressure? Because his dad thinks he's not man enough?

And what'll he do now that he's told *me* all about it? Will he regret it and hate himself even more so he'll come after me for real?

And he can pull whatever he wants. No matter who he is inside or out, he's still king of football and his dad's still a cop.

What have I got? Art?

The camera and folded tripod weigh down my backpack, making my clenched shoulder blades ache even more. Guess

I *do* have something more than just my art. It's not the confession I expected, but a confession nonetheless.

I go straight to the nurse's office and get there just as the first bell rings. Maybe she can make this bruise less obvious? Stop the pain and swelling? Stop people from asking so many questions?

It's not lying when I simply tell the nurse, "I slipped and hit my nose. Stupid accident."

She sits me down and checks me out. "Pretty banged up but not broken."

Thank Obi-Wan.

After I assure her yes, everything's all right at home and no, I didn't pass out or have a concussion, she has me lie back and hands me an ice pack to hold over my nose.

Ahh. It's so cold it almost burns.

I close my eyes and replay what happened in my mind. I've captured everything on video, but what the hell do I do with it?

My head hurts, my brain hurts—this is all too much.

Okay, focus on the cold ice pack, the freezing cold.

After a while the swelling goes down some. The bruises are still there, but at least I'm not puffy and as scary-looking. My headache is better too.

The nurse releases me with a note. The halls are empty, but I keep an eye out for anyone, anything as I head to class. As soon as I step through the doorway, Madame Pauline stops and gasps. She questions me, but I give her the note and explain all's good, I just fell. So embarrassing, right? Then I settle in and attempt a smile at Lev, but he looks freaked. I mumble, "I'll explain after class."

As Madame Pauline resumes, I pretend to hear what's said but don't listen.

As I pull out my notebook, my eyes land on the camera buried deep in my bag. I could show the video to McConnell, wipe that smug smile off his face and open his eyes. "Boys will be boys," my freakin' ass.

Or I could post it, send it into the world and show who Doug *really* is and what he truly did to Kobe. It'd be like unmasking him, showing how he feels about his dad, how he feels about everyone's expectations, showing him losing control again and again. He always has his impenetrable mask so firmly in place—I doubt many have ever glimpsed what's behind it. It'd be so easy to edit the video to hide my identity, blur my face, distort my voice, but keep Doug and his voice crystal clear.

My stomach drops.

Doug would kill me. He would flat-out kill me.

No. I've gotta keep this secret, from *everyone*. It can't slip out.

Right?

The bell rings, and as we step into the hall, Lev pulls me aside. "What happened to you?"

I shrug. "No biggie. Just slipped in the hall and got a little bloody nose."

"Little bloody nose? You've got black eyes!" Scrunching his forehead, he lowers his voice and says, "Was it Buddy?"

"Buddy?" My pulse speeds up.

"Well, after what happened yesterday with him and you before school . . ."

"Oh. No, haven't seen him." My voice is nasal. "Told you, I fell."

"Did you trip on something?"

I grip my backpack straps. "I'll tell you later—so embarrassing. I'd rather not focus any more on how I got this ugly face."

Softly, he says, "There's no way you could ever be ugly. It just makes you look *tough*." He grins.

"*Tough?*" I grunt. "Don't know about that."

He pulls his hair back behind his ears. "I should go. Be careful!" He gives me a questioning look, and we head our separate ways to second period.

I *hate* lying to him, but I gotta figure this out.

All I do through the next few classes is recycle the same crap in my head, over and over. I dash between periods as fast as I can, then sit in class trying not to go insane.

But nothing makes sense.

At last it's lunchtime. As I walk to the cafeteria, I keep my head down but stay on alert. I turn a corner and—coming this way, Audrey.

I spin around and walk in the other direction.

But then I slow down. Should I tell *her*?

No. Remember, I tell no one.

But I turn back around and go right up to Audrey anyway. After everything I've been through this morning, being grilled by her is *way* better than no Audrey in my life at all.

I wave.

She spots me and puts her hand to her chest. "Oh, Lord!"

"Uh, hi." I turn my face away.

Mouth hanging open, she looks me up and down. Taking my arm, she pulls me over to the wall.

"What *happened* to you?" Her expression is so intense, so worried.

My face heats up, dull throb around my nose. I glance at her but can't look in her eyes. "Nothing to make a big deal over. Just a little accident."

She arches an eyebrow. "Accident?"

"Look, I can't go into it now."

"Uh-huh?"

I check over my shoulder. "Really."

"Adrian, this is serious. If someone did this to you, then you have to go to the office, tell the principal. You can't just . . ." She tilts her head. "Why are you grinning all of a sudden?"

"I miss you." Just comes out.

She blinks, puts her hands on her hips. "Then why've you been so wacko?"

I put my hands on *my* hips. "I'm not the only one."

She flashes me the Audrey Eye. But I wrap my arms around her and squeeze, resting my chin on her shoulder.

She hugs me back and I let go.

Lamely attempting to stifle a smile, she readjusts her light-green blouse. "You're lucky you didn't wrinkle this. Imported silk."

That makes me laugh.

"So," I say, "coming to lunch?"

"*Oh*, yes. You've got lots of explaining to do!" She hoists her purse over her arm and we make our way to the cafeteria.

Entering, I take a deep, deep breath. Safe zone—I lower my shields. Doug and Buddy and their friends don't have this lunch, and I've got Trent and maybe even a table of drama kids on my side. And, it seems, Audrey again.

It takes a few minutes for Trent's eyes to reenter his head after seeing me and Audrey come in together, especially with me looking, well, like a raccoon. I'm much better than this morning but still "tough."

I give Trent my usual "I fell but can't go into it now" talk, but he's kinda freaked.

And he looks wiped out. I'm dying to ask if his mom lost it again last night, but not with Audrey here.

Everyone's got so many screwed-up secrets.

Since I brought my lunch, I can stay here and face the wall to avoid as much notice as possible. With Audrey chatting away, she and Trent head to the cafeteria line.

Once I pull out my lunch bag, I place my backpack on the floor and slip my legs through the straps. I'm never going to let this camera out of my sight.

Damn! I hate hiding anything from them, but this secret is too toxic.

My fingers itch for a pencil. I need Graphite.

Trent and Audrey return. Dropping her tray on the table in front of me with a *smack!*, Audrey settles in her chair and says, "Ooooookay, now. Catch me up." She points to my face. "And start with this."

Instead, I start with "Actually, there's something you need to know first."

I look at Trent and lower my voice so only they can hear. "She doesn't know about Lev and Teen Drag Queen Bingo."

Her eyes pop wide open. "Say what?"

I knew that would change the subject. And it's so good to tell her at last.

Making sure no one overhears, I take my time detailing everything from the start. Except for the parts I didn't share with Trent, either, of course. Those are *healthy* secrets, between Lev and me.

The bell rings and I haven't even finished recounting the whole date.

Trent downs the rest of his iced tea and gathers his trash. "I didn't know about the little kid giving you a 'unigiraffe' painting. This I gotta see."

"It's cute," I say.

Audrey stares at me and shakes her head. "All this happened in a week? Well, seems I gotta personally thank this Lev."

"For what?" I untangle my backpack from my legs to stand.

"For giving you something better to do than taping up eyeballs all over the place and tryin' to get yourself killed."

I almost say, "I'm actually trying to keep myself *alive*," but instead just smirk.

She pushes up from the table. "No wonder you're distracted,

though. He is cuuuuute." She picks up her tray. "Too bad all the cute ones are gay."

I smile. "Why, thank you."

Trent points at himself. "Uh, exsqueeze me? Way-too-tall but somewhat cute straight guy standin' *right here.*"

She rolls her eyes.

I explain I have to run but I'll look for them later. So I dash away before either of them can bring up my nose again.

Head down, I weave through the halls, dodging people like an obstacle course.

In my remaining classes I avoid eye contact and thus don't see the what-happened-to-your-face stares. But my mind has already left the building and is soaring through space with Graphite. I just need to get home with my pencils and let him out onto paper.

He'll know what to do.

The last bell rings and I hustle toward my locker. I just need to drop off—crap! Doug *never* comes down my hall after school.

I hang to the side.

He walks slowly, doesn't see me yet. Buddy's not with him.

Through the general laughing and rushing around the hall, I watch Doug. He turns his head side to side, red cap like a beacon. What, is he looking for me? Has he come to make sure I keep my mouth shut?

I stare at his face. That macho mask is back on. He isn't the confused, out-of-control kid from this morning but wears the same Doug face as always.

But Kobe's face isn't the same. Neither is mine. All because of Doug.

I could just slip away as usual. But that's not me anymore.

Standing tall, setting one foot in front of the other, I move through the crowd. Stop right in front of him.

His eyes go wide as he scans my bruises, then looks down at the floor. The brim of his cap covers his expression, but his shoulders sink just a bit. Then he puffs up, checks around, and catches my eye one last time. He steps past me, picks up his pace, and walks away.

What the hell?

People give me curious looks, so I make a beeline to my locker. I need to tuck away some books, then get the hell home and unload this camera and possibly my brain. I cannot handle anything else.

I spin the lock and—*really?* Another note.

I scoop it up and, making sure Doug's not hanging around watching me, open it.

Written on plain notebook paper in that same disguised Doug handwriting is just one simple phrase.

It's not easy being green

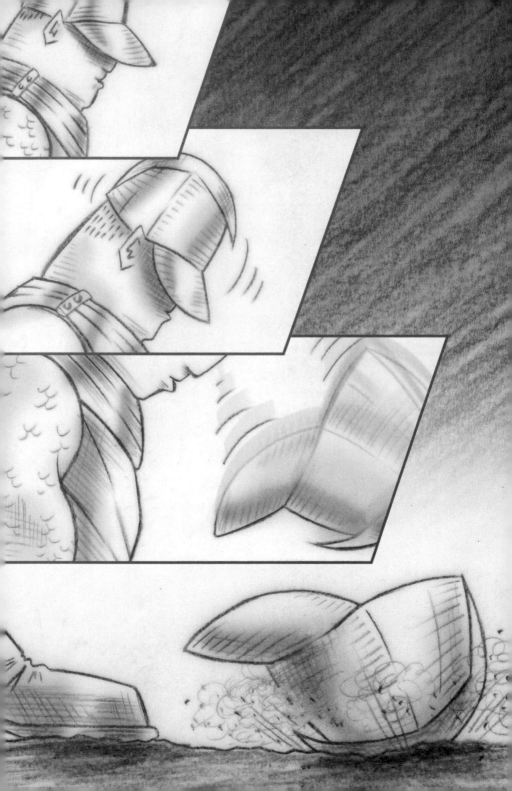

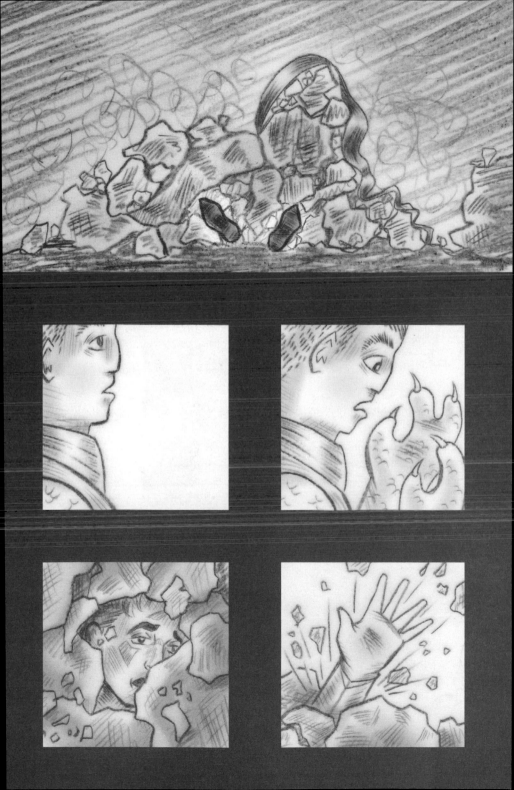

In his haste, Thug doesn't see that he leaves behind a part of his Innermost Secret.

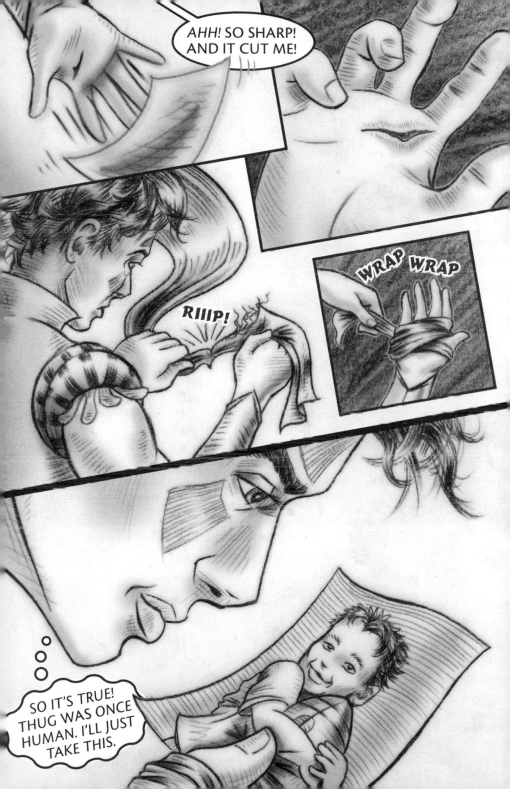

Fleeing the alien cave planet and soaring toward Earth, Graphite ponders whether to show his discovery to the humans.

With the Dark Rage and revenge infecting his very bones, Graphite grapples . . . *with himself.*

Even as he races through space, Graphite's True Heroic Self is locked in battle with the villainous Dark Rage that creeps its way into *his very soul.*

WHICH WILL WIN?

Adrian

Thirty-five

I HOLD HARLEY, SCRATCH HER BETWEEN THE EARS, AND PEER OUT my bedroom window. Over the houses across the street, the morning sun breaks through thick clouds. Bright golden light shines between the naked tree branches in my yard and right in my eyes. I squint but don't look away.

I'm up, dressed, and ready for school, but it's early so there's no rush.

When I first woke up I checked in the mirror, and my face looks somewhat less scary. Still a dull throb underneath the skin around my nose, but the swelling has gone down a bit and the bruises under my eyes are now slightly lighter, like ink smears someone's trying to erase.

I still look "tough," though.

Harley wiggles, so I let her loose on the bed, then go to my computer. Blinking away the afterimage of the sun, I stare at my screen.

Two files are open.

One contains my new comic pages, signed, scanned, and set to upload to my site.

The other has the video of me and Doug.

As soon as I dashed home yesterday, I downloaded the video from the camera to my computer. I skimmed forward to when Doug entered the balcony but—I stopped watching. Then I shut down the computer. If I hadn't, I think my head would have exploded.

So I drew, breaking pencils and ripping paper, racing through one sheet after another. Graphite was even more confused than me.

I paused only for a quick dinner, where I finally revealed my swollen and bruised face to Mom and Dad. I explained that I just slipped and fell "but it's no biggie. No damage. The nurse checked me out and all is fine." That wasn't good enough for Mom, though. It's hard to eat spaghetti while holding an ice pack to your face, but it did help cool me down.

After dinner, with my door shut and a *Batman* soundtrack in my headphones, I sketched and sketched. I let Graphite guide me, show me what the hell to do, make everything clearer.

Then around midnight I gave in. I was ready. Turning on my computer, I opened the video, watched and listened. I was so sure it would enrage me, bring back the anger, make me post the whole video then and there. But it didn't.

Seeing myself, grainy in the dark balcony, was like stepping outside my body. But this time I wasn't some screaming, wimpy kid like in that other video. I was simply me. The real me.

And Doug, confined in that frame on my screen, wasn't scary at all. He was just pathetic, like some freaked little boy pretending to be tough.

Watching it one time was enough.

If I posted that video, whether I altered it to mask my identity or not, the tables would turn. *I'd* be the villain, letting my hate take over, seeking revenge, finding ways to hurt and destroy.

But I don't destroy—*I create.*

So I turned away from the computer, back to my drawing table. I kept sketching, shading, refining my art until each scene was clear, each panel truly finished.

Then, just before going to bed, I decided to make one last illustration. This time, not for my website, but for Doug himself—a drawing in the form of a challenge. I sketched it fast, then tucked it into my backpack.

At last, I finally got some sleep, four hours or so.

And now, here I am.

Doug's latest locker note rests on my drawing table. I pick it up.

It's not easy being green

It's not easy for Kermit the Frog, for sure, probably not for the Hulk, and evidently not for Doug. But guess what? It's not so easy for me, either. I tuck the note with the others in the back of my desk drawer.

Plopping down in my chair at my computer, I click the mouse and close the video window. I eject my camera and erase the video from it. My muscles relax in relief.

But I *keep* the video copy on my computer. Just in case. There's a lot on there Doug wouldn't want anyone to know. And with the angle and low light, it kind of did look like he caused my bloody nose—tried to beat up another "gay kid." But enough about this damn video.

Okay, time to log on to my website.

Here we go. Uploading last night's comics takes only a few minutes. I check to be sure they posted, and wow, they look awesome: panel after panel of Graphite battling with himself, taking action and tossing a dark secret in the air . . . then watching it explode.

Now it's my turn to throw a secret into space.

And man, will it ever explode.

My heart speeds up, so I take a deep breath. Then I open the editing screen for my home page.

"Oh, boy." I put my hands in my lap and stare out the window, out at the world filled with blazing sunlight.

It's time. No more toxic secrets.

I turn back to my screen and place my fingers on the keyboard. Then, on the home page under my banner that says *The Amazing Adventures of Graphite*, I type three new words:

By Adrian Piper

401

I hit Save . . . and light the fuse of my own truth bomb.

Standing, I step back and look at the screen. I cross my arms and exhale.

Harley leaps on the chair and curls up.

Shutting down the computer, I bend and kiss her on the head. "Okay, little girl, wish me luck."

I go to grab my jacket and look down at what I'm wearing. Hold up, I can't wear gray again. Not today.

I pull off my charcoal-colored sweater and dig through my shirt drawer. I used to have a long-sleeved—ah, here it is. Pulling it out, I hold it up in the light, my only shirt that's bright red.

So it's crazy wrinkled, who cares? I put on the shirt, then kick off my battered old sneakers and slip into my barely worn red shoes, the ones I wore on my date with Lev.

Red may psychologically mean angry and sexy, but it also means "don't screw with me." Well, today I'm ready to be all of the above and more.

I put on my jacket and pick up my backpack, checking to be sure I have both Doug's keys and that drawing I made tucked inside. I zip it up and head out.

One last check in the hall mirror, and hey, I do kind of look tough.

Both Mom and Dad check me out before I can leave. But they give their approval when I assure them yes, I'll be sure to watch my every step and not fall again.

And boy, ain't that the truth.

I head out the front door and the crisp almost-Halloween

air slaps my cheeks. Curled brown leaves roll across my path as I make my way down the street, so I stomp on as many as I can with a *crunch*. Passing this one yard, I notice they've raked the leaves into a huge pile. I look around, but no one's in sight.

Like a little kid would, I speed up and plow right through it, making that fabulous swooshing-crumpling sound, kicking up leaves. The air smells like earth and nature and magic.

Yep, it's a red day for sure.

Approaching the school, I pause. My insides do a little flip. Can I really do this, face the world after I've just exposed my art and myself?

Out of habit, my hand goes to my pocket. But I don't have a freakin' phone anymore, so I couldn't take my name off my site even if I wanted to.

Making my way to the parking lot through the schoolyard, I crunch through more leaves. Watching them whip around my legs makes me think of Carmen and all her papers, tossed in the wind like the aftermath of a crime scene.

Yes, I can own up to my creations and the truth they show . . . and I *must*.

No more secrets.

And no more games.

Good, I timed it just right. Doug must be inside the school already—his truck is here.

Hanging out at the edge of the lot, away from all the kids heading toward the building, I pull out the drawing I made for Doug last night and look at it for the first time this morning. It's a portrait of Thug, in full-on attack position with the

Dark Rage pulsing through his veins. At the bottom I wrote my website, *AmazingGraphite.com.*

When I drew this in the middle of the night, it seemed perfect. But it's not enough.

I pull out my red pen from my bag, sit cross-legged on the grass, and add a note to the drawing:

> Thug.
> Is this who you really are? You don't think so. I'm still not so sure. You like the Hulk, but remember, even though he has a dark side, the Hulk is a superhero, not a villain. What the hell do YOU want to be? In your alter ego football costume you're a "hero," so why can't you be that out of costume?

This note probably won't do crap, but at least he'll see it and maybe it will even make him think a little. Hope it doesn't piss him off even more, but what do I know at this point?

I've just gotta do what's right for *me.*

Slipping the pen in my pocket, I fold the paper and stand. Here goes. I grab my bag and walk through the lot, right past his truck, and hang out on the little steps by the cafeteria and the stinking Dumpster. I hope to Obi-Wan I'm never over here again. Ever.

As people amble by, I sit like I'm waiting for someone and stare at his vanity plate. INEBG. I still don't get it. Maybe it's not beer-related after all? I Never . . . hmm. I'm Not Even Big . . . Green?

Oh. Oh!

It's Not Easy Being Green.

It has to be that. Crap, he really means it. He put it on his freakin' license plate! Wow, I know way too much about this guy. I'm definitely about to do the right thing.

The last bell rings, but this is worth being tardy for.

The remaining stragglers disappear around the corner of the building at last. I reach in my bag and bring out Doug's keys. When I hit the unlock button the truck goes *bwoop!* I scan the lot, but no one's around.

Opening my note for him, I place the keys right in the middle and fold the paper around them, like a little package.

I've got to be quick. Putting on my backpack, I get up, go to the truck, and open the driver's door. I place the note-wrapped keys on the seat, right in the middle where he won't miss them.

I check but there's nothing under the seat; his sketchbook is gone. He must have figured I'd be back, which I am.

Manually hitting the lock button, I shut the door and move on. I check over my shoulder, but I'm safe. There's not a soul in sight.

I make a beeline around the corner and right to the main entrance. As I hop up the front steps, my backpack bounces against my back. It's so light. No video camera, no notes, no keys—just papers and books are inside, like it's supposed to be.

My shoulders relax.

Taped to the outside of the doors are two orange Halloween Hoedown flyers. Pulling my pen from my pocket, I write

AmazingGraphite.com in big letters across the top of them.

I click my pen shut and grin.

It's definitely a red day.

I yank open the doors and go inside.

Thirty-six

"WHAT'S UP WITH YOU?" LEV SAYS AS HE AND I LEAVE FIRST PERIOD. "You were so jumpy all through class."

"Come on, follow me." I lead us through the noisy hall and out into the quiet courtyard. The dead grass is trampled flat out here now, so the ground is cold and hard. I stop by the same tree where I read that first note—*Doug's* first note. I check the cafeteria windows, but this time he's not there.

Wow. I wonder if he was watching me then, thinking I was looking at his note.

Lev elbows my arm. "So?" He puts his hands in his pockets to keep warm.

I elbow him back, keeping my arm on his. Even just like this, touching him is electric. Makes me want to grab and hold him, pull him to me, like I did against that wall Saturday night.

"Wish I could kiss you right now" comes out of my mouth.

He smiles, looks around, then says through a sigh, "I know."

I eye the rows of windows that surround the courtyard and inhale. "This is *so* not the way I wanted to tell you about Graphite, standing under a shriveled-up tree while we have, like, just a few minutes. But it can't wait. Can I see your phone?"

He scrunches his forehead. "Huh? You're speaking in tongues."

"You know how you wanted to see my art? Open a new web page on your phone."

He eyes me but gives me his phone, so I type in my site and my home page appears. Even on this little screen my newly added name pops out.

I hold the phone to my thumping chest. "His name is Graphite. He's my hero. I mean, he's my superhero—I created him. And this website."

Lev looks at my hand clutching his phone. "Can I see?"

I start to hold out the phone. "Wait!" I pull it back again. "There's something you should know. Um, okay, it's that he has friends? You know, superhero friends? And one of them is, like, *more* than a friend? And he kinda looks like you."

I hold my breath.

He grins. "Is he cute?"

"Very."

I hand him the phone and watch over his shoulder.

"Oh, no," I say, "my art looks so much better on a big screen. You need—"

"Hush, let me look!" He bumps me, then focuses on the first image. Mouth open, he looks at me, then back at the screen. "Adrian, you drew *this*?"

I nod.

He flips through panel after panel. "When you said you were an artist I didn't imagine comics. This is freakin' amazing! You're so talented. I mean, like, professional. Look at this! And Graphite—way cool name, by the way—is *hot*. He looks just like you."

I shrug. "I dunno."

He gives me a sweet smile, then studies my face. "Even with those bruises under your eyes. They kinda resemble the *A* markings on his face."

Whoa. I didn't even think about that.

"His eyes are—" Lev studies the screen and then me, his mouth shaped like an O. "It was you."

"What? It was me what?"

He glances around. "You put up those flyers in the halls! Those eyes."

I cross my arms. "Yeah, but it didn't quite work out as planned. It was supposed to intimidate Doug, not start a new damn fan club hashtag."

"Still, that was gutsy."

"I guess."

"See, more proof you are *the* Adrian." He keeps swiping the pages, then stops. "Who's this hottie, Oasis?"

I swallow. "Uh, that's . . . you?"

He enlarges the image and studies Oasis's face. Then turns and looks me in the eyes.

Oh, god, he hates it.

"No one's ever drawn me before. Ever." He looks down at the phone again. "This is how you see me?"

I lean my shoulder against the tree. "Uh, yeah."

"Really? But he's so . . . beautiful."

I study Lev's face, his jawline. Arms. "Looks just like you."

He blushes, clicks off the phone, and slips it in his pocket. "Don't know about *that*."

"I do."

"*Oasis,*" he says, gazing past me. "No one's thought of me like that either." His face turns even redder.

People are racing inside before the bell, so we hoof it across the courtyard toward the opposite doors.

"I wanted to let you know because today"—my throat catches—"today I put my name on my site. Until now it's been anonymous."

"Why today?"

Okay, Adrian, you can do this.

I stop, grab his sleeve, and lean close to his ear. "I have a lot to tell you. And I really want to show you my art in person. So . . . you wanna come over after school?"

He turns to me. "Your dad'll be all right with it?"

"I think he likes you. You actually talked with him. And it's not like he has to know what *kind* of friend you are."

He smiles. "Okay."

"Really?" My insides jump like they're on a trampoline. "Excellent."

I open the door for him and we step inside. Waves of chatter, locker slams, and squeaking sneakers hit us all at once.

We make a plan to meet after school and I tap his shoe with my foot. He taps back. As we turn to go our separate ways he says, "Oh, and great shirt. You look good in red."

I smile and head off.

OHmygodohmygod. Lev is coming to my house. Today!

As I dash to algebra, my brain whirls.

Good thing Mom works tonight so she won't be around.

Bad that I'm on Dad Duty and he *will* be around.

Good that I can tell Lev about stuff and show him my art.

Bad that our house is the opposite of fancy and my room is a mess and looks like crap.

Good that who freakin' cares about any of this because Lev and I will be alone . . . *in my bedroom!*

All through second period I ponder the possible outcomes of this and my body is all tingly, especially in certain areas south of the border.

Oh, boy, I've gotta distract myself here.

It doesn't take long since algebra equals the opposite of horny. After a while I calm down—in *all* senses of the word.

While we work out an especially tricky problem the teacher's writing on the board, I look around at everyone. I barely know any of these people. No one, really, just faces and voices and maybe a few names—and what categories they could fit into, what cliché boxes.

And they don't know me. To them, I'm just categories and clichés, too. The geek. The gay boy. The wimp. Even though I screamed at Doug in front of everybody at Boo, what have I done since then that anyone knows about? I'm happily a geek and happily gay, but I'm no longer a wimp.

My art is my superpower—and I'm not afraid to use it.

I take a sheet of paper and rip it into small sections. Then, with my red pen, I write *AmazingGraphite.com* on each piece.

As the bell rings and I get up, I leave one behind on the desk.

Heading through the hall to my next class, I slow down. Observing people, I watch their faces, look right in their eyes.

How many secrets are in there?

It's strange to be the one staring at others for a change, watching them stare back or scowl or look away. Some even say stupid things, like "What you lookin' at?" But I just keep staring.

It's a red day, after all.

And it's so good to let go, open up.

Come out . . . in more ways than one.

Of course, there'll be the haters, but my art is my own. And if they don't like that Graphite's a weird, sexy superhero/ Renaissance hybrid creation—and *gay*—then screw them.

And who knows, I bet some might actually like him.

As I pass through the halls, I wedge some torn bits of paper with my site written on them in the frame of a display case, stick a few on a couple bulletin boards, and place them next to the water fountains. Then, when third period is over, I drop a couple on the desks as I leave.

At lunch, both Trent and Audrey are already seated at our table and eating when I get there.

Trent holds up his hand. "Hail, O woodland creature."

"Huh?" I plop my backpack and lunch bag on the table.

"Lookin' better," he says. "Not so raccoony today."

Oh.

Audrey stands and puts her hand against my forehead. "Somethin's not right."

I squint at her. "What do you mean? I feel fine."

She shakes her head and points at my red shirt. "You're wearing . . . a *color*."

Suppressing a smile, I shrug. "And why not?"

Trent leans forward. "Well, allow me to elucidate the many many reasons—"

"Nuh-uh." Audrey cuts him off. Then she inspects my face. "Much better. But you aren't off the hook." She points to a chair. "Sit and spill the beans. What happened?"

I do sit but don't spill anything, just explain I'll fill them in later. I'm still not sure what the hell to do, who to tell what.

The ball's in Doug's court. I've made my moves, so now it's his turn. He claims he doesn't want to be the "dumb-ass thug," so let him prove it. I'm going to wait until he finds my note—my challenge to him—and sees I've put my name on my site and am spreading the word, that I'm not a wimp and won't just go away. Then I'll decide whether it's time to put Thug to rest, no longer draw him and take him off my site—or not.

I'm not invisible anymore.

As I eat my squishy peanut butter and jelly sandwich, I tell Audrey and Trent about putting my name on my site and spreading the word. Then I rip up another piece of paper and write my website on the torn sections like before.

Audrey snatches one up and eyes it. "Are you crazy? Why are you doing that?"

Holding his taco halfway to his mouth, Trent leans over to look. "Maybe not the wisest move there, Señor El Asking For It."

I sit up and look at them. "Do you know what everyone at school thinks about me?"

They glance at each other.

I put down my pen. "Seriously."

Trent blows the hair from his eyes. "Who gives a crap what they think?"

"I do," I say, "when I have to always hide. When random assholes stare at me, yell at me, slam me into lockers. When all anyone knows is from lies or their own ignorance."

Audrey surveys the noisy, crowded tables around the cafeteria. "How's going public with Graphite going to change that?"

I lean back in my chair. "I'm not going to let people put me in some stupid category anymore, be a blank canvas for them to put on me whatever they think I am or want me to be. *I'm* going to show who I *really* am."

"Hey, wait a minute," Trent says, swallowing a bite of taco. "I'm in your art too."

"Willow's pretty awesome, you know. Great outfit, right?"

He squints at me, then nods. "I'm cool with that. But I

don't know if Sultry here can handle going public."

"Ha!" Audrey checks herself out in her phone and reapplies her deep-purple lipstick. "If anyone connects the dots that *she's* supposed to be *me*, then they're delusional. No way I look like that."

"You're right," I say.

She shoots me a sideways look.

I turn to face her. "I could never draw a character as sultry as you really are. Face it, you're hot."

She caps her lipstick and holds up her hand. "We're not goin' here—"

"*I* am," I say. "You're special. You've got style, class, and sass."

She arches her eyebrows and says to Trent, "You hearin' this babble?"

He sits back. "Gotta say, dude's right."

"No offense," she says, "but I wouldn't call either of you an expert in what makes a woman hot."

I grin. "Audrey, you can come up with all the excuses you like. But I draw the truth."

She clears her throat and lowers her voice. "Speaking of which, all that art you did with Doug beating up Kobe—or at least their character versions, which anyone with a quarter of a brain could figure out—it's still on your site?"

"Yes."

She looks at my bruises. "I'm surprised I'm saying this, but you should probably take that down. What's gonna happen when Doug sees—"

"No." I ball up my trash. "Doug may not like it, but I can illustrate my own damn life any way I want."

And, of course, he already knows my site all too well.

"What about Buddy?" Trent says. "*Bootlicker?* Dude, you drew him like a dog. A *wiener* dog."

I cross my arms and nod. "I'll be honest, I'm trying to not think about that. But he already wants to kill me and—guys, let me finish—he gets away with whatever the hell he wants to." Like scrawling *God Hates Fags* across *my* locker. "Someone needs to call him out for the dog that he is."

"Dude," Trent says. "You got balls, I'll give ya that."

Audrey snorts. "That's the problem with this planet. *Way* too many balls."

I laugh. Then I stand to gather my stuff and—damn, Manuel's staring right at me from across the cafeteria. "What is his deal?"

"Who?" Audrey scans around, then scowls. "Oh. *Him.*"

Manuel sees me notice him, then looks at Audrey and averts his eyes. Starts talking to his buddy next to him.

I drop my backpack in my chair. "Hold on, I'll be right back." I stride past our table and start across the room.

His eyes go wide as he sees me coming, and he grabs his bag and waves bye to his friends. He's trying to act casual but scoots out of the cafeteria, fast.

What the hell? He didn't write those notes, so what is it?

But he's gone. I spin around and go back to Audrey and Trent. I pack up my bag, toss my trash, and tell them, "Listen, just trust me about my website. I know what I'm doing."

Audrey studies me as she tucks up a few loose strands of hair in the poufy bun she wears today. "You know, Adrian, I'm beginning to think you do."

Trent pushes up from his chair. "Like I said, *balls*."

He gets the Audrey Eye.

I say bye and move on.

On the way out, Carmen catches up to me. "Adrian, I saw your comics!"

I blink. "You did?"

"Yeah. *So* cool. I mean, like, way awesome!" She holds up her phone. "A few people forwarded it to me."

Already? A *few* people? My pulse skips. That was fast.

She grabs my sleeve. "It's supposed to be Kobe, right? That character, Kerosene?"

I nod.

"Amazing," she says. "Does he know?"

Oh. "No, but he should. Will you send him the link? I don't have my phone."

"Of course." She smiles, then turns away.

My art is being looked at, exposed to the world with my name front and center.

They'll know it's me, all the bystanders, heroes . . . and villains.

There's no turning back.

Thirty-seven

AS LEV AND I WALK TO MY HOUSE AFTER SCHOOL, THE WIND KICKS
up and makes the almost-bare tree branches sway and dance.

"October's not usually like this, right?" Lev pulls up his
shirt collar and crosses his arms.

I take off my Windbreaker. "Here, wear my jacket. I'm
okay without it."

"No, you'll—"

"Seriously, I don't need it." I hold it out, so he puts it on.
"And anyway, we're almost to my house."

And we're almost to my bedroom.

These aren't just butterflies flapping around in my stomach, but every winged species known to man.

"Weird seeing you in my jacket," I say. "Looks good."

"Feels good." He grins, then looks away.

Oh, man. I'm already getting way too excited.

But one block later the excitement is gone. Here's my house, which means here's my dad, and here's major awkwardness.

I take out my keys, which jangle. Keys. My heart skips— Doug will have found *his* keys by now, and my note. Or maybe he won't see them until later, after football practice?

Okay, push that aside. Don't go there. Stay here.

I inhale and open the door. The sound of some blaring TV commercial greets us.

I've rehearsed this Dad conversation in my head all afternoon. I awkward-grin at Lev and close the door.

I exhale. "Dad, I'm home."

Using his cane, he shuffles out of the kitchen holding an iced tea. "How was—oh!" He goes over to the remote and mutes the TV. Silence.

Lev does a little wave. "Hi, Mr. Piper." His voice cracks.

Dad's fully dressed, shoes and all. What's that about?

"Bone-joor. Come on in." He gestures toward the living room.

Obi-Wan, *why?*

"*Bonjour.*" Lev steps from the entry hall into the room.

I stand next to him. Guess the place doesn't look *too* bad. Mom and I keep it pretty clean, but Dad's area is a mess. And this furniture is ancient.

I talk fast. "We've got this big test coming up in French, so we're going to study in my room."

Dad looks at Lev. "Well, I'd offer to help, but I never took French."

"What did you study?"

Lev, really? Let's get moving.

"Well, I went to school to be an architect. But math and I aren't such good friends. So . . ." Dad waves his hand in the air. "You don't want to hear about all that. You guys go par-lay in French and have fun."

"Thanks." I move toward the hall and Lev follows.

Dad turns. "Oh, Ade?"

Damn, don't call me that. "Yeah?"

"My buddy Pete's pickin' me up soon and we're gonna watch the game at his place again. I'll have dinner there."

What! Really? This is too good.

"Hey, Lev," Dad says—wow, he remembered Lev's name—"you a football fan?"

Lev glances at me, then says, "Kinda, but it's not my favorite."

Dad smiles and shakes his head. "Sounds like a certain kid of mine."

With Lev right behind me, I head down the hall and call back, "Have fun, Dad!" My voice comes out too loud.

I glance back, but he just settles in his chair.

We're at my door, which I always leave open just a little for Harley to come and go. "Okay, I, like, didn't clean up or anything. It's a total—"

"Don't worry." Lev nervous-laughs. "You haven't seen *my* room. Bet I've got more binders and folders and papers piled up than you."

From the living room, the TV sounds resume.

I take a deep breath. "Welcome to my messy-yet-cozy Hobbit Hole."

We step in and, so Dad won't suspect anything, I leave the door open a tad. For now.

Just us.

Lev and me.

Alone.

Lev nods toward the door and says softly, "You said your parents don't know about you, right?"

"Not yet." My turn to nervous-laugh.

Hands in his pockets, he checks out my room. My cluttered, tiny room.

He eyes the bed for a moment, then too quickly turns and points at my sci-fi and superhero action figures lining the bookshelves. "You have quite the collection there of, you know, those things."

"Uh-huh." Throat's so dry. I reach out to grab my vintage Caesar figure from *Planet of the Apes*. "Some of these are really old—" I bump the shelf and knock a whole row of action figures domino-style all over the floor. Crap!

As I bend to pick them up, so does he and we bonk heads. He grimaces. "Ooh—sorry!"

"No, no, my fault." I rub my head, then shove the figurines into a little pile and to the side.

His eyes travel around my room. "You sure like sci-fi stuff."

My brain thinks of words but my mouth won't budge. Instead I scoop up dirty clothes that litter the carpet and dump them in the clothes basket in the closet. A pair of glowing eyes stares at me from the shadows. I bend down and pet Harley. "It's all right. He's nice."

"Huh?" Lev says.

I stand. "Talking to my cat, Harley Quinn. She's shy with new people, but she'll come out. Just gotta give her time."

"Sounds like me." He nervous-laughs again and comes over to peer in the closet. "Aww, she's cute."

That sounds like you too.

We're just a couple inches apart. There's that spicy cologne he wears. My insides vibrate.

One touch and I know I'd burst into flame.

He must feel it too. He steps back and turns away. "Hey, you put it up," he says, pointing to my bulletin board, where I pinned little Jimmy's unigiraffe painting.

I eye the open door and say in a low voice, "Still can't believe they have art classes at the gay center."

Damn. Look at him. His hair's pulled back in a thick ponytail, exposing that jawline, that neck. Lips.

"So," he says. "Can I see your . . . you know . . ."

My *what*?

He clears his throat. "See your art?"

Oh! "Right, yes. My art." I step over and shut my door, somewhat quieting the TV sounds that bounce down the hall.

From my bookshelf I take out *Elements of Renaissance Architecture*. Standing next to Lev, I click on my drawing table lamp and open the book to where I've tucked some art between the chapters on arches and domes. Stop it, hands! They're shaking like crazy as I spread out my drawings on my table. "This is Graphite's origin story. Some of the first art I posted on my website—"

My stomach drops. My website! Oh, my god, how many people have seen it by now? I eye my computer. Should I look? No. The comments can wait, good or bad. How often is Lev here? *Never.*

Hands behind his back, he leans over my art.

"So," I say, shrugging. "What do you think?" I bite my lower lip.

He hesitates. "Well . . ."

The longer he's quiet the more my face heats up.

Crap. He thinks it's stupid.

"I don't really know comics and stuff like that." Now he's blushing. "So I'm kinda out of my league here? Your art is SO cool and, I don't know, I just don't want to say the wrong thing."

"Oh, you won't! But . . . do you hate it?"

"*No!* It's just that—ah! I'm all nervous."

He's not the only one.

Holding up the sketch of Graphite's Moon Palace, he says, "Seriously, you're crazy talented. Have you always been able to draw like this?"

"I've always drawn," I say, "but I guess you just get better as you go, right?"

He shakes his head. "I don't know anyone who can do *this.*"

I turn on my computer, but not to go to my site. I scan through my music and put on the soundtrack from Miyazaki's

Spirited Away. Those magical opening notes flit from the speakers, piano and synthesizer lifting us up.

"Wow." Now he's holding a sketch of Oasis. "Look at that ass. And those muscles. No *wonder* you like to draw so much."

Oh, man. When does that freakin' football game start?

My midsection sizzles as I lean against Lev and look down at the drawing table. "See, he does look like you."

"Me? Oh, that's Oasis?" He swallows. "No, he's *much* hunkier than I am."

I whisper in his ear, "You're wrong."

Our shoulders are locked as if by superconductor magnets.

Harley slinks out from the closet and settles nearby on the bed.

"Ya know," Lev says, studying more sketches, "Graphite's not a superhero."

"Why not? What do you mean?"

"He's, I don't know. . . . Superheroes are pretty common. There are so many and it's easy to mix them up. But Graphite, he's different." He faces me. "He's not like anything I've ever seen. He's special."

With those amber eyes staring into mine, I'd almost agree with anything he says. But I've got to ponder that one.

"And," he says, "Graphite's body is frickin' hot. Look at those hands." He's staring at mine.

KNOCK! KNOCK! KNOCK!

We both jump away.

"Coming!" I yell, glancing at Lev. "Um, I mean, just a sec!"

I turn off my drawing table lamp, then sweep my art into a quick pile and place the book on top. I open my bedroom door.

Dad peers in. "How's the French goin'?"

I nod. "All's good." My voice squeaks.

"Well, Pete's here," he says, "so I'm headin' out."

Somehow I missed hearing the doorbell and Dad shutting off the blaring TV.

"*Bonne chance*," Lev says. "Hope your team wins."

"They'd better!" Dad totters down the hall and out the front door.

I close my door and cross my room to look out the window.

Lev comes up behind me. "So, how long will he be gone?"

"Forever. Those games are endless," I say to the window. "And Mom doesn't get off work until late, so . . . just you and me."

Oh. My.

Taking his time with his cane, Dad makes it to his friend's car and they drive off.

I exhale. "Well, they're gone." I turn and bump right into Lev. He pulls back.

The *Spirited Away* soundtrack playing through my speakers is bouncy with horns, playful and dramatic.

Lev glances out the window one more time. "Do you think he suspects that, well, you know?"

I swallow. "That you're my boyfriend?"

His cheeks flush and he looks at the carpet, a few loose

strands of wavy hair falling over his face. "Am I? Are we?"

"I don't know." I cross my arms. "What do you think?"

He grins. "I'd like that."

"Me too." My insides quake.

He tucks the loose hair behind his ears, then takes off my jacket that he's wearing. "Hot in here." His eyebrows shoot up. "I don't mean that as some line. I'm really hot." His face gets redder. "You know what I mean."

I sure do.

All of me does. *Boner* is definitely the most accurate word in all of the English language.

I reach out. "Here, I'll grab it." My voice squeaks. "My jacket! I mean."

He steps over and hands it to me, but doesn't let go.

We look at each other for a moment, holding the jacket together.

Then, at the same time, we drop it to the floor.

I slide my arms around him and he wraps his around me. I taste his lips.

"You're shaking," he says.

"I know."

"You okay?"

I pull back and hold his hands. "Have you ever, like, been with a guy before?"

He swallows. "Yes. I mean, kind of. Haven't done much. Well, some, but not, you know, *that*."

I nod. "How many?"

"Just one. It only lasted for the summer. I met him at the

LGBT center, but it didn't mean anything—all right, it did, but not like this." He smiles and looks in my eyes.

I clear my throat.

He frowns. "Does that bother you?"

"No, it's just that . . . well, I've never . . ."

He moves his hands up my arms, holds my shoulders. "I don't care. This is just you and me here. We do whatever we want. Or don't."

I reach down, grab his belt loops, pull him to me. "I want."

We kiss. He holds my face, and our tongues slide and play.

I press my crotch into his.

Whoa.

I'm still shivering but heating up, too.

The world fades out as we take our time, kissing in different ways.

We slowly swivel our hips in opposite directions, back and forth, rubbing fabric together, hardness to hardness. Back and forth.

MAN.

I gotta take a breath. "Whew."

He's panting too. "Yeah."

I step away, turn my back, reach down and adjust myself in a flash. In the corner of my eye I see he does the same.

"Okay. Gotta sit. Harley, move." I gently push her off my pillow. She slinks back into the closet. I plop down on the corner of the bed.

Lev sits beside me. He rubs his hand in circles over my back, sending voltage through my veins.

My pulse is racing.

I slide my hand up his back, scrunch my fingers in that gorgeous hair, and pull on the elastic ponytail band to free his—

"*OW* ow ow ow! Ow." He throws back his head and reaches around, grabs my hand. "Stop."

I let go. "Ohmygod—sorry! Didn't mean to hurt you."

"It's okay, I got it."

As he untangles his mass of hair, I get up, close the curtains, then switch off the lights.

Early-evening sun makes the curtains glow. A soft golden haze fills the room.

I turn up the music a little. Sounds of slow horns and violins and echoing notes swirl around us, gentle and haunting.

On the bed, I lie down next to Lev. He lies down too, and rolls on top of me. Heavy, pressing into me. It's hard to breathe but feels so good.

He holds my face again and our mouths lock together.

"*OwOwOw!*" I cover my nose.

He pushes up on his elbows. "Ooh, sorry! Sorry!"

"Still tender is all. I'm all right." My nose and the skin under my eyes throb.

But so does the rest of me.

I move my hands down his back to his ass. Whoa.

He kicks off his shoes, so I kick off mine and press my toes on top of his.

We fit so well together.

Is this really happening?

OH, my. He nibbles my neck.

This is so happening.

We roll over, me on top.

He pulls my shirt and gently peels it off. With my hand, I protect my nose from the red fabric sliding over my face.

I grab his shirt and, with him arching his back, wiggle it off his body. It's so tight, though, it's stuck around his neck. I yank harder—

"*Gurgg,*" he chokes out, grabbing the fabric. "Hold up!"

Tugging, we both slip it over his chin and face and toss it to the floor.

I smell his sweat and that spicy cologne, stare at his chest. "Look at that."

He hums, staring at mine. "Look at *that.*"

We lock eyes. I ease back down on top of him. It's like we're melding, skin to skin, beating heart to beating heart.

I grab his hair, his amazing gorgeous hair, and gently push my fingers through it. It lies around his head on the pillow like an electric crown.

Time, everything, disappears. It's as if we're swirling through space, just him and me.

Closing my eyes, I nestle my head between his neck and shoulder. Listen to him breathing, like the notes of music that fill the room, scaling up, down, then up and up.

And up.

Thirty-eight

OKAY. I'D BETTER STOP DRAWING NOW. IF I KEEP GOING THIS'LL TURN into *that* kind of art pretty quick.

I drop my pencil, stand up from the drawing table, and look over at my bed, where Lev and I were naked together.

"Naked!" I holler.

Harley's eyes snap open.

I scratch her head, warm from my drawing lamp where she's curled up under the light. "Sorry, just can't help my happy freak-outs."

Poor kitty has had to endure me screaming *Oh my god oh my god!* at random ever since Lev went home about, what, thirty minutes ago? As long as I still have the house to myself before Dad or Mom gets home I might as well shout and let it out.

My whole body is warm and tingly and buzzing, like I just stepped off a two-hour roller coaster on the surface of the sun.

We didn't go *all* the way, but what we *did* do . . .

"OH MY GOD OH MY GOD!"

I look over my sketches, which were fun to draw from memory. I glance over at the rumpled sheets on the bed. Oh, boy, I'm getting excited again.

No way I'm scanning or posting these new sketches—oh, crap, my website. I didn't even think to check it!

I sit, log in, and take a deep breath. How many people have seen Graphite by now? Here comes my home page—holy crap. Eighty-seven new comments. *Eighty-seven!*

I maybe get that many in one year, never in one day.

I wanted this, right?

I scan through but looks like a bunch of anonymous or bullshit usernames. Okay, focus, Adrian. One at a time.

you really are a freakin' fag

Asshole. Delete.

wtf is this site? and ummm why?

Delete.

Burn in hell faggot.

Really? Well, back at ya, asshole. Delete.

Haaaaayyy Adrian. Youre soooo fagulous!!! (how do you type with a lisp?)

Delete!

I'm gonna break this mouse if I hit Delete any harder. I expected this, though, didn't I? No surprise, and it's not like people writing crap on my site is new.

But it's the first time they've used my name and know exactly who I am. It's so easy to spew hate anonymously.

Well, screw you if you can't even own up to it.

I take a deep breath and keep reading. Delete and delete and delete and—wow.

HO-LYyy fluffy pancakes from heaven! This is beyond EPIC-NESS! Adrian you drew all THIS?

Yay, some love. Username is just Princess. Someone I know? I reply: *Thanks! Yes, been creating this comic for a long time. So glad you like!*

I go through a few more baffled comments asking what Graphite actually does, then read more likes, even a few loves, mixed in with more stupidity.

What's this?

Listen up, haters. Until you can draw THIS good and do something more in YOUR OWN damn life than be a troll, you should just SHUT THE HELL UP.

I check the username. Has to be . . . yes. *Sultry.*

Wow. Audrey's amazing, and finally admitting she *is* sultry!

I reply: *You got that right, my friend!*

I sit back in my chair and roll my head around, stretch my neck, then keep scrolling through the comments. Here's one saying *Graphite is SOOO HOT.* Love that.

But not this, posted by Anonymous:

How friggin STUPID can you be? Thug? Bootlicker? Supposed to be Doug Richter and Buddy Jones? Your ass is gonna be shredded.

I inhale and stare at the screen. I almost reply *Screw you, ANONYMOUS, if you can't handle seeing the truth.* But, instead, I hit Delete.

My art speaks for itself, speaks for me.

Maybe I *am* stupid, not for drawing my life, but for hoping Doug might do the right thing and pull back, keep Buddy in line, and leave me and my friends the hell alone. And, as unlikely as it is, maybe he'll even come clean about how he beat Kobe *not* in self-defense. He says he's more than just a thug, but he's got to prove it.

And if not, I still have that balcony video. In case.

"Bye!" I holler from the front hall.

Holding her breakfast yogurt and spoon, Mom peeks out from the kitchen. "Have a good—oh, don't you look nice? Glad you're finally wearing that shirt I got you, *last* Christmas."

I shrug. "Just seems like a good day for yellow."

She scans my face. "Thanks heavens, that bruising is almost gone. Your nose feel all right today?"

Every part of me feels all right today. I touch my nose, which is a tiny bit tender but no biggie. "Yep, all good."

I head out the front door and down the block. The bright sunlight and crisp wind make the air buzz. Or maybe it's me sending out shock waves since my whole body is *still* humming from being with Lev last night.

Being. With. Lev. Last. Night.

Between that and attempting to make sense of all those comments on my site, I've been so distracted: bumping into things, leaving faucets running, losing my toothbrush only to find it was still in my mouth. It's like I'm a toddler again, learning basic motor skills.

But the sidewalk seems to stay under my shoes and I'm heading the right way to school. Thinking about seeing Lev in French makes me pick up my pace.

Crossing the school's front lawn, I scan the side parking lot. Standing out among all the boring cars, there's Lev's lemon-yellow Beetle. Guess I match it today with this bright-yellow shirt.

Doug's parking spot is still empty. My stomach drops. He's had a whole night to think about my note. There were no comments on my site from BigGreenBro and none of the anonymous ones sounded like they were from him either.

It's still his move.

Since it's about ten minutes until first period, there are tons of people arriving and goofing around. How many have seen my site?

I pass by a cluster of giggly girls who don't even glance at me. Most people keep to themselves.

As I make my way to the entrance, I pass three guys huddled, sitting on the grass. I recognize them from the geek boy table at lunch. They're writing in sketchbooks on their laps and notice me. One with bleached-blond hair looks up and says, "Hey."

"Um, hey," I say.

"You're Adrian."

I stop. "Yeah?"

He nods. "I checked out Graphite. He's cool."

I exhale and smile. "Thanks."

He holds up his sketchbook pages with portraits of some manga characters. "You like Naruto?"

"Sure, but I don't follow it." I step over and look at his art. Thin, sketchy inked lines with colored-pencil shading. "That spiked hair is great."

One of the other guys points to his drawing of a sexy girl in a school uniform. "I can't do clothes. How do you do fabric like in Graphite?"

I shrug. "You have to think of it as in motion like—"

AH! I'm shoved from behind. I fall, palms and knees slamming into the dirt. I jump up and spin around.

Buddy.

He scowls and his nostrils flare. "You freakin' asshole fag!"

I shake out my wrists.

The three guys grab their stuff, scramble up, and get back. People move away from us.

I stand my ground. "What's your problem?"

"You take that shit down."

"Take what down?" I breathe heavy and pull my shoulders back.

"Don't screw with me, faggot. That *Bootlicker* shit you did about me." He pushes up the sleeves of his Saber Cats jacket.

I sneer. "There's no character named Buddy on my website. What makes you think that's supposed to be you? You see a resemblance?"

He grits his teeth. "I ain't no bootlicker." He eyes the crowd watching us. Spitting on the ground, he turns and storms inside.

I brush the dirt from my hands and jeans, which, dammit, are streaked with stains at the knees.

One of the guys blinks at me. "Man, you pissed him off."

I inhale deep and let it out. "No, he pissed *me* off."

From the parking lot, Doug's red pickup catches my eye. The motor rumbling, he pulls into his spot.

What's up with him and Buddy not coming to school together anymore?

I so want to know what he thought of my drawing and note, but not here, not now. I head up the front steps and inside, stepping into the din of the hallways.

In the bathroom, I wash off my scraped wrists, which sting from the soap. If Doug doesn't do something about Buddy, I will. But I've no idea what.

The first bell rings. Making my way to my locker, I watch faces and listen to voices to discover who might have seen my website. From the variety of reactions I get—smiles to quizzical looks to wide-eyed stares—I can tell a lot of people have. Excellent.

Swinging open my locker, I grab my stuff, then get to class.

I walk through the doorway, and just laying eyes on Lev's beaming face, I can tell this is going to be torture. How am I supposed to sit so close to him but act normal, whatever the hell *normal* means? He's right here, but I can't even touch him.

I plop into my seat and he nervous-giggles. "Hi."

"Hi." Is it possible for my face to smile *too* big?

I check around as more people arrive and the general talking gets louder.

"Hey," I say, "give me your French book."

"Why, you forget yours?"

I put out my hand. "Just give it to me."

With a curious look, he reaches into his backpack and hands me his textbook.

Opening my bag, I pull out a folded paper.

Last night before going to sleep, I had to stop all that website crap from swirling in my brain. So I drew a quick portrait of Oasis, floating against the stars, his sexy eyes staring right out at the viewer.

I slip the drawing inside the book's front cover, hand it back to him, and lower my voice. "Look at it later."

"Okay," he says, but goes ahead and peeks at my art anyway. He slams the book shut and covers it with his arms. "Wow."

I grin and turn around.

And, just like I thought, the rest of class is pure torture.

After the bell we head into the hall together. He bumps my shoulder and whispers, "*That* was fun last night."

"And holy freakin' how!" I bump back.

He eyes me. "Your parents suspect anything?"

"No. By the time they got home I had everything all cleaned up." My face heats up like someone flipped a switch.

His pocket buzzes, so he pulls out his phone, reads a text, then looks at me. "Wish I could text *you*."

I sigh. "God yes. I HATE this no-phone crap."

"I've been thinking, your mom said you have to pay for a new phone yourself, right? And you have to get a job?"

"Yeah."

"Well, I have an idea. I called Maria, you know, that woman I volunteered for at the LGBT center?"

I stop walking. "Okay . . ."

"I told her how much you liked the art room there and what a freakin' amazing artist you are. She said she'd connect you with that art teacher we met. Maybe you could help teach the kids or something?"

"I . . . I wouldn't have thought of that."

He bites his lip. "You don't mind I asked her, do you? It's just an idea."

Turning away from everyone zooming around us like fish in a stream, I lead us over to the wall. "Would they really pay me?"

He shrugs. "You're so good and you'd be a great teacher, I bet."

So many thoughts pop up, like how would I get there and, well, what do I know about little kids?

He watches my face. "Look, tomorrow's Saturday and the art teacher should be there like she was last week. I could pick you up and we'd go together. You could bring some art to show her. It'd be fun!"

"I don't know. It's kinda scary." I check the wall clock and we start moving.

He nods. "Maybe it's a stupid idea."

"No, it's a good idea. Better than anything I've thought of. I really need a phone."

We come to the corner where we have to go in different directions.

I breathe in deep. "Okay, why the hell not? Doesn't hurt to ask, right?"

He smiles. "And we'll get to drive around together, alone."

"I like this idea more and more."

We tap shoes and go our ways.

Then it hits me. Oh, man. If this actually works, how the hell do I explain to my parents I got a job teaching kids . . . at a gay center?

Thirty-nine

"WHOA." TRENT HOLDS HIS HAND IN FRONT OF HIS EYES. "THAT'S some shirt you're sportin' there, Señor Sunshine."

"Felt like a yellow day this morning." I drop my lunch bag on the table, sit down across from him, and take out the tuna salad sandwich and Pop-Tarts I packed this morning. The sounds of chairs scraping the floor and people chattering bounce all around the cafeteria.

His tray is covered with three huge slices of veggie pizza and an iced tea. He checks me out. "Guess that shirt distracts the eye from those bruises *Doug* gave you."

I look up at him. "What?"

"Why didn't you tell me how you got that bloody nose? Seems like you should've told *me* before putting it on your website."

"I meant to tell you first," I say, "honestly. Everything's just happening so fast."

"I'm not the only one who saw it and gets what it means."
He eyes Audrey as she carries her tray our way.

Oh, man.

She places her slice of pizza and a latte on the table, plops
her purse beside them, and slides into the seat. She's wearing
a necklace of deep ruby-red glass beads, which pop against her
black dress.

"When did you get that necklace? It's gorgeous."

She shoots me the Audrey Eye. "Uh-huh. Go ahead, try
and butter me up. You've got *lots* of explaining to do."

"Look, I'm sorry I didn't tell you sooner. I meant to."

She takes a sip of her latte. "Well, tell me now." She looks
hard at my face, at the last of the bruising under my eyes.
"What did he do to you?"

I scoot my chair closer to the table. They scoot in as
well.

"Oh, boy," I say. "There's so much more than just
that. And I'm only going to tell you if you promise not
to freak."

Audrey arches an eyebrow. "I ain't promising nothin'."

Trent points a slice of pizza at Audrey. "What she said." He
takes a huge bite.

"Then I'm not telling you everything."

She groans and looks at the ceiling. "Fine, I'll stay calm.
But now you have me worried."

I glance at Trent.

His mouth full of pizza, he gurgles some noises and points
the crust at Audrey.

I take a deep breath, lower my voice, and tell them all about Doug writing the notes, my plan in the balcony, and what happened there.

Audrey keeps interrupting with "Oh, no, he did *not* write those notes" and "Why didn't you tell me about this?" Trent just keeps saying "Dude" in various tones.

This is so good to let out. Why *didn't* I tell them sooner?

Audrey interrupts me as I explain about my trap to get Doug's confession on video. "What were you thinking? I would *never* have let you do something so stupid."

Ah, yes. That would be why I didn't say anything sooner.

I ignore her and keep going, finally saying why he wrote the notes.

Trent drops his pizza. "Well, even if he does give a crap if Kobe's okay, it sounds like he really wants—"

"To cover his own damn ass?" Audrey shouts.

"Shhhh!" I scan around. A few people heard her but just give us curious looks, then turn away.

I speak softly. "You said you'd stay calm."

"How can—" She drops her voice. "How can I stay calm when you lay that on me?"

"Dude."

I hold up my hand. "As weird as this sounds, I could tell he really meant it when he asked if Kobe is better. There's *some* humanity in there. Has to be. Otherwise . . . I don't know. There'd be no hope."

Audrey crosses her arms. "I ain't buyin' that."

"Well then, hang on, 'cause it gets weirder." I get antsy

describing how Doug freaked, kicking the seats and flipping out, losing control.

Then how *I* freaked and fell and got the bloody nose.

I even describe how, in his scary, effed-up way, he tried to help me. Well, kind of help.

They stay quiet.

I keep going and finish bringing them up to date, ending with my last note to Doug, wrapped around his keys.

Trent just shakes his head. "My friend, you are an enigma enclosing a mystery, inside a, well, all that. But like I keep sayin', you got balls." He takes a bite of pizza and wipes his black-nail-polished fingers on yet another napkin. "Not so sure that's a good thing, though. For you."

Audrey gawks at me. She hasn't touched her pizza. "You had Doug's car keys? How the hell did you get Doug's car keys?"

"Oh, right, you *are* behind." I inhale. "Well, after   "

She flaps her hands in the air. "Never mind, don't tell me now. I'm gonna pass out cold on this very floor if I hear any more." She fans her face and takes a long drink of latte.

Trent blinks. "Graphite Boy—I can say that in public now, yes?—either you really are a superhero or you're just a wacko magnet."

I laugh. "Well, I'm stuck to you guys."

He nods. "I rest my case."

"How can so much happen to you in just a few days?" Audrey says.

I beam. "Well, something *else* happened too. Something

awesome." Memories of me and Lev in my bed come to mind. My insides crackle.

Audrey looks up at the ceiling and drops her arms on the table with a *thud.* "Oh, Lord, what now?"

Trent eyes me through his bangs.

People talk loud all around us, but I lower my voice and lean even closer. "So—"

"Hold up! I need sustenance." She takes a huge bite of pizza, chews, and swallows. "All right, lay it on me."

And I do. Not the details, god no, but just that Lev and I had some fun last night.

Audrey sits back. "Oooooooh! I like *this* story. Don't leave me hanging with that. Tell me more."

"No, don't." Trent holds up half a pizza crust. "Still eating."

In the corner of my eye, I notice Carmen coming our way. I sit up as she stops at our table.

"So," she says, "this may sound weird, and you can completely say no, okay?"

I shift in my seat. "Okay . . ."

"Those superheroes you drew on your Graphite site? Oh, my god, they're *so* crazy awesome." She looks at Audrey and Trent. "You guys must love your characters. They're so cool and look just like you."

Audrey plays with her beaded necklace. "Don't know about that."

Trent nods. "They're cool."

"Yeah. And . . ." Carmen pinches her lips. "Those scenes

with Kobe's character are so intense. Still can't believe you did that. A lot of people are talking about it."

Audrey eyes me. "I bet they are."

I ignore her.

Carmen adjusts her big neon-orange glasses. "So, I was wondering . . . You can say no, just thought I'd ask. But would you do a drawing of *me* as a superhero?"

I sit back in my chair. "Really?"

She talks fast. "Not for your comic, just for me to have. I don't draw or anything, so I can't do a trade, but maybe I could pay you something? Only if you want!"

"That's so cool you're asking," I say. "Uh, let me think about it?"

She grins. "Sure, that's awesome. Thanks. No rush!" She giggles and goes back to the drama table.

I turn to Audrey and Trent. "How cool is that?"

"You're getting a little fan club going there, Graphite." Trent takes a swig of iced tea.

"Yeah, well, not everyone's a fan. You should've seen most of the comments people wrote on my site since yesterday."

He blows the hair from his eyes. "I did."

"First," Audrey says, "that's pretty impressive that Carmen wants you to make her a superhero. You should do it—"

Trent cuts in. "And charge her big-time. You don't come cheap."

Audrey shoots him the look. "What are you, his agent all of a sudden? *Anyway,* second, ignore all the haters. You got a lot of positive comments on your site too."

I smile. "Yes, and thanks for what *you* wrote, Sultry." As I down the rest of my lunch, I ask, "So, enough about me, what's up with you guys?"

Trent laughs. "Man, my life is sooo freakin' boring compared to yours."

Audrey puts her hand in the air. "Amen to *that* and praise the Lord!"

"In fact . . ." Trent's smile fades. "I wouldn't mind if my life was more boring, if you know what I mean."

I do—his mom. We look at each other, and then he turns away.

The bell rings, so we clean up and I move on.

As I pass the geek boy table on my way out, they nod at me and the bleached-blond one says, "Hey, Adrian." I "Hey" him back.

Cool. Maybe they're not so bad after all.

On the way to chemistry, I go by my locker and check for a note, but nothing.

The rest of the day I go looking for Doug between classes. I even walk by his locker a couple times, hoping for some sign of what he thought of my note. But we don't cross paths. This sure is a big switch from *me* always trying to avoid *him*.

Since it's Friday I'll have to wait all weekend having no clue.

I don't run into him or Buddy again.

Freakin' Buddy.

After school, Audrey's got a family church dinner to go to and Trent's all excited about a new video game he needs to play "a-sap." I'm not into either of those options and Lev has some Pep Club meeting, *of course*, so I just head home. After last night, I wish Lev would just skip Pep Club and be with me.

I take a long route home, walking along the edge of lawns and crunching on leaves.

When I walk through the front door, I find both Mom and Dad in the living room in front of the TV, the volume low. Late-afternoon sunlight streams through the windows, making glowing geometric patterns on the carpet. Dad reclines in his chair and Mom's dressed in comfy clothes, sitting sideways on the couch with her legs up, her back propped against the armrest.

"Hi, honey," she says. Her eyes are tired.

I plop my backpack on the floor. "You're home."

"Thank heavens." She drops her arms to her sides. "I've been running around all day, and coming up this weekend, I have hotel shifts and three showings. *Plus*, I have to make a ton of cookies for the church bake sale on Sunday. Since I'm off tonight, I came straight home to *relax*."

"Well, you deserve to." I step into the living room and pet Harley, who's curled up on the couch next to Mom.

"Adrian, honey?" Mom says. "I could really use your help with those cookies."

"Why don't I make them all for you?" I say.

Her eyes go wide. "Really? That's so much work."

"I know, but maybe my friends could come over tomorrow and help. Well, maybe not Audrey—can't see her thrusting her manicured fingers into a bowl of batter."

"She could just sit back and dictate what to do." Mom slaps her hand over her mouth. "Sorry, did I say that out loud?"

Dad and I crack up. Still curled in a ball, Harley opens one eye to see what's going on.

"True," I say. "But Trent might help, and my friend Lev."

Dad and Mom glance at each other. Dad mutes the TV.

Uh-oh. What's that about?

Mom shifts on the couch to face me, bringing her feet to the floor. "I haven't met Lev, have I?"

I swallow. "No, not yet."

I look at Dad. He guessed. Was it that obvious?

Mom asks how I know Lev and for how long.

No way. Is this the we-know-you're-gay talk?

Right now?!

My heart speeding up, I cross my arms and just say we've gone to school together awhile and are in the same French class.

Mom wants to know his last name and about his family.

Oh, god. This *is* the we-know-you're-gay talk!

This is actually happening at this very moment.

I tell them what I know, that his family sounds really nice and all that stuff.

This is so weird!

Mom listens while Dad stares down at the TV remote, turning it over in his hands.

Clearing her throat, Mom says, "So, can I ask?"

No way, really?

She continues. "Is he your special friend?"

I stifle a laugh, comes out like a snort. "Sorry. 'Special friend' just sounds funny."

My cheeks heat up.

Here we go.

"It's okay, you can say it. He's my boyfriend."

Time stops. Mom and Dad look at each other, then at me. I hold my breath.

From her perch on the couch, Harley stretches, then snuggles back into a ball.

After a moment, Mom stands and takes my hands. Since she's not wearing shoes, she's a little shorter than me. "Is that what you want? Are you happy?"

I squeeze her hands. "I am."

She looks right in my eyes. Her stare is intense, but so completely opposite from the way Trent's mom glared at me, knowing I'm gay.

I hug my mom.

We let go and she wipes her eyes.

Dad keeps turning the remote over in his hands.

"So, uh, Dad?"

He nods but doesn't look at me. "Seems like a nice guy."

"He is."

He takes a sip of his beer and unmutes the TV.

I go and pick up my backpack from the hall. "I'm gonna study in my room."

Mom gives me a tight smile and sits back down, her hands in her lap.

Harley jumps off the couch and follows me into my room.

I take a look back; Mom's watching me go down the hall.

I close the door, drop my bag, and exhale a blimp's worth of air.

Is that it? That's the yes-I'm-gay conversation I've been dreading for so long?

I go sit on the edge of my bed, gaze out the window. Harley leaps up into my lap, settles in, and purrs.

Outside, the street is calm. No cars go by. But the wind is whipping all around, leaves swirling and bare trees dancing in the gusty air.

Like the world finally stopped holding its breath.

Forty

LAST SATURDAY I WAS STANDING HERE IN FRONT OF MY CLOSET
mirror figuring out what to wear for my first date. *This* Saturday
I'm here trying on way too many shirts again, but for my first
job interview. Or my first I-don't-even-know-if-you-have-a-
job-for-me-but-here-I-am-so-please-like-me interview.

Lev called his friend Maria at the LGBT center again and
set up a time for him and me to meet with the art teacher we
saw there.

Mom's at work, but Dad will be here when Lev picks me
up in a couple hours. *That'll* be interesting.

Neither Mom nor Dad has said a word about Lev or anything gay-related since our "talk" yesterday. But of course,
every conversation since has purposefully *not* been about it, so
we all might as well have been saying *gay, gay, gay* the whole
time.

At least now it's in the open. I'm not sure what that means, though.

So . . . what shirt says "Hey, gay center art teacher who doesn't know me *at all*, I create comics, so I can easily teach little kids how to draw, now pay me money"?

Maybe long sleeves are best, but rolled up at the cuffs to show I'm casual? White says neat and calm, but blue is honest and true.

"Harley, it must be nice never having to care what people think about you or stress about what to wear." Stretched across my pillow, she's half asleep in all her kitty nakedness.

"Of course, you have a teeny brain and no opposable thumbs, so I guess it evens out between us."

The phone rings. I dash to the hall and grab it before Dad can.

It's Lev's cute, gravelly voice.

I holler, "It's for me!" and take it back to my room and shut the door.

I jump right in. "So, what do you think I should wear to this? It's so hard."

"Um, listen," he says. "I'm SO sorry, but I can't go after all."

"What? But . . . what happened?"

"There aren't usually Pep Club meetings on weekends, but we just decided we need one today. You know, the Halloween Hoedown is just a week away. Oh, my god, we have so many decorations to do by then!"

I grip the phone. "But me talking to that art teacher was your idea, and you already set it up with your friend Maria. They're expecting us at three p.m."

"I know, but you could still call and talk with the teacher on the phone, right?"

I flip through the sketches and drawings I gathered in a folder to use as my portfolio. "No. It's not the same. I have all this art to show her. And I thought we were going together so I'd get to see you today. Plus, I'm going to help my mom make some cookies she needs for tomorrow. Since you're in the Baking Club and all, I thought we could do it together. You could teach me some tricks."

"Adrian, I'm *so* sorry." There's rustling in the background. Is he even listening to what I'm saying?

"Where are you?" I ask. "What's that noise?"

"Oh, I'm at our kitchen table cutting out bats, you know, from black paper? We need about a hundred or so to put all around the gym."

I look at the ceiling. "How about if we go tomorrow?"

He makes a sad sound. "It sucks, but I can't. We're going over to my grandma's in the morning and then I have more Pep Club stuff to do after that."

"What about the Adrian Club?" I sink onto my bed.

The snipping sounds stop on his end and we're both silent for a moment.

He clears his throat. "I have another idea. I wanted to ask you before, and since we're talking about the dance . . ."

"Yeah?"

"So I know we've only really been together, like, a week, but by next Saturday it'll be two weeks."

I sit up. "Uh-huh."

"Do you want to go to the Halloween Hoedown?" He lets out a breath, then says fast, "I mean with me. With me."

My stomach flips. "Like, as a couple? At *our* school? But weren't you telling me how glad you are no one's figured out you're gay? This'll sure clue them in."

"We don't have to dance together or hold hands or anything. It'll look like we're just there as friends. But it would be fun. I mean, I'm putting a lot into this event and I want to enjoy it with you. And . . ."

I hold the phone closer to my ear. "Yeah, and what?"

"Well, I mean, look at *you*. You're out there now and not hiding, putting your name on your website and all. Maybe it's time I stop dreading the day someone figures *me* out."

Wow.

"And there's something else I wanted to tell you." He clears his throat. "I already thought of our costumes!"

"You did?"

"We could go as Bert and Ernie."

"*What?*" I stand so fast Harley jumps. "But . . . but wouldn't that make it kinda obvious we're more than just friends?"

"Don't worry, it's not like a prom. People don't have to go as couples. Kathleen could go with us. She could be Cookie Monster, maybe. And Trent and Audrey could be, I don't know, Big Bird and Oscar the Grouch? He's tall and she's, well . . . anyway. We'd be a group!"

I snort. "Trent and Audrey? As she would say, '*That* ain't happenin'.'"

He gets quiet, then sighs into the phone. "Maybe it's a stupid idea."

"Let me think about it." I reach over and scratch Harley behind her ears. "If we do go, I'd be Ernie, right?"

"Um, I thought *I'd* be Ernie."

Really? "I need time to wrap my head around this." I look at the pile of shirts on the floor. "So, what's the number for the LGBT center?"

I write it down and tell him not to call and cancel the appointment. I'll call myself. He repeats how sorry he is over and over and for me to think about Halloween.

After we hang up, I lie back on the bed and close my eyes. Maybe he does want to be with me, but do they really need a hundred freakin' bats on the walls? Is that more important? But he does want to go with me to the dance, which is holy-crap-terrifying. And Bert and Ernie? If I'm going to a costume party, there's only one character I want to be.

Speaking of which, I get up and log in to my Graphite site, bracing myself for more crap comments.

And there they are. But wow, more good ones, too. One from ShikamaruKicksButt says: *I don't draw as good as you, Adrian, but check out my stuff.* I click the link and, hey, it's that bleached-blond-haired kid at school who showed me his sketchbook yesterday. He's got photos of himself in cosplay costumes. His drawings are a lot of Naruto fan art—a whole lot—and some are really good. I comment on his page that I like his art a lot.

I go back and scan my comments. Nothing from Lev. Has

he even looked at my site again? Probably too busy weaving homemade spiderwebs on a loom for his hoedown.

No comments from BigGreenBro, either.

But there is another from Audrey, yelling at the haters again. I love her.

I eye the LGBT center number I wrote down, then jump up, grab the phone, and dial Audrey. She answers right away.

"So," she says, "are they going to let you teach young artistic minds how to draw moody superheroes on the moon?"

"Not yet. The appointment's not till three this afternoon. And there's a problem."

I fill her in on the details of how Lev backed out of his promise to take me.

"Typical male," she says.

"Well, I don't know about that. Do typical males ditch plans to take their boyfriends to the gay center so they can stay home and do arts-'n'-crafts?"

She laughs. "Okay, you got me there."

"So will you take me instead? I could use your good energy. Well, and your car. It'd be fun and we could hang out after." I'll tell her about baking cookies, but later.

She gets all excited and starts asking what she should wear. I explain that's exactly my problem, so she says, "Ooh, I'll be right over."

Before she arrives I decide to go with honest and true, so I wear the blue shirt. As soon as she gets to my house, she points at me and says, "Yes, that's perfect."

She's all in autumn earth tones with very little jewelry,

for a change. "I went with Saturday casual," she says.

I call Trent to see if he'll join us.

"Accompany you to the Lesbian Gay Bisexual Transgender Community Center?" he says. "I thought you'd never ask."

So I grab the folder with all of my art and we head out to pick him up.

As we drive up, Trent's waiting for us outside, thank Obi-Wan. There's no way I want to go near that house again.

I say "Hey" and step out of the front seat so he can take it. I eye the windows but see no sign of his mom.

He glances back at the house too. "Don't worry, it's still as joyous as when you were here."

"I'm sorry. I wish . . . well, you know."

"I'm tryin' to be that stoic Willow." He looks at me and shrugs. "Besides, only five hundred and eighty-nine days on the Graduation Countdown Clock." He folds into the front seat.

Damn. At least maybe getting out today will be a good distraction for him. I hop in the backseat and we take off.

Twisting to look at me, he says, "So . . . is this the *fun* thing you said we'd do this weekend?"

I smile. "Woo-hoo!"

We make a stop for car snacks, but I'm too nervous to eat a thing.

"All righty, then," Audrey says. "More for us!"

Bouncing along to Audrey's current peppy playlist, we're on our way.

I fill them in about Lev wanting me to go to the Halloween

Hoedown with him. When I say he thinks they should go too, dressed as Muppets, Audrey almost drives us off the road. "He said *what*?"

Trent grips the door handle. "Whoa there, Audrey. I don't wanna go to some stupid dance either, but I do want to live."

I laugh. "I told him neither of you would be interested in going at all."

"Understatement," Audrey says, back in our proper lane.

I tell them about Lev's Bert and Ernie costume idea but that, if I do decide to go, I'd rather be Graphite.

"Aww." Audrey smiles at me in the rearview mirror. "But you'd be an adorable Bert."

"Ernie! I'd be *Ernie*."

Trent says, "Well, whatever you do . . . have fun with that."

Following Audrey's GPS, we arrive in the gay neighborhood. As we drive down the main street, I spot a boy couple walking hand in hand down the sidewalk.

Lev should be here with me.

We turn down a side street. "Hey, there it is." I point to the center and we pull into the parking lot, which is pretty full. A couple guys come out of the building and go to their car. "Looks so different in the daylight."

"How?" Audrey glides into a space and parks.

"Well, looks smaller, maybe, and more like a regular building, I guess."

Trent scans around. "Yeah, where's the rainbow unicorn parking valet to greet us?"

"Ha-ha," I say.

"That'd be cute." Audrey turns off the car and opens her door.

I grab my art folder and we get out. As we head toward the entrance, I spot the wall off to the side where Lev and I made out, pressed against the brick. Remember his amazing lips. And the moonlight. Getting all tingly.

Maybe I shouldn't be so frustrated with him. He does have a lot to do and he did set up this whole meeting, right?

Just before going in, I take a deep breath. "Okay," I say to both of them, but look at Audrey. "Let me do the talking."

She holds up her hand. "I'll be quiet as a mouse."

Trent smirks at her.

I open the door and we enter. The little lobby looks the same but is much brighter, filled with sunlight from the front windows. I glance at the wall clock: 2:52, we're right on time.

I clear my throat. "Hi," I say to the same woman who was at the desk last week. "You're Maria, right?"

She smiles. "Yes?"

I explain I'm Adrian Piper but that Lev couldn't come so I'm here with other friends. She's really sweet and points us down the hall. My heart speeds up as we turn the corner.

Alone in the art room, the same bright-red-haired woman is pushing stacks of little chairs into the center of the space. She spots us standing in the doorway. "Hi, I remember you. Jimmy gave you his painting." She offers her hand. "I'm Clare."

We shake and I introduce myself and my friends, explaining that Lev couldn't make it. I tell her I still have Jimmy's art on my wall at home.

"That's really sweet. Well, come on in. Sorry there's nowhere to sit, though." She gestures to all the little-kid chairs. "After the adult art class ends I always have to move the grown-up chairs into the hall and bring in these kid ones. They look small, but they're surprisingly heavy." She mops at her forehead.

The smells of turpentine and oil paints and charcoal linger in the air.

Trent and Audrey check out the room and the art lining the walls. "So colorful!" Audrey says.

"We have a lot of talented kids. And talented adults." Clare gestures to the corner, where, resting on easels, there are some serious paintings in progress, the styles so loose and free. There's even an oil painting of two guys holding each other.

Trent blows his bangs from his eyes. "Expressive."

"So," Clare says, "I understand you're interested in helping out with art classes?"

I nod. "You may not be even looking for someone, but it'd be fun to work with the kids and I'm an artist." I hold up the folder of my drawings.

"Let's take a look."

Standing around one of the big drawing tables, I place the folder in the middle. "Now, you may not like comics or stuff—"

"Oh, Adrian," Audrey chimes in, "hush up. Your art is amazing."

I shoot her a look, but she just raises an eyebrow at me.

I inhale and take out my sketches, drawings, and some printouts of what I posted on my site, explaining who Graphite is and about his world.

Clare leans in and pores over everything. "Wow, this is impressive. How old are you?"

"Sixteen."

She looks me up and down. "Your skills are really advanced."

"Right?" Audrey peers over Clare's shoulder.

Trent elbows me.

I beam. "I'm glad you like it."

She asks what media I use and how I learned to draw so well. I explain my process and that I've just always drawn but haven't taken classes since middle school.

She scrunches her forehead. "Why not?"

"Let's just say no one ever got what I was doing." I eye the paintings in the corner. "I'm not so worried about that here."

She smiles. "I think you're right." She turns to face me. "So let's talk about what you could do for us." She explains that she doesn't know Lev, but that Maria thinks the world of him and says anyone Lev recommends must be special.

I tell her I'm super-honest and work hard and think I could be a good teacher.

"Well, you wouldn't be teaching. That's my domain." She points to the chairs. "You'd be stacking and moving chairs, tables, setting out art supplies, cleaning up, making sure no little ones run out in the hall . . . that sort of thing. Not so glamorous, I'm afraid."

Oh. Still . . . "That's okay."

She goes through all sorts of details, like how most jobs here are volunteer. But she's really overwhelmed with the classes and does need the help, so my timing is great. She thinks they could pay something, even if it's not much. It would have to be on a trial basis for a few weeks to be sure. "And, of course, I'll need to speak with your parents."

I sense Trent and Audrey glancing at me.

"Really? But I'm sixteen."

She smiles. "I understand. But let's just say we've had a couple of surprises in the past when certain parents found out *where* their kids were working. I just need to make sure everyone understands from the start."

"That's no problem," I say. "They'd love it if I got a weekend job. Even here. Oh! I don't mean *even* here, just—um, they'll be fine with it."

Clare stifles a smile and nods. "Great. So we'll take it one step at a time."

I gather my art and we exchange info, make plans to talk again, and say bye.

It hits me—this may actually happen.

No idea right now *how* I'd get here every weekend. But, as Clare said, one step at a time.

Out in the parking lot, Audrey and Trent start talking all at once.

"Hold up, hold up!" I put my hands in the air. "First things first. Tex-Mex. All I want right now is a gargantuan plate of nachos, dripping with way too much cheddar cheese."

Trent's eyebrows shoot up. "I'm in."

Audrey smiles. "You had me at Tex-Mex. But we have a *lot* to talk about."

"Yes, we do." I turn and hop through the lot to the car like some bouncy little kid, clutching my art to my chest.

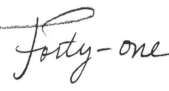

IT'S SUNDAY MORNING, SO I SLEEP LATE LATE LATE. AS DOES TRENT,

who stayed over.

He probably hasn't slept this soundly in forever, never knowing which Mom he'll be waking up to—happy or hungover?

But I guess this morning counts as a surprise too, since he wasn't expecting Harley to walk across his face at 6:00 a.m. He kinda freaked but then fell asleep again just fine, even though he was sleeping on the floor.

By the time we get up for real, Mom's already left for her church with all the cookies we made after we got back from the LGBT center.

Shockingly, Audrey jumped right in and helped. It turns out she knows how to bake awesome cookies. Who knew?

After dinner, I offered Trent peanut butter peppermint

pretzel ice cream as promised, but he declined. It's no wonder, considering his main contribution to the cookie making was eating a whole batch that kinda burned.

"I'm just assuring that your carbon footprint doesn't go to waste," he said.

I splash water on my face and run a toothbrush through my mouth.

Trent and I stumble to the kitchen and I throw together a ton-o-pancakes for us and Dad. Sunday means all-day non-stop football on TV, oh, joy, so Dad's all settled in for the long haul. While we devour pancakes—god, I love pancakes—we sit on the couch with him and watch for a while, because why not?

As he has since I was a teeny toddler, he attempts to explain what's going on. I nod and ask questions, but I don't get it. It's probably not too hard to understand. It's just that I *really* don't care.

At least there are those tight tight pants running around to watch.

I want to show I'm trying, though, so I talk about the uniform color choices and the team logo designs on the helmets. "I like the pissed-off red bird better than that blue lion. That one's got no personality."

He laughs. "Just like the team. See, you may have some football instincts yet."

"Oh, good." I guess.

Trent just sinks into the couch. And smiles.

I contemplate bringing up my potential part-time job with

Dad, but I don't want him telling Mom before I do. So when we're done I clean up, and then Trent and I head back to my room. Since I'll soon be needing to use Mom's car—our *only* car, as she likes to remind me—and Clare needs Mom's approval for me to work at the *gay* center, I'll have to find the right time to tell Mom about it. I'll definitely need to catch her in the right mood. Oh, man.

Because I have a mountain range of homework about to collapse and bury me alive, Trent says he'll head home so I can attempt to catch up.

At the front door, he pats his belly. "Thanks for the fluffy pancakes."

"My pleasure." I lower my voice. "And thank *you* for going with me yesterday."

He bows. "I'll send out positive vibes in the general direction of La Señora Clare."

Once he's off, I get to my room and sit at my computer. Dive in.

Holy crap, there's a lot to do.

Just as my eyes glaze over from staring at the periodic table of the elements for too long, a new message pops up.

Oh! From Kobe: Hey, you around to talk? Then he wrote his phone number.

Uh-oh, what's this about? I grab the phone and dial.

"Hey," I say. "It's Adrian."

"Wow, talk about instant gratification," he says.

"Well, I saw your message, and is everything okay?"

There's a pause. "No."

I sit up in my seat. "What is it?"

"I've been reading all the comics on your site."

Uh-oh. "Yeah?"

"Don't ya think you could've drawn Kerosene a lot hotter than that? I mean, come on."

"*That's* what's wrong?"

He sighs. "I'm serious. You and Lev, oh, excuse me, Graphite and Oasis—get dreamy much?—are superstuds. What about poor me? Couldn't I be more hot? I mean, c'mon, you named me *Kerosene*."

I laugh and lean back in the chair. "I'll see what I can do."

"Excellent."

He sounds so clear, so like the old Kobe. Maybe he's cut down on the pills? Or maybe he doesn't need them so much?

"Speaking of dreamy Oasis," he says, "I've been hearing rumors about you two from an unnamed source, by which I mean Carmen. What's the deal?"

Wow, guess Lev and I have been more obvious than I thought.

Since I barely have anyone to talk to about this, I go ahead and tell Kobe about our date at the center. "Oh! By the way, I met LaTrina."

"Yes, I heard, from another unnamed source that you just named, otherwise known as David, out of drag. He stopped by this week, *unannounced.* You gotta stop sending people to my house!"

I spin back and forth in my chair. "I'm glad she—I mean he—came by."

Where's that bracelet LaTrina gave me? Oh, here, looped around my drawing lamp. I slip the bracelet on my wrist.

I tell Kobe about Lev planning for the Halloween Hoedown. Kobe asks if I'm going and I say yes.

"Good. You should," he says. "I had my whole costume planned and everything. I was gonna rock that thing."

"What's your costume?"

He grunts. "Who cares now? I still look like crap and, oh by the way, ain't never stepping foot in that school again."

"Don't you feel any better?"

He goes through a long explanation of his healing over the week and a half since I saw him. Sounds *much* better, actually, for such a short time.

While he's talking, I stand and stretch, walk to the window, and gaze out.

"So, listen," he says. "I know you're gonna make Kerosene super-hot and all, but I wanted to say . . . otherwise, those scenes are just right."

"What do you mean?"

"Now that you're pointing neon signs at your website—yes, I heard about that, too—your art of Doug beating the crap out of me is getting attention. I've heard from all sorts of people, even a couple teachers, believe it or not."

"Um, is that a good thing or a bad thing?"

His voice is soft. "It's good."

"I'm glad."

After we finish talking and hang up, I go to my drawing table, shuffle through the folder I took to the center yesterday, and find a portrait pose of Graphite. It's one of him in full glory, floating weightless, fabric flowing. I pin it to my bulletin board right in the center.

"You know, Graphite, Kobe's right. . . . You *are* a stud."

In class this morning everyone's got their I-hate-Monday faces on, but in his seat behind me, Lev's perky and awake. Buzzing with Halloween excitement, he says. He called last night and we agreed to meet before class, so I got to hear all about his ongoing Halloween decorations and he got to hear all about what Clare said to me.

He was very cute, apologizing over and over, and so excited for me. I forgave him. It's hard to stay mad, looking in those eyes of his . . . and at the rest of him.

After class, Madame Pauline asks me to stay for a minute. Lev has to dash, so he takes off. I go over to Madame Pauline.

Staying in her seat, she motions for me to come around the desk and speaks in a low voice. "I heard about your online artwork, so I checked it out."

Oh, crap. "I can explain—"

"Hold on a minute, let me finish."

I swallow.

"You're a very talented artist. I'm not going to discuss the content of your art right now, but I would like to hear what you have to say about it. Maybe stop by one day after school?"

"Okay."

"In the meantime, I want to give you a commission." She

smiles. "I'd very much like to see what kind of superhero you'd make of *me*."

I blink. "Are you . . . ? You want me to draw you as a super-hero?"

She nods. "Does that interest you?"

"Well, uh, sure. It's funny, you're not the first person to ask me that."

"And I bet I won't be the last." As a couple kids come in for the next class, she stands. "You certainly don't have to say yes if you don't want to. But think on it and, if so, let me know what you charge."

Holy wow. "I'll let you know soon, okay?"

Big grin. "Tray bee-yayn."

I head out. Yay, more moneymaking opportunities! New cell phone, here I come.

This is *crazy*.

I hurry down the hall and turn the corner—there's Manuel Calderón.

I walk right up to him. "Hey."

He stops and eyes the busy hallway around us. "Yeah, I'm in a rush, okay?"

"No," I say. "We gotta talk. Now."

He checks over his shoulder.

I motion for us to step to the side, away from people. We go to the wall.

"So, come on, what's the deal?" I say. "Really."

"Listen, I don't know you and all, but . . ." He shrugs.

I brace myself. "Yeah?"

"Your friend Audrey. She, like, hates me, right?"

"Huh?"

He shifts his backpack on his shoulder. "Okay, so I think she's hot. And funny and, like, so smart. But she just ignores me. Or worse." He looks at the floor.

I blink, then stare at him. "Waitwaitwait, are you saying you *like* her?"

"Crap, I knew it. She's got a boyfriend. It's not that goth kid, is it?"

I lean against the wall, take this in. "Goth kid . . . Trent?" I smile. "God, no! We're all just friends. But if you like Audrey, why have you been so freaky around *me*?"

"Well, I didn't wanna ask the goth dude. And since you're, like, a gay guy—no offense, bro!" His face turns red. "But I was thinking maybe, ya know, you could put in a good word for me?"

Oh. My. God. This is too awesome.

He's cute, has a wrestler's body, and is adorably awkward. "Sure, I'll talk you up with her."

"You will? Great. But don't be, like, obvious or anything, okay?"

"No, not at all. I'll be subtle."

He lets out a long breath. "Thanks, bro." He holds up his palm, so I give him a high five. He practically slaps the bones out of my hand.

Ow.

Turning, he says, "Oh, I saw your website. Weird, but some funny stuff!"

He thinks it's funny?

Checking over his shoulder, he says, "And hey, I get why you made Doug like that after what he did to your friend. And Bootlicker?" He grins. "That's good. Buddy really is a dick, isn't he?"

"Yeah," I say. "A dick without a dick."

He snorts.

Look at me, using straight boy humor.

His face gets serious. "Audrey. Don't forget. We're cool, right?"

"Don't worry, bro," I say in a low voice, "I'll talk with her and be, like, all over the downlow. 'S all good. Dude."

He looks at me funny but nods and we go our separate ways.

Holy fluffy pancakes from heaven. Wait till Audrey hears about *this*!

"Ugh, where is she?" I stare at the cafeteria wall clock. Lunch started five minutes ago.

Sitting next to me, Trent ponders his tray of two bowls of spaghetti, deciding which one to devour first. "Why're you so hyped up for Audrey to get here?"

I smile. "You'll see."

I arrived early and got all set with my lunch and with my back to the wall. This way she'll have to sit facing me while I have a clear view of Manuel at his table. He's there now with his usual buddies, glancing my way from time to time, avoiding eye contact with me.

I take a bite of peanut butter and blueberry jelly and spot Audrey in the lunch line. At last, with a big salad and a latte on her tray, she comes over and sits down.

"There you are," I say. "What took you so long today?"

She points to her face. "You think this much beauty maintains itself? Why?" She starts in on her salad.

His silver-and-black goth rings glinting, Trent lifts a fork twirled with spaghetti, trying to find the end of one long noodle. "Okay, Graphite Boy, what's the big news?"

I check and Manuel is eyeing us from across the cafeteria.

Trying not to smile so big, I say, "I found out why Manuel Calderón has been weird with me. I cornered him in the hall."

Audrey smirks. "Well, we know he wasn't writing those notes to you, just like I *told* you all along."

I roll my eyes. "No, he's not the note writer. But . . ." I lean in. "Audrey, Manuel thinks you're hot!"

She arches an eyebrow. "Say what?"

"Hot and funny and smart." I tell them all about what he said to me. "See, like I keep repeating, you *are* sultry! Here's proof."

She crosses her arms. "You're makin' this up." She turns around to scan for Manuel.

I sit up straight. "No, don't look don't look don't look! He's staring over here."

She faces me, eyes wide. "This for real?"

"Yes, but I said I'd be subtle and not tell you, like, everything I just told you. So act casual."

"Oh, who cares?" She scowls. "In AP history he's always going on about himself, thinks he's so smart, so funny. He's a jerk."

"A cute jerk," I say. "And maybe it's just that he's nervous and trying to impress you? He was so adorable and awkward, the way he talked about liking you."

Trent wiggles his eyebrows at Audrey. "And he's a wrestler. Just think about that."

She points at him. "Do not go there."

I smile. "Nothin' like a man in a singlet."

She grunts. "Sultry, huh?" Turning in her seat, she spots Manuel across the cafeteria. He notices and they lock eyes for a split second.

She spins back around. "Lordy."

"Oh, another point in Manuel's favor," I say. "He saw my site and gets why I drew Doug like Thug after what he did to Kobe. No, really, he said that. And he thinks Bootlicker is funny and said Buddy's a dick."

Trent slurps down a few noodles. "I like this guy."

Using her phone like a mirror, Audrey reapplies her lipstick. "We'll see."

Bell rings and we move out, Audrey making sure Manuel leaves before she does.

I can't *wait* to hear what happens in her AP history today.

I fly through the halls and swing by my locker—oh, boy. A note.

Wait, the handwriting is different. It's from Lev!

I unfold the paper. There's a golden-yellow leaf taped inside.

Hi! I went by the library to visit your old
friend Roald Dahl yesterday. He misses you.
So do I.
-L

My blood gets all tingly in my veins. Wow.

I reread it, then carefully fold the note and slip it into my front pocket.

Beaming, I get my chemistry homework and shut my locker. Then I go to cut through the courtyard.

I follow a couple girls out the door into the chilly air.

Oh—Doug and Buddy are right here, sitting at the top of the steps to my right. Buddy leans against a trash can.

Keeping my head down, I move past them, close enough to hear Doug say, "I told you, I ain't going."

Buddy makes a face. "C'mon, we could just be bloody zombies like the other guys or some shit. It's all about what the girls wear, anyway. Remember those 'nurses' last year?" With a fist, he pops the side of the trash can.

I jump. He notices. I'm just a few feet away at the bottom of the steps. The girls keep walking, oblivious.

Buddy squints at me and spits out, "What're you lookin' at, faggot?"

Doug turns, sees me.

We eye each other for a second, and then he looks away.

I keep going, but Buddy jumps up and leaps off the steps after me.

I spin and grit my teeth. "Back off."

Doug stands and grabs his duffel bag. "C'mon, Bud."

Buddy looks up at Doug but points at me. "You've seen that shit this asshole did about you? And *me*?"

Still at the top of the steps, Doug puts his hand on the door handle. "Move it. We're gonna be late."

"No! Fag's right here. What's your deal?"

Doug glances at me once more, then opens the door and goes inside.

"What the . . . ?" Buddy turns and shoves me.

"Hey!" I catch myself and jump away.

He checks over his shoulder where Doug was, then looks right at me. "I told you, take that shit down."

I glare at him. "I'm not doing anything for *you*."

"Well, then maybe you'd do it to save your little boyfriend."

What?

He smirks and storms off, toward the opposite door from where Doug went.

Oh, no.

Forty-two

I FIND LEV AT HIS LOCKER AFTER THE NEXT CLASS, AND EVEN THOUGH Kathleen's here too, I tell him what happened with Buddy and to be careful. He's freaked.

So am I.

But there's no way I'm taking down my comics.

Kathleen puts her hand on my arm. "Maybe you should, though. Just the sections about those guys?"

"No, I'm not going to censor myself."

Lev takes a couple books from his locker. "I don't know. If it would keep them from—"

"But it won't," I say. "Buddy's an asshole and was way before I drew anything. Taking down a few comics from my website won't stop him from being a dick."

"Yeah, but he just threatened *me*." He shuts his locker.

I look down. "That's true."

Kathleen hugs her books to her chest.

Dammit. Why did Doug just leave like that? Is that all he's gonna do now, walk away? I guess it's something, though. At least he didn't join in.

I sigh. "Okay, I'll think about it."

We start down the hall and Lev hoists his backpack onto his shoulders. "I guess this week there's not much chance of me running into Buddy after school. I've got Pep Club every day."

"Every day?" I say. "But I thought we'd hang out this week."

"Yeah," Kathleen says, "me too."

"Guys! Our Pep Club has, like, *so* much to do before the Halloween Hoedown. We're way behind."

"Speaking of Halloween . . ." I clear my throat. "I thought about it and, well, I want to go with you."

He squeezes my arm. "Excellent!" He starts planning how we'll coordinate our costumes, insisting that I'm definitely much more of a Bert than an Ernie.

I clear my throat. "Listen, please don't get mad, but I have a different costume I want to wear."

He stops walking. "But why? What do you mean?"

I turn to him and smile. "I'm going as Graphite."

"Oh." He looks away. "When did you decide that?"

"Kinda just after we talked on the phone. But you could still go as Ernie if Kathleen is Cookie Monster—that'd be fun."

Kathleen leans her head on Lev's shoulder. "Well, like

Adrian said, don't get mad." She lifts her head again. "But I actually don't love the Cookie Monster idea. Sorry."

He groans. "But I . . . okay, fine, whatever." He starts walking again, so we follow.

Picking up his pace, he says, "This could be good, actually, since I don't have *time* to make something new. I'll wear what I bought before I had the Bert and Ernie idea."

The bell is about to ring, so we speed along.

"What is it?" I say.

"Since you and I won't match, I'll keep it a surprise."

Kathleen does a little hop. "Me too. There's a costume I've wanted to make since last year." She giggles.

We turn to go our separate ways. "Hey," I say, "it'll be fun."

He gasps, eyes wide. "Crap! I was supposed to buy more balloons."

Kathleen and I look at each other, and then I hoof it to class.

The rest of the day I spend pondering my costume. Certain parts should be easy to make, but that sculpted mask knee armor . . . that's tricky. And the flowing fabric?

I get home and jump into sketching and plotting and planning the various elements of my transformation into Graphite. This is going to be harder than I thought. I need a *lot* of materials.

When I message Audrey to see if she'll drive me to buy everything, she says she can't. Her mom's cousin is getting married this Saturday, the same night as the Halloween Hoedown, and Audrey has to go shopping for a new dress.

When I ask how it's possible she, the Queen of Fashion

herself, doesn't already have a dress she could wear, I get a lecture in the variations of last fall's necklines compared to *this* season's.

I make the mistake of asking if she could take me tomorrow after school and, oh, my god, "Then when exactly do you expect me to shop for the *shoes*?"

So I wait up for Mom and, since she doesn't work tomorrow night, she says she'll take me. She gets excited and asks what my costume is going be. I say it's a surprise and leave it at that.

Guess this is the week I introduce them to Graphite. And with everyone else knowing about him now, why not?

Tuesday morning whooshes by at school. I never thought I'd actually look forward to going to anything called a hoedown, much less wearing a costume, but I can't wait to start making it.

At lunch, as I approach our table, Trent's already there and gives me a weird look.

"What?" I ease into a chair and pull my lunch bag from my backpack.

He leans in. "Overheard a couple kids in class say how some of the football guys started calling Buddy Bootlicker."

I smile. "Really?"

"Wouldn't be so happy if I were you. Seems he went ballistic."

I sit back in my chair. "Was Doug there?"

He shrugs. "They didn't mention him."

I sigh. "Well, even if I took that art down from my site,

it's too late now. Besides, it's got everyone seeing what a dick he is."

"Yeah, and makes him want to annihilate you even more."

And maybe go after Lev. "Buddy's such a damn . . . asshole."

Trent lifts his iced tea in the air. "I'll drink to that."

"Really? Eeew."

Audrey saunters over with her tray. I glance across the cafeteria at Manuel, who's watching her.

"Whoa," I say. "Talk about sultry. That the dress you bought last night?"

She shoots me a what-are-you-crazy? look. "This thing?" She slides her tray onto the table. "First, no way I'm wearin' that evening dress I bought last night to *school*. Second, you've seen this outfit before, nothing special."

Trent leans way to the side and looks at her. "You grew."

She rolls her eyes and sits. "They're called high heels. Not a new invention."

A slow smile crosses his face. "Methinks this ensemble may be because of a certain wrestler dude?"

She clicks her tongue. "Oh, come on."

I put my hands on the table. "So what happened in class yesterday with Manuel?" Over at his table, he's talking with his friends now and not looking at us.

She shrugs and nibbles on a French fry. "He's a jerk."

"Why?" I say. "What happened?"

"He was overly ignoring me, then babbling at me, then

ignoring me again. If he's gonna talk to me, he should just talk to me. Guys are such wackos."

Trent blows the hair from his eyes. "He's probably just scared of you."

She props her hands on her hips. "Now, why the hell would he be scared of *me*?"

Trent and I bust out laughing.

She stifles a smile, checks over her shoulder toward Manuel, sees he's not watching us, then changes the subject to this wedding she's going to. We get to hear all about family gossip and which side of the family isn't talking to the other side until the bell rings and we get to class.

Before sixth period I catch Lev again at his locker. "Any problems with Buddy?"

He shakes his head. "Passed him once, but he didn't notice me." Lev shoves some books in his backpack. "I see you didn't take anything off your website."

"Look, at this point everyone's seen it and knows the truth about what happened with Kobe. Kobe himself even told me he likes what I—"

"So if everyone's seen it, then why not just delete it?"

I lower my voice. "First you tell me I'm a hero for standing up to Doug and Buddy, and now you're pissed about it. I don't know what else to do."

He looks down at the floor, then at me again. "Okay. But now that everyone's seen what you already drew, it's not like you're backing down if you delete it from your site. It's just moving on to new—"

"Graphite's story is my story, and I have every right to tell it like I—"

"But it's not just *your* story! It's mine, too. And everyone you decide to put in it for the world to see, whether you change our names or not. Just because your friends are okay with it doesn't mean everyone is. Doesn't mean *I* am." He slams his locker shut. "Have you even asked me how I feel about it? About strangers seeing what you think of me or what we do together?"

Oh, man.

"I'm sorry. You're right." My face burns hot. "That's . . . It's not fair to you. I'll take down the art of Oasis. Maybe I should take the whole thing down."

He leans against his locker, closes his eyes, and exhales. "No, don't do that. You don't even have to change what you did of me, I guess. Maybe. I don't know."

"No, I will. I should've realized . . ."

He nods. "I gotta go." And he does.

Damn.

I shuffle to class and get there after the bell. I apologize to the teacher.

It's starting to be an afternoon of apologies.

Do Audrey and Trent hate their characters too, but are just being nice about it? I've never asked *anybody* if they minded that I open up their personal lives for all to see. I'd be pissed too.

How did I not see this before? And now I'm putting everyone in danger.

That's it, I'm taking down the whole damn site. And screw this stupid costume idea. Bet Lev wouldn't even want me to go to his dance at all now.

When I get home, Mom's not there yet. As soon as she gets back from work, I'll just say never mind; no need to go shopping after all. She can have the night to do whatever she wants.

I shut my bedroom door and throw my backpack on the floor. Sitting in front of my computer, I pull up my freakin' site and stare at the screen.

People left more comments. Might as well read them before I pull the plug.

There's a lot of the same hate crap but more amazing ones, too, liking my art, liking my stories.

Dammit, what do I do?

I rest my head on my arms. Maybe what I've posted is important. Kobe said it is, and the most personal part is about him. He doesn't mind.

I sit up, take a deep breath.

Okay, think about this. I look through it page by page, art panel by art panel. I take down all of Oasis first. All the scenes of him and Graphite swirling through the air, joyous.

I leave all the scenes of just Graphite. *I* sure don't mind they're here. Obviously.

Guess I'll leave the Sultry and Willow scenes for now.

Then I go through all the Thug scenes, and freakin' Boot-licker, pull them down, one by one. Except for the beating section, with Kerosene. That stays.

As I take down the Thug scenes, I read the comments on each, one last time. I guess I'm getting desensitized to reading anonymous threats and hate, since reading the bad stuff only makes me feel numb right now.

I get to the last Thug scene I posted, when Graphite discovers Thug's Innermost Secret. There's a new comment.

Wait a minute.

BigGreenBro: *i like how you drew thug's secret human face. makes him a better character than just some stupid villain like you did before. how are you going to draw him next? maybe show more of what he's like as a human. that would be good. he's probably not as dumb as a brick wall with a missing brick where you throw the trash.*

Holy crap. I stand and pace my room. What's Doug trying to tell me? I reread his comment. Does this mean *he* likes being in my comic? Can't be. That would be too bizarre. Right?

And why the weird, horribly written sentence about the brick wall? Maybe he just wants to prove BigGreenBro really is him.

I sit back down. Okay, not taking down this scene. No.

I write a reply: *Well, BigGreenBro, guess it all depends on what Thug does next. These characters have a life of their own, I don't control them. I'd like it too, a LOT, if Thug showed Earth more of his human side. That would be fun to draw. What do you think?*

I click the mouse and it's posted.

I look up at the Graphite portrait I put on my bulletin board, next to little Jimmy's unigiraffe.

Graphite, what would you do?

I study his intense expression, the energetic swoops of fabric, the bold lines and swirls. He's no wimp.

Oh, my god. He'd *so* go to the Halloween Hoedown, even on his own, and show everyone what a badass he really is.

GRAPHITE
COSTUME

(¡¡ Yay !!)

Sleeve puff
shoulder ~~epolettes~~
epaulets (sp?)

Cut white
cardboard
w/ black
electrical tape
stripes?

— OR —

More puffy like
real Renaissance
doublets would have.
How???

• Sew felt
shapes w/
tissues stuffed
inside?

Roll over arm & tape
w/ duct tape

Forearm armor:

• cut from
cardboard &
cover with silver duct tape (?)
— OR —
cover in foil (?)

Sew on collar from cut-off old shirt?
V-neck T-shirt
cut sleeves
Add black ribbon
Knee face armor
???
HOW?
(EVERY ARTIST'S FRIEND!)
• Sculpt from foil??
OH! → Build on KNEEPADS!
attach w/ silver duct tape!

TO GET:

⊗ = must buy #

DOUBLET ⊗ • V-neck t-shirt (that I can chop-up.)
- old shirt with collar (⊅)

⊗ • black ribbon

- cardboard - OR - felt ⊗

- electrical tape (in garage?)

- needle & thread →

(MOM has)

[HARLEY MADE ME DO THIS - CAT ASSISTED ART. JUMPING ON DRAWING TABLE]

ARMOR • cardboard
- aluminum foil (kitchen)

⊗ • knee-pads
- duct tape (garage? - OR - ⊗)

MISC ⊗ blue sheet for flowing fabric - OR - satin? ⊗ # —!
fabric

⊗ • tights (OH BOY! 😮)

⊗ • eye-liner? face paint? for "A" on face.

(WOW #!)

SO MUCH STUFF!

Forty-three

"MOM, DON'T BRAKE SO HARD, I MIGHT CRUSH MY KNEE ARMOR. I spent all day making these."

From the driver's side, she glances at my legs, lit by the glow of the dashboard. "Well, move your seat back, Adrian. Armor or not, I'm going to keep stopping for red lights."

I pull the seat handle and push back, away from the low knee-bumping glove compartment. My seat budges only a few inches. Well, we're almost to the gym anyway, where I'm about to appear in front of the whole school wearing makeup, dressed in tights, wrapped in flowing fabric, and with giant aluminum foil faces on my knees.

How come superhero costumes are so uncomfortable in real life—and don't turn out the way you planned?

Even though I rushed home from school every day to work

on this, I could still use another week. How'd it get to be Saturday night so fast?

The light turns green and Mom accelerates. "Honey, relax. You're going to have fun, and you look adorable."

Great, adorable is hardly what I'm going for here. I was aiming for epic.

She glances at me. "I wish you had shown us your cartoons before—"

"Ugh, they're not cartoons. I create *comics*. So different."

"Okay, I'll get it right. But whatever they are, it would have been nice to have seen what you've been drawing all along. You draw so beautifully."

I tug back the seat belt shoulder strap before it crushes my sleeve puff. "It wasn't ready to be seen. Like I said, I only put my name on my site a few days ago."

"Well, you showed that teacher at the, the GLB—oh, I don't want to say it wrong."

"It's the LGBT center."

She sighs. "Yes, that. You showed *her* before you even told me or your dad about any of it."

She turns right and we're almost there—the school is all lit up and coming toward us.

My stomach flips.

I look at her. "So you'll call Clare tomorrow about me working there, right? You promised."

"Yes, I'll call her tomorrow." She eyes me. "So many new things I'm learning about my own son!"

With lots of other cars, we drive around behind the school

and turn into the brightly lit parking lot. Above the gym entrance up ahead, strings of little orange lights outline a huge painted sign that says RHH HALLOWEEN HOEDOWN! And in front of the building, fake cobwebs cover the bushes, flashing from what must be at least twenty strobe lights spread out and tucked in the branches.

"Wow," she says, "can't wait to hear what it's like *inside* the gym. Oh, look at all those black and orange balloons they tied on the trees."

Yeah, and I wonder who spent all week blowing up those balloons instead of being with me?

Oh, my god, there he is up ahead. Lev's carrying a ladder and wrestling with a few balloons in the wind. Shouldn't he be finished decorating by now?

"Oh, wait, Mom. Drop me off here."

"But we're not even near the door."

"Right here by this little building, this is good. I need to adjust my costume before I go in." And before Lev lays eyes on me.

She pulls off to the side of the lot and I ease out of the car. Wow, they don't call these *tights* for nothing.

I close the door and, through the rolled-down window, assure her I'm fine and will have a blast, and okay, whatever, take one more picture but make it quick and don't be obvious. She gets out of the car and, of course, is more than obvious. But, still taming the balloons, Lev doesn't even look our way.

I say bye to Mom and, as she drives away, adjust the damn tights. Ooh, that's better.

I'm by a little utility shed that smells like fertilizer and engine oil. Stepping into the shadows, I rewrap the fabric around me and attempt to make it look flowing like I draw it on Graphite. But it only droops like a lame blue satin toga.

What the hell am I thinking, going as Graphite? All I'm gonna do is trip on this thing and smash my nose again.

And oh, yeah, get mocked mercilessly.

Halfway between me and the gym, Lev seems to have conquered the balloons, tying them to a lamppost. He's wearing a long cape but no hat or mask. His costume must be underneath?

Things have been good with him since I took down the Oasis art. Well, it's actually hard to say since I've barely laid eyes on him. But after tonight, it'll be time for him to start coming to Adrian Club meetings.

Past Lev, by the entrance, car headlights illuminate a variety of arriving zombies, sexy witches, and . . . is that supposed to be a samurai or a giant armadillo?

The *boom boom boom* of some hip-hop song bounces out the doors each time someone goes in. Obi-Wan, give me strength.

Wow, a T-shirt, tights, some aluminum foil, and a strip of fabric aren't so warm. I inhale deep. Okay, Graphite, let's do this.

Lev picks up the ladder and carries it to the side yard between the shed and the gym.

I step out of the shadows and follow behind him into the

side yard, dead grass crunching under my black boots. A tall parking lot lamp casts dramatic yellow light on him as he drops the ladder and puts stuff in some plastic bins by the bushes. He must be done decorating at last.

As I get closer to him, I check behind me in the lot. I wait for a few people to walk past on their way to the gym entrance.

With his back to me, Lev's focused on packing up. As soon as those people are gone, I approach him. It's hard to walk in this costume, though.

I strike a grand Graphite pose. "Greetings, human!" With the music spilling from the gym, he doesn't hear me.

With a twirl of my draped fabric, I'm about to wave my arms. But from the direction of the stadium on the far side of Lev, a guy dressed like a zombie football player is coming from the shadows. Talk about ruining my entrance.

He weaves as he walks. Looks like the party already started for this guy. He spots Lev and stops. Staring at him, he hollers, "Holy shit! This is too perfect." He then goes right for Lev, pushes him into the bushes.

"Hey!" Lev yelps, scrambling to get out of the branches.

I start to rush over, but damn this draped fabric.

"Get away!" Lev frees himself.

Oh, my god. "What are you *doing*?" I yell. Gathering up the fabric under my arm, I run.

Laughing, Buddy shoves Lev again, hard.

Lev slams into the ground on his side.

I dash over and get between Lev and Buddy. "Get the hell away from him."

Buddy gapes at me and cracks up, claps his hands.

I eye the parking lot, but no one's walking by. A new song comes blaring from the gym doors around the corner.

"Oh, *man!*" Buddy yells. Then he drops the smile and comes for me.

I run right at him and trip him. He rolls on the ground, then stumbles as he tries to stand. So drunk it takes effort.

It gives Lev time to get up and steady himself. He holds his side but stands by me.

"You okay?" I ask.

He pants but nods.

I grit my teeth. "I won't let him hurt you."

Movement catches my eye. I glance over where Buddy came from the stadium. Two guys head this way. Both big, but one is obviously Doug.

"What's this?" Doug booms as he approaches us.

Buddy turns to him. "Check it out! Look what's here in little fairy dresses."

With Doug is another football guy, half-assed smears of camouflage paint on his face, wearing army fatigues, an open beer can in his hand.

Doug's not in costume. He looks the same as always. But under that cap brim his eyes are glazed.

Just like they were at Boo.

He focuses on me, then Lev. "What's the deal?"

Lev breathes heavy beside me.

The other guy blinks at us, sees my costume. He barks out a laugh. "Ha! Oh, shit!"

Over by the parking lot a few people in costumes walk by, talking, not glancing this way. They keep going.

I turn to Buddy. "What is your fucking problem?"

"Screw you, faggot."

"I can do math." The guy in the army costume takes a swig from his beer, then places it on the ground. He points at himself, Doug, and Buddy. "One, two, three of us can whup, let's see, the one, two of you little assholes."

Buddy pops Doug on the arm. "Right?"

Wavering in a tipsy way, Doug bumps Buddy away from him.

I look at Lev. "Let's go in."

Buddy steps toward me. "Where do you think you're goin'?"

"Look, we're leaving." I glance at Doug. "Right?"

Ahhhhh! Buddy slams me to the ground. I land on my back.

He's on top of me, digs his knee in my side.

I grab his wrist.

Twisting and kicking, I push on his slimy face.

Doug stomps over. "Fuckin' idiot." He grabs Buddy, pulls him off me.

Buddy falls back on his ass. "What the hell?"

Lev helps me stand. I'm twisted in my costume but brace myself.

Scrambling up, Buddy screams at Doug. "What the hell's wrong with you?"

The army guy steps to Doug. "Dude, c'mon. Show this fag he can't screw with you."

Three people walk by in the parking lot. They see us. "Adrian?" a girl says.

No mistaking that voice.

Audrey and, oh, my god, it's Trent. And someone else, wrapped like a mummy. They start across the grass toward us, then notice Doug and Buddy and stop.

I turn back to Doug.

Buddy spits on the ground and scowls at Doug. "Shit! We had this."

The army guy grunts. "Check out all the *freaks*."

"Adrian, you okay?" Audrey says from a few feet away.

I look over. What are she and Trent doing here? And who is that mummy with them? "Oh, my god, Kobe?"

In the light from the parking lot, the strips of gauze crossing over his forehead and chin cast shadows, making his bruises and still-swollen face look like a mask. He glares at Doug, eyes on fire.

Doug tries to focus, squints. Then his eyes go wide. He takes a quick step back like from an electric shock. He turns to the side, looks at the ground, and lets out a long breath.

Buddy and the other guy take it all in.

No one says anything.

I scan all around. Everyone's watching Doug now.

I walk right to him. "I like your costume."

"You . . . huh?" Doug scrunches his eyebrows. "I ain't wearin' no—what costume?"

I say in a low voice, "Your *human* side. Looks good."

Buddy steps over. "What's he saying to you?"

Doug looks from me to Kobe. Then to Buddy. "Let's move." He turns to go back toward the stadium.

"Screw that." Buddy spits at me.

I jump back in time.

Doug spins, grabs Buddy's arm, and hurls him to the ground. "Fuck you!"

Buddy scoots back along the grass. "What's—"

"Grow the fuck up!" Doug kicks him in the side. "Sick of your shit."

The army guy puts up his hand. "Doug, bro, cool it."

Doug wheels around. "You got a problem?"

He backs down.

Pushing from the ground, Buddy's up on his feet. He clutches his side, eyes wide.

Doug turns and punches him in the stomach.

"Oooh!" Buddy doubles over.

I run at Doug. "Stop! Just stop!"

He glares at me.

"Doug, listen. Enough." I glance back at Kobe, take a quick breath. "Enough. God, I can't believe I'm saying to *not* kick Buddy's ass, but . . . enough." I look in his eyes. "Right?"

Buddy's hunched over, grimacing, watching us.

I check over my shoulder at my friends. Everyone stares.

I focus on Doug.

Nothing moves, like the earth stopped turning.

Doug peers over at Kobe. Then me. He puffs up his chest, turns to Buddy and the other football guy, points at each of them. *"Move out."*

With baffled scowls, Buddy and the other guy slump off to where they came from, away from the gym, toward the stadium. Doug follows them.

I realize I'm standing with my hands on my hips in some cliché superhero pose.

Doug turns back one last time, looks at me. I give him a little nod.

He flips me off.

So I flip him off.

He disappears into the shadows.

forty-four

I TURN FROM WATCHING DOUG DISAPPEAR AROUND THE BACK OF THE building.

Audrey, Trent, Kobe, and Lev all gawk at me.

"That was, like . . . whoa." Trent stands at full height with his arms out to his sides.

"Guys?" Audrey gestures toward the parking lot. "Let's maybe move into the light?"

More and more costumed kids pass by. Some look our way but don't care.

I grab Lev's arm. "You okay?"

He pushes his hair out of his face. He's pale. "I'll be—yeah. You?"

Still catching my breath, I say, "Yeah."

I look down at my costume. "Dammit! That asshole." My knee armor is crushed, shoulder puffs practically ripped off. I'm sure the *A* symbol on my face is smeared beyond recognition.

Kobe stares at me. "What *the hell* just happened here?"

I study his face. "You look better."

"Oh, please. Bullshit."

"You do. I mean, you're *here* . . . and why are you here?"

"After whatever *the hell* just happened, wish I wasn't." He flaps the mummy bandages that dangle from his hand toward Audrey and Trent. "It was their idea."

Audrey raises her voice. "Come on, people, let's move away from this spot." Now that I really look at her, she's gorgeous, dressed up more than I've ever seen.

Lev turns. "Wait, I can't leave the ladder and all that stuff. What if—"

"Trent," I say, "help us move this?"

He, Lev, and I grab it all and drag it into the lot, in full view of everyone hanging out at the gym entrance. The doors are open now and a thumping beat bounces across the pavement.

I touch Lev's arm. "Let's just leave it all here. Get someone else to deal with it. You're done."

He nods. "That's for sure."

The five of us stand in a little huddle under the big parking lot light.

Audrey glances back at where we came from. "What just happened?"

"Buddy attacked Lev, and then Doug and that other guy showed up." I look at Lev's side where he hit the ground. "You hurt?" I probably should have let Doug pummel Buddy into oblivion.

Lev pulls his hair behind his ears and wipes his forehead. "No, I'm all right. Just knocked the wind out of me."

He scans my face, then takes hold of my shoulder. "You. Are. *Awesome*." He kisses me, full on the mouth—the best sweaty, electric, freaked-out kiss I'll ever know.

Oh, *man*.

After ten high-voltage years go by and he pulls back, I exhale.

"Oooooh." Audrey fans herself. "Gettin' hot out here."

Trent studies his black-fingernail-polished hands.

I put my arm around Lev and look at everyone. "Main thing is we got them off our back."

Audrey points at me. "*You* got them off our back, Graphite. I don't know what all that was, but I'm scared a'you, superhero."

Graphite. I hold up my ripped fabric. "Yeah, well, not very 'super' now."

Trent scans my costume up and down, nods. "I like what I think you were trying to do."

Lev squeezes my arm. "You're a superhero no matter what you wear."

Kobe grunts dramatically. "Oh, *god*."

I turn. "Okay, let's get the hell inside the gym."

"No way, I'm outta here." Kobe looks at Audrey. "Please take me home? Maybe Kerosene would be ready for this. But I'm not. *Bad* idea."

Trent nods. "I'm with the mummy dude."

"No." I face Kobe. "You have as much right to be here as anyone. We *all* do."

Kobe flaps his fabric hands. "Nuh-uh. I can't."

I point to the side yard. "Well, *I* can't let those assholes get away with it. If we run and hide, they win. Right?"

"Amen to that," Audrey says.

Kobe blinks. "I'm not so—"

"Look," I say, "we earned it. This is *our* school. This is for us. We *deserve* a fucking dance!"

"Yeah!" Lev says. "And wait till you see the decorations. They're awesome."

Trent cracks up.

Audrey rolls her eyes. "Let's get inside. This girl is ready for some *fun*. Enough drama."

I drape my fabric over my shoulders. "All right, head in. Let's TAKE this school."

"Oh, please." Kobe sighs. "Fine. But do not tell *anyone* who I am."

With Audrey's help, he rewraps the strips of gauze like a mask over his face so he's not recognizable. He only leaves a slit for his eyes to peer through the fabric.

As we start walking toward the gym, I take in what Lev's wearing. His cape is hanging off one shoulder and his costume looks like . . . "Are you Prince Charming?"

He smiles. "Oasis."

"Really?"

"Okay, it is Prince Charming, but it was the closest thing Party City had left that looked like what you drew."

I grin. "Prince Charming works just fine."

"Ugh," Kobe mumbles. "Get a room."

Audrey laughs.

I turn to her. "Hey, weren't you supposed to be at that wedding? You look *amazing*. Like, holy crap."

Her elegant, low-cut sapphire-blue dress has a long skirt with a slit up the side. It looks like it's made of a hundred separate satin panels. Her hair is dramatically piled on top of her head and she wears dangly silver jewelry.

Strutting in her high heels, she says, "Don't you recognize me? I'm Sultry, bitch."

Kobe cracks up as much as he can wrapped in gauze. "Ooooh, you sure are."

She smiles. "Okay, I did come here directly from the wedding ceremony—and yes, you'd better be appreciative that I'm skipping the reception to surprise *you* instead. But I think Sultry would wear this, yes?"

Beaming, I nod. "She will now."

She looks down at herself and frowns. "Even though this color makes me look as big as a house."

"Audrey, it doesn't." Lev lowers his voice. "And you have three gay boys here telling you you're hot. Believe me, you turned it out."

She waves him off but stands a bit taller.

We get to the crowd forming a line at the gym doors and pull out our school IDs.

Ahead of us, a couple jocks are lamely dressed as cheerleaders. Sexist, homophobic pricks. They notice me, take in what I'm wearing, and bust out laughing.

Audrey glares at them. "If anyone gives *you* trouble, Adrian, just remember—I'm trained to use a high heel as a weapon."

"Ooh," Lev says, "teach *me*."

"So." I spin my finger in a circle. "How is it you guys—"

"We all talked behind your back," Audrey says. "Not so unusual, I might add. We decided to surprise you. So, surprise!"

"Guess who I am?" Trent says.

I study him, fully in black as always. "Hmm, new coat, right?" It almost touches the ground and has little silver skulls running up the sides and sleeves.

Trent slowly turns in a circle. "I call it Willow-inspired haute couture soup du jour."

"I . . . Wow." Overwhelmed. "You guys are . . . Wow."

The line moves forward.

I spot a guy and girl looking at my costume. Oh, great, why don't they just—oh. They both give me a thumbs-up. Cool. I give them a thumbs-up too.

I turn to Kobe. "I'm really glad you came. And I love the mummy look."

He grunts. "I went for the irony. But then thought I could be Mummy Dearest."

Lev laughs.

I squint at Kobe. "What do you mean?"

His shoulders slump. "Oh, my god, you *really* need to brush up on your gay references."

Lev touches my arm. "You do."

As soon as we're through the doors, we step into the gym and pulsing music.

Ghosts hang from streamers, spinning lights splash colored spots on the walls and floor, fog machines make the air thick and spooky, and "Hey, look at all your bats!"

Lev smiles. "You like?"

I tap his shoe, yell over the noise, "This is wild."

My insides flip. Wow. My first dance with a boyfriend.

In fact, my first dance *and* my first boyfriend.

Lev blushes. He must feel it too.

The crowd pushes around us, so we all keep walking.

I spot Kathleen through the mass of costumed kids across the foggy room. It's hard to miss her—she's dressed in a bright-pink full-body leotard and tights with a little kid's plastic chair strapped on top of her head.

"What is she?" I ask Lev.

He peers at her. "You got me."

Audrey hooks Kobe's arm. "You doin' okay?" she says over the music.

I barely make out his words through his face fabric. "Maybe let's hang over in that corner?"

Trent elbows Audrey. "Check out who's coming through the doors."

We all do and it's Manuel, barely dressed in a toga. Whoa.

Audrey's eyes pop, and then she turns and stares ahead to the drinks table. "They wouldn't happen to serve Chardonnay at this thing?"

Kobe pulls her arm and starts walking. "I wish."

We get drinks (of the non-Chardonnay kind) and sit on some chairs against the wall off in a corner.

Kathleen comes over and says to us, "There you are!"

Attempting to not bump the teetering child-sized chair strapped to her head, Lev gives her a hug. "I don't know what you are, but it's cute."

"Wait," Trent says loudly, "let me guess. You're the naïve, idealized dream supporting the mass education of innocent youth before it crumbles into a hollow shell and dies."

"Um . . . no." She spins around. "I'm bubble gum that someone stuck under a chair."

Trent shrugs. "Okay, that works too."

Lev whispers to Kathleen that the mummy is Kobe. She gasps, but Kobe doesn't notice. He's gazing at the crowds, taking it all in, after everything he's been through. Can't imagine.

I clear my throat. "Hey, mummy dude. Welcome back."

Kobe blinks, nods.

Kathleen bounces, the wobbly chair-hat practically taking out her eye. She tightens the strap. "Come on, y'all, let's dance." A little group has already started dancing in the middle of the gym.

Lev and I look at each other. My heart beats louder than the boom from the speakers.

Okay, the Adrian? he mouths.

I smile. "Okay."

Before going over, I try to fluff my ripped costume as best I can. "I look like a mess," I yell. "You can't even tell who I'm supposed to be."

"Don't worry, Nurse Piper." Kobe's eyes smile at me through his wrapped bandages. "We know who you are."

"Truth," Lev says. "Now, who's dancing?"

Kobe sits back, shakes his head.

Trent settles in the chair next to him and salutes us. "Have fun, kids."

Lev and Kathleen go toward the dance floor and Audrey grabs my arm. "C'mon, I wanna dance my ass off tonight."

So we do.

Forty-five

"YOU THINK YOU CAN HANDLE IT THIS TIME?" AUDREY EYES MY BBQ
turkey burger with Boo's special sauce.

It really is massive on the little plate in front of me. "Sure.
What could possibly go wrong?"

"Gravity," Trent says, biting into his quesadilla.

Lev and Kathleen crack up.

We're all five at a table against the wall near the front of
Boo. The usual Sunday-night dinner crowd chatters all
around us and funky music drifts through the air.

"Hold on. Let's get a photo before you pick up that burger
and make a mess." Audrey goes for her purse, but it slips off
the back of her chair. She reaches down to get it and grunts.

"Here." Trent scoops it up and hands it to her.

She arches her back and winces. "Next time, remind
me not to wear brand-new heels to a wedding *and* a dance,

okay? That hoedown last night almost knocked me flat."

Kathleen wipes pasta sauce from her mouth. "Why didn't you just take off your shoes?"

"At school?" Audrey arches an eyebrow. "I ain't that tacky."

"And," I say to Kathleen, "in heels she's taller than Manuel. It's a power struggle thing."

Audrey gives me the Audrey Eye and, from her purse, whips out her phone and takes my picture.

A waitress I don't recognize refills our water, then moves on.

I sigh deeply. "So surreal being here again. They haven't changed anything, but it looks so different. Smaller." I gaze out the front windows. No one's hanging in the parking lot, and in the setting sunlight, all looks peaceful.

But that nightmare is seared in my brain.

I still can't wrap my head around what Doug did before the dance last night. I mean, obviously he doesn't want to be the villain. And he wasn't. But he wasn't a hero, either.

No matter what, things are different now.

So this morning I made the choice—I deleted that balcony video. It no longer exists.

I let my shoulders roll back against the old beat-up seat.

Lev squirts ketchup on his fries. "Can't believe Kobe actually came last night. That was awesome."

"Wish he'd come back to school for real, though," I say.

Audrey purses her lips. "Maybe he will."

"Wonder what he'd say about your new coif?" Trent stares at my head. "It's growing on me, pun intended."

I smile and run my hand through my hair, now all buzzed

on the sides and spiky on top. Taking my time this morning, when I was fully awake and of sound mind and body, I carefully cut my hair. Even though I still can't get that Graphite flip in the front, it turned out pretty awesome.

Lev bumps my shoulder. "I think it's cute. Even in the back."

"Why? What's wrong with the back?"

"Oh, nothing."

I run my hand over my scalp and look around the table. "What's wrong in the back?"

They all glance at each other and grin and shrug.

"Really, guys, what—"

"It's not so bad," Audrey says. "Just a bit, um, uneven?"

Great.

"Anyway," Lev says, "I want to tell you something. I kind of miss seeing Oasis on your site."

"But you had me take it down."

"I know, but I was thinking maybe you could draw some new stuff that could be more public. Like, I don't know, Oasis saving an endangered species or something."

Leaning close to his ear, I whisper, "But I'll still draw some new stuff for your eyes only."

"Oh, get a room," Kathleen says.

To my right, the wall here has a great open spot, not yet covered by what anyone's written.

"Hey, Audrey, can I have a pen?"

She fishes a blue one from her purse and hands it to me.

While everyone talks and eats, I draw Graphite in a power

pose, his paintbrush brandished in the air. I sketch the flowing fabric so it swirls around the other doodles and writings that surround him, integrating Graphite into the space.

I sign my name and drop the pen on the table. There, freakin' at last.

Trent nods. "Awesomeness."

Audrey eats another fry, then readies her phone. "Go ahead and eat. I'm ready to document the mess you're about to make with that turkey burger."

I smirk, pick up my fork and knife, and cut it into pieces. With the fork, I stab a chunk of turkey patty and twirl it in the BBQ sauce, then hold it up to her. "Ha-ha. I'm not even going to use my hands at all." I bring it to my mouth and—

"*Crap!*" A blob of sauce lands right in my lap.

They all crack up.

I quickly eat the bite and drop my fork on the plate.

Audrey wiggles her phone. "Got it!"

"Do not post that!" I say.

Damn I need a phone. Here's hoping that job works out.

I sop up the blob on my pants with a napkin. Not too bad.

I eye all the happy faces around me. "Hey, Trent, your arm's the longest. Take a selfie of us."

He's on the end of the table, so we all scoot and lean in from both sides. Put our arms around each other. We're all linked.

"Okay," he says, aiming the phone at us. "Ready?"

Audrey speaks up. "Everyone say 'Graphite!'"

We scream it out loud together as he hits the button.

Click.

Acknowledgments

If not for the real superheroes who populate my world, Adrian's life and adventures would not exist. I am so thankful to the cast of characters that helped bring this book to life:

Superhero name: THE BUNNY GROUP
(a writing critique group like no other in all the galaxy)
Real names: Kathy Bieger Roche, Stephen Alan Boyar, Gail Carson Levine, Selene Castrovilla, Roberta Davidson-Bender, Karen DelleCava, Michelle de Savigny, Sheila Flynn DeCosse, Alice Golin, Emily Goodman, Michele Granger, Deborah Heiligman, Sherry Koplin, Patricia Lakin, Arlene Mark, Sheila Nealon Ramsay, Judy Rosenbaum, Vicky Shiefman, Marcia Shreier, Erika Tamar, Susan Teicher, Seta Toroyan, Pat Weissner, Niki Yektai, and Adrian's first "mom," Margaret "Bunny" Gable
Superpowers: towering talent, x-ray insight, limitless energy derived from the planet's very core, nuclear-powered kick-you-in-the-butt-when-you're-full-of-self-doubt designer boots, hugging arms of titanium

Superhero name: CAPTAIN MARVELOUS
Real name: David Gale (a.k.a. The Reviser, a.k.a. The Friend)
Superpowers: faster than any e-mail, more perceptive than Sherlock, able to expertly edit massive manuscripts in a single bound (with intense respect for every word)

Superhero name: THE LITERARY LEAGUE
Real name: Simon & Schuster Children's Publishing
League members: Jon Anderson, Justin Chanda, Liz Kossnar, Sonia Chaghatzbanian, Dorothy Gribbin, Martha Hanson, and many, many other superamazing superhumans

Superpowers: megadazzling design, Kryptonite-proof copyediting, maximum-warp production, laser-beam marketing, supernova-like publicity, heat-seeking sales, all-around awesomeness

Superhero name: AMBASSADOR FABULOUS
Real name: Brenda Bowen (a.k.a. The Not-So-Secret Agent)
Superpowers: bubble of calm, voice of reason, support of steel

Superhero name: THE TRIBE
Real name: Society of Children's Book Writers and Illustrators (scbwi.org)
Tribe leaders: Lin Oliver, Stephen Mooser, and the L.A. Jedi Team
Superpowers: limitless inspiration spells, rechargeable enchantments of encouragement, formidable deflector shields to protect tribe members against naysayers everywhere

Superhero name: SANCTUARY
Real name: Chris Spinelli
Superpowers: most potent empathic powers in the galaxy, singular ability to wield the Dome of Tranquillity, mighty laugh of disarmament

Superhero name: THE FELLOWSHIP OF THE FAMILY AND FRIENDS
Real names: Lizzy Bromley, Katrina Groover, Phil and Hilda Jackman, Stephen Linn, Peter and Marlene Linz, Angela Matusik, Danielle Obinger, Carmen Osbahr, Marjorie Shik, Caroll and Debi Spinney, Polly Stone, my Muppet and *Sesame Street* families, and *many, many* other superheroes of mine
Superpowers: incredible strength and support over the years in helping me boldly carry *Draw the Line* to journey's end

Superhero name: THE MIGHTY READER
Real name: YOU!
Superpowers: singular abilities to tell your own tales, find your inner truths, and change the world

31901059375594